tulsa
LIBRARY TRUST

ADVANCE PRAISE FOR

Love and War in the Jewish Quarter

"Dora Levy Mossanen is a master storyteller of historical fiction. In *Love and War in the Jewish Quarter* she serves up yet another feast, telling this tale with sensitivity and insight that makes the novel infinitely rich and nuanced. Fascinating characters, truly beautiful prose that is a Mossanen trademark and an incredibly complex plot make this book simply unforgettable."

—**M.J. Rose**, *New York Times* bestselling author of *The Last Tiara*

"Dora Levy Mossanen's new book commands our attention, not only for the range of its subject matter and literary artistry, but for weaving in a personal narrative within the context of Iran's historical, political history and cultural practices. *Love and War in the Jewish Quarter* is both lyrical, informative, and very moving—an extraordinary addition to depiction of the lost worlds of Iranian Jewry."

—**Angella Nazarian**, author of four books and the newly released: *Creative Couples: Collaborations That Changed History*

"With the signature lush economy and exuberant precision of her prose, which any poet would envy, Dora Levy Mossanen explores the intricacies of history's lesser known side streets, as she introduces a new cast of unforgettably colorful characters, not all of them fictitious, including Iran's Queen Fawzia, and the city of Tehran, itself, as it was in WWII. In full command of her uncanny powers of observation and inexhaustible imagination, Levy Mossanen crafts an exquisite balance between drama and comedy, idealism and worldliness, strength and weakness, risk and triumph, set in the midst of humanity's two polar constants—love and war."

—**Leslie Monsour**, poet, author of *The Alarming Beauty of the Sky* and *The House Sitter*

"With a love and gift for language, Dora Levy Mossanen lushly paints a tale of life, love, and war during mid-twentieth century Tehran. Right from the start, she captures your curiosity as she whisks you into opulent Persian palaces, colorful bazaars, and flourishing fields of opium. This is an intoxicating tale that takes place in Iran during the tension-filled years of World War II. A fascinating read."

—**Esther Amini**, author of *Concealed: Memoir of a Jewish-Iranian Daughter Caught Between the Chador and America*

"*Love and War in the Jewish Quarter* is Dora Levy Mossanen's best book yet. Set against the backdrop of World War II, the author shows mastery in blending Iranian history, the European turmoil, and Jewish life in Iran with a subtle touch of erotica. Trained in Europe, Soleiman Yaran, a humble but capable dentist, brings together the opposite worlds of Iranian royalty in gilded rooms and that of the Jewish minority consigned to the crumbling Jewish ghetto. Above all, this is also a story of women's lives, of their fears, desires, ambitions, love, lust, loss and hope. *Love and War in the Jewish Quarter* is an enchanting rendition of how life may have been in Iran at that time. Although love, lust and desire palpitate throughout the novel, Mossanen masterfully controls its scope in favor of a more dramatic historic novel."

—**Farideh Dayanim Goldin**—author of *Wedding Song: Memoirs of an Iranian Jewish Woman and Leaving Iran: Between Exile and Migration*, and founder of www.foodmemory.net

"Set in an Iranian Jewish Quarter during World War II, yet seemingly drawn from the Arabian Nights or Persian Book of Kings, two worlds collide in this tale of impossible love between a Jewish doctor and the Muslim Governor's wife. Dora Levy Mossanen's novel *Love and War in the Jewish Quarter* is at once down-to-earth and fantastical, modern and ancient. It is full of atmospheric and astonishing detail, whether she is describing a dental procedure or an exotic palace, and keeps the reader riveted until the redemptive end."

—**Lyn Julius**, author of *Uprooted: How 3000 years of Jewish Civilization in the Arab world Vanished overnight* (Vallentine Mitchell)

"An utterly captivating and poignant tale that braids history, religion, and an improbable love story. *Love and War in the Jewish Quarter* offers the reader entrée to a world at a crossroads and the people who are caught between their own deeply rooted pasts and the unknown future. A mesmerizing read!"

—**Angela Himsel**, author of *A River Could be a Tree*

"*Love and War in the Jewish Quarter*, the newest novel by the very talented Dora Levy Mossanen, is pure pleasure from start to finish. It is a perfect blend of historical fiction set in one of the most crucial periods in modern history—World War II—and the tale of a marginalized Jewish dentist who is indispensable to those in the highest echelons of power, including the Queen of Iran. Striking the exact balance between the intimately personal and the crushing sweep of human history, this enchanting novel is steeped in an intoxicating mix of flavors ranging from Persian culture and history, to Jewish rituals of mourning, to touches of magical realism. *Love and War in the Jewish Quarter* is a story of worlds that are far from our own and, at the same time, evergreen truths of human nature. It grabbed me on page one and stayed with me long after I closed the book."

—**Deborah Goodrich Royce**, Award-winning author of *Ruby Falls* and *Finding Mrs. Ford*

"The setting, dialogue, and details create the ideal backdrop for the tension and intensity of this lush and lusty tale of beguiling romance. A captivating historical gem."

—**Steve Berry**, *New York Times* bestselling author of *The Omega Factor*

"With her lyrical, evocative prose, Dora Levy Mossanen transports the reader to Tehran in the 1940's and delivers both a love story filled with passion and forbidden love and a novel rich with history and the turbulence of another era. *Love and War in the Jewish Quarter* is perfect for book clubs and for anyone trying to understand the strife that is still so relevant today."

—**Anita Abriel**, author of the international bestseller, *The Light After the War*

Dora Levy Mossanen has been called "an Isabel Allende of Persia" for her elegant and exotic historical novels. Born in Israel, raised in Iran, and living in the United States, she credits the intriguing characters and compelling plots of her bestselling novels to her experiences in such diverse cultures.

Her widely acclaimed novels *Harem*, *Courtesan*, *The Last Romanov*, and *Scent of Butterflies* have been translated into numerous languages and distributed worldwide.

Her novels have been praised by many celebrated authors, among them: Amy Ephron, Steve Berry, Jonathan Kirsch, John Rechy, Robin Maxwell, and M.J. Rose.

Her awards include: San Diego Editors' Choice Award, Barnes and Noble Editor's Pick, Selected best Historical Novel of the Year by the *Romantic Times*, and Editor's Top Pick from the *Romantic Times*. She has also been featured in various media outlets, including the *Los Angeles Times*, KCRW, Radio Iran, Radio Russia, and Jewish Women's Theater, and has appeared on several television programs.

LOVE AND WAR in the JEWISH QUARTER

LOVE AND WAR in the JEWISH QUARTER

DORA LEVY MOSSANEN

A POST HILL PRESS BOOK

ISBN: 978-1-63758-556-6
ISBN (eBook): 978-1-63758-557-3

Cover design by Alan Dingman
Interior design and composition by Greg Johnson, Textbook Perfect

Post Hill Press
New York • Nashville
posthillpress.com

Published in the United States of America

To Nader
For making it all possible
and to David Ascher
for being there

In memory of Paulita Shtrum

Nothing is the same

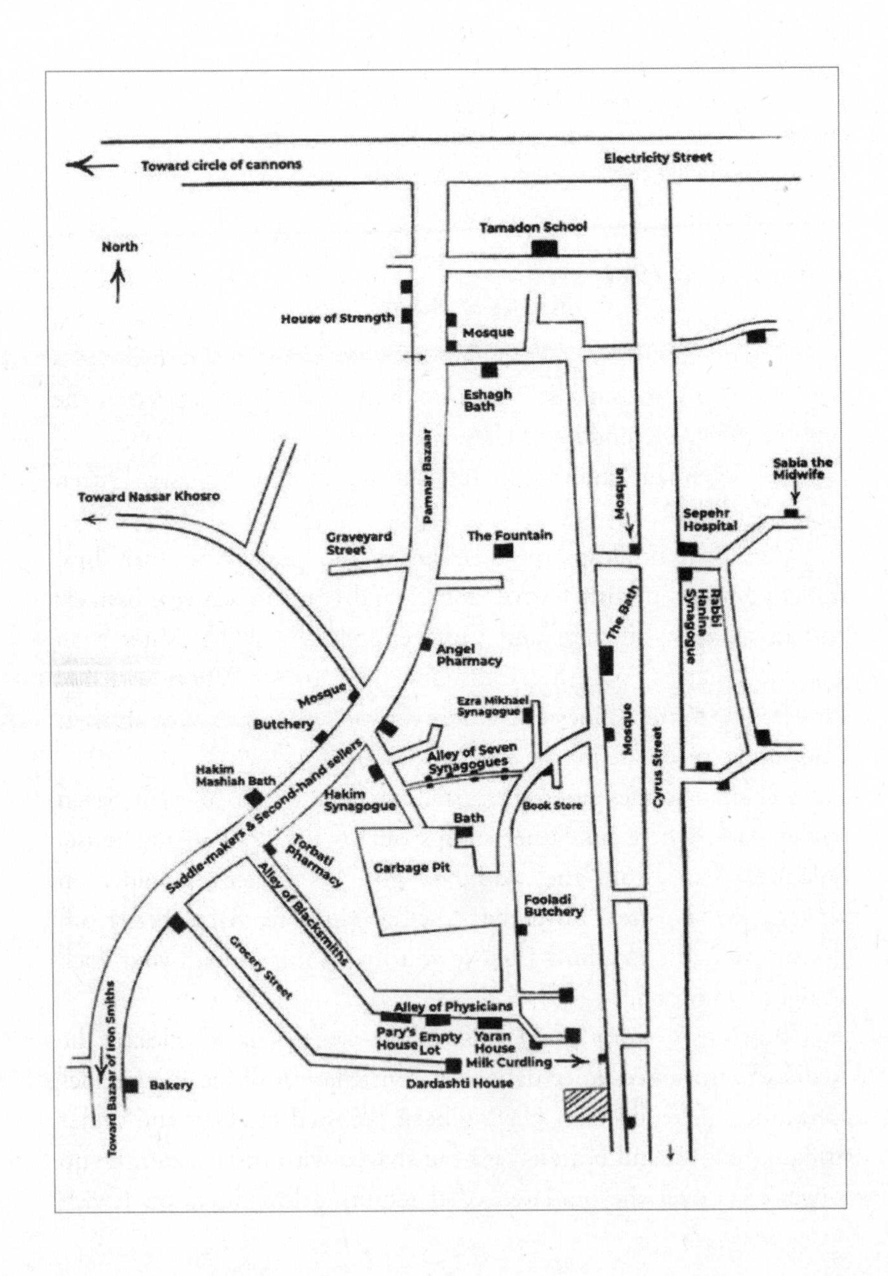

Toward circle of cannons
Electricity Street
Tamadon School
North
House of Strength
Mosque
Eshagh Bath
Parmnar Bazaar
Toward Nassar Khosro
Mosque
Sabia the Midwife
Sepehr Hospital
Graveyard Street
The Fountain
Rabbi Hanina Synagogue
The Bath
Angel Pharmacy
Mosque
Ezra Mikhael Synagogue
Butchery
Mosque
Cyrus Street
Alley of Seven Synagogues
Hakim Mashiah Bath
Saddle-makers & Second-hand sellers
Hakim Synagogue
Book Store
Bath
Torbati Pharmacy
Garbage Pit
Alley of Blacksmiths
Fooladi Butchery
Grocery Street
Alley of Physicians
Pary's House
Empty Lot
Yaran House
Milk Curdling
Toward Bazaar of Iron Smiths
Bakery
Dardashti House

CHAPTER ONE

Tehran, Iran, 1941

Pride and fear travel fast in the Jewish Quarter, where everyone's nose is in someone else's business, and gossip gets trapped in the low-roofed shacks and blind alleys.

Dr. Soleiman Yaran is on his way to see Her Majesty, Queen Fawzia Pahlavi.

Men with skullcaps on their heads and prayers on their lips, ululating women with festive clothes and colorful scarves, bankers and merchants, butchers and fruit vendors, the shah's Water Man and the Quarter Fool, the rabbis, and the Quarter Whore with her bleached hair and rhinestone-studded slippers are out to wish their beloved doctor a safe journey and a safe return.

Soleiman guides his restless stallion toward the Alley of Seven Synagogues, where his father stoops out of the door of his house. Soleiman leans from the saddle to give his father's shoulder an affectionate squeeze. "I'll be back before nightfall, Baba, better off, I hope, and able to afford a house you'd walk out of with your back straight and proud."

"Bowing to *goyim* is the least of my worries, son." Eleazar the Redhead's unruffled voice defies the constellation of blazing freckles sprinkling his pallid face. Having been accosted in alleys and under bridges, spat on and beaten, his head shaved with rusty razors, he no longer frets over the outdated edict requiring low doors on Jewish houses so that the occupants genuflect like servants when they step out. He slips a small *Tehillim* prayer book into the pocket of Soleiman's coat. "Bottle up your pride, son, keep your eyes open and your mouth shut at all times, or you'll end up hanging from a tree in a deserted alley. Don't forget that even if you become the Queen's dentist, to them, you're still a *najes* Jew."

Aunt Shamsi stoops her way out of the house as she swings a mesh fire-turner with crackling seeds of rue to ward off the evil eye. A backhanded slap on Rostam's flank. "What did you eat for breakfast, Soleiman? Donkey brains? Look at you! Trotting to the Queen, all high and mighty on that smug stallion of yours."

"Good morning to you, too!" Soleiman calls back to his aunt as he points his stallion toward Jacob Mordechai, who is rinsing the steps to his house, the paisley patterns on his silk, velvet-collard robe flickering in the wash of light tumbling out of the open door. He drops the hose and crosses the alley to greet his friend, grabs the reins, and lowers the stallion's head. "It's a big day, Rostam. You're on your way to the palace."

Soleiman prods Jacob with a playful tap of his riding crop. "And you, my friend, must have heard about the Queen's toothache even before she felt it."

Jacob steps back, clicks his crimson slippers, and raises his hand in a military salute. A member of the Jewish Agency for Palestine, his sharp ears and eyes are tuned to Tehran's pulse, which currently pounds with indignation at the court's choice to elevate Soleiman Yaran above all the Muslim dentists in the country. "Good luck, Soleiman. Use your new position wisely. Travel permits for Palestine aren't being issued, and negotiations with the British are at a stalemate. But the agency keeps sending me more orphans. Plead their case with the new Queen before she's hardened like the others. Go now, and don't you dare come back feet first."

Tehran has expanded beyond her old walls, all the way north toward the foot of the Alborz Mountain range. Neoclassical buildings, designed by European and Iranian architects, line avenues newly widened to accommodate the passage of cars. Gone are the charming gates that once led to streets and surrounding hamlets. Gone are the buildings of the Qajar dynasty, with their ornate mosaics and intricate woodwork. Gone are the inner courtyards with cooling turquoise-tiled fountains. In their place, block-like houses face the wider streets that buzz with pedestrians, donkey and horse-drawn droshkies, trucks and buses, and the two-car passenger train running along the center of town.

The din of hawkers can be heard everywhere—juicy pomegranate and quince for veal stew, crunchy cucumbers, ripe watermelons, grilled beets and corn on the cob, sun-dried fruit, and jars of shelled walnuts swimming in saltwater. A blind man, amulets displayed around his neck, wrists, and fingers, peddles his wares—turquoise pendants, evil eye bracelets, and prayer pouches—at the side of the street.

British soldiers patrol in khaki overalls and shirts, sleeves rolled up, the stomping of their dusty boots an insult to the ears. Hard-eyed Russian soldiers bark and spit and crush foreign cigarettes under their boots as if this is their home and all is well.

All is not well!

The Second World War is in full force, and Iran, despite her declaration of neutrality, has been invaded by the Allies. The Trans-Iranian Railway that winds its way through the Alborz Mountains has come under the control of the Allies, serving as a major corridor through which tons of war matériel are transported to the Soviet Union. Hundreds of American engineers are working day and night to render the treacherous highways and archaic ports operational, so as to transport added supplies and ammunition to the Red Army, which is overwhelmed by the massive German offensive.

Most of the country's harvested grain is impounded by Russian and British soldiers. Bread, rice, and most other food is scarce, as is gasoline and clean air to breathe. Lootings have become rampant, and the populace lives in perpetual fear of famine, influenza, and typhoid.

Soleiman observes the squeezed faces of children that peer out of the opening of a tarp-covered Red Cross truck on its way to one of the hastily erected Polish refugee camps around Tehran. Thousands of refugees, who fled the German occupation of Poland, drowned in the Caspian Sea on their journey to the port of Pahlavi. Those who survived became sick with malaria and typhus and were so desperate for food that thousands more overate, when food became available, and died from dysentery. The luckier ones found temporary refuge in the homes of residents like Jacob, who is in talks with the British authorities to allow the "Tehran Children," as they are called, entry to Palestine.

The beats of hope in Soleiman's chest echo the footsteps of an assembly of Imperial Adjutants in red and blue uniforms, who escort him into the grounds of the Golestan Palace of Flowers. He, a Jewish man, is welcomed into the royal compound, where, for more than two-hundred-and-fifty years, edifices have been erected, added, and destroyed to accommodate the visions and ambitions of kings. He will prove worthy of the Queen's trust. The Muslim society will see his people for who they are and accept them in their own land.

Crested helmets aglitter in the sun, the adjutants escort Soleiman into the magnificent complex of royal buildings—the Ivory Hall, Brilliant Building, Mirror Hall, Diamond Hall, and Marble Throne. A walled citadel during the reign of the Safavid King, Tahmasp I, and the official residence and governing hub of the last reigning Qajar Dynasty, this is where formal receptions, royal weddings, and coronations are held now.

Riders trot about the perimeter of the grounds, around the Wind Catcher Building, its golden cupola a dazzle in the sun, its summer hall cooled by breezes directed down by four towers.

Deep in conversation, men in western three-piece suits and somber-colored cravats stroll in and out of the columned Khalvat-e-Karimkhani, its domed terrace a place for peaceful reflection, far from the mayhem of war and chaos outside the walls.

Soleiman is accosted by an imposing man of the Ghashghaei Tribe, tall and wide-shouldered, a black handlebar mustache slashing across his face like double scimitars. A nasty rumble in the man's hulk of a chest, he signals to the doctor to open his medical case. "Inspections!"

Grip tight around the handle of his case, Soleiman tugs at a chain looped through a buttonhole across his vest and flips open the top of his pocket watch. "I don't have time for petty inspections, *Agha*. Her Imperial Majesty expects me in six minutes."

A bald, full-bearded adjutant steps forward to inform the inspector that the doctor is authorized. The inspector growls something under his breath and marches away. The adjutant waves to a groom who, wide-eyed with wonder, offers a sugar cube to the magnificent thoroughbred he will be in charge of. A grunt at the groom's feathered helmet, an indignant whinny, and the stallion allows the groom to steer him away.

With a confident gait that conceals the slight shortness of his left leg, a result of childhood polio, Soleiman follows the adjutants into the palace, resplendent with magnificent carpets and antique furniture, the walls decorated with miniature paintings by Persian masters, Sevres vases and bowls displayed on buffets and consoles.

A set of interior doors open, and Soleiman steps into the Hall of Mirrors, where the Peacock Throne was housed before it was moved to the Treasury of National Jewels. The dazzling lights of thousands of brilliant arrows shoot back and forth from intricate designs of cut-mirrored ceiling and walls. Everything is multiplied ten-fold, the grand chandeliers, the latticed windows, the gold-leafed furniture, and the twenty-year-old Queen Fawzia, who leans back in a cushioned chair, one leg crossed over the other, her white summer dress tumbling just below her knees to reveal shapely legs and varnished toes peeping out of satin shoes.

None of her photographs do justice to the stunning beauty he faces, the torrent of black curls framing her translucent complexion, the brightly painted lips, the turquoise eyes regarding him with detached curiosity and arrogance.

The grandeur triggers anxiety. But there is pride and awe, as well. Among the many dentists Her Majesty could have had her pick of, she chose him, a young, newly minted dentist from the Jewish Quarter.

Ill-prepared for the formalities and complexities of court, he wonders how to address the recently crowned Queen. How close should he step to bow his respects? Aware that Muslims consider Jews *najes* and impure, he clenches his hands at his sides and waits for a clue.

The Queen solves the problem by raising her hand to him. He kisses the air a few centimeters above the back of her hand, close enough to detect the scent of lavender on her royal skin.

The lace handkerchief she coils and uncoils around her fingers grants her a measure of innocence, which clashes with the fierce stare maintained steadily on him. "Good afternoon, Doctor Yaran." Her voice originates deep in her throat, the words sounding more Arabic than French.

"Good afternoon, Your Majesty," he replies in French, having read that the Queen has given up the study of Farsi and prefers to communicate in French with her husband and the royal court.

Like ghosts bleeding into the heavy curtains, a wall of attendants surveys the Queen's every move as she rises and makes her way across the room toward a German-made Ritter Dental chair, fully equipped with a control panel, cuspidor, drill, tray table, saliva ejector, and air and water syringes.

The Queen waves her handkerchief toward the chair—behind which two liveried men stand at attention. "Will this do?"

"Perfectly, Your Majesty." Aware of the many eyes on him, he crosses the room and arranges his medical equipment carefully on the table. Is he expected to wear rubber gloves? He hopes not. They are thick and cumbersome and would make it difficult to feel and diagnose the condition of the gums and the underlying bones, but the

Queen, too, might find the touch of a Jew repulsive. "May I have Your Majesty's permission to check your teeth without gloves?"

She nods, shuts her eyes as if his asking permission is a waste of her time.

He is relieved. It is true, then, that the Queen, like most Sunni Egyptians, is more tolerant than Shiite Iranians. Still, he feels the need to bring to her attention that he is wiping his fingers with alcohol and disinfecting his medical instruments, his every move slow and deliberate as a magician's.

A white longhaired spaniel skips in to settle at the Queen's feet. She slides one bare foot out of her shoe and strokes the dog's groomed hair with her manicured toes.

Egyptians, unlike Shiite Muslims, do not consider dogs dirty, Soleiman is aware; even so, he is surprised at the liberties this court allows the Queen—her bold, unflinching stare, red lips, bare toes, her skirt barely covering her knees.

He recalls the unprecedented fanfare surrounding the royal union of the then seventeen-year-old Princess Fawzia, the eldest daughter of King Fuad I of Egypt and Sudan to Mohammad Reza Pahlavi, the twenty-year-old crown prince of Iran. The wedding ceremony was held at the Abdeen Palace in Cairo and repeated in the Marble Palace in Tehran. Commemoration medallions of the royal marriage were minted, and *Tagheh nostrat* triumphal arches graced every street. Such a magnificently handsome couple, so deeply in love. May they be blessed with a son in nine months, Insha'Allah.

Fate had other plans for the young couple. Princess Fawzia gave birth to a daughter. And when the allies ordered her father-in-law, Reza Shah, the progressive and once powerful king of kings, who had forged close ties with Hitler, to abdicate, the heavy responsibility of ruling the country was forced upon her green husband, Mohammad Reza Pahlavi.

The weeks before the abdication and exile of Reza Shah to Johannesburg are forever tattooed in Soleiman's mind. All ears were tuned to the news; Jews stayed with friends who owned a radio. Hitler was at the border. If he succeeded in invading Iran, it would have been the end of them all. Reza Shah, despite the forceful demands of the Allies, refused to expel German residents from Iran. Nor was he inclined to allow the Allies the use of the 788-kilometer Trans-Iranian Railway to transport war matériel to the Soviet Union.

The enraged Allies handed Reza Shah a diplomatic ultimatum:

Would His Highness kindly abdicate in favor of his son, the heir to the throne? We have a high opinion of him and will ensure his position. But His Highness should not think there is any other solution.

Her Sultanic Highness Princess, Fawzia bint Fuad, was crowned the Queen of Iran.

An impatient tap of the Queen's finger on the armchair. "You were educated in Paris, Doctor Yaran. You have a *Diplôme du Baccalauréat Professionnel* in dentistry. You introduced Novocaine to our country. Yes?"

"Yes, Your Majesty," Soleiman replies as he places his disinfecting paraphernalia on the table. "I have a valuable supply I brought from Paris."

"This is why I asked for you."

"I am honored, Your Majesty. I will not disappoint."

"You left Paris to return here." A dismissive gesture of her royal hand as if Iran is not worth naming. "Why?"

"Out of duty, Your Majesty."

She nods, gauges him with added interest. "Duty to whom?"

"To my father, Your Majesty, to my people who financed my trip to France, so they would have the benefit of my education."

The Queen questions him through narrowed eyes. "You have a wife, Doctor Yaran. She is expecting, yes?"

"Yes, Your Majesty, Ruby, my wife. She is expecting our first child." A flicker of a rare smile in Soleiman's eyes. God willing, Ruby will give him a son for whom he will purchase a stallion like his own. A gift from the first patient he had injected with Novocaine.

Grateful beyond words at the novelty of having a molar extracted painlessly, the patient led Soleiman to his breeding farm and handed him the reins of a liquid-eyed purebred named Rostam. The Jewish Quarter was no place for a splendid stallion named after the mythological warrior of Ferdowsi's *Shahnameh*, Soleiman had reasoned, an imperial animal such as this would be a liability. Had Rostam not lowered his muzzle to sigh furtively in his ear, he would have refused the gift.

The Queen gestures to the dental explorer in Soleiman's hand, prompting him to explain that the instrument is used to check for decay or any other abnormalities. *What*, he wonders, *is the proper way to ask a queen to open her mouth wider?* "Are you in pain, Your Majesty?"

"Yes, Doctor Yaran." With her handkerchief, she wipes a speck of lipstick from her teeth as if she noticed it in a mirror. "I am in terrible pain."

"I might be able to help Your Majesty."

She spreads her hands in a gesture of surrender. His heart thumps with pride. He has been deemed worthy of the Queen's trust. "May I ask Her Majesty to open her mouth wider?"

The Queen rests her head against a pillow an attendant brings in for that purpose. She shuts her eyes and slightly parts her lips, as if opening her mouth wider would expose some vulnerability.

He lifts her upper lip, noticing the slight tremble of his hand, but before he embarks on checking all her teeth, he sees the problem—a black, perceptible dot on her upper front tooth, which will require far more sensitive work than he had anticipated. This is not good. The Queen will not like her beauty marred. He taps on the tooth. A royal flinch. A spark of disapproval scuttles across the blazing eyes. "I apologize, Your Majesty, pardon me. I found the problem. A decay on your upper front tooth."

Again, that unsettling half smile. "My indulgence in baklava, I'm afraid. It must be easy to fix. Yes?"

"I am not sure, Your Majesty. I am concerned about the aesthetic result. Gold filling is best, but Your Majesty will not like the look of it. Amalgam is even less attractive. We don't have any material that will look natural, I am afraid."

"Nonsense!" The Queen stares him down as if he uttered blasphemy. "What is it you need, Doctor Yaran? Whatever it is, it will be arranged."

"No doubt, Your Majesty. But it might prove difficult. Such material has not been invented."

"Invent it, then. And make sure it is the color of my teeth. You are an inventor. I have heard nothing but praise about you. Do not disappoint me." The Queen snaps her manicured fingers to demonstrate the speed with which she expects him to accomplish the task.

CHAPTER TWO

"My royal dentist!" Ruby walks into Soleiman's embrace. "Tell me all about the palace...no...about the Queen first."

Soleiman strokes his wife's child-heavy belly, lifts her in his arms, and digs his face in her raging hair, the shade of polished copper. "How is *my* beautiful queen?"

"As beautiful as Queen Fawzia?"

"Far more beautiful, Sweetheart." He unspools her red scarf from around her neck and gathers her hair back with the scarf he ties into a neat bow. His mouth travels up her neck, nips at her earlobe as he carries her across the garden, past a feast of mint, lavender, basil, oregano, and thyme in a box she painted the shade of ripe cherries, past the two Shabbat candles that flicker behind the kitchen window, and sets her in one of the metal chairs under the ancient mulberry tree, where the air is laced with the scent of ripe berries hanging from branches overhead and the many squashed underfoot.

She lifts both arms and twirls six gold bangles on each wrist, displaying the gift he had given her for having tolerated his distracted behavior in the last months.

He slips from his vest pocket a gold watch with etching on the back, her gift to him for discovering Ruby Magic.

Their laughter echoes around the small garden as they recall the months of experiments Soleiman conducted in his laboratory after he learned that the Novocaine he brought to Iran could be deadly to an immune system compromised by long years of opium abuse.

He tested all kinds of bitter ointments on his own gums, applied them so often and for so long that his gums turned purple and remained numb for three days straight so he could not eat or drink properly. When he lost six kilos, Ruby marched across the garden and into his laboratory. Her cheeks flushed, her fiery mane chaotic, she planted a cage on his working table. "Enough, Soleiman, you're killing yourself. Here! Experiment on these if you have to."

A couple of pink-eyed rabbits stared at him like forlorn convicts through the cage's tightly wound metal mesh.

The experiments on his gums continued but less often and in lower doses. Wary of bothering Ruby with the drone of his dental tools, he switched them on late at night and after she was asleep. In rare moments of respite from the endless computations of his hectic mind, he was content to sip tea in silence with his wife when she delivered two cups of cardamom tea with a plate of *koloocheh* cookies.

In the end, he invented a mixture of opium, lady slippers, oak bark, tea tree oil, and wild indigo, which he hoped would prove effective as an anesthetic for the large Iranian population of opium addicts, who could not tolerate Novocaine.

It took another month of adding and subtracting extracts of dates, molasses, and the sweet stevia rebaudiana plant to eliminate the bitter taste. He named the ointment Ruby Magic for his wife and, to thank her for reminding him of what really mattered, gave her his most precious possession—his mother's twelve gold bangles, still wrapped in the original fading silk she had kept them in.

Ruby, too, had a gift for him: a gold pocket watch with 'Ruby Magic' engraved on the back.

Soleiman tucks his watch back into his vest pocket. "Tell me, Sweetheart, did you really think I could test my ointment on those rabbits?"

Ruby wraps her arms around her belly. "That, Soleiman, was your business. Mine was to make sure you don't lose your teeth."

He regards the white tablecloth covering the round iron table, the freshly baked challah, bowl of pickled herbs, a dish of pomegranate-rice and eggplant stew. "Everything smells delicious, Sweetheart. You shouldn't tire yourself."

"Tired? Never. I'm in love." Despite chopping herbs from her garden box, despite mincing the dates and seeding the pomegranate Soleiman received in return for his services, despite having to manage the Quarter Fool's every move when he came to hose down the garden earlier today, she is not tired.

"You need to take better care of yourself. That's the doctor's orders. Promise?"

She presses a palm to her eye. "Promise, *Agha* doctor."

"The butcher's holding some veal shank for you. Make a meat dish for yourself, Sweetheart."

A twinge of anger scuttles across Ruby's face. "They take advantage of you, Soleiman, the butcher, the Water Man, the greengrocer, every single one of them. Don't go performing miracles on rotting teeth in return for two measly eggplants, a pomegranate, and a few grams of meat." She ladles eggplant stew into his plate. "I'll stop eating meat too."

Soleiman cups her face in his hands. "The baby needs protein, Sweetheart, you too. The war will end soon, we'll have lots of meat."

The day he stopped consuming any type of meat or poultry remains alive in his mind with startling clarity. Hardly ten, he had accompanied his father on business as he walked around the Jewish Quarter, the legs of four chickens gripped in one hand, their racket sending housewives out to squat at the threshold of their homes. After thrusting a finger into the backside of one or another chicken, they handed the plumpest to Baba Eleazar to perform the kosher *shechitah* of slaughtering chickens for food. The quick metallic flash of the sharp knife slashed the chicken's throat, tossing the dying bird into a blizzard of bloody feathers. Soleiman doubled over and vomited what was left in his stomach of last night's dinner. He vowed to shape a different destiny for himself, make enough money to have Baba Eleazar retire from the thankless jobs of slaughtering chickens for a few dinars or shoveling snow off Muslim rooftops, his compensation more often than not a stinging slap at the back of his head accompanied by an expletive.

Soleiman fills to the brim a silver goblet with kosher wine. He rises, recites the Kiddush, drinks from the wine, then brings the goblet to Ruby's lips for her to take a sip.

Ruby says the *HaMotzi* blessing over the challah and sprinkles it with salt, plucks a small morsel from the bread, and feeds it to Soleiman with such care and patience he says, "Soon you will be nursing your own baby."

"Our son," she whispers, disarming him with the wonderful strangeness of her dazzled gaze.

"A healthy child, Sweetheart."

She fills his plate with pomegranate rice. "Tell me about the Queen. How did she treat you?"

"Far better than I expected. Don't give me that jealous look, Sweetheart. I've eyes for you only. You should have seen how impossible it was to coax the Queen into opening her mouth."

Their laughter is muffled by the roar of approaching airplanes, the rumble of engines overhead vibrates in their chests. The onslaught of black aircraft emblazoned with red stars turns the skies the color of soot and steel. The stench of smoke and gasoline sends them into fits of coughing.

A barrage of leaflets tumbles out of the planes, flaps, twists, and flutters mid-air, crowding the skies like drunk birds. They land on Ruby's herb box, the roof of the laboratory, mulberry branches, and plates of food, soaking in pomegranate juice, olive oil, and kosher wine.

Attention Tehran!

The Soviet Air Force Commands.

Surrender!

Or suffer massive air raids and annihilation.

The faraway rumble of trucks crossing the main street shakes the small garden. The crack of gunfire in the distance. Three consecutive explosions propel Ruby out of her seat and into Soleiman's arms.

"No one will bomb Tehran, Sweetheart. They're waging a psychological war, trying to destroy our morale. The last leaflets warned us against cooperating with the Germans. These demand our surrender." But he knows better. Germany has invaded the Soviet Union, forcing Britain and the Soviet Union into an uncomfortable alliance in their fight against the Third Reich. The Soviet Union and Britain have launched a full-scale invasion of Abadan to keep vulnerable oilfields from falling into German hands. Tehran might be next.

Soleiman lifts Ruby in his arms and carries her into the house, grabs a radio from the hallway table, and descends the steep basement stairs, lowers her onto a mattress and covers her with one of the blankets piled against a wall.

He turns on the radio, extends the antenna and adjusts it horizontally, this way and that, but the reception is weak. He drags a stool under the cellar window and climbs up to place the radio on the ledge, then adjusts the knob.

Zeesen, Nazi Germany's propaganda station, comes to static life. "Jews! Communists! Hitler, the Shiite Messiah has arrived. Just as our Prophet Mohammed struggled against Jews, Hitler will—"

Hot winds slam the window shut, startling a cloud of flies and drowning the broadcast. A single branch of the ancient mulberry tree in the garden breaks loose from the trunk, sways in the wind, and scratches against the window like a gnarled finger.

Soleiman turns the radio knob in search of another station—Tehran Radio announces the advance of the Red Army deeper into Iran to the North. *The British-led Indian army is marching into Iran from Iraq to take control of precious oil fields.... Massive invasion by air, land, and sea...heavy airstrikes on cities and airfields...staggering fatalities.... Palang, the 950-ton gunboat sloop, is sinking in the harbor of*

Abadan. Soviet armored units have invaded Tabriz. American airplanes on the ground in Abadan airfields are ready to be delivered to the Soviet Union. The warship, Babr, torpedoed in Khoramshahr.... Commander of the Caspian flotilla killed in the line of duty...tanks infantry and artillery under the command of General Shahbakhti.... Stand by...ten seconds an important announcement from...five seconds...I repeat...Rear Admiral Bayandor, commander of the Iranian navy...an amphibious attack— another burst of static explodes in Soleiman's ears. Are the broadcasts reliable? How could the Iranian army, the pride of the exiled Reza Shah, surrender with such speed?

"Soleiman." Ruby pulls herself up to lean against the wall. "Pary's all alone. Go and bring her here."

"Pary is safer where she is, Sweetheart, try not to worry." But he *is* concerned. Pary, their next-door neighbor, is a strong and independent woman and not prone to being easily alarmed. Still, it is difficult to be alone with the threat of fighter planes overhead and the rumble of tanks and artillery so close. Hardly a month has passed since Pary lost Monsieur André, her French husband, to typhoid. Ruby was at her side the entire week of Shiva. And he, too, did what he could. Administered Valerian drops when needed, tonic of passion flowers and lemon balm leaves to calm the nerves, and a sleeping pill or two when Pary became inconsolable. A week after Monsieur André died, a superstitious rabbi claimed that he had seen Pary's door shed tears at the exact hours of morning and evening prayers. Before long, the Alley of Physicians became crowded with people from near and far, who came to pray to the green door, encroaching on Pary's need for solitude and making it difficult for her to step out of her house to purchase groceries or visit the bookstore for a book. *Well, each to his own*, Soleiman muses, as he steps down from the stool and carefully lowers himself next to Ruby, wraps his arm around her shoulders, and draws her close.

They are startled by the clang of the gate opening and the hasty bang of it closing. Soleiman jumps up, climbs the stool, and wipes the fogged-up window, but it is low and narrow and all he sees are the black shadows of two figures, hurrying across the garden toward the house.

He quickly silences the radio, descends from the stool, and goes back to Ruby. A burst of gunfire outside. A nearby explosion lights the basement from wall to wall. An acrid stench seeps in through the window and into their lungs. He gathers Ruby in his arms.

"We should have locked the door," she whispers.

I should have fixed the broken lock of the gate, he thinks.

Heavy footsteps clamber down the stairs.

"May the black plague strike Hitler and his descendants. May pus-filled boils devour every stinking Nazi!"

A torrent of curses spill out of Aunt Shamsi's mouth as she lumbers in, behind her Eleazar the Redhead, breathless, curls springing in odd directions.

Soleiman starts to his feet. "Baba! Why are you out? It's dangerous."

"Shamsi thought Ruby might need her." Eleazar the Redhead greets his daughter-in-law with a resigned smile and a calm nod. His usually ruddy face is gaunt, the lines around his eyes deeper. He lowers himself into a cross-legged position on the floor and leans against the wall. From his coat pocket, he pulls his shechita knife out of its leather glove and, with the same quick and precise movements he has been performing the kosher *shechita* for thirty-two years, polishes the sharp, nick-less blade with his handkerchief.

"It's hell out there, Soleiman, hell!" Aunt Shamsi wails. "Hitler opened his stinking *koon* bottom and vomited black smoke and filthy leaflets. People are running around like lunatics with their tails on fire. Ruby? How are you? You're paler than death."

"Calm down, Aunt Shamsi," Soleiman says. "You're safe here."

"Of course," huffs Aunt Shamsi, "With Eleazar brewing all kinds of nose-burning alcohol in our basement no one's safe there. May they all choke on their *aragh*."

Eleazar the Redhead folds his knife and tucks it back in his pocket. "Some peace, Shamsi, please."

"Peace? Not until every single Nazi drowns in Hitler's stinking shit!"

Hours pass in the cellar heat. It is hard to breathe, and their clothing is damp with sweat. Wary of further agitating Ruby, Soleiman does not turn on the radio. He arranges a folded blanket behind her back, but she rests her head in his lap and shuts her eyes.

Dawn breaks out of the fogged window and an odd silence descends upon the outside world. Despite the growing heat, Ruby shivers like a new-born kitten. Soleiman covers her with another blanket, kneels by her side, checks her pulse, and runs his hand over her face. Her cheeks are drained of color, her plump lips dry and chapped. Her belly distorts with a strong spasm, and she stuffs her scarf into her mouth to stifle her cry of pain. His heart lurches into his throat. The shock of the last hours has thrust Ruby into early labor. He lifts her in his arms. "I'm taking you upstairs, Sweetheart. Aunt Shamsi, prepare for delivery."

Aunt Shamsi pulls herself to her feet. "Bring Ruby upstairs, Soleiman, then find something useful to do with your time."

"Let Soleiman be." Eleazar the Redhead climbs the stairs behind his sister. "He's a doctor, Shamsi, he knows what he's doing."

Aunt Shamsi aims a string of curses—plagues, boils, and runny bowels—at every ignorant husband who made her life miserable in the last eleven years. What good is Soleiman, when he doesn't know a fart about delivering babies? "Leave matters concerning women to women, Soleiman. You shouldn't see your wife exposed in that immodest way."

"May Hashem bless you with Noah's patience," Eleazar the Redhead tells his son, "I'll be home if you need me."

Soleiman lowers Ruby onto the cot in the bedroom, tells Aunt Shamsi to boil water on the coal stove, scrub her hands clean, and dip everything in the boiling water.

Shamsi washes her hands with great fanfare, grumbles under her breath that she, the most competent midwife in the Quarter, does not need directions from her nephew. "Step out, Soleiman, so I can check her. The birth won't be anytime soon, not before her water breaks."

Soleiman strokes Ruby's hair away from her damp cheeks. "I'm not going anywhere, Sweetheart."

A racket at the gate and a series of urgent bangs sends Aunt Shamsi to the door. She tiptoes back into the room and quietly closes the door. "Someone's asking for you, Soleiman."

"Can't you see I'm busy? Send them away."

"You better see for yourself, Soleiman, someone in uniform with very important medals all over his *takhteh mordeh* uniform."

At the garden gate, Soleiman finds a huge man with coarse hair slicked back over a protruding forehead. From behind a thick mustache, his loud, deliberate voice appears to pronounce a fatwa: "His Majesty the *Shahanshah*, *Aryamehr*, and *Bozorg Arteshdaran* orders Doctor Soleiman Yaran to call on His Excellency, the Governor General!"

A peculiar silence descends on the Alley of Physicians. The shah's Water Man and his donkey, the beet and cucumber seller, even the hungry stray dogs abandon their tasks and survey the royal messenger with dread-tinged curiosity.

Refusing royal orders is out of the question, Soleiman knows, as is escaping the long reach of the powerful Governor General, better known as the Land Eater, whose ruthless behavior has gripped Iran's populace with fear.

"Is the Governor General in pain?" Soleiman asks.

"His Majesty commands!" the man declares.

"I understand," says Soleiman. "But is it an emergency?"

The messenger lets out a roar of outrage from behind his hardly moving mustache. "By His Majesty's command!"

"All right, then. I shall visit the Governor General first thing tomorrow. Right now, I'll have to take care of my wife."

The royal messenger's mustache jumps once at the unexpected audacity confronting him. He draws his baton from its holster, stares for a long time at the neighbor's mythical door, in front of which the greengrocer and his son have stopped praying, and threatens to smash their heads, unless Soleiman saddles his stallion right away and speeds to the Governor General.

CHAPTER THREE

Soleiman's concern for Ruby mounts with every flick of the reins distancing him from home. Aunt Shamsi is an experienced midwife, better equipped than most doctors in Tehran's filthy hospitals, where infections and contagion are prevalent, but her tendency to rely on antiquated superstitions—incantations, potions, blessings and curses—is no consolation. He will make sure to be back in time to deliver his child.

Rostam snorts and pants up the governor's steep dirt-packed road, which had disrupted life for years. Continuous blasts shook Tehran day and night as hundreds of laborers dynamited through limestone and beds of lava, jackhammered, and shoveled to widen this private road to accommodate giant trucks that transported tons of construction material to build the governor general's blue mansion, which rises like a ghost ship in the center of a sea of red poppies.

Soleiman observes with a blend of astonishment and disgust the private kingdom the governor general has created. It is no small feat to carve a plateau on top of such a mighty mountain. No small feat to erect a mansion here, along with two opium refineries, which are poisoning the air with smoke and ash. But to cultivate opium poppies in such a hostile environment is an achievement beyond comprehension.

The vast fields surrounding the mansion throb with workers in loose skirts and trousers, who collect opium in earthenware pots held at their waist with ropes. They mark with *nishtar* lancets the skins of the ripening poppy pods—horizontal incisions to manipulate the plants into shedding milky tears, which will dry to a sticky brown resin they will harvest at dawn. The harvested opium is hastily refined in the governor general's crude laboratories, packed in falsely labeled boxes, and shipped with war supplies across the Trans-Iranian Railway to neighboring countries, Azerbaijan, Turkey, and Afghanistan.

Soleiman watches with dismay as from time to time the laborers take a break and lick accumulated resin off their blades, addicting themselves.

A uniformed chauffeur is polishing the gold trim of a black Lincoln Continental parked by wide-open gates bordered by massive stone pillars on top of which two cannons aim at the surrounding fields.

A woman emerges swiftly out of the gates, a golden comet blazing a path through the red poppies. Her yellow chador swells in the breeze as she breaks into a run, gathering speed as if borne on winged sandals. She comes to a breathless stop in front of the stunned Soleiman and his stallion. A few impatient tilts of her elegant neck, and the chador slips off her head to reveal a shock of corn silk hair, as dazzling as her silver eyes.

Soleiman touches his hat in salutation. "*Sarkar Khanom*, honorable Madame." Who is this exquisite creature, this unexpected vision, who has the audacity to accost a male stranger with her face revealed like this, her hair flirting with her face in the breeze, the glint of her eyes as assured as those of a queen?

She steps closer, so close she can sense the faint scent of mud the stallion's hooves stir as he trots in place, the horse sweat in the air, the quiver of the animal's flank against his master's thigh on which rests his silver-handled crop. It is not wise to be out here, she knows, but she had to see for herself the doctor who has aroused such hate and admiration. Now and then dignitaries visit to pay their respects to the governor general, bribe him with gold coins, gift him valuable clocks to add to his collection of precious clocks. But a Jew? Never.

Her gaze wanders up his high-waisted trousers and the red suspenders peeking from under his European-style coat, across his clean-shaven face up to his hat. She knows she will not find any proof of the horns the governor general describes with gleeful detail, jagged and sharp and more ominous than an Arab's dagger. Curious, nonetheless, her eyes rest on the determined lines of his generous mouth, his carefully trimmed hair, grazing the starched collar of a white shirt with cuff buttons. Her silver eyes acquire a jubilant air as she drapes her yellow chador around her shoulders. "*Salam, Agha* doctor from Paris. You have a magical pain medicine, I hear."

An imperceptible smile at the manner he is addressed. His right palm against his heart, a gesture of respect. "I have, *sarkar Khanom*."

A wave of one hand toward the gates behind her. "Good luck *Agha* doctor from Paris." She tugs the chador up to cover her hair and floats back toward the mansion, scattering the scent of roses in her wake.

With growing trepidation, Soleiman coaxes the grunting stallion toward the gates and into the gardens, where a host of men in army fatigue plant and prune a chilling landscape of twisted trunks and prickly shrubs dotted with purple lilies. Drops of water from the surrounding Persian junipers tremble on the animal's back as his hooves sink into a pebbled path that leads to the governor general's mausoleum-like mansion on top of which is a gold dome flanked by a pair of minarets depicting Islamic motifs.

A platoon of guards in military uniforms emerges from behind the dense landscape, marches in formation toward the stallion and his rider, and squeezes tight around them in a pincer movement. Rostam rears with a shrill neigh, scattering the men. A series of barked commands from a bald, thick-lipped guard, and the men scramble to regain their footing and formality, clicking heavy boots as if saluting an army general, rather than a doctor.

The thick-lipped guard steps forward, cracks his trunk of a neck this way and that. His slit eyes assess the visitor. "Doctor Soleiman Yaran?"

"Correct." Soleiman hands Rostam's reins to the groom, stops to take a good look at the groom's face. *Salak*, a flesh-eating bacterial disease that originates from contaminated waters in reservoirs and aqueducts, has chewed off the man's nose. "A moment, please," Soleiman says to the thick lipped guard, "I will inoculate the *Agha* before the disease consumes the rest of his face." Noticing the guard's hesitation, he adds, "None of you are immune, either. Not even the governor general."

The guard stares at the doctor as he attempts to grasp the facts. The doctor must surely know about the governor general's tendency to foam at the mouth when kept waiting. "Another time, please." The words whistle out of the guard's dry lips. "Maybe *Agha* doctor will pay a special visit to inoculate us all."

Soleiman is marshalled toward the mansion, up a flight of marble steps to a vast limestone veranda. A dead bird lies on its back in a corner, its eyes burned by the sun. The faint odor of its decay leaves a sour taste of worry in his mouth. The royal Palace, despite all the elaborate tile work, extravagant woodcarvings, and latticed windows, was far more welcoming than this garish mansion, perched ominously on top of the mountains as if to ridicule the poverty below.

The grand entry door slides open, and a tall woman steps out. She adjusts the silk turban covering her hair. A flash of her amber, turquoise, and emerald ringed fingers dismisses the guards. She glides across the terrace toward Soleiman, her flowing pants and ankle-length overcoat of crushed silk rage about her satin-clad legs, gold anklets and a cascade of gold chains around her neck chime in unison.

Soleiman is surprised. If women in his household are free to reveal their faces to male strangers, then the Land Eater must be a more progressive man than rumored.

"Welcome, Doctor Yaran, welcome." The woman raises a penciled eyebrow, tilts her head, and smiles. "I am Tulip."

The doctor is momentarily startled into silence. Something about the woman, with her cardamom-laced breath, delicately blushed cheeks, and kohl-rimmed eyes is not quite right. The long arms, large hands, slightly stooped shoulders are proof nature has been tampered with.

How could his eyes so utterly deceive him? The talk whirling about town is true, after all, talk he refused to believe from Baba Eleazar, from Aunt Shamsi, even from Ruby. Yet here he is face to face with the governor general's eunuch.

"Come in please. His Excellency is waiting. We mustn't try his patience," the soft-footed apparition sings in her melodious voice, and Soleiman has a sense of being led into a long-ago harem in the palace of a Qajar Shah.

Tall windows puncture impenetrable walls that resemble the mountain on which the mansion is built. The dark panes reflect the two figures walking side by side, the flurry of maids and servants bustling about like shadows in the night. Stone-cold halls pulse with the synchronized tick-tocks of an army of clocks that look down from walls, mantles, and pedestals. Clocks in different shapes and sizes—gold and silver, enameled and jewel-encrusted, a rotating globe, a zebra with a pendulum tail, one with soldiers for numbers, another with a background of poppies turning and tumbling at the stroke of the hour, and above a doorframe, a red-cheeked sea captain burrs and whirrs and gongs to announce the passing of two hours since Soleiman left Ruby. He snuffs the urge to reach for his own pocket watch. Firstborns take longer. He will make it on time for the birth.

A feminine voice recites poetry from somewhere deep inside the mansion, breathing a measure of warmth into this forbidding place, as does a burst of carefully arranged roses in a crystal vase, an enamel tea set and a collection of china dolls in a glass cabinet, a bowl of cherries next to a lipstick-stained teacup, a lace handkerchief forgotten on the marble top of a commode.

The odor of opium intensifies with Soleiman's every advancing step, as does his fear that the governor general's addiction is more serious than rumored. *What if the governor needs an injection of Novocaine*, Soleiman wonders, *a medication that could be lethal to a man whose blood is poisoned with opium?* He mentally rummages through his medical case for the fresh batch of Ruby Magic he had prepared for the Queen. Yes, it is there with the rest of his medical supplies. Having tested its efficacy on less than a handful of his patients, the anesthetic ointment is relatively new, but there is nothing else to rely on.

The eunuch taps the doctor on one shoulder. "*Salavat* thanks to all the imams for leading you here, *Agha* doctor, but I need to rest for a minute."

Soleiman forces himself to stop. Castration is known to disrupt the normal balance of the glands, weaken the bones and muscles, and cause the arms and legs to grow long and ungainly. "Are you in pain?" he asks the eunuch.

A slight tremble of red lips. A flutter of long lashes. "Truth be told, every single bone aches." He makes a sweeping gesture up and down his magnificently attired self. "Allah's will, I guess, and my kismet."

Soleiman takes a small packet from his medical case, shakes a fist-full of pills onto his palm, and drops them into Tulip's pocket. "Try two a day with food. It will help."

The eunuch grabs a few cardamom seeds from his other pocket and tosses them in his mouth. He does not know how to react to such kindness, something he did not experience as a child and has difficulty accepting as a twenty-one-year-old adult. The sweep of his perfumed sleeve momentarily masks the sickly-sweet smells in the air. "*Moteshakeram* thank you. May your kind hand never feel pain."

They come to a stop in front of a grand door carved with religious verses. An ivory elephant clock with bizarre, diabolical tusks, grins at them maliciously from above the doorframe.

Soleiman is escorted into a vast salon crowded with heavily carved furniture upholstered in crimson velvet. Crystal drops of a grand chandelier reflect like bloodstains on a silk carpet bordered with arabesque motifs. Displayed in a gold-leafed armoire are a wealth of daggers and scabbards, enameled and bejeweled, engraved with gold Arabic lettering, valuable scimitars twinkling like silver-toothed grins.

"I am right here if you need me," Tulip tells Soleiman, after which he slips behind an elaborate stand made of deer antlers on which leans a gilt-edged book of poetry bound in Moroccan leather.

The governor general is seated in a throne-like chair behind a massive agar wood desk. He is busy signing one document after another with his infamous pen, the cap crowned with a diamond as large as his thumbnail. A single signature of this pen has sent innocent attorneys to the gallows, locked families in prison, and shut thriving businesses. No one is exempt, not even the powerful administrator of Railroad Crossing who, having questioned the legality of transporting the governor's opium across the country, finds himself at the mercy of the governor, who has banned the import of Sulfamide on which the administrator depends.

The sight of the governor's skeletal frame strikes the doctor with renewed concern. Not that he is unattractive. On the contrary. His waves of dark hair frame strong features, high forehead, wide-set eyes, and arched eyebrows that endow him with a certain unapologetic masculinity. But other than his fleshy lips, his face lacks a gram of fat, proof that the man is far beyond enjoying a few daily puffs from the opium pipe, or a tiny pellet consumed in the morning for a lift of energy.

The governor screws his pen shut, twirls, tilts, and swings it between thumb and forefinger, the diamond reflecting latticed patterns on the walls and ceiling. A sudden twist of his wrist aims the pen toward his visitor. "I can't suffer pain, Yaran! Understood?"

"Yes, Your Excellency, I understand," Soleiman replies.

"Good!" The governor general reaches for a bowl on his desk and slides it toward the doctor. A drop of liquid spreads like spilt blood on the desk, which he blots with a grinding fist. "Come closer, Yaran, please. Wash your hands for me in this bowl of permanganate, right here where I can see you do it."

Soleiman attempts to muster a steady voice. "No need, Your Excellency. I always sterilize my hands with alcohol."

The governor's face wobbles on the surface of the permanganate solution as if drowning in the Red Sea. "Do as I say, Yaran. Wash your Jewish filth off before you probe my mouth."

The room is still. The clocks appear to have gone into collective sleep. Tulip holds his breath behind the gilt-edged book of poetry on the stand.

A stab of anger shoots through Soleiman. He could wear the gloves he brought from Paris and save himself from this humiliation, but they are thick and will hinder his ability to work fast, and all he wants is to do his duty and leave this suffocating place. He rolls his sleeves up and, his eyes meeting the governor's black stare, starts to scrub his hands with rubbing alcohol. "This, Your Excellency, is what doctors do. If you find it inadequate, a Muslim dentist will better serve you."

A torrent of confusion explodes in the governor's veins. His orders have never been refused. Yet. The impudent Jew continues to rub alcohol on his steady hands. Lower lip curled in contempt, the governor leans back in his high-backed chair and, as if it is the weight of his pen he is puzzled by, balances it on his open palm. A flick of two fingers and the pen rolls on the desk and cradles in a groove next to an issue of *Iran-e-Bastan* with a swastika on the cover. "I will let this one go, Yaran, but disobey me again, and I will yank your tongue out with my bare hands and fry it in pig lard."

CHAPTER FOUR

"Curse the devil's black heart!" Hours of probing and coaxing and no sign of the stubborn baby's head. Aunt Shamsi unfastens a safety pin from her blouse and blows between her breasts. The room is humid with breath and sweat and steam from the bowl of boiling water Soleiman left on the stove. How long does it take to fix That-Cursed-Land-Eater's teeth? She aims a string of silent curses—black plagues, puss-filled boils and runny bowels—at the evil man's untimely toothache.

"Now, now, sugar, it's me and you and God here." Aunt Shamsi attempts to soothe Ruby, who with every merciless spasm cries out for Soleiman. She grabs a fistful of salt from her pocket and rubs Ruby's belly as protection against *Mal'ach ha-Mavet* Angel of Death, who crouches around every dark corner, ready to pounce upon the innocent. "May *Hashem* bless Soleiman with a son to say the Kaddish over our graves."

So desperate was Ruby for a child, she had suffered a concoction that looked and smelled like rotten liver, which according to Aunt Shamsi, was made of a breed of half-fish, which cost its weight in gold, had to be dried in the sun, then pounded with a single pearl and two grams of pulverized turquoise to bribe *Sheitan* the devil into unlocking Ruby's womb.

The bitter concoction accomplished its purpose; Ruby became pregnant. But Aunt Shamsi was far from done. She appeared every morning with a fist-full of foul-smelling foreskins she smuggled from circumcision ceremonies around the Jewish Quarter and told Ruby to gulp them down. But no matter how hard and long Aunt Shamsi beat on her own chest and insisted that boys were not made out of thin air, Ruby refused to eat the foreskins. Instead, she agreed to consume the *sirabi* stew of sheep hooves and entrails. Having simmered for forty-eight hours on a slow cooking stove, the gelatinous stew was known to make the uterus slippery in preparation for an easy delivery.

All that, while Soleiman shook his head in disbelief and threw his hands up in surrender. His medical knowledge and sound advice were doomed in the face of his wife's desire to have a son and his superstitious aunt's old wives' remedies. But when Aunt Shamsi insisted Ruby drink the milk of a she-dog, he demanded an end to this farce, threatening to deliver his own child, which he intended to do anyway.

What, Aunt Shamsi wonders, is disorienting her experienced touch? She bends closer to check for herself, nearly topples off the stool. She has delivered hundreds of babies, some breech, others preferring to enter the world feet first, face up, or not at all. The quick gliding motion of her hand is known to successfully reposition in the mother's womb the most contorted babies. But this she has never seen. A sheer veil is blocking the opening of Ruby's cervix, which by her estimation, is more than ten centimeters dilated.

Is Ruby still a virgin? Is her stomach large with her imagination? Will she, after eight months of pregnancy, give birth to a half-formed creature? A deep breath, another close look. A tentative poke at the veil. It is slippery like sheep intestines and gives like the inner membrane of an egg.

At an interval of relief, Ruby props herself on one elbow to peer between her thighs and find out why Aunt Shamsi is suddenly quiet. But the hill of her stomach obstructs her view of Aunt Shamsi back on the stool at the foot of the pallet.

Finding herself in unchartered territory, Aunt Shamsi decides to treat the delivery as any other normal one. Her flat-tipped fingers dip in a bowl of olive oil, spread the labia, and knead the lip of the cervix in an attempt to widen the birth canal and facilitate the birth. Her touch edges about the veil, careful not to rupture it, afraid of opening a door to unknown calamities. Damn the *Sheitan*! The sly creature recoiled further up the canal. Her bloodstained fingers struggle for renewed grip, explore the position of what feels like a gelatinous mass and, one hand in Ruby's womb, the other applies pressure from outside. There! Firmly trapped in place.

One fluid movement of her wrist and something slides out like an eel fished out of oil to land in her outstretched arms, startling her up to her shaky feet.

"Aunt Shamsi!" Ruby attempts to reach for her baby. "Is it a boy?"

"Patience, sugar. Calm down, or your afterbirth will stick to your womb and rot."

Aunt Shamsi gazes with wonder at what looks like a water-filled balloon in which the baby is packed tight in the fetal position. A tentative push of her forefinger at the transparent membrane encasing the baby, the soft indentation at the crown of the head, the ear cartilage bending under her finger, the beats at the right temple—erratic and hardly noticeable. A human baby, by its look, but won't last long squashed underwater like this.

The child unfurls a fist, fans its perfectly formed fingers and punctures the membrane. A splash of water wets Aunt Shamsi, releasing the familiar odor of birth into the room.

Smart baby. This is how every child should enter a world, where misfortune sneaks up on you like an assassin's blade, safe and protected in the amniotic sack. En Caul births are rare, she knows, so rare less than one in thousands and thousands of babies are born with the amniotic sack intact. Yet she, Shamsi the Midwife, has been deemed worthy of the rare blessing of welcoming a magical child into the world.

She peels the wrinkled membrane off the child, careful not to cause injury. The caul is stuck to the face like a mask, and she attempts to remove it more slowly and cautiously, so as not to leave permanent scars. A quick check—two arms, two legs, ten fingers, the ears clean, surprisingly strong gums to suckle. Such a gorgeous child! Curly, sable lashes and a head-full of onyx-black hair.

"You hatched a gift-wrapped miracle out of your womb, sugar. Wait and see, your child will have supernatural talents. Patience, Ruby, patience, you'll have your child after your afterbirth is out." Aunt Shamsi places the baby at the foot of the pallet, pokes Ruby's belly to release the afterbirth and trapped blood clots, examines her breasts for properly swollen milk ducts. At the feel of the youthful breasts, firm and shamelessly proud, the nipples beginning to darken, a bitter seed of sadness sticks out its stubborn fangs, and she briefly forgets why she is fondling Ruby's breasts. Her own breasts are done suckling. Her womb is a useless coffer of grief. Will a time ever come when she'd deliver a baby without mourning the loss of her own child?

Another cramping of Ruby's uterus and the afterbirth slides out. Aunt Shamsi cups the still warm, blood-veined placenta in her hands and allows herself to relish this special moment, a miraculous birth, this one on her own birthday. She is thirty-six today. She survived the death of her daughter. Survived the abandonment of a husband who did not know what to do with his grief but shove it down his dumb throat, turn his sorry back, and run.

May this marvel of a child bring a semblance of peace, not joy, no, that is too much to ask, but some temporary reprieve from sorrow, this much she will ask.

She approaches the pallet and spreads the charmed baby's legs wide above Ruby's face.

CHAPTER FIVE

Flies haunt the tall windowpanes flanking the governor general's throne-like chair. One lands on Soleiman's dental probe, and he chases it off with an impatient flick of a hand, then drops the probe in a container of alcohol. The flat disk of the sun is high in the sky and the summer afternoon shimmers with heat. Arabic numbers embossed on the copper face of a grandfather clock announce the passing of yet another hour since he left his wife in Aunt Shamsi's care. He waves away the rosewater sherbet Tulip offers him in a tin cup set aside for his sole use. He will not be delegated to the rank of filthy pigs and dogs.

The Land Eater's opium-ravaged teeth are beyond saving. Most of the molars are rotting and the gums have receded. The tooth causing the pain is fortunately loose, eliminating the need for an injection of Novocaine. "Your upper left third molar is loose, Your Excellency, and needs to be extracted."

The governor stiffens in his armchair. "Speak human language, Yaran! Which tooth are you talking about?"

"Your wisdom tooth, Your Excellency, it's causing you pain. I'll have to pull it out."

"You have some nerve, Yaran! No Jew will pull out my wisdom. No! You will not play tricks on my brain."

Soleiman taps on the crumbling molar with the probe and catches a loosened enamel chip on the surface of the mouth mirror. "Look, Your Excellency, it's just a tooth. Nothing to do with your brain. If I don't pull it out it might fall and get stuck in your throat and, God forbid, clog your windpipe and cause serious trouble."

The Land Eater rests his head against his high-backed chair, shuts his eyes, and weighs the pros and cons of losing a wisdom tooth, whether he can afford to lose a fraction of his knowledge. He does this the same way he calculates the net profit from the sale of opium after having determined the operating cost, the inevitable waste, loss, and theft during the process of planting, harvesting, refining, packaging, and shipping. "All right, Yaran, go ahead. My remaining teeth hold more wisdom than you and your entire people put together. But no pain. Understood!"

"Understood," the doctor replies, knowing full well that if Ruby Magic fails, he might have just signed his own death warrant and handed it to a man who is known to scorch, with a sizzling poker, the tongue of any peasant who refuses to transfer to the governor the deed to his plot of land, in return for a fraction of its worth. Soleiman digs a dollop of Ruby Magic out of its container and is about to rub it on the governor's gums, when a voice like a chorus of angels, swells through the open window:

I dreamed that in my drunkenness
I might achieve success:
And kiss his ruby lips; but all
I drank was grief and gall—to no effect.

The governor jumps out of his seat, leans across the window ledge, and shades his eyes to bring into sharper focus the audacity confronting him in the courtyard. "Velvet!" he calls out. "Cover your face. There's a male stranger in the house."

Soleiman, too, can see the courtyard below, the landscape entirely different from the abrasive wildness of the front gardens. The lovely woman he had encountered in the poppy fields on his way here, her sun-splashed hair flirting with the breeze, dances from one branch to another to collect roses.

The governor lowers his voice, a kinder tone. "Cover your hair, Velvet, please."

Her blazing gaze leveled on the governor, Velvet flings her yellow chador into a puddle of mud. A soft whistle, and a nightingale abandons its post on a branch and, with a frenzy of chattering, comes to perch on her shoulder. "*I have learned that every heart gets what it prays for most*," she recites the poem of Hafiz, and for an instant her silver eyes, bright with trapped tears, travel past the governor to land with such intimacy on Soleiman, he feels the need to look away.

The mocking clang of the gate Velvet kicks shut behind her jolts the governor like a slap. He slams the window shut and glares at Soleiman as if all this is his fault.

"Come, Your Excellency, sit back in your chair." Soleiman attempts to restore a scrap of professionalism into the scene. "Thank you. Please open your mouth wide." He is late and Ruby will chide him, and no matter his hurry, interruptions keep occurring.

Pressing his thumb and forefinger on the inner and outer gums at the root of the molar, he expertly vibrates to replicate an electrical current to stimulate the nerve, hopeful that the nerve stimulation will improve the numbing effect of Ruby Magic.

The frantic quiver of the governor's firmly shut eyelids, prompts Soleiman to distract him with tales of far-away Paris, where a man named Alexander Gustave Eiffel built a skeletal iron structure with a moving room to lift visitors three hundred meters up to its top. Where the Arc de Triomphe was erected to honor those who fought the Napoleonic wars. The serene beauty of the Pére Lachaise Cemetery, where Molière, Oscar Wilde, and Chopin reside, and the eerie silence of cold catacombs with maze-like underground graveyards that house millions of human skeletons.

The Land Eater waves a hand in the air, gestures toward his mouth.

"Your Excellency?" The doctor's fingers are numb with the anesthetizing effect of the ointment he's rubbing on the governor's gums. "You want something?"

"Enough about towers and cemeteries. Tell me about those infidel women with bare hair and painted faces—"

"Are you sure, Your Excellency? I don't want to offend you. Or your wife."

"No offense will be taken, Yaran. My wife's back in the inner quarters, where she belongs. And our friend here." He waves toward the eunuch, who remains in his silent stance behind the book on the stand of antlers. "He's deaf and blind when it comes to women."

With a furious clatter of gold bangles, Tulip grabs a fistful of cardamom seeds from his pocket and begins to grind them in his mouth.

His words chasing his fingers as he massages the governor's gums, Soleiman recounts stories of Parisian nightclubs where naked dancers swing on trapezes, flaunt quince-colored hair and bat eyes the shade of turquoise. "There's a place in Paris called Pigalle, Your Excellency, where out in the streets and inside dark rooms, on satin sofas behind heavy drapes, red-lipped, cigarette-smoking women solicit the attention of men with thick wads of francs in their pockets." He rubs another bead of Ruby Magic on his patient's gums, secures the extracting forceps at the base of the molar and applies just enough pressure, taking care not to break the tooth. Forceps clenched in his fist, he directs a reassuring glance at the governor who, having sunk deeper into his chair, stares at him with eyes shining like black moons in a muddy sky. "Close your eyes, Your Excellency, and imagine you're there."

Soleiman rocks the tooth back and forth to break the ligaments and widen the supporting bone. He holds his breath and extracts the molar.

The man's jaws lock with a dry clack.

Soleiman displays the decayed tooth from different angles to his unbelieving patient.

"My wisdom?" the Land Eater asks, "Are you sure?"

"Yes, Your Excellency, all yours." Soleiman drops the tooth into the Land Eater's palm, before stepping away in search of fresh air.

The governor general abandons his throne and comes to face the outrageous dentist with his *farangi* western-style suit, too-long hair, and restless eyes. An urge to chop off the doctor's head to reduce his height overcomes him, and his hand shoots up, hesitates for an instant above the doctor, then comes crashing down with great force on his shoulder. "You are good at what you do, Yaran! A rare Jew. But we have a problem."

"Your Excellency?"

"Don't be surprised, Yaran, even a good Jew is impure, and permanganate and alcohol can go only so far before the unspeakable happens." He rubs his hands as if to rid himself of the doctor's filth. "But there's a simple solution. Very simple. Convert to Islam, and you will become as pure as Hazrat Ali's spring water."

Soleiman reaches out for his medical case and begins to collect his instruments. "That is out of the question, Your Excellency! You will not want a traitor to take care of you. And a man who turns his back on his faith is a traitor."

The tongue of the tiger clock on the desk sways back and forth with cheerful malice.

"Put those down, Yaran! I am not done with you!"

The doctor twists the jar of Ruby Magic shut and drops it in his medical case, locks the top, and clasps the handle. "I'm not done with Your Excellency either. Rest assured I will not abandon you until I fix every one of your wisdom teeth so that not a gram of your precious brain leaks out from anywhere."

CHAPTER SIX

Pebbles scatter and ricochet with dry pings under Rostam's frantic hooves as he gallops across the poppy fields and down the rocky mountain path. The sun has set behind the mountains, and the sky is slate-gray. The river below Tajrish Bridge swells and foams to vomit its flotsam over its banks. Traffic is lighter and activity less hectic than it was this morning. Vendors have shuttered their stalls and congregate for one last cup of tea, a puff of cigarette, hookah, or opium pipe before heading home.

Soleiman steers the stallion around a mule-drawn cart stuck in the middle of the road. Ruby will not forgive him for not being there to usher his first child into the world.

The screech of brakes. A truck swivels to avoid three drunk Soviet soldiers, who stagger across the road, their holsters dangling from their necks like leather yokes.

They have all settled here, Soleiman fumes, *Russians, Americans, and the British, as if they are welcome guests, rather than enemies whose assaults have robbed the populace of sleep. The British marched into Iran from Iraq to take control of precious oil fields. American airplanes are on the ground in Abadan airfields, ready to be delivered to the Soviet Union. And a bunch of no-good Germans continue to stick their filthy noses in every affair.*

A short, flat-nosed soldier stops in the middle of the road, removes the holster from around his neck, pulls out his pistol, and shoots aimlessly above his head. Cars and trucks screech to a stop in the middle of the road. Pedestrians crouch for shelter behind vehicles. Soleiman attempts to steer Rostam in a different direction, but the reins are suddenly yanked out of his grasp.

Rostam protests with a long-drawn grunt and a violent shake of his neck.

The trigger-happy soldier aims his pistol at the stallion. A smug smile distorting his red face, he shouts, "*Stoyat' na kolenyakh*! Kneel!"

Soleiman digs both knees into Rostam's flanks. A piercing whistle through clenched teeth, and Rostam rears with a frightening neigh. A hoof crashes on the man's foot and catapults him to the middle of the road. His pistol flies into the waters of the *joub* aqueduct at the side of the road that transports a soup of water infected with urine, tossed away chicken legs and sheep entrails, wide-eyed carcasses of rats, cats, and dogs that ferment in the water that flows south toward *abambar* private reservoirs, where the water is used for cooking, filling samovars, washing dishes, bathing, and laundry.

The stallion speeds toward the Jewish Quarter, whipping swells of dust as he skirts the Square of Cannons, where hangings and political rallies are held, and clatters past the Pamnar House of Strength, where *pahlevan* wrestlers are practicing.

"Follow me," Soleiman tells the Quarter Fool who canters across Graveyard Street like a bewildered rabbit. Sunburned and leathery from constantly roaming the alleys, the Quarter Fool trots next to the stallion as he speeds toward the baked mud wall surrounding the communal stables.

Soleiman dismounts, hands the reins to the Quarter Fool with instructions to walk the stallion around to cool him down, feed him, and fill his water pail.

Soleiman rushes past moth-haunted windows and locked doors reinforced with metal studs to discourage break-ins, past the quarter prostitute, who leans against her door, a red chador wrapped around her waist, her bleached hair held up with rhinestone-studded combs. To avoid a group of women gathered at the entrance to the Hakim

Mashiah public bath, he escapes to the Alley of Seven Synagogue and, oblivious to the chant of *Maariv* evening prayers, speeds past the dilapidated synagogues, which, in fear of raids, bear no religious symbols.

"Thank God you're back!" The voice of the shah's deaf Water Man silences the racket of crickets. With his long legs and the upper body of a wrestler, he sprints forward and grabs the fleeing doctor, who has a cure for everything—an attack of the hiccups, a nasty growth, or an outbreak of the flesh-eating-disease. "My back is splitting, *Agha* doctor!" He nods toward his rickety donkey-pulled cart. "Hard to handle this—"

Soleiman tosses a packet of painkillers toward the Water Man, but thanks to his blaring voice, a crowd has emerged from all corners, clapping Soleiman on the back, asking him if rumors about the cruel governor general are true. Is his wife the most beautiful woman in Iran? Is a eunuch imprisoned in his mansion? Is it true that the blue mansion on top of the mountain is a den of opium addicts?

"Let the man go!" Jacob lands in the center of the mayhem. Having returned from one of his clandestine missions, his grey suit, shirt, cravat, even his hair meld into the surroundings, as if he is sculpted from ash. He swoops one woman off her feet and out of Soleiman's way. "Go home, Soleiman, go!"

The clatter of wheels and the hum of the crowd are replaced by silence in the Alley of Physicians; nothing but the buzz of insects and the shadow of a scurrying rat. An anemic moon hangs low over his house, the jagged shards of glass on top of the surrounding walls a sporadic spark in the dark. Neither the cries of a newborn baby nor the usual string of blessings and curses from Aunt Shamsi can be heard.

He dashes toward his house and down the three steps leading to the wide-open gate. He comes face to face with his aunt, whose hair has come undone, an open safety pin dangling from the buttonhole of her blouse.

He drops his case and charges into the room to find Ruby huddled on the pallet with the crying child clutched to her breasts. She turns to him and attempts to part her pale trembling lips in a smile.

"You're back," she whispers.

"Always, Sweetheart, always." Her red scarf has fallen from her hair and is tangled around her neck. He unties the scarf, tucks her wet hair behind her ears, and checks her bloodstained face and the baby's blood-matted head for injuries. None. Where is the blood from? He disengages the baby from Ruby's arms and hands her to Aunt Shamsi, then tosses the blanket off the mattress. It is soaked in blood. In the weak light of the Primus oil lamp, he separates Ruby's thighs to discover the source of bleeding. He attempts to stem the gush of blood with his hands, with the sheets, tears his shirt off his back and bunches it between Ruby's thighs.

Her pupils are dilated, and her pulse races against his thumb. Her skin is turning icy and moist under the hands he runs over her body.

Shamsi wails behind him. Water bubbles in the pot on the stove. His child whimpers. And his heart is breaking in his chest.

His wife's uterus has ruptured.

Her vital signs are dwindling. Ruby is in the last stage of shock.

"Fight, Ruby," he pleads over and over again, "Look at me! Keep your eyes open."

"Soleiman." She grabs his coat, draws a labored breath.

"Yes, Sweetheart, I'm here." He presses his ear to her cold lips.

"Name her Neda—"

"Whatever you like, Sweetheart. Neda is a beautiful name."

He slides next to her on the wet mattress and folds her tight in his arms. "Remember the first time we met on Yom Kippur in Ezra Mikhael Synagogue? You wore your red scarf around your neck. I told you you'll become my wife. Remember the herb box we built together? You talked to your herbs as if they were your babies. Now you have your own beautiful baby. Remember when you ordered two kebab *barg* and one *koobideh* from the kebab seller in Shemiran? I told you too much meat is not healthy. You said death won't touch you because you're in love. You promised to live forever. Don't you dare break your promise."

Her grip on his coat is weakening, but she will not let go. Her body shakes with the effort to summon the strength to hold on to him. She digs her face into his neck, into his damp hair, her breath in his roaring ear.

"Soleiman, my love," she gasps. "Neda needs a mother."

CHAPTER SEVEN

The last thirty days and nights have been so long, so filled with thunderous grief that Soleiman could not hear the beat of his arteries, Neda's sleeping breath in the next room, Aunt Shamsi's grumbling in her sleep, and the endless scratching at the door of Pary's cat, Mademoiselle.

Nor does he now hear the cheering of boys playing dodge ball in the alley, the rush of water in the *joub* canal, the bray of the overloaded donkey, the cry of the mattress beater, or the racket of chickens being slaughtered at the threshold of houses.

What he hears are Ruby's last whispered words and the scream of his own conscience. He should not have left her alone that day. He should have stood his ground and refused to go to the governor general. Yes, he would have been punished, locked behind bars, perhaps tortured and maimed. Far better than losing Ruby.

Yet, even now, he is not allowed to mourn in peace. A squadron of stiff-backed giants strode into the Alley of Physicians this morning, rattling the Quarter to no end. The Queen's impatience was relayed to him with boisterous fanfare: "Her Royal Majesty expects Doctor Yaran at the palace in three days," they had announced like a chorus of executioners.

Soleiman collects his scattered bits, shaves his thirty-day beard, and washes his face. He wears the suit and shirt forgotten on his chair and forces himself to step out of the house.

He walks past the ancient mulberry tree, which lost its leaves when Ruby died, lingers in front of the red box of wilting herbs, and grabs a handful of lifeless mint. They have lost their scent.

The room at the end of the garden, which he transformed into a laboratory, is surrounded by windows and crowded with the most modern dental equipment, much of which he had devised to accommodate his own needs—a mixer for his numbing ointment, a portable drill, extra-sensitive scales to measure ingredients up to a nanogram, a grinding machine to gauge the durability of different filling materials.

He embarks on the challenging task of creating a composite resin, which must be as strong as enamel as well as esthetically pleasing to the Queen. He adds and subtracts different materials, adhesives, fine glass, and porcelain particles to match the shade of Her Majesty's teeth, which is difficult guesswork, since he is relying on memory.

Hours pass. Evening fog licks the windows outside, steam collects inside. He discards one batch of composite after another. The harder he tries, the less he is pleased with the outcome of his work. The discarded heap of composite multiplies in the trash can.

Once again, he cleans the porcelain container and begins experimenting with another set of resins. The rumble overhead of war planes. The porcelain bowl falls and shatters at his feet. It no longer matters whether the planes that constantly roar over the city are Russian, British, or American, whether they're about to drop leaflets or bombs from skies foul with the smell of smoke and gasoline and panic. The murderers frightened Ruby into premature labor.

He collects the broken pieces of porcelain and drops them in the wastebasket, shuts the laboratory door behind him, and steps out into the Alley of Physicians, where the chatter of crickets has replaced the call of street vendors. Up and down the alley he walks, past the empty lot in the center of which stands an ancient willow, its branches weeping into the earth, past Pary's house with its mythical, green door, which draws superstitious believers. Back and forth he marches, furious at himself, furious at the war, at Hitler, at the Allies, and at the universe and all its inhabitants.

The green door sighs on its heavy hinges. A kerosene lamp in hand, the young widow steps out into the pallid gloom of the night and gazes up, as if searching for her dead husband on the mottled face of the moon.

Soleiman retreats into the shadows of the empty lot. It is enough that Pary's solitude is disrupted by ignorant people who congregate to pray at her door at odd times. He observes his neighbor with a measure of sadness and compassion. They both suffered devastating losses in the same year. Both bear their losses alike. She withdrew from the world after her husband died. He, too, locked the doors to his laboratory after Ruby died, assigning Aunt Shamsi the task of announcing the tragic news. Affluent clients he normally called on at home were informed he would be unavailable for the next twelve months. Patients no longer come in the mornings. He no longer works in his laboratory in the evenings.

When the governor general's messenger arrived at the garden gate and raised his threatening voice from behind his thick mustache, Aunt Shamsi rounded her eyes with fear and gestured for him to keep his distance. Her voice shaking, she announced that the doctor had fallen mysteriously ill with symptoms resembling typhoid. The messenger turned on his heels and fled.

The Queen, on the other hand, had exhibited uncommon patience. Until this morning, when her emissaries left no doubt that she will not tolerate any further delay.

Soleiman is about to return to his task when he notices the faint glint of two metal cans Pary sets at her feet. From one can she retrieves a brush, dips it in the other can, and, with surprising speed and vigor, attacks the door to her house with white paint.

He steps out of the lot. "May I help, Pary *Khanom*?"

"People say the door killed him. They say the doors shed tears. Plain superstition, Doctor Yaran, isn't it?"

"Yes, of course. Doors don't cry. I am sorry, Pary *Khanom*, like many others, Monsieur André lost his life to typhoid."

In silence and slightly leaning on him, she hands him another brush. She runs a palm over the white paint she splashed on the door.

"Easy to fix," he says as he dips his brush in the can and smooths the running paint. They work together side by side in the dim light of the kerosene lamp; Pary paints the lower half of the door, Soleiman works on the upper section. He attempts to do a thorough job, hopes a coat or two of white paint will succeed in tarnishing the false allure of the door and allow Pary to grieve in solitude, but there is not enough light to do a proper job. Pary raises the flame of the lamp, and they continue for another hour until, content that not a peek of green is left, he lifts the cans and follows Pary into the house. Finding no place to deposit them, he remains standing in the center of the living room, surrounded by books and cotton-lined baskets of all sizes that overflow with the wood figurines Pary cherishes. A pall of solitude shrouds everything, prompting him to wonder whether among the countless visitors, who come to pray at her door, even one might have thought of crossing the threshold to share a glass of tea with the owner.

From a basket, Pary retrieves a miniature hookah pipe with blue bands painted around the body and a spiraling wisp of smoke from wood shaving rising from its charcoal tray. One by one she relives her memories as she shows him the wood figurines her husband fashioned for her, a speckled cat, a replica of Mademoiselle, Rapunzel with blue eyes and blond braids, and Rudabeh, Rapunzel's Persian counterpart, with eyes and hair darker than grief, the braids of both dolls cascading down twin towers carved from exotic woods.

Soleiman stands there and listens because this is what the young widow needs, to conjure happier days and nights, when her husband labored with a weasel hairbrush over each figurine to make sure every detail was true to life. "Maybe you'll allow Neda to play with your dolls one day. When she's older, of course, and understands their worth."

"Yes. Ruby would have liked that, I am sure. They were too young, Ruby and André, weren't they?" A quick, self-effacing gesture of the back of her hand across her face as if, accustomed to silences that come with living alone, she regrets the uttered words.

"Yes, they were." Soleiman puts down the cans in a corner of the room. "But nothing will bring them back."

CHAPTER EIGHT

Soleiman is announced at the threshold to the Saheb Gharani-e-Palace War Room. In the warm sepia hue of sconces and chandeliers everything appears to be cast in gold—the sixteen high-backed chairs, the glossy mahogany conference table, and the detailed globe in the center. The room is far too formal for the business at hand, but Soleiman is pleased that this time he has been invited to the royal couple's private residence.

The Queen welcomes him, as she had on his first visit, reaching out her royal hand for a kiss. She seems more at ease in these surroundings, yet there is an even deeper sadness than he remembers. A white gardenia is pinned at an angle in her piled-up hair, three chains of pearls on display around her neck. His eyes rest on the embroidered brocade belt girding the Queen's slim waist. His two hands could nearly circle Ruby's waist to lift her over one shoulder as he sprinted across an overflowing *joub* or rode a high wave on their visits to the Caspian Shores.

The gaze the Queen directs at Soleiman is as sharp as icepicks. "It took you more than thirty days, Doctor Yaran!"

"My apologies, Your Majesty. My wife died in childbirth the day the governor general summoned me. I have not been myself since."

"My condolences, Doctor Yaran." The Queen opens her arms wide as if to include him in her royal circle. "We belong to Allah, and to Allah we shall return. Your wife was young. Yes?"

"Only twenty-three, Your Majesty, and healthy."

The Queen toys with her pearl necklace. "You have a child, then?"

"Yes, Your Majesty, a daughter, Neda."

It is whispered that the Queen is desperate to take her two-year-old daughter to Egypt, but the shah will not permit Princess Shahnaz to leave the country. The Queen misses her life in Egypt, where she was the favorite of her brother, King Farouk, a beloved princess pampered by a retinue of adoring aunts, ladies in waiting, and servants. Many say she finds the Iranian court colorless and inferior to the Egyptian court and that she considers Iran a backward country.

The Queen's eyes glisten. She dabs her lace handkerchief at a pearl of perspiration above her lip. "You have a daughter to raise. How will you manage?"

"It will be difficult, Your Majesty. But Neda is more fortunate than many other children. Like the thousands of Polish refugee children, who lost entire families in the war and are reduced to begging in our streets for food and shelter."

A slight tilt of the royal head, a spark of interest in the intelligent eyes. "You are referring to the Tehran Children, Doctor Yaran. The refugee camps around the city are full to capacity, we hear. One of our private gardens has been converted into a makeshift camp to accommodate a number of them."

"Thank you, Your Majesty." Soleiman attempts to contain the excitement in his voice. The Queen appears to be interested in the plight of the orphans. "It is a dire situation, Your Majesty. Malnutrition is so common; their teeth sometimes fall out of their mouth when they talk."

The Queen purses her mouth. Studies him with dismay. "This cannot be true, Doctor Yaran! Is it?"

"It is, Your Majesty. I've seen it myself. I tend to a group of orphans who currently lodge with a friend of mine. It is hard to believe what these poor children have experienced. The war has traumatized them beyond repair." He has overstepped his permitted boundaries, he knows, but the Queen might never be as interested as she is now.

"They are in desperate need of a permanent home, Your Majesty, or they will have to be transferred to Isfahan orphanages due to food shortages."

The Queen turns away to gaze out the window. The subject is too painful to pursue. "Have you invented the material, Doctor Yaran?"

"I have, Your Majesty."

She snaps her lacquer-nailed fingers. "Of course, you did. The exact color of my teeth. Yes?"

"I hope so, Your Majesty."

"Hope?" The Queen utters the word as if it is an insult. "You are a scientist, Doctor Yaran, you do not rely on 'hope'." She turns her back to him and walks toward a Dental Ritter workstation with all the necessary modern equipment.

A royal aid stands at attention behind an antique table placed next to the dental chair. Soleiman is about to suggest that the table be covered to protect the fine wood but, having already talked more than he should have, he takes out his dental tools from his case and arranges them on the table.

The Queen settles in the chair. Adjusts the silk hem of her skirt above her knees. *She favors sandals*, he observes, these with golden straps revealing her red toenails.

He gestures toward the tightly drawn curtains. "May I have Your Majesty's permission to open the curtains? The light here is not ideal."

A flourish of the Queen's sheer-sleeved arm, and the attendant opens the curtains, splashing the room with sunshine. A loft of pigeons abandons the window ledge and lands on an ancient sycamore tree. A white-gloved hand appears behind the window to wipe pigeon droppings off the ledge.

Reluctant to ask the Queen to remove her lipstick, Soleiman rubs Ruby Magic on her gums. He tests her teeth for any pain and is pleased to discover there is none and she will not be needing Novocaine. He has fashioned a somewhat smaller but more sensitive dental burr to remove the decay from the front tooth in order to create space for the restorative material and fill the tooth with minimal damage to the surrounding enamel.

Impatient to discover the result of three days and nights of hard work, he works fast. Now and then, he wipes the Queen's lipstick off his dental tools. The erosion is more extensive than he first assessed, making it necessary to bore closer to the dentine than he would like to. He removes the decay with meticulous care, cleans the area, and prepares it for restoration, layering different shades of the white composite to achieve the desired cosmetic look, which is easier now that the color can be compared to the Queen's teeth.

Drawing a deep breath, he begins the delicate process of recreating the original contours of the tooth, which requires patience and a keen, artistic eye, as is achieving the esthetics of a refined, glassy layer that would reflect light as natural teeth do.

A blow on the windowpane startles them both. A crow has crashed against the glass, leaving a bloody smear.

The Queen sighs. Shuts her eyes. "Bad omen, these birds," she murmurs, forcing Soleiman to momentarily stop his work.

Perhaps they are, he muses, having descended on the palace grounds like the Allied troops on Tehran, loud and rude and syphoning local resources without a grain of consideration for anyone.

Once again, a white-gloved hand is at work outside to wipe off the crow's blood from the bay window and, in a matter of minutes, order is restored and the manicured world outside is spotless again, and, to make sure it remains so, a soldier appears to scare the crows away with a pellet gun.

Why, Soleiman wonders, *are pellet guns not banned after the accident some years ago that nearly blinded the young Mohammad Reza?* He had come across a pellet gun in his private classroom in the palace and was playing with it when a friend snatched it. The gun went off. A pellet missed the crown prince's eyes and shot through his hat.

Soleiman checks the Queen's tooth through the magnifying glass, then without it. The shape is perfect, but the color is lighter than her other teeth. Just a hint. Enough to cause him alarm. He gives the dental chair a slight turn to take advantage of a ray of sunlight cutting through the window, fixes a small rubber bowl to his forefinger, and begins anew, his eyes tearing with concentration as he adds, subtracts, and mixes different shades.

The Queen reaches out for the mirror on the table.

A tap of his dental probe on the mirror. "May I beg Your Majesty to be patient? It will not be long. I am about to polish the tooth."

A sleek, violet-colored Bugatti rolls into the palace's manicured grounds, a splendid gift from the French government on the occasion of the marriage of the shah to Queen Fawzia. A footman runs to open the door, but before he reaches the car, the shah steps out. He is dressed in a striped, gray suit and a dark cravat. His combed black hair is parted in the center. Fixing a cigarette in an enamel cigarette holder, he takes a deep draw and gazes at the window of the War Room.

The Queen observes her husband beyond the window. Her eyes are suddenly leached of their confidence. There is a shift in her, a sense of fragility.

People are talking about the shah's infidelity. From the very beginning, when he was a young prince engaged to princess Fawzia, and now that they are married and he is king, he continues to neglect his wife's emotional needs. His roaming eyes are aimed at, and his deep pockets open to, other women. And there's the matter of the king's dictatorial mother and possessive twin sister, Princess Ashraf, all piercing nails and fangs and full of venom. Above all, the Queen's failure to produce a male heir to the Pahlavi throne has further poisoned the young couple's relationship.

Certain that the king is on his way to check on the result of his wife's dental work, Soleiman quickly resumes polishing the tooth. He places his dental tools on the table and, grateful he is not required to wear the cumbersome gloves, slides his forefinger around the Queen's gums, the front, the back, and edges of the tooth. All is smooth to his sensitive touch. With his handkerchief, he wipes remnants of lipstick from his finger. Steps back to assess the result of his work. He offers the mirror to the Queen, clasps his hands in front of him, and observes her with anticipation as she inspects her teeth in the mirror for an unbearably long time. The clang of a shutting car door, the salute of an adjutant, the revving of the car's engine. Soleiman glances up to see the shah walk toward another building.

The Queen puts the mirror down, presses a forefinger to her mouth as if to stop herself from speaking. Deep in thought, she dangles her pearl earring, an innocent gesture that renders her vulnerable. Then, before he has a chance to tell her to wait for a few hours before drinking anything, she raises her teacup and sips. Her mouth puckers in distaste. The tea has been sitting on the silver tray and is cold and undrinkable. The attendant steps forward with a pot of steaming tea, and, to the doctor's relief, she waves it away. "The sun is too bright," she tells the attendant, and he draws the curtains.

She shifts in her chair, rests her head back. The Queen is pale, and her breathing shallow.

He steps forward to check her pulse. "Are you all right, Your Majesty?"

Her eyes are fierce again. "I am now."

"It sometimes happens, Your Majesty. The body's reaction to certain medications. Please try to rest today."

A tap of the Queen's forefinger on the tooth he had worked on. "You will be rewarded."

He bows, rests his palm on his pounding chest. "Attending to Your Majesty is an honor as well as my reward."

An imperceptible lift of her royal eyebrow. "There is something you want, Doctor Yaran. Yes?"

"If it pleases Your Majesty. It concerns the Tehran Children, the orphans we discussed earlier. They are desperate for food and shelter, but our country, unfortunately, is limited in her ability to provide that." He hesitates, his every muscle on alert. The silence is so deep, he can hear the cooing of pigeons outside, the slap of a broom behind the window, the sigh of wind in the trees. "May I beg Her Majesty to put in a good word with the Immigration Office to issue permits for the children to leave the country?"

The Queen stares at the universe beyond the window where, in spite of the pellet-gun wielding soldier, another murder of crows has congregated on the lawn to peck at seeds. "Where can the children go to when the entire world is at war? They will not find a better home than this country." The Queen reaches out her hand for a kiss. "Farewell, Doctor Yaran, and be well."

CHAPTER NINE

Aunt Shamsi navigates the small house, Neda tucked in the pocket of a sheet wrapped around her shoulders and waist. She wipes rat droppings off window ledges, yanks sheets off Neda's crib and Soleiman's bed, and tosses them into the metal washing bucket.

Six months have passed since Ruby died, and the memory of that day has burrowed deep roots. Soleiman became a different man, as if a streak of bitterness crept into his blood and made its way into his heart, so that he resented everything and everyone for having the gall to go on living after Ruby.

He refused to eat or sleep, and if it were not for his pacing through the small house, she would have thought he'd simply decided to stop breathing so he'd join his wife. Once in a while, he mumbled under his breath as he stood over the crib and stared at his daughter. She was quiet, just whimpering like a motherless kitten when she was wet or hungry, as if she felt the deluge of misery dripping from the walls and ceilings and didn't want to make it worse with her own tears.

So, she took pity on her nephew and his motherless daughter and moved in with them until they could stand on their own feet. She placed her steel banded storage trunk, which held a few of her belongings in a corner in Neda's room, not caring to empty it because this was a temporary arrangement. Even the brass lock is left open, since there is nothing of value in the trunk other than the silver purse she inherited from her mother, which is of no use to anyone in this house.

Every now and then, she checked on Soleiman in his dark room to inquire if he needed anything, which he never did. Every day, either Eleazar or a neighbor brought homemade food and helped with feeding and bathing the child. Even Pary, the mourning widow next door, baked two challah breads every Shabbat and had the Quarter Fool deliver them.

Then, the Queen summoned Soleiman back, and Aunt Shamsi wasn't sure whether to curse or thank her for forcing Soleiman to push his grief deep inside and step out of the broken gate to confront the world with an expression that scared *Sheitan* himself. All because no Jew with a bit of *khokhma* brain in his head would refuse a royal command.

With Neda, however, he is more patient than Job, as if she has the exclusive right to all the love he had reserved for his wife. He spends hours telling her stories and reading her books, while her lips mouth his every word, as if to press it into her memory.

Well, Aunt Shamsi sighs, she might have thought it was temporary, but when Neda began to stomach-crawl behind her like a newly hatched duckling, she was in no hurry to pack her trunk and move back with her brother. The truth is that after her own loss, she doesn't mind being needed by another sweet child. Especially a child who can stomach-crawl when she's hardly six months.

Aunt Shamsi fires the coal iron. She starches and irons Soleiman's shirts as Neda's head nods against her breasts as if the child agrees with everything she grumbles under her breath: in a country where Jews are wise to disappear, it is foolish of Soleiman to call attention to himself with his shirt collars standing up at attention and his handkerchiefs folded like the deed to the shah's palace. Useless work, this constant ironing, when the stink of the toilet will kill them all if she doesn't get to scrubbing it.

A stack of folded shirts under one arm, she opens Soleiman's drawer. Ruby's red scarf lies on top of Soleiman's shirts like a bolt of fire that might flare up and consume everything. She spools the scarf out and drapes it around Neda's shoulders. "Your mother used to wear it all the time. Too red for her own good, if you ask me. But that was your Madar, Little Leech, everything about her was bold. She wrapped this scarf around her shoulders the same way men wear their prayer shawl to synagogue. Then, one Shabbat, she decided to go and sit right next to your father in the men's section. Vaiii! What *gereftary* it caused! Men swore to stay away until Ruby went back where she belonged with the other women in the back of the sanctuary. But deaf to the uproar of rabbis and congregants, your parents sat smiling and holding hands, as if they had all the right to sit next to each other in the holy sanctuary and so close to the Torah. The men's section became emptier and emptier week after week. Until Rabbi Elihu the Compassionate stepped on the bimah on the sacred day of Rosh Hashana and announced to the empty sanctuary that if men were not ready to suffer Ruby's presence among them, Soleiman and his wife will move to an affluent neighborhood in the north. Child! When I saw the sanctuary filled with men on the eve of Kol Nidre with your mother sitting next to Soleiman, like the Queen of Sheba, with her red scarf covering her bare shoulders, I thought it was the end of time and the *Mashiakh* had come."

Aunt Shamsi slides the scarf off Neda, folds it with great care, and puts it back on top of Soleiman's shirts. "We don't want your Baba to turn the house upside down searching for it. Stop it, child! Don't you look at me like that. I tried to save your Madar, but no, she took one look at you and stopped fighting. Who knows? Maybe she knew you'd be different, the way you entered the world breathing underwater like a wide-eyed fish. Maybe things went wrong because you poisoned her from inside. Stop punching me with your iron fists!" Aunt Shamsi pats Neda's curls into place, wipes her tears off with a corner of her headscarf. "*Basheh* okay, you win. Have the scarf. I can't blame you for wanting a piece of your Madar." She takes Ruby's scarf out of the drawer, folds it into a square, and tucks it under Neda's head. "Here, all yours. I'll deal with your baba later."

CHAPTER TEN

The sun is not yet out to draw bees and butterflies to rosebushes rich with nectar, and the courtyard beyond the windows is eerily shadowed. Yet it is not dark here, in the *andarūnī* women's inner quarters, where the aroma of melting wax rises from candles kept alive at all times.

There was a past, Velvet recalls, when the dark held no demons, and her vivid dreams rang with the laughter of her own children. All that ended when her father pressed her hand into the governor general's, and her proud mother, who deemed him one of the few eligible men worthy of her daughter, burst into joyous ululation and dispensed sugarcoated almonds to mark her wedding celebration. She was an innocent sixteen-year-old then, with a high school diploma, who loved the poems of Hafez and Saadi, Rumi and Molana. It didn't matter to her that the governor general was twenty years her senior. He was tall and slim, all muscles and prominent cheekbones, his uniform rich with gold braids and important medals. She was impressed by his voice like thunder and the imposing way he carried himself, the way his gaze softened when he promised her father to take good care of her, and the way his long fingers cuddled his diamond-capped pen as if he held a precious secret in his fist. Little did she know then how she would come to fear the pen.

Tehran celebrated their wedding for seven days and nights. The city was on fire with colorful lights, music blared from speakers on top of buildings, banners flapped in the spring breeze. Bakeries gave away free sugar-coated almonds. Sacrificial sheep were slaughtered at their feet.

On their wedding night, the governor general carried her in his arms to his private chambers and laid her on a divan tented with gold-threaded fabrics. His black eyes gleaming with love and passion, he flaunted his naked body in the red light of the chandelier, then took his time to undress her—first the garland of fresh jasmine, then her gauze head-cover, tulle wedding gown, and high-heeled satin shoes—removed each piece with such tenderness, she trembled under his touch as he stroked the tiny goosebumps on her arms, soft and slow and loving, his warm lips lingering on her mouth. He licked her nipples and blew on them until the fluttering in her belly settled, and she opened herself to him. He drew back. Observed her for a long time in silence and with unbearable intensity, so long, her skin turned cold and began to shrink under his gaze.

He lifted her wedding gown from the carpet, asked her to dress, and, promising to fulfill her every desire, locked a splendid chain of pearls around her neck, before walking her to the door.

Stunned with shame at her failure to arouse him, she stood behind the door, unable to move her trembling body. She heard him curse under his breath and certain it was directed at her, she carefully nudged open the door he forgot to shut in his haste and peered in to find him distracted and muttering angrily to himself. What had she done, other than trust and believe, to deserve his ire? She was about to step back in to ask him that question, when he tugged at a rope above the divan.

The connecting door to the adjoining bedroom opened, and a tall woman floated into the bloody light of the chandelier. The gown of gold tissue under the endless folds of her veils, the feminine sweep of her hips, the golden sandals on her feet, the lavish tune of her many bangles, and the voluptuous contours of her body were magnificent as were the rich layers of sequined tulle that fell over her slightly bowed head and concealed her face. She draped the governor's cape about his shoulders to cover his nakedness and, without turning this way or that, the two of them walked toward the adjoining bedroom and melted away like lingering shadows of a nightmare.

It became his ritual. Each Friday, before the maids, servants, and cooks are done mopping, polishing, and cooking, two guards lead her through the dimly lit corridors of the stony house—across the hall of carpets and courtyard of roses, past the ablution room and the second wing of the house, through the Hall of Precious Clocks—to deliver her to her husband.

The guards accomplish the task with as much subtlety as their crude background allows. Their loyalty is to Velvet, who treats them as equals, so different from the bite of the governor general's poisonous barks. Little do they know that behind the closed doors of his private chambers he bids his time at his desk, signs a stack of documents, raises his head now and then to stare at his wife with a mixture of resentment and compassion. Once the clocks announce the passing of half an hour, he caps his pen, abandons his desk, and dismisses her with a perfunctory gesture of a hand, then pulls the rope and summons the Friday Night Woman.

Why he goes through the trouble of keeping up appearances in front of his household remains a mystery to Velvet.

Five chest-drumming bongs of a clock startle her back to the present. Who could have snuck a clock here while she was asleep? She pushes aside the amber mosquito net and sits at the edge of the pallet, wraps herself in a sheet, and, with growing trepidation, enters the living room. A mahogany grandfather clock confronts her in a corner like the ghost of an abandoned soldier with a loud brass pendulum and brass hands that mourn the passing of her life.

She will not tolerate a clock in her sanctuary, not when the only time her husband sets foot in here is to give her a meaningless gift—an emerald ring the size of her thumb, a bracelet of Burmese pigeon blood rubies, pearl earrings too heavy to wear—only to pamper her as he does his valuable clocks, dust and buff them once in a while to keep them clean and lustrous, so they won't reflect badly on the owner.

At the echo in the distance of the Clock Master's boots, she tightens the sheet about her. "Damn the man!" He has no business in her quarters, with his loud boots and winding tools that keep her husband's precious clocks alive.

Each time Velvet hears the sporadic pleas of one or another dying clock, exiled to the attic because it no longer merits her husband's loving attention, each time she hears one last grinding bowel, one last quake, groan, or belch of a cog, she feels a certain giddiness, as if it is not merely one of her husband's cherished clocks, but his mistress who is exhaling her last breath.

"Zahra!"

Zahra, the restless sixteen-year-old maidservant, who has made it her business to eavesdrop behind porous walls, closed doors, and low window ledges, materializes like a wisp of smoke. "You need something, *Khanom*?"

"A moment of peace."

"*Ey Vaai, Khanom*!" Zahra rolls her eyes toward the grandfather clock. "How did *this* beast get here? I swear on all the imams I'm up twice a night to make sure the candles are burning. I didn't see a soul." Zahra checks the clock from all sides to assess how to remove it. "How did they attach it to the wall, *Khanom*? Why didn't we hear anything? Caused such damage, too. But don't worry, please, I'll take care of it in a blink."

The maidservant runs down to the cellar and comes back with a can of paint, a brush, and a ladder and, scrambling up the rungs like a multi-skirted squirrel, embarks on the task with great joy and energy, attacks the nails and chains that anchor the clock, yanks and pulls with her small ferocious hands until, concerned the girl will injure herself, Velvet hands her pliers, a nail puller, and a hammer.

Zahra studies the tools with puzzled contempt, drops them back into the toolbox, and finishes the job with her own reliable hands. In the end, the wall is patched and painted with such professional speed, no sign of the antique grandfather clock remains, not even the slightest indentation on the carpet on which it stood. "Happy, *Khanom*? Shall I shut it up with this?"

"Not with a hammer! Let's send it up to the attic."

Zahra solicits the help of the massive, mustachioed guards stationed at the entrance to Velvet's quarters to haul the clock up the narrow stairs and squeeze it into a hidden nook of the crowded attic.

Pleased, Velvet goes to the window, props her elbows on the ledge, and gazes at the world beyond. The cannons, perched as they are on two giant stone pillars that flank the gates, glow under the sun like bonfires, their intent to scare off intruders. Pointless! No sane person will risk this mountain unless ordered to do so.

Time passes, and, unaware of Zahra and the guard waiting in the shadows to be dismissed, she is swept away into the powerful tide of her dreams, hopes, and desires. A tenderness impossible to contain brings tears to her eyes, and she reaches out for one of the embroidered handkerchiefs Tulip keeps handy for such times. A stanza Jahan Malek Khatun, a Persian Princess, jotted down on paper more than five centuries ago, repeats itself in her mind:

My love's an ache no ointments can allay now:
My soul's on fire—how long you've been away now!
I said, "I will be patient while he's gone."
(But that's impossible…it's one whole day now…)

At the distant clatter of hooves, she presses her forehead to the window. Dr. Yaran trots through the gates on his white stallion like a foreign dignitary from a mysterious world, dismounts, and hands the reins to a groom, who hurries to greet Rostam with a treat and a pail of water.

"Anything else you need, *Khanom*?" Zahra whispers behind Velvet's back. "May we leave?"

"Of course, thank you," Velvet mutters. "You were all a great help, like always. I won't forget," she adds, turning her attention back to the doctor.

A ray of sunshine glints on his wind-ruffled hair and the silver handle of his riding crop as he cleans clods of mud off the stallion's hooves and exchanges a few words with the groom. And then, instead of taking the gravel path toward the mansion, as he has week after week for the last year to climb the stairs, with that slight limp she finds endearing, he steals a quick glance this way and that, then turns left and vanishes among the dense gathering of Persian junipers at the edge of the walkway.

She dashes down the cellar stairs and into the inner quarter, where colorful shawls are strewn on a cushioned divan and roses crowd *barfatan* opaline vases. A paisley tablecloth on the Isfahan carpet is set for her breakfast with hot *sangak* flat bread, pistachio halva, sheep cream, Tabriz cheese, quince, and fig jams.

She grabs her book of poetry from a stack of books by her pallet and, her heart flipping with excitement, her chador billowing behind her like a tent, hurries through the mansion's corridors.

An elderly maid hums under her breath as she polishes picture frames with yellow wax. A pubescent girl in a black headscarf carries hot-house roses in a tin bucket to replenish the vases. A hunchbacked servant on hands and knees mops gleaming floors bordering valuable carpets. Velvet presses two fingers to her lips, and they discreetly withdraw.

She flings the entry door open, sprints down the stairs and across the gravel path toward the grove of junipers, fights serpentine branches that threaten to close around her. A sharp-nailed branch scratches her cheek, and she lets out a cry of pain. Frightened and disoriented under a densely woven canopy of trees, where little light penetrates, she extends her arms in front of her, attempts to find her way around without slipping on the underbrush. A ray of sunlight from between the tight gathering of trees punctures the dark, revealing a clearing she stumbles into. A few stumps of axed trees here and there, cut branches piled around. Patches of yellow, green, and purple wildflowers. Loose stones make a low wall around the perimeter of the clearing. Leaning against the stones are paper bags filled with fruit—sour cherries, glistening mulberries, tiny, blossom-crowned cucumbers, and blushing pomegranates—two burlap sacks, one packed with potatoes, and another with onions. A watermelon sits on the dirt next to a basket of walnuts in their green shells.

A cloud fleets over the sun, and she is tossed back into a dark, demon-crammed abyss. Her knees buckle, and she falls far and deep, until fear gives way to a soothing, dream-like state into which she curls like a baby. Someone calls her name, powerful hands break her fall, and, reluctant to face her truth, she fights to free herself. Blood rushes back to her head, and her eyes spring open to the sight of a set of pearlized buttons on a white shirt, the gleam of a gold chain, and, beyond a shoulder, on a tree stump lies open his medical case, the contents of which she so often wished she could browse through. Her cheeks are on fire and her neck throbs. Sweat trickles down her back. Her husband will kill her if he finds her clinging to the doctor like this. "Thank you," she says, the instant she is able to stand on her own feet. "I'm fine now."

He loosens his hold on her. Tilts her face onto his hand. "Your cheek is bleeding."

"I didn't see a branch," she exclaims as she attempts to adjust the chador that slipped off her hair. "Why are you here, Doctor Yaran? What is this place?"

"A clinic of sorts. For when your employees need medical help." The shadow of a smile fleets across his face. "Zahra visits, too, although I can't cure her of her curiosity. But for this cut, Velvet *Khanom*, I have a cure."

"I am afraid of the dark," she says with an apologetic tilt of the head.

With a square of medical gauze, he pats the pearls of blood on the gash on her cheek. "Must be difficult living here when you're afraid of the dark."

"Yes, it's miserable." Feeling a tenderness long forgotten, she leans into his healing touch as he rubs a salve on her cheek. "Ruby Magic?"

"It is," he replies, and, for a heartbeat, he fears he might draw into his embrace this forbidden woman, the thought of whom has been stalking him in the last months.

She touches her cheek where he has rubbed the ointment. "After whom is your ointment named, Doctor Yaran? Is the ointment magical?"

"After Ruby, my wife. She died a year ago. And on your cheek, Velvet *Khanom*, the ointment is pure magic."

A year has passed since she ran out to the poppy fields to see the *Agha* doctor from Paris for herself, the despised Jewish doctor her husband said had sharp horns sprouting out of his brainless head. Now here she is, so close to him, his blood seems to pound in her own veins.

At the crack of breaking branches underfoot, Soleiman adjusts her chador over her hair, tucks in a few errant curls, and inclines his head toward the twisted trunk of a tree. "Until next Monday," he whispers.

"I've something for you." She strokes the book of poetry she has been clutching so tight, her moist fingerprints shadow the cover. "I hope you like it." She drops the book into his medical case and, with a dancer's leap, conceals herself behind the tree.

Branches are pried apart and, kerosene lamp in hand, out steps the only groom on the premises who is allowed to care for Rostam.

The sun has changed position in the sky, and the sporadic flashes of sunlight no longer penetrate the braided branches. Soleiman examines the man's nose in the light of the lamp he hangs on a branch. He works fast, explains that he is drawing pus from the wound and transferring it to the groom's arm to inoculate him from *salak*, the flesh-eating disease, the spread of which he managed to slow in the last year. "There, it didn't hurt much, did it? Make sure to keep the area clean until it dries." A tap on Velvet's book of poetry before he locks his medical case, a discreet farewell wave to her, and he makes his way out of the clearing and toward the mansion to examine the governor general's teeth.

CHAPTER ELEVEN

"Indigestion is not my specialty," Soleiman tells the governor general, who has become increasingly dependent on him, expecting him to tend to his every ailment—a minor rash, a creaking joint, chronic constipation, or a stomachache. "I will be happy to introduce you to a competent doctor."

The governor bursts into a bark of laughter. "Stop talking, Yaran, and rub that pain medicine on my stomach."

"Ruby Magic numbs the gums, Your Excellency. It does not cure a stomachache."

The door opens soundlessly, and Velvet enters carrying a glass of sherbet. She approaches her husband who, propped up against cushions on his divan, studies her with suspicious eyes. She sets the glass on the side table and draws the chador tighter around her face to cover the scratch on her cheek.

"Velvet! Have you lost your mind?" The governor general splutters. "We have a male stranger here."

"I brought you some rosewater sherbet," she replies.

A violent sweep of his arm cuts her off. "Sherbet! I don't want sherbet. What I want is for you to—" For a few long-drawn seconds he grapples to find words other than the string of obscenities threatening to spit out of his mouth. "To make me one of those stews you make. Go now, please, and don't you come barging in again like a loose woman."

Glass of sherbet in her hands, bare feet hesitant on the carpet, Velvet makes her way toward the door. She rests her hand on the door handle, lifts her eyes to Soleiman, and there is such pain in her imploring eyes that he is unable to turn away.

"Women!" The governor says the instant Velvet shuts the door behind her. "Can't live without them, Yaran, can we? But they need a teaching sometimes. Of course, they do. How did you manage to keep yours in line?"

"By showing her, I couldn't live without her. Your own words, Your Excellency."

"And how do *you* show that?" The governor's voice oozes scorn.

Soleiman recoils from the flames of hatred that spring into the man's dark pupils. "I couldn't possibly advise someone of your stature, Your Excellency. All I will say is I named my numbing ointment after my wife. This is how highly I thought of her."

The governor's teeth grind with indignation. "Not much, Yaran. My wife's name is on dunams of land, lucrative fields of healthy poppies. I give my wife expensive jewels you've never seen, permission to read those silly poetry books."

This conversation will lead to nothing but trouble, Soleiman knows, but Velvet's tear-filled eyes have robbed him of all caution. "Jewelry is nice, Your Excellency, but flowers are more personal, especially if you choose them yourself."

The governor's glare dissects the doctor like a coroner's scalpel. "Only straw-brained idiots prefer flowers to diamonds. That's what I think. You are serious, Yaran, aren't you? What kind of flowers do they like?"

"This, Your Excellency, you should ask your wife," Soleiman says, surprised to glimpse a sliver of humanity behind the simmering eyes.

"*Mozakhraf* nonsense!" The governor unbuttons his shirt, tugs his pants slightly down, and pats his stomach. "You better stick to your profession."

"I shall do just that." Soleiman scoops a generous amount of Ruby Magic from the jar and, turning away from the hairy sight of the man's belly that threatens to repulse years of medical knowledge out of him, drops a dollop onto the governor's palm. "It will be more effective if you rub it yourself, Your Excellency."

CHAPTER TWELVE

The governor general is in a foul mood. The pain of indigestion is becoming intolerable. The arrogant Jew was of no help, neither are opium and *aragh*, and he feels caged in the fetid air of his quarter. He pushes the opium brazier aside and stares at Velvet, who stands in front of him as she had earlier today—full of defiance and impossible to yoke and offering him a glass of sherbet he does not want.

His eyes scramble up her chador-clad body, rest on her breasts, the soft curve of her throat, the arrogance of her full mouth. A silent groan wells up. Such a waste of beauty, when he is not aroused by it, when however hard he tries he is unable to enjoy her. He rips away the chador she clutches under her chin. His stare travels across her face and lands on her cheek. He examines the bruise, rubs off the ointment, pinches the greasy residue between two fingers, and sniffs it closely. "What is this?"

Her head jerks back in fear of his identifying the scent of Ruby Magic Soleiman applied to her cheek this morning. "Something Tulip rubbed on. I scratched my cheek on a branch."

The tiger clock above the door comes to life with rolling eyes and a red, swollen tongue, joining the Clock Master's noisy boots behind the door as he goes about the endless process of winding the clocks.

"You went out in the fields in daylight? With all these workers around? I told you not to!"

"Am I a prisoner here? Not even allowed some fresh air sometimes. What else can I do but wait for you to show me off in your Lincoln?"

The tremors, clangs, and rings of clocks echo against the stone walls. One is not synchronized with the others. The governor general cups his ear and listens as if his life depends on his clocks operating in unison. He walks from one clock to another, checks each, retrieves his ever-present master key, unlocks the glass cover of the guilty clock, and takes his time to adjust the hand.

Her husband's obsession with clocks, Tulip tells her, has to do with his being locked in time or having to control time. Poor Tulip, how could anyone guess what transpires in the governor's crooked mind? For all she knows, the clocks might have a way of measuring the circadian health of the governor's opium poppies or else he might be suffering from an affliction of the brain, which might explain his fits of anger when the clocks are not synchronized.

Having made sure the clocks tick in unison, the governor scoops his pen out of its resting groove on the desk and signals with it for her to step closer. His tone is gentle, even kind. "No, you are not a prisoner, Velvet, of course not. Here, give me your hand. Don't be afraid, please, I'll be gentle. It's necessary if you want to go out for fresh air in the fields."

He wets the tip of his pen in his mouth and, wielding it like a sword, digs the tip into the soft flesh on the back of her hand and, careful not to puncture her skin, signs his name with black ink.

Horrified, she attempts to erase his name, rubs it with her palm, but the dark letters are embedded in her skin like poisonous tentacles. "Why did you do that?"

"So you remember you are mine. Don't worry, it will wash off in a few weeks. Behave yourself and you won't need a reminder."

In the center of the room, under the red glare of the chandelier, she shrugs off the rough woolen overcoat he demands she wear when she steps out of the mansion, peels off her long-sleeved dress, slips out of a shell pink gossamer camisole, the embroidered shoulder straps threaded with silver ribbons the color of her eyes, and stands naked and vulnerable in front of him. "Look at me," she says with confidence she does not feel. "Look carefully, my husband, check every centimeter of your wife's body. This flawless body belongs to a pure woman who does not need reminding that she belongs to her husband."

He turns her this way and that as he does a coveted clock he is about to purchase, a collectible piece he likes to brag about. Her skin shrinks under the violating weight of his prodding hands that crawl like strange creatures up and down her nakedness, the skin she pampers with warm oils and unguents of *khashkhash* seeds and sheep yogurt when she dreams of being in Dr. Yaran's arms.

"Flawless as a newborn," the governor murmurs, kissing his stamped name on the back of her hand. He cuddles her shoulders and tells her to shut her eyes while he goes to his desk to fetch a box.

"Open your eyes, Velvet. Look what I ordered. Queen Fawzia's jeweler made this especially for my beautiful wife."

He swings a magnificent necklace in front of her face and before she has a chance to take a good look at the chain of diamonds, locks it like a noose around her neck. She lifts her clothing from the carpet, her torn camisole, her dress and heavy overcoat, slips into them, and tosses the chador over her hair. Her palm runs over the row of diamonds, the same way her husband's hands had just crawled over her naked body. She appraises another costly jewel she will be expected to wear when he parades her around the city in his Lincoln, a reminder of her position as an ornamental wife.

She unlocks the necklace from around her neck and tosses it at his feet, darts out of his reach, and hurries toward the door. She is hardly out of the room when he utters her name with such unexpected mildness, she turns around to face him.

"Maybe you prefer flowers." he says. "Do you? Tell me what kind you like, and I'll get them myself, a room full of the most expensive flowers you'll find in this country."

"Give your jewels and your room full of flowers to the woman you love," she says, turns on her heels, and flees out the door.

CHAPTER THIRTEEN

Aunt Shamsi releases her skirt from Neda's grip, plops herself on a stool in the kitchen, and plants Neda between her thighs. "Poor Little Leech, a year old and stuck to me like *srishom* glue." She snatches a dishrag from a peg overhead and wipes sweat off her own armpits. "Look at me, drenched to my marrow and I've not even started preparing for your Madar's *yahrzeit*. Can you believe it's a year already?" She unfurls Ruby's red scarf from around the child's neck and ties it around her waist. Soleiman is coming home soon, and she won't hear the end of how the scarf could choke the child if it's anywhere close to her neck, on and on, as if she is a useless turnip to let such a thing happen.

Six months back, when she told Soleiman how Neda had burst into a deluge of tears when she took Ruby's scarf away, he sat down and held his head in his hands for so long, she regretted her decision. Then he stood up and went straight to her crib, where the scarf looped at her feet like a *chahar shanbeh souri* bonfire. He raised the scarf with tender care, knotted it into a floppy bow around her waist and talked to her as if she was an adult. "Take good care of it, Sweetheart. Your Madar wore it the first time I saw her on Yom Kippur in *kenissah*. I told her she'd become my wife one day. And your Madar, the brave woman she was, looked into my eyes and said she'd have me as her husband right there and then. We were married in three months."

Aunt Shamsi grabs a bunch of herbs on the kitchen counter. Damn herbs, she hates cleaning the sticky bugs off and chopping,

chopping, chopping. How in the world did she get herself into this never-ending mess, when all she wanted was to tend to her flesh and blood until they could fend for themselves. "Let go of my sleeve or I'll chop off your finger. Listen to me, Little Leech, we better find a wife for your Baba, or you'll be stuck to me forever."

Neda digs her nose into a fistful of herbs. "Smelling bugs," she announces.

"*Zaban deraz* long tongue!" Aunt Shamsi stabs the tip of the knife into the cutting board. "Since when can you smell bugs?"

Neda hangs onto Aunt Shamsi's neck and forces her face down into the hill of chopped herbs. "Smell, Aunt Shamsi!"

"Bugs! I washed them until my hands became raw like monkey bottoms. All your Baba's fault to teach you to speak like this. Okay, okay stop slapping my hand, not your Baba's fault. Just saying a good spanking on your stubborn *koon* now and then will take care of your long tongue."

Neda jumps off Aunt Shamsi's lap, runs out of the kitchen, across the hallway to the garden, and hops into her father's arms. Her Baba smells of That-Cursed-Land-Eater man's mountain dust and tiredness and a different kind of sweet-smelling flower Neda doesn't have in her garden.

Soleiman tosses Neda in the air, holds her tight, and waltzes around the yard while Mademoiselle, Pary's cat, spins like a Hanukah dreidel at his feet.

"Did you have fun today?"

"No fun," Neda says.

"Why, Sweetheart, what did you do that wasn't fun?"

"I cook. I cut foods. I clean all your room."

"That's no fun." He laughs. "Come, we'll play after dinner."

The three are seated around a wooden table by the kitchen window, a naked bulb casting a half-hearted glow on a platter of herb rice, a basket of *sangak* bread, and Neda's favorite, a dish of mushrooms fried with onions and seasoned with rosemary, thyme, and bay leaves.

Mademoiselle, who has made it her business to appear at mealtime, having had her fair share of fried mushrooms Neda fed her under the table, is snoring contentedly.

Soleiman gazes at the outline of the mulberry tree behind the rain-streaked window which, after a year of mourning, is beginning to grow leaves again. A fat moon sprays a silvery light on the patch of mushrooms that blossomed after Ruby died. Tiny tombstones commemorating his wife's death or small candles heralding his daughter's birth. Whatever they represent, they attract Neda in ways he does not quite understand. He spears a piece of mushroom omelet with a fork. The mushrooms are edible, he is certain, having checked their gills and spores under a microscope, consulted an encyclopedia to identify their variety, and consumed the first and second batch. For good measure, he revisits the mushroom patch at frequent intervals to make sure that no poisonous spore has found its way there. He takes a bite of the omelet. "This is excellent, Aunt Shamsi, have some."

She waves the plate away. It is the month of Mehr, and fat, funereal clouds herald the arrival of yet another wet season, when her bones begin to shift and crack and moan at the memory of the black night of Noah's flood, when her daughter, Azar, left her bed and sleepwalked out into the torrential rain and straight down the twenty-two moss-covered steps and into the five-meter *abambar* private water reservoir under the house. Her swollen body was found floating on the surface in the morning.

He pats his aunt on the back. "You look tired, Aunt Shamsi. Why don't you hire a housekeeper?"

Aunt Shamsi rolls her eyes in terror. "And spend your hard-earned money on a stranger! Never. You need a wife, Soleiman, not a maid."

"I do *not* need a wife, Aunt Shamsi. Look for help, please. You'll have more time for yourself, more time to spend with Neda." He blows on a spoonful of herb rice to cool it off. "Have some, Sweetheart, before I eat it all."

"Smell all the so many bugs," Neda declares for the second time today.

Soleiman sets the spoon down. A discreet glance at the chopped herbs mixed with rice. "Tell me, Sweetheart, what do bugs smell like?"

"Funny, Baba!" Neda's blue eyes gauge her father as an adult would a fascinating child. "All the so many bugs smell like *Agha* Fool's sugar cane when Aunt Shamsi shout all loud, 'Wash the mud off that stupid thing.'"

"What about the mushrooms? Do they have bugs, too?"

"Stop with your stinking bugs!" Aunt Shamsi drops her fork in her plate. "Cooked like a slave, so you find bugs in my food! Why don't you look for worms?"

CHAPTER FOURTEEN

The inhabitants of the Jewish Quarter have come bearing traditional gifts of ties, button-down shirts, flannel, wool, and gabardine fabrics for suits. They have come with smiles and firm handshakes, with encouraging pats on Soleiman's back, and affectionate kisses on his somber cheeks.

It is the *yahrzeit,* one-year anniversary of Ruby Yaran's death and Soleiman's living room has been emptied of furniture to make space for rows of metal chairs.

Rabbi Elihu the Compassionate tells Soleiman it is incumbent on him to set his grief aside. To prolong sorrow beyond the acceptable year of mourning is a sin. The rabbi glances around and lowers his voice. "Our religion is not a religion of mourning, Doctor Yaran. Cherish and enjoy the life God gave you."

Eleazar the Redhead gives Soleiman's arm an affectionate squeeze. "Rabbi Elihu is right, son. Ruby's soul won't be at peace until you are."

"Get lost everyone!" The Quarter Fool springs up behind Eleazar the Redhead. "Or *Agha* doctor will kick your stupid *koons* all the way back to your mother's *cos*."

Soleiman suppresses a smile as he guides the Quarter Fool to a chair, thinking the Fool is the sanest of them all.

Rabbi Elihu the Compassionate digs into his lungs to raise his voice above the prayers of other rabbis echoing in the garden and the alley outside, which teems with a crowd the small house is unable to accommodate.

May His great name be exalted and sanctified in God's great name in the world which He created according to His will!

May He establish His kingdom and may His salvation blossom and His anointed be near during his lifetime and during your days and during the lifetimes of all the House of Israel, speedily and very soon!

And say Amen.

"Amen," they all chant as they sway back and forth on their heels.

Neda looks around. So many people come for Madar, but no one come with birthday presents for Neda. Baba Eleazar with his hair on fire around his head and his always laughing voice is here with the shah's Water Man with his gold tooths, donkey smells and too loud voice that hurt Neda's ears. A fat-*koon*-woman Neda doesn't even know keeps giving Baba peeled apples and cucumbers, mint and rosewater for prayer, and too many glasses of tea. Maybe the fat-*koon*-woman thinks it's Baba's birthday instead of Neda's. Even Rabbi Elihu the Compassionate, with his smell of mildew and mothballs, his always-sliding-on-his-head kippah, and his voice like a woman with a cough stuck in her chest, come to tell Baba to live another kind of life Baba doesn't ever like to live. The Quarter Fool with his hair sticking out like a very angry porcupine, and his sticky hands smelly with sugarcane he sucks and sucks all the time, kneel in front of Neda and give her a new not-sucked-on sugar cane for her birthday. But all other people only pat her on the head and pinch her poor cheeks, ouch, and tell Baba she is very special because she speak like grownup peoples and not like all little one-year-old girls that can't ever speak. Neda puts her hand in Baba's hand because he is not very happy right now because everyone tell him to forget Madar and begin again some different kind of normal life.

Soleiman shakes hands, attempts to smile, and thanks everyone for their gifts, which he has no use for. Ruby is here, and he wants her here to remind him of the enormity of his folly. How could he have been so reckless in the juniper grove, almost embraced Velvet, encouraged a future visit, given life to words he should have stifled before they left his lips. Unable to sleep all night, he leafed through the book of poetry she left him. A note was tucked in the end flap of the book. A poem by Anonymous:

Brought to this town's bazaar today, I'll be
The best "companion" here—so who will hire me?
Though I don't care for those who want to have me,
And those I like the look of don't desire me.

How else would Velvet feel but undesirable with that cruel husband of hers in that desolate mansion? Soleiman re-arranges his face and rises to greet a family he does not recognize. He thanks them for their words of sympathy, bows, and is about to leave when Masud Benyamin introduces his wife, Pouran, and his fifteen-year-old daughter, Angel. Pouran opens her short arms and, to Soleiman's surprise, hugs him so tight that her hennaed curls, piled stiff above her head, squash under his chin.

"Come, Angel Joon," Pouran turns to her daughter. "Come, say *salaam* to *Agha* doctor. He studied in Paris; you know. He is the Queen's dentist."

Soleiman inclines his head in respect as he wonders whether Pouran Benyamin is a distant relative he should remember.

Pary steps into the living room, casts her eyes down, and settles in the chair closest to the door. Dressed in white for the first time since her husband's death, she crosses one slim ankle over the other and lowers the hem of her crepe de chine skirt over her knees. She spent the last two days cooking lentil rice, fried fish, and herb omelet for tonight, but aware that the superstitious Aunt Shamsi would not want a widow to prepare food for the occasion, Pary asked the Quarter Fool to deliver the platters to the Yaran home.

Shocked out of her seat, Aunt Shamsi rolls her eyes in Pary's direction. "Look at her. No shame, bringing her cursed widow's feet here."

"Drink, Shamsi." Eleazar the Redhead hands his sister a glass of wine. "The poor woman's feet are like yours and mine."

"You forgot, didn't you? But me, I'll never forget how her bad luck door drove Monsieur André and Ruby to the grave." How could anyone forget how Monsieur André, Pary's ignorant French husband, drove all the way to Asghar Sarvary's orchard in Ramsar to chop a truck full of defenseless mulberry trees, which supply cool shade, sweet fruit, thin paper, and a feast of leaves for silkworms, to build that green door, better suited for a citadel or a caravanserai, with its brass knocker in the shape of a fang-toothed cat and that insult of a *gholamrow* access door for their feral cat with her fancy French name to shoot in and out at will to find her way to Neda. No sane person will forget how the moment Monsieur André polished the door with a last coat of linseed oil, an angry rash spread up from the tip of his toes to the top of his feverish head, he coughed his insides out, and just before Shabbat candles flickered behind windows, he took his last breath and succumbed to typhoid. Hardly had the cold pallor of death settled on Monsieur André, when the Quarter Fool darted around the alleys, announcing he had seen the green door shed big, fat tears of mourning.

Rabbis of all seven synagogues gathered in front of the door in the heat of summer, fanned themselves with their bare hands, wiped sweat off their bearded faces, and waited patiently. At the peak of noon, when steam rose from the ground and the rabbis were embarrassed at their own gullibility, they cast their eyes down and were about to leave, when they heard the wood moan and gazed up to witness the door shudder twice on its hinges. First one, then four, and then a rush of green tears slid down from the very top of the glaze-tiled doorframe, washed dust and fingerprints off the engraved bronze plates and medallions, then pooled at their feet.

A miracle, the rabbis announced, prompting people from near and far to travel to the Alley of Physicians to pay homage to the door, behind which Pary grieved the loss of her husband. Those who arrived after sundown and in time to recite the evening prayers swore on the graves of their ancestors that they were cleansed of their sins, as if they had made a pilgrimage to the Western Wall in Jerusalem. But Shamsi is not fooled. No matter what the rabbis say, the bad luck door brought nothing but death and misery to the Alley of Physicians.

"Collect yourself," Eleazar the Redhead tells his sister. "We can't expect Soleiman to go on with life when you keep telling him bad luck's prowling around every corner."

Aunt Shamsi's gaze swivels around the room—men on one side, women on the other. Soleiman rises for the mourner's kaddish, Neda in his arms, Ruby's red scarf knotted around the child's hair like a wilting tiara. Shamsi takes a large gulp of wine, coils her bun into place at the nape of her neck. "You're right, Eleazar. A *simchah* celebration will turn our luck around. Look at Angel Benyamin. See how she's following the Torah. She's educated enough for Soleiman, don't you think?"

"Let's hope so, Shamsi, let's hope so." Eleazar the Redhead observes the Benyamin Family stand in unison, pray, or sit according to the demands of the Torah. Angel is a good match for Soleiman, but his son does not like being taken by surprise, even if this is how marriages are arranged from generation to generation.

Blessed and praised, glorified and exalted, extolled and honored, adored and lauded be the name of the Holy One, blessed be He, above and beyond all the blessings, hymns, praises and consolations that are uttered in the world!

And say Amen!

"Amen!" Aunt Shamsi shouts as if God is hard of hearing.

Neda runs across the room and flies into her grandfather's arms. His puckered lips make bubbly sounds against her neck. "You must be bored, *boubaleh*."

"So bored, Baba Eleazar," she says between hiccups of laughter. "No one give me happy birthday present. Aunt Shamsi say many time she give me her silver purse, but she don't give me anything. Where's my happy birthday present?"

"You're something else, *boubaleh*. How do you know it's your birthday?"

"*Agha* Fool know it's Neda's birthday. I want a birthday like *Agha* Fool's birthday so everyone give me nice presents."

"Tomorrow, *boubaleh*, you'll get your presents tomorrow."

"No, Baba Eleazar, I don't want tomorrow happy birthday. May tomorrow never come!"

"Oy!" Eleazar the Redhead slaps his thigh, breaks out into laughter. "Don't you start talking like Shamsi, or we'll all be in trouble. 'May tomorrow never come' is what old people say when they've nothing to look forward to. But you, *boubaleh*, have many, many wonderful tomorrows ahead of you, so don't you pay attention to Shamsi. And don't wait for her silver purse, either. It's from her mother, and she'll never part with it."

Everyone falls silent, chairs creak, and gazes turn toward the door. Jacob Mordechai announces himself with a mix of audacious colors—pinstriped navy suit, yellow pocket square, suspenders, and bowtie. He scrutinizes the gathering, takes out a wrinkled pack of cigarettes from his shirt pocket and fixes a cigarette between his nicotine-stained fingers, lights the cigarette, and, moving with efficiency and purpose, approaches Pary and offers her the cigarette, which she refuses with an apologetic half-smile. "Ah, Madame, you don't smoke." He bows with an exaggerated flourish of nobility. "Perhaps I might have the honor of being your cavalier for a pleasant day in the city sometime." A gallant kiss on Pary's hand and off he ambles to sit next to Soleiman.

"You're not in Paris." Soleiman grins. "Remember yourself."

"Lovely, isn't she, and living right next to you. What are you waiting for, Soleiman? Time's too precious to squander like this. Who knows where we'll be tomorrow."

"Not tomorrow, Uncle Jacob." Neda climbs onto Jacob's lap. "Give me my happy birthday present."

Jacob crushes his cigarette in an ashtray. "*Salaam*, Neda. Look at you! Talking like an all-grown-up girl."

"Like a little miracle, Uncle Jacob."

"You sure are," he says, his expression softening. Neda reminds him of his own niece, who was slightly older, but with the same blue eyes, curly black hair, and naïve belief in miracles. But no miracle saved his niece or her parents from Hitler's ovens. He rummages in his coat pocket, his hand emerging with a silver coin he fans between his fingers to appear and disappear in front of Neda's astonished eyes. He tickles her palm with the coin. "For a *lavashak* fruit roll." Another trick of the hands, and two blue marbles drop from his sleeves. "And these are for *tileh bazi* game." In no time, a paper carnation pops open like a red fan behind his collar, which he sticks in her red scarf. "Happy birthday, Neda."

"All for my today happy birthday?"

An affectionate tap on the tip of her nose. "All for your today happy birthday. Now give Uncle Jacob a big hug," he says, his gaze following her as she goes to Aunt Shamsi to ask her to tighten the red scarf, which is sliding off her hair. "Your daughter is different," Jacob tells Soleiman. "Quite advanced for her age. It's unusual for a one-year-old to understand the concept of a birthday, or the difference between today and tomorrow. Children usually don't talk until they're two, and when they do, they start with a couple of words, not phrases. Having said that, it's common for children to understand before they speak, so be very careful what you say in front of Neda. Now off I go to tend to my other children. And come visit us soon. We're moving to a larger house."

Dinner is being served, and people squeeze out of the house, through the gate and into the garden.

It is not a large garden. Soleiman measures the eighteen-meter length and fifteen-meter width by the count of footsteps it takes him to reach his laboratory and by the sum of the cut-glass on top of the walls, which are there to deter thieves and Jew-hating invaders. Aunt

Shamsi measures it by the number of hours it takes the Quarter Fool to sweep and water the place. Neda measures it by the distance it takes her to walk to her Baba's laboratory, the mushroom patch, and the box of herbs she nourishes with discarded tea leaves and eggshells, which the neighbors now skirt as they hurry back and forth into the Alley of Physicians, past the Garbage Pit, and in and out of the Alley of Seven Synagogues to fetch serving dishes heaped with golden halvah sprinkled with almond slivers, fried, crispy white fish, bowls of *fesenjan* ground walnuts and pomegranate stew, veal and quince stew, rice laced with orange rind, almond and pistachio slivers. A wealth of food for which the populace has sacrificed much time, money, and precious rations.

But Soleiman has no appetite. He sits in one of the chairs set in rows in the garden and begins to snap the cover of his pocket watch—a growing habit when Ruby's voice becomes particularly loud in his troubled mind: the Soleiman she knew would have burned Velvet's book before she charmed him out of his senses, the Soleiman she knew would not fall for a married, Muslim woman, but would have honored his wife's last words and would have done what is right for his daughter.

As if sensing her father's sadness, Neda makes her way back to him and climbs into his lap. She slaps her hands on his frantic fingers. "Baba, you break your watch!"

"No, Sweetheart, I won't. It's very special." He displays the engraving of "Ruby Magic" on the back. "Your Madar gave it to me when I made Ruby Magic to take people's pain away."

"How you take people's pain away, Baba?"

"I rub Ruby Magic on their gums, Sweetheart. It's a very special ointment, a mixture of all kinds of herbs and plants and medicines." He rises to his feet to greet Pary who, a small glass dish cupped in both hands, crosses the garden toward them.

"I hope it's not too late, Doctor Yaran, but I want to thank you for helping me paint André's door. I wouldn't have forgiven myself if I destroyed its esthetic beauty." She hands Neda the container, in it a small chocolate cake on top of which a tiny wooden cat made of balsa holds up a red candle. "Happy Birthday, Neda," she whispers with a youthful glitter in her black eyes, which is at odds with the melancholy image of the widow, who has been carrying her grief like an honorific crown. A self-effacing gesture across her face, before she walks out of the garden and back to the refuge of her home.

Neda like Pary's wood dolls and her lullaby voice and all the fairy tales she tell Neda when she sometimes sneak to Pary's house when Aunt Shamsi snore-sleeps in the afternoon. But she doesn't like the smell of paint of Pary's white door or her always sad eyes that make Neda's tongue taste like radishes Aunt Shamsi puts in sour vinegar. Neda like the creamy sweetness of Pary's chocolate cake, the stickiness of caramel, the slippery melting of butter and dancing smells of vanilla and rosewater. Why Pary says happy birthday and give Neda cake and a little cat doll, but no one else want to give Neda presents, only Uncle Jacob and maybe *Agha* Fool too because his sugar cane is only half a present.

It is after eleven o'clock, the flame of kerosene lamps sputter and stoop in exhaustion. Fog seeps into every nick and cranny, the sigh of ghosts rise from the Garbage Pit, and the night exudes a sour smell. People begin to trickle out, at last. They bid Aunt Shamsi and Eleazar the Redhead farewell. Kiss Soleiman on both cheeks. "May your future be filled with joy," they say. "May you live one hundred and twenty years."

"*Moteshakeram*," Aunt Shamsi says over and over again. "May good fortune follow your departing steps."

Rabbi Elihu the Compassionate rests one veined hand on Soleiman's shoulder. "May this be your last grief, Doctor Yaran. May I officiate your wedding in the near future."

The Quarter Fool hops out of the gate, his shrill voice trailing behind him, "May dogs feast on the bulging eyes of Jew-haters. May donkeys munch on their black livers. May they hang upside down from their shriveled testicles."

The garden has quieted down, but the Benyamin Family has congregated by the geraniums Ruby planted two springs ago under the mulberry tree. The geraniums have grown long-legged and sparse for lack of care, and Soleiman makes a silent vow to bring them back to life.

"Say good night to Baba Eleazar and off we go," he whispers to Neda. "Not polite when we've guests, but I've had enough for one day."

The moment he lifts Neda from his lap and rises to his feet, his father and aunt are at his side, telling him to take a good look at the lovely fifteen-year-old girl talking to her parents.

"She's been praying all evening like a born rabbi," says Eleazar the Redhead.

"From a good family, too," says Aunt Shamsi, "a perfect mother for Neda."

Baba look at the lovely fifteen-year-old girl Aunt Shamsi say is perfect Madar for Neda. Baba's face is all suddenly red like spoiled cherries. Neda look hard at the lovely fifteen-year-old girl with so much black hairs sticking out of her big head and her bigger mouth that munch, munch something with her long teeth like Rostam. The lovely fifteen-year-old girl's stink of must-not-eat mushrooms burn Neda's nose all the way from other side of the garden. Neda grabs Baba's leg, so he won't go tell that lovely fifteen-year-old girl to become Neda's Madar.

Neda's hysterical sobs ricochet around the garden. She wants to run to the mushroom patch and tell everything to her Mushrooms Friend that lives in the mushrooms all the time, but Baba push chairs out of his way and lift Neda hard in his arms.

"Sweetheart! What's wrong?" Soleiman says.

"No, Baba, no!" Neda cries out between punishing belly hiccups. "I don't ever want any new Madar. I want Aunt Shamsi."

Holding his daughter at arm's length, Soleiman looks at her with deepening concern. "Don't listen to other people, no one's becoming your new Madar. Listen to me, Sweetheart. I'm not getting married again. Do you hear me? I promise."

Big people make many promise all the time and forget many promise all the time like Aunt Shamsi make promise to give Neda her Madar's silver purse on her birthday and *Shahreh Farang* man with picture stories in his golden box who make promise to come to Neda's birthday and show new stories in his golden box. But Aunt Shamsi don't give Neda her silver purse and *Shahreh Farang* man forget and don't come to today birthday that *Agha* Fool say is Neda's real birthday.

Neda's sobs grow louder.

Soleiman rushes into the house, lays her on one of the sofas, checks her from head to toe, asks her if she's hurting anywhere. Her sobs more urgent, she turns from him and rubs her eyes so hard he fears she'd break capillaries. He lowers her fists from her eyes. Lifts her from the sofa and sets her in his lap. "You'll have to trust your Baba, Sweetheart. I'm not getting married again, not to this girl out there or to anyone else. Come now, Sweetheart, give Baba a big smile." He takes his handkerchief out of his pocket and wipes her eyes, stares at the handkerchief in his hand, then tilts her head up and studies her eyes as his fingers slide over both cheeks, the corners of her eyes.

Fear sets his eardrums thrumming. His breath coils in his aching chest.

Something has gone terribly wrong with his daughter.

Her face is contorted with crying, but her eyes, face, and the handkerchief he bunches in his fist are as dry as his mouth.

His daughter's eyes stopped producing tears.

CHAPTER FIFTEEN

It is eight in the evening, and cinemas, cabarets, burlesque clubs, cafés, and theaters hum on Lalezar Street, the Champs Élysee of Tehran. British and American soldiers stroll, the women on their arms in pricey nylons, knee-length skirts, and fashionable hats perched on their swept-up hair.

The rare Russian soldier who has money, and the generosity to spend it, is faced with a vendor's deceptive smile, a ridicule of a bow and a chain of exaggerated niceties as he is handed a tumbler of inferior vodka and a silent curse in the wake of his retreating steps. It is one thing to serve British and American invaders with money to burn. Entirely different to serve mean-spirited Russians, whose sole intent is to devour the country's rich reserves of oil, copper, iron, and ore.

Soleiman and Neda pass the Grand Hotel, where Ghamar-Al-Molouk Vaziri holds concerts on Friday evenings. A tiara winking on her Parisian coiffed hair, naked arms exposed to adoring audiences, she has been dominating the grand ballroom stage years before any woman dared appear in public without a chador.

On Meli cul de sac, Soleiman stops to check the address he scribbled on a piece of paper, then the numbers glazed on a turquoise tile on top of the door he faces. "Uncle Jacob's new house," he tells Neda, who squeezes to her chest a wood doll bundled in Ruby's scarf.

Four years in Paris, he shared a room with Jacob while he obtained his *Baccalauréat Professionnel* and Jacob studied psychoanalysis. For four years, every single Sunday, their landlady climbed the stairs to the third-floor attic and left them a week's supply of cheese, better suited for cooking, so that they still cringe at the sight of a slice of French cheese.

They spent hours studying at Café La Rotonde in Montparnasse, where the kind-hearted owner looked away when they pocketed a piece of baguette left in an abandoned breadbasket.

Jacob joined the Parisian *Hashomer Hatzair* Jewish Youth Movement. He prepared Jewish orphans in underground schools for *aliyah* to Palestine. A chameleon, adept in inhabiting different guises, he managed to navigate the most difficult situations with hope and a sense of humor. They shared each other's ups and downs, their successes and failures, their struggles to make ends meet.

But nothing predicted the fact that Jacob could afford a handsome fired-brick house nestled behind tall walls and ancient plane trees. Soleiman lifts the larger of the two knockers and drums, a louder knock to reveal the gender of the guest and warn the homeowner to dress properly before opening the door.

A soothing fountain trickles into a round pool in the center of the courtyard they enter. Steps lead to a balcony that connects several rooms in which children can be seen playing or studying. Neda lets go of her father's hand, tumbles up the stairs, and into Jacob's open arms.

"Everyone!" Jacob claps as he winks at Neda. "To the salon. Neda is here." He adjusts the satin lapel of his gold-buttoned blazer. "Took your father six months to get you here."

"Enough time for you to rob a bank," Soleiman replies. "Or inherit this house?"

"Both, my friend, both." Certain information is too sensitive to share, even with Soleiman. All he, himself, knows is that the house was obtained by the Zionist Organization to accommodate the Tehran Children as they prepare for *Aliya* immigration to Palestine and that the expenses are paid from a fund to which he has no access.

A rush of laughter and chatter precedes six children as they pour into the large salon, which is sparsely furnished. A few chairs here and there. Two sets of low tables with four chairs around each. A sandbox in a corner. Art materials, fairytale books, puppets and stuffed animals, molding clay, and building toys are scattered on the carpet and on tables. This safe environment is where the children have a chance to interact freely with each other and with their toys, recreate traumatic events in their games, reveal what is hard or impossible for them to voice, and, in so doing, release negative emotions and acquire healthier behaviors.

Sahar, the children's young teacher, tries to save the four-year-old Anna's silk-blonde hair from dipping in the icing of a pistachio cake she carries. Jacob catches the cake, balances it above his head on one palm, takes the girl by the hand, and walks her toward Neda. "Come everyone, introduce yourselves to Neda."

"Jacob *Agha*," Sahar says, a dimple appearing in her right cheek. "The children were in the middle of their lessons."

"I know, Sahar, thank you, just a short recess to meet a new playmate."

The children crowd Neda. A chorus of voices shout out their names. Anna reaches out to touch Neda's doll, amazed at the fine details, the small nose, lined lips, eyes so lifelike. A pale, round-eyed boy attempts to grab the doll.

"No!" Big hands break Neda's dolls. "No!" Neda hides the doll behind her back, then wraps both arms around it and grips it tightly against her chest. Such loud, pitiful sobs burst out of her; the children scatter in different directions.

Jacob's eyes rest on Neda for a while before he turns his attention to his children. This is what he calls them, his orphaned children, whose shattered emotional health might take a lifetime to mend. He studies Ludwig, a chubby, red-haired boy, as he folds his legs under him, rests his elbows on his knees, and presses his hands to his ears to muffle the sound of Neda's sobs. Anna, having lost interest in Neda, is sucking her two middle fingers, which went numb the day she was yanked away from everyone and everything she knew in Poland.

Antoni, whose papery, lower lips are blistered from constant chewing, retreats to a far corner of the room, dismantles a toy car, and begins to smash the broken pieces under one foot.

"Come, Antoni, let me have a look at your lips." Jacob lifts Antoni into his arms, pulls a small tube out of his coat pocket, rolls it between the fingers of one hand, and makes it disappear in his sleeve. "Now, where did it go?" He asks Antoni as he peers into his mouth and produces the tube as if from there. He twists the tube open and puts some salve on Antoni's lips. "Go, play now, everyone's waiting." He turns his attention to Soleiman, rests a hand on his shoulder. "Worrying won't help, my friend. Come, it's not the end of the world. The children will figure it out between them."

Soleiman settles in one of the two chairs; Jacob moves to an abandoned table in a corner.

"Talk to me." Jacob leans forward. "What kept you away for six months?"

"Neda did. She cries, even sobs, without shedding a single tear. I've dragged her to the best ophthalmologists and retina specialists. They all say the same thing. The retinal cones, the rods, the shape of the cornea are normal, as are the optic nerve, retinal ganglia, and tear ducts. One doctor after another assures me that nothing is wrong with her eyes."

Jacob moves a few story books on the table, a bowl of rice cookies, slides domino blocks in no specific order. He lowers his voice, a kinder tone. "They might be right, Soleiman. Have you considered that?"

A dismissive wave of Soleiman's hand. "Something *must* be wrong. Healthy eyes shed tears. Healthy eyes are not dry, itchy, and painful. My daughter needs proper medical help. Just like your children need a proper home. And neither can be found here."

Jacob rakes his fingers through the furrows of his combed-back hair. "No, these are two entirely different problems. There *is* proper help here for Neda. You might not believe in psychotherapy, but I've seen and continue to see miraculous results right here with my children. Fine, fine, you're not even ready to hear me, and I respect that. So, back to my orphans who need to settle in a suitable home, which they won't find here. Somewhere permanent, where they will be properly taken care of. And that will not be possible unless I get my hand on travel permits." The British bastards had intercepted the last ship to Palestine and had sent his previous group of orphans back to Europe. The war on illegal immigration is at its peak, and the Cyprus detention camps are teeming with stateless Jews. But as fast as the British Patrol turns shiploads of refugees away, the Mossad Aliyah Bet, having no alternative, turns around and drops them back on the beaches of Palestine. Jacob nods toward the children. "I can't keep them here much longer. Another ten are scheduled to move in soon. Any news from the Queen?"

Soleiman lets out an impatient grunt. The initial pride he experienced when he was first summoned to the royal court is fading, but not the optimism he felt on his second visit. "She appeared sympathetic. She even mentioned a temporary refugee camp the court erected in one of the royal gardens. I will hear from her."

"Don't be so certain." Jacob fishes out another cigarette from his shirt pocket, lights it, and takes a pensive draw. After months of being tossed from one consulate to another, one department to another, pleading with and bribing countless authorities to acquire visas, it has become amply clear that nothing much happens in this city without the governor general's blessing. "I've been trying to get an appointment with a certain Colonel Motamedi in the British Embassy. He has a heart somewhere in his bony chest, I'm told. But he won't give an appointment unless the governor general demands one."

Soleiman's thoughts unspool as he gazes at Neda inching her way toward the girl who brought in the cake. "There might be a way, Jacob. Far-fetched, but worth a try. I'm thinking of Tulip."

"The governor general's eunuch? Are you serious? You trust him?"

"I do. He's the voice of reason in that dreary mansion. The only ally I have. And I'm doing everything I can to keep his pain under control while I'm working on a hormonal substitute to ease his imbalance. No one has the governor's ear more than he does."

"Then do what you can, Soleiman, we don't have much time. Europe is being crushed under Hitler's tentacles, and Iran is next. Hitler has his eyes on Iran's oil fields. There's no end to the bastard's vitriol. Parisian Jews have been ordered to surrender their radios, phones, bicycles. The Gestapo bombed Synagogue Nazareth."

Sorrow clouds Soleiman's mind. Years ago, he and Jacob attended Yom Kippur services in Synagogue Nazareth when they were students in Paris. How impressed they had been by that gilded sanctuary with its high ceilings, the ornate women's gallery, and the rousing notes of an organ they did not expect to hear in a synagogue. Despite their empty pockets and brutal schedules, they were happy then, optimistic about their future. "I'll talk to Tulip tomorrow when I visit the governor."

"Thank you, Soleiman, and good luck," Jacob says, his gaze seeking Neda, whose sobs have subsided and, her doll still clutched in her hands, inches her way toward Anna. "Does this happen often," he asks Soleiman "Neda's fear of sharing her dolls and her whispering under her breath like this?"

A deep bone weariness overwhelms Soleiman. "Yes, it does. I think there's a connection between the dolls and her mother."

"That is normal. At her age a child will associate everything to her absent mother. Listen to me, Soleiman. Neda needs a mother. And you, my friend, need a wife."

Soleiman slaps his knees. "As if Aunt Shamsi, Baba Eleazar, and Ruby aren't enough, you, too, need to tell me to get married."

"And why not? It's been a year and a half. It's time."

"I don't want a wife." Soleiman nods farewell, rises, and turns to fetch his daughter. At the gleam of fear he notices in her wide eyes and the sense of urgency with which she continues to squeeze the doll to her chest, he settles back in his seat and adds: "My heart is with someone else."

Jacob's smile erases the concern off his face. "But that's great news, my friend. Why didn't you tell me before? Who is she?"

Soleiman tugs at his shirt cuffs, twists an onyx cufflink. "Her name is Velvet."

"Velvet! Nice name. I like her already. Velvet." Jacob riffles through the file of his memory for names of eligible girls in the Jewish Quarter. "Interesting! Why don't I know her? I must have lost my knack for sniffing out things around here." He rubs his hands with delight as he leans back in his seat. "Go on, Soleiman, start from the beginning. Tell me all about her. Is she educated?"

Soleiman's white-knuckled hands grip the arms of his chair. "I believe so. She recites poetry in a lovely voice. She is kindhearted. Vulnerable. Has irresistible silver eyes…"

"Enough!" A flash of excitement illuminates Jacob's face. "I'm falling in love with her, myself. Who is this Velvet?" He shifts in his chair. "Well? I asked who stole your heart."

Soleiman's voice is low. "Velvet. Velvet, the governor general's wife."

"Who?" Jacob slides to the edge of his seat. He is suddenly aware of the thumping of his heart and the bitter taste of nicotine in his mouth. "Who did you say she is?"

"I said the governor general's wife, Jacob. You heard me right. The wife of the governor general."

The children, sensing an escalating tension, stop playing and turn their attention to the adults. The stunned silence is pierced only by the drunken cries of a British soldier on Lalezar Avenue and the mesmerizing voice of Ghamar-Al-Molouk Vaziri, which comes all the way from the ballroom of the Grand Hotel: "The country is a mess. The nation is asleep. Women of Iran rise and revolt."

Jacob draws a deep breath and, incredulous eyes trained on his friend, says, "Tell me it's a bad joke, Soleiman. You did *not* fall in love with the Land Eater's wife." The silence levitates undisrupted in the heavy air, long enough for Jacob to rein in the buzz in his ears and construe Soleiman's reply. He jumps out of his seat and, years of training and discipline forgotten, shouts, "Have you lost your mind? Falling in love with the wife of that ruthless Jew-hater! Putting yourself, your daughter, and your entire community in danger. What happened to the levelheaded man I knew in Paris?"

"Sit, Jacob, please. I don't know what to tell you. I wish I was not in this impossible situation, but I am."

Jacob drops himself into his seat, pats his shirt pocket for his pack of cigarettes, and draws deep puffs. He was an active underground guerrilla fighter of the *Hashomer Hatzair* Jewish Youth Movement. He established underground press and schools in Paris. He prepares Jewish immigrants for illegal *aliyah* to Palestine. He is trained in controlling the secretion of his adrenaline glands under stress. Yet. At no other time did his breath feel as painful in his chest as it does now.

Dominoes clatter on the table around which two children are playing. Antoni piles in his arms the broken parts of the toy car and sets them like peace offerings at Neda's feet. She smiles her first smile of the evening, sifts through the pieces, and, sitting cross-legged next to each other, they try to put the toy car back together.

Time passes. Jacob's probing gaze emerges from behind a riot of smoke. He crushes the empty packet of cigarettes in his fist, slides his chair closer to Soleiman, and stays like that for a few moments. "What a terrible position you're in, my friend."

CHAPTER SIXTEEN

Tulip lifts layers of veils off his head and studies his image in the mirror above the fireplace in the governor general's private quarters. It never fails to shock him, his painted lips lined like rose buds, wide eyes the shade of smoke, lashes thickened with crushed berries and soot. What is he? A young, handsome man painted like a woman? Born a man and turned into a woman. Or someone all wrong. Someone who depends on Dr. Yaran's pills to keep his brittle bones functioning and his prematurely graying hair from falling.

Who, he can't help but wonder, is to blame for his suffering, his stepfather or the governor general, who appeared in the arid, palm-dotted village of Kanakan thirteen years ago?

Clad all in black, except for a white turban covering his lush, black hair, the governor general planted his tall, lean figure in the gathering center of the small village and, wielding a fat bag of gold coins above his head, announced he was there to find a servant. Anyone interested in a wealth of gold, anyone who wanted to save their young ten-year-old son, nephew, or cousin from the misery of village life, was to seek the governor in private at *Rahmat* Mercy Inn.

The populace was divided. For some, no amount of gold was worth approaching this man's evil orbit. For others, the temptation proved hard to resist. By evening, the village buzzed like a hive of mad bees. Why did the governor general come all the way to this poor hamlet to hire a servant? Why didn't he dispatch one of his many employees to do the job for him? Why did the few greedy folks who entered the caravanserai leave with pressed lips, glazed eyes, and dragging feet? After two days, once the wave of excitement and the volley of unanswered questions died, a dark cloud descended upon the village, and people found it prudent to roll their curiosity into a tight knot and swallow it whole.

His stepfather, however, clutched the bag of gold to his chest and assured the governor general that it was entirely possible to fulfill his wish. He will hand the governor a pubescent boy with flawless skin, delicate features, and light-colored eyes, who would possess the qualities of a woman. However, in order to do the job himself as well as keep his mouth forever shut, he demanded an additional fifteen gold coins. Face twitching with glee, he counted the coins, then bowed low until his head hit his arthritic knees and begged the governor general's pardon for having to ask him to leave the room for a short while, which the governor happily obliged.

Strapped to the dining table, the ten-year-old Hassan nearly choked on the scorching *aragh* forced down his throat to numb him. His stepfather fondled his genitals to assess how best to accomplish the task delegated to him. His gaze pinned to a spider that scrambled across the stained ceiling, Hassan grabbed the edges of the table and, his face burning from shame and fear, experienced his first and last orgasm.

A thin wire was knotted around his penis and testicles after which they were amputated with a razor. The urethra was plugged with a cork to prevent closure and the wound covered and wrapped with paper moistened salves to stop the bleeding.

The governor general converted the *Rahmat* Mercy Inn into a makeshift hospital, hired a tight-lipped doctor, and cared for Hassan for eight days and nights until he was well enough to tolerate the ride from Kanakan to Tehran. In the back seat of the Lincoln, the child's head resting in his lap, the governor whispered, "My beautiful, beautiful boy. You deserve a beautiful name like yourself. I will call you Tulip! Yes, my Tulip, my innocent Tulip, we'll keep our secret to ourselves, won't we?" Hassan closed his eyes and, his pain momentarily forgotten, slept for the first time in more than a week.

In Tehran, up in the mountains, it was not hard to deceive the workers in the fields or the rare visitor into believing that he was born like this, an aberration of nature, whom the governor general had saved from a miserable life after his mother died from accumulation of desert dust in her lungs, and he was left in the care of his cruel stepfather. But convincing Velvet, the governor general's young bride, whose boundless compassion demanded an honest response, was far more difficult than he had imagined. Until, unable to tolerate the lies, he decided to reveal part of the truth and begged her to stop the questions because an honest reply will conjure a time he would rather forget.

Tulip sighs. Best to delegate Hassan to the past where he belongs. Life, in the end, has been kinder to him than to others, who roam the war-ravaged streets begging for a kilogram of coal to warm their braziers and a slice of bread to fill their growling bellies.

He sets the bowl of hot water on top of a heavy trunk on which two saddle and harness makers worked day and night for eight months to complete the tooling, silver banding, and brass tacks, which gleam like the thousands of gold coins contained inside. Coins to bribe one authority or another in return for turning a blind eye to thousands of kilograms of rolled opium the governor general regularly dispatches by train to Afghanistan, Iraq, Pakistan, Azerbaijan, and Turkmenistan.

The lid is unlocked, and the governor is in deep afternoon slumber on his divan. Good. Visitors are not expected. Asking for a favor requires the indulgence of time. He wipes off a drop of water, so it will not stain the exquisite leather, collects the foaming skirts at his heels, and settles cross-legged on the carpet.

From his satin purse, he removes a plate, two candles, a matchbox, a small bowl, and a container of paste made from the highly prized kernels of black walnuts from Ghazvin. Black walnuts cured under the sun in aromatic oils and pounded to obtain a fistful of fine paste more precious than life itself.

He sends a prayer to Allah, lights the candles, fixes them on the plate, and begins the slow process of squeezing and kneading the paste. Now and then he warms the paste above the candle flames to tempt drop by precious drop of black walnut oil that trickle down like tears from his clenched fist to pool in the miniature china bowl at his feet. It is an agonizing job, normally delegated to a mortar and pestle, but he prefers to rely on his hands which, at the service of the governor, have developed into efficient machines capable of squeezing secrets out of rocks.

The somber orchestra of clocks announce the passing of another hour. These are the heartbeat of the mansion, the ceaseless metallic bongs in which the governor general hears the toll of his own quickening footsteps across the narrow bridge of time, hears the bejeweled gates of heaven open to welcome him to his final destination, where he hopes to be absolved from the sins of his flesh. It must be exhausting to have one's ears endlessly cocked to the clocks, as his master does, to count every second like a miser who collects small increments of coins in an earthenware *ghoolac*. It must be exhausting to kneel five times a day in prayer and fast so rigorously on Ramadan, all in hope of being pardoned on the day of Judgement. But Allah, the all merciful, Tulip muses, will not so easily absolve a man who robbed a young boy of his manhood.

Tulip dries his hands and prepares to awaken the governor general. He strokes his cheeks, wipes sweat off his neck, and dries spittle off his lips.

Still attached to his dreams, the governor reaches out for the pen under his pillow.

"It's only me, Your Excellency." Tulip drops a date into the governor's mouth, raises his head as he chews, then spits the pit into Tulip's palm.

"It isn't Friday night? Is it?"

"No, Your Excellency, it is not," Tulip replies as he drops the pit into a silver urn. "But the weather is hot, and I thought you wouldn't mind a bath."

"A bath? Want me to take a bath, Tulip?"

"Yes, I want it very much."

An affectionate tap under Tulip's chin. "All right then, I will."

"A massage too?" Tulip displays the china bowl like a trophy. "Look what I have for you. Pressed drop by drop with my own hands." He dips one finger in the oil. "Still warm, Your Excellency. Shall we?"

"You naughty boy! How in the name of the imams did you find black walnuts on a weekday? No! Don't tell me. Do with me as you please."

Tulip cherishes these moments—a fond gaze, a direct question, a tender word distributed like the sweetest of baklava. He helps the governor step out of his loose pants and collarless shirt, helps him stretch out on layers of towels spread on the carpet next to the trunk and washbasin. Daily calisthenics have held the ravages of opium at bay, so the governor remains lean and firm muscled, his mane of hair shinier than oiled onyx. But his sallow skin is like a porous sponge that exudes the odor of opium and burnt smoke, which can be temporarily moderated with only the strongest of lye soaps and a vigorous scrub that leaves Tulip's hands dry and itchy.

Tulip gives his master a thorough rub behind the ears, under his arms, around his thighs, between every crooked toe. He drops the washcloth and the cone of soap into the bowl and begins to knead the governor with aromatic oils, each protruding vertebrae and well-defined rib, the firm, double-hills of his buttocks, then turns him around and rubs his chest and belly, mindful of the pressure and rhythm of his hands, the delicate dance he has fine-tuned to perfection, attentive to the slightest sign of pleasure or annoyance, until every muscle is receptive under his touch.

He warms the oil between his palms, applies it to the dark bush, the hairy creases, flips his master's scrotum to the left, the right, circles the puckered sack, adds more oil, and rubs the flaccid penis.

Opium addicts have difficulty reaching orgasm. For the guilt riddled governor general, release is cause for celebration. And for

Tulip, the rousing of impossible longing for the man he could have been.

"My beautiful boy." The governor general lifts himself on one elbow. His lips graze his servant's mouth. "What would I do without you?"

His master firm and alive in his greased fist, Tulip takes a deep breath, as if he has come up for air. "Don't worry, Your Excellency, I'm here and will always be here. May I speak?"

"Yes, my boy, yes, anything you want...pearls...emeralds..."

"It's about Doctor Yaran."

"Faster, my boy! Faster!"

"May I ask you to order Colonel Motamedi to issue visas?"

The grinding of the Governor's groin becomes more insistent. "Squeeze harder, my boy!"

"Doctor Yaran is out of important medication and—"

The governor's eyes spring open. "You're sick, my boy?"

"No, Your Excellency. I'm talking about a medicine Doctor Yaran needs for your teeth. He's out of it and can't find it here and he shouldn't travel alone because—"

The governor slaps away Tulip's hand, as if swatting off an irritating mosquito. He gestures toward his shriveling penis. "So, you've become the Jew's messenger? Is this why you're here?"

"Allah forbid!" Tulip scrambles to reestablish his connection. "I came because I am worried about you. You need this medicine and... what if, Allah forbid, may I go mute, there's an emergency and the pain is intolerable and there's nothing to be done."

A breeze from the window shifts the chandelier's red crystal drops, dappling the governor's face with sprinklings of blood. "Don't worry, my boy. Yaran is a smart Jew. He always finds a way."

The last remnant of oil a puddle in his cupped palm, Tulip stops lubricating, squeezing, and rubbing. "Please, Your Excellency, do it for me. I'll die if something happens to you."

"Don't stop, my boy, more oil."

“Shall I tell Doctor Yaran you’ll lift the ban on permits?” Tulip says, teasing his master with soft strokes.

“Harder,” The governor shouts as he writhes about. “Harder, I said!”

Another drop of warm oil, another soft lick. “Better, Your Excellency?”

“Ah, my boy, my beautiful boy. You’re mine. Say I’m yours.”

“I am your beautiful boy, Your Excellency.”

“Louder, I said! Louder!”

“I am all yours,” Tulip raises his voice. “Will you order permits issued?”

“Anything you want, my boy! Anything!”

CHAPTER SEVENTEEN

Soleiman checks Rostam's shoulders for cuts from the juniper branches, then checks his hooves and pries free with a hoof pick yesterday's mud and manure lodged in each hoof from the trip back from the governor general's mansion. He smiles at the memory of Velvet's wine-stained lips and silver eyes that had snuffed out all sense of reason. She had snuck into the juniper grove like an ethereal angel, not caring to wait until Tulip had ended delivering his message. He, too, was reckless and, despite Tulip's nervous warnings, nestled her lovely face between his hands and was about to seek her mouth, when a series of coughs from Tulip brought him back to his senses.

Tulip had come to the juniper grove to inform him that he had managed the impossible feat of arranging an appointment with Colonel Motamedi, the top governmental officer in charge of issuing permits.

Soleiman oils Rostam's hooves, grooms his coat with a curry comb, and, with a damp sponge, wipes his eyes—dirt crumbs from the inner corners, bits of hay stuck to the lashes, seeds wedged in the ears. "We're going to get visas, Rostam. The orphans will have a home, at last, and Neda will see the best specialists."

He saddles his stallion and spurs him out of the Quarter and around Toop Khaneh Square of Cannonballs, his hope multiplying with each clop of Rostam's hooves. He passes a knife-sharpener, his wheel a torrent of sparks, a donkey buckling under a cartload of salt, and a woman with an empty birdcage on top of her head, then circles

Naderi intersection, where the iron roof of the British Embassy comes into view.

Accounts of the mishaps that plagued the building continue to make the rounds with malice-tinged glee. Part of the British-manufactured roof was lost during sea passage. Bandits detained large caravans of camels that transported other parts of the steel roof from the port of Bushehr. When the caravans were finally freed, they were ambushed and robbed again, an escort shot, and the steel nuts for the roof covering stolen. The next load was stranded in Baghdad due to a shortage of mules. In the end, most supplies had to be carried over treacherous mountains on the shoulders of porters. The supplies reached Tehran during a time of famine. Cast iron gutters arrived broken, the locks were wrong, and the doors and windows were designed for large sheets of glass, which could not be found in Tehran. When the "SS Mesopotamia," which had carried the joinery and glass, caught fire in the port of Bushehr, Iranians were certain the embassy was cursed.

More than seventy years have passed since then, yet the British have not been forgiven for tapping into Tehran's resources of land, water, and labor to build the British Embassy, into which Soleiman, armed with a bottle of expensive whiskey and a roll of the finest yellow opium, is escorted.

Portraits of British dignitaries line the oak panels. The bitter odor of cigarettes in the air. Farsi and English are spoken behind half open doors. The thump of boots on carpets is a constant reminder of war.

Colonel Motamedi is seated behind a metal desk littered with ashtrays overflowing with cigarettes, a stack of folders on the right, on the left a gilt-framed photograph of the shah in full regalia. The colonel is a small, atrophied man with a waxy complexion and a twitch at the corner of one drooping eye. A few strands of henna-tinted hair are combed over his freckled scalp. He draws deep from his cigarette and grinds it in an ashtray. Tobacco flakes scatter on the table. A repetitive curling of a forefinger invites his guest to enter and sit in a cushioned chair next to him behind the desk.

Soleiman crosses the room and settles in the chair. A quick glance at the half open drawer confronting him like a wide yawn, empty and lined with red felt, as Tulip had explained. Soleiman tucks the paper bag discreetly into it.

The colonel folds his sleeves up to his elbows and opens the paper bag. An acrid stench seeps out to join the rancid smell of cigarettes trapped in the room. He checks the roll of opium, deep yellow and of the highest quality. Lifts the bottle of whiskey by the neck, reads the label, returns it to the bag, and shoves the drawer shut, then taps a cigarette out of its crumpled packet, lights it, shakes the match out, and tosses it in the overflowing ashtray. His chalky dentures clack in his mouth like out of tune castanets. "Our governor general needs medication, I am told. And you, Doctor Yaran, will get it for him. Right?"

"That is right." Soleiman attempts to ignore the colonel's dentures.

"I am baffled on so many levels, Doctor Yaran. Why would our governor endanger your life, when our inbound and outbound flights are controlled by the British and traveling is dangerous? You know that, don't you?"

"I do," Soleiman says. The situation is more dire than the colonel cares to mention. Planes are often redirected to a besieged Europe. Paris is under German occupation. German soldiers invaded Tuscan villages and executed 200 civilians. Britain is at war on land and at sea and the Allies are advancing into Italy. An infamous pamphlet titled "The Jew as World Parasite" is circulating around Europe, where Jews have been ordered to wear a yellow star on their clothing, right over their heavy hearts.

The colonel's cigarette-stained fingers drum on the desk. "Why, Doctor Yaran, do you need to travel to get this medication? Tell me the name, and I'll see if we find it right here or have one of our British friends get it from Europe."

Soleiman frowns. "I will not break physician-patient confidentiality, Colonel. What I will say is that the governor general prefers that I go to Palestine. It's closer than Europe, less dangerous, and it will be faster and easier to get his medication."

"Palestine?" The Colonel chews on his cigarette. "Wouldn't have thought in a thousand years. Palestine is a tragic mess—the Irgun and the British are at each other's throats. Daily shooting and bombing and all that." He grins, taps on the locked drawer. "Having said that, I'd do anything for our governor. Lydda Airport is controlled by the British and predominantly used for military air transport and cargo planes, but give me the prescription and I'll have a British army personnel bring it back from Palestine." He hiccups a child-like laugh. "Do convey my utmost respect to our governor general, tell him I'd move mountains for him, climb the top of Damavand, get him chicken milk, if possible, swear on my precious daughter's life."

The room is still, dense smoke, cigarette stink. Arguments come from the next-door office. Dust motes dance in a ray of sun making its way through the bare window.

Soleiman's mouth is dry. "The truth, Colonel, is that I want to take my daughter to Palestine because doctors here can't find a cure for her eyes. And I need another nine visas for homeless Polish orphans; whose only hope is to find a home in Palestine. You have children of your own, Colonel, you must understand."

The colonel shifts to the edge of his seat, tilts one ear toward the doctor. He is unable to bear the suffering of children. "Terrible! To be orphaned in war. I want to help every single child, I really do. But it's even riskier with small children. Not safe at all." He presses his hand to his heart. "I'd put them on the first passenger plane if there were one, but only cargo planes fly there."

"We will travel as cargo, then."

"Cargo?" The colonel levels his forefinger at the doctor. "Impossible! An adult maybe, but I won't have the blood of orphans on my conscience."

"They will not be alone, Colonel. I am a doctor. I will know how to take care of them."

"You don't understand the brutal conditions. No heating system! Below freezing temperatures for seven, eight, sometimes more than twelve hours. The turbulence guts your insides like sheep innards."

Soleiman taps on the drawer, an assurance of future bribes, more valuable than the ones here. "I take full responsibility."

"No!" The colonel shouts. "I will not put your daughter or any other child in such danger. Never!" His lower denture springs out of his mouth and lands on the desk in front of him. He pops out his upper denture, drops it onto his palm and wags a finger at it as if scolding a dog. Once his well-oiled tongue rids his gums of lunch residue, he sucks the dentures back into place. "Torture, Doctor Yaran, pure torture. They make my life miserable. Can't say a word without their popping out."

"Ill-fitting dentures can destroy your digestive system, colonel, wreak havoc on your health, cause cancer, and make you look years older. I can make you proper dentures."

"Yes, very kind of you. I've heard about your excellent work, of course. These became loose when I lost weight."

"The right fit will change the quality of your life, Colonel. You'll be pleased." He takes out a container of Ruby Magic from his medical case. "In the meantime, rub this on your gums before you wear your dentures."

"Thank you, thank you." The colonel's dentures click in his mouth like jolly marbles. "How long will it take to make them?"

The doctor's heart settles again. "For you, Colonel, only two days. Wouldn't take longer to arrange for a plane, would it?"

"Not sure, let me look here," he murmurs, riffling through a stack of papers on his desk. He taps on a page. "As luck has it, dear doctor, a plane will leave for Palestine next week. I'm sure Captain McKenzie won't mind moving a couple of tires to make space for all of you."

Soleiman unclenches his fist, shakes the colonel's hand. "I am indebted to you, Colonel."

"All settled, then. Now, here's what *you* will have to do. Buy a kilogram of black walnuts. Not the kind you find in just any grocery. With luck and a few extra *touman*, the merchant will spare a kilo or two." He smacks his lips as if tasting the walnuts, scribbles directions to Mullah Ghazvini's grocery in the Bazaar of Nut Sellers, and hands it to Soleiman. "Our governor will do anything in return for that stuff. You look surprised, doctor."

"I was under the impression that the governor general already agreed to this," the doctor says.

"Yes and no. I agreed to see you and issue one visa because Tulip *Agha* said our governor needs medication. But if he discovers the real reason you are going, which he will, and that I agreed to issue eleven visas, we'll all be in great trouble. But our governor general is quite fond of you, I hear, so give him these nuts, and he'll grant your wish."

Soleiman crumbles the note in his fist and drops it in his pocket. He should have known that in the end every crooked alley would lead back to the Land Eater.

CHAPTER EIGHTEEN

1942

The harsh winter of 1942 has made life more difficult. Tons of vital war matériel—Studebaker US6 trucks, jeeps, blankets, American canned food, and ALCO diesel locomotives to replace existing steam locomotives—set sail from the United States and the United Kingdom, circle the Cape of Good Hope, and land in various ports in the Persian Gulf. The supplies continue their journey northward on icy roads by railroad or long truck convoys toward the Soviet Union to bolster Joseph Stalin's fight against Adolf Hitler.

Hundreds of American military forces maintain and operate the Trans-Iranian-Railway, adding to the woes of a country buckling under the needs of a heavy inflow of troops and Polish refugees. The Soviet Union is embezzling Iran's harvest produce, causing bread riots in Tehran. People blame Ahmad Qavam, the British-appointed prime minister, for food shortage, mismanagement of the economy, and the steep rise in inflation. The shah, too, is blamed for having signed a treaty, which guarantees non-military aid to the allies.

The country's economy is on the brink of collapse. Martial law is declared.

Neda is two years old. She is taller, her hair darker, her tearless eyes more susceptible to infections, and, as if to compensate for her lack of tears, her sense of smell is growing keener. Her second birthday was a happier event than her first birthday. Convinced that Ruby would not mind having her *Yahrzeit* held a day late, Soleiman decided to celebrate Neda's birthday on the day she was born. The guests, aware that Neda was far more mature than her age dictated, brought gifts geared toward a much older child. Neda was delighted.

Eleazar the Redhead and Aunt Shamsi are increasingly puzzled by Soleiman's behavior. He might not be ready to replace Ruby with another woman, they speculate, but a wise man such as he must surely understand his daughter's need for a mother. And Jacob, aware of the ongoing quarrel between Soleiman's heart and mind, is feeling uncharacteristically helpless.

After years of living in fear of landslides, falling rocks, and an avalanche of limestone and soil that landed in the river or buried homes, communities at the foot of the mountains let out a sigh of relief. The governor general, having dynamited, hacked, and leveled all possible mountain space, has directed his bottomless greed to the outskirts of Tehran, where he is wreaking havoc on farmland, replacing much-needed pistachio, almond, saffron, and cucumber crops with the more lucrative opium poppies.

Every week, for two years, Rostam has trotted up and down these mountains, but he still shies at the sight of the poppies waving in the wind, shakes his neck, and digs his stubborn hooves deep, preparing to dash back down. Soleiman, on the other hand, no longer pays much attention to the workers in the opium fields, their habit of licking opium residue off their lancets, or to the two cannons at the gates that appear to change course and aim at him each time he canters through the gates on his stallion.

He scans the surroundings for Velvet, never knowing whether she will appear in his path in the fields, in one or another of the mansion's hallways, or in the wild juniper grove, where he continues to secretly attend to the medical needs of the governor's employees.

Soleiman steers the stallion across the fields and toward the wrought iron gates where Velvet, alerted by Rostam's clopping hooves and grunts of protest, steps out. Tulip is at her side, a load of gold chains on his chest, his cape swaying in the wind. "Look there, Rostam," Soleiman whispers to his stallion. "Here comes our favorite lady. Go say hello." The restive stallion slows to a trot, stirs beneath his rider, lets out a soft snicker, and canters ahead to meet Velvet.

Tulip tucks Velvet's hair under her crimson chador, a richer red than the surrounding poppies. It is not wise for his mistress to welcome the doctor out here, but it breaks his heart to deprive her of the excitement of her transgressions that keep her sane in this punishing place. "Don't, *Khanom*, please. Don't look so eager. The mountains have eyes and ears." But Velvet is running toward the doctor and his stallion, so Tulip fastens the gold buttons of his sable-lined cape and follows her.

"*Salaam*, Rostam." Velvet's laughter is like a ripple of bells. "You are late today."

Rostam raises his head and neighs his delight toward the sky, then bows his head in salutation and hooves the earth at her feet, as if digging for some hidden treasure to offer her.

She feeds Rostam a sugar cube, lifts herself on her toes to stroke his mane, which she had braided with red and gold ribbons last week. A poppy pod rolls under her shoe. She loses her footing, flails for balance and before Soleiman has a chance to sprint down from the saddle Rostam, in an act of acrobatic agility, maneuvers his powerful neck and succeeds in breaking her fall.

Pale, ragged breathing painful in her chest, Velvet rests her forehead against the stallion's lowered muzzle and, for an instant, Soleiman is consumed by such longing and desire, his hand curls so tight around the reins, Rostam bares his teeth and stamps a hind leg.

Tulip steals a look at the laborers dotting the fields. A tentative tap on Velvet's shoulder. A soft warning. If the governor general finds his wife's face, naked and palpable with emotions and pressed to the doctor's stallion, they will all be hanging from the gallows with their innards fed to hungry vultures.

Velvet strokes Rostam's flank, a shy glance at Soleiman, and she steps away, teases out from under her wool sleeves lace ruffles she wears next to her skin, but even this small show of femininity is taboo in this place, so she conceals the lace again. A gust of wind sends her chador flying off her head, letting loose a riot of corn silk hair. She gasps. Lunges to snatch the chador. Too late. It has landed on Soleiman's lap. He tucks both hands under the red silk and lifts it as if it is something sacred, leans low from the saddle, and, with his steady gaze on her, sets the chador in her slightly trembling arms and, in an instant which will bleed into the rest of their lives, presses his lips to the wild pulse on each of her wrists.

Tulip grabs the chador from Velvet and quickly covers her hair. He bows with extravagant formality. "Our governor general's wife," he warns as he slides four fingers across his throat. A terse reminder to the doctor that His Excellency is waiting. A discreet kick on the stallion's shin, and Rostam turns around and gallops toward the mansion.

CHAPTER NINETEEN

It is the ten days of Repentance between Rosh Hashanah, the Jewish New Year, and Yom Kippur, the day of Atonement. *Shochetim* walk up and down the dust-filled alleys. One by one, they circle sacrificial chickens above the heads of the inhabitants of the Jewish Quarter as they recite: "This is my exchange. This is my substitute. This is my atonement." Having been trained in the slaughter of animals in accordance with Jewish law, the *shochetim* check their sharp knives before they subject the birds to a quick, painless death—an ancient blood ritual of *kapparot,* which promises absolution from last year's sins and the hope of being inscribed in the Book of Life.

Soleiman sidesteps the puddles of spilled chicken blood, which will seep into the dirt and cake in a day or two, until the arrival of the Feast of Tabernacles, when the Quarter will be hosed down with precious water from underground cisterns. He turns into the Alley of Physicians and walks past Pary's white door, where an emaciated man is praying. Perhaps, he, too, should pray to the door. What else is he to do when no one can find a cure for Neda's tearless eyes and the prospect of taking her to Palestine is becoming unlikely? He gives the small gate to his yard a push with his riding boot, surprised Neda does not come running to greet him. Then he sees her, seated next to Ruby's herb box and surrounded by her miniature dolls. At her feet is an iron mortar and pestle, too heavy for the child to have carried all the way from the kitchen.

She digs into the earth and studies a mushroom, the tiny cracks at the edges, the dark blemishes on the cap, blows a layer of dust off, licks the mushroom, and drops it into the mortar. Do the mushrooms carry her mother's scent?

Every now and then she tugs at Ruby's scarf tied around her waist and mouths "Madar" as if she is having a serious conversation with her mother.

Ruby swims in front of his eyes, her presence so real it is difficult to dismiss Aunt Shamsi's fantasy that Neda is drawn to this patch of land because her mother's caul and afterbirth are buried under the mushrooms that sprouted overnight after her death.

The next instant, it is not Ruby, but Velvet who floats about like a moth, her aura illuminating her surroundings, the sweet lilt of her laughter sending his senses reeling. So often has he leafed through the pages of her poetry book, they are frayed at the edges, every poem chiseled into his heart.

Come on now, dearest, heal me, you know how
To make my doctor's headache disappear.
(Jahan Malek Khatun c.1324–c.1382)

How long will you be like?
A cypress tree,
And lean your lovely head
Away from me?
(Hafez)

Neda mixes and pounds something in the mortar with great focus and patience, as if the monotonous act is a respite from the bombardment of endless scents and emotions she is subjected to.

She drops the pestle in the mortar, rubs her hands clean with her skirt, and tugs at the muddied red thread Aunt Shamsi tied to her wrist to ward off the evil eye. Finding the red thread secure, she checks the safety pin attached to the string as a precaution in case she is struck with the evil eye, in which case the safety pin will snap open and blind the evil eye.

She brushes mushrooms off her skirt and, as if summoned by invisible forces, walks across the garden, up the three steps into the Alley of Physicians, and turns into the empty lot next door.

Soleiman assumes she's on her way to visit Rostam, but she is interested in the willow tree. Her fingertips, which seem to have grown sensors to help her discover the healing properties of plants, push aside the branches, then drum up and down the bark, her ears cocked to any hollow sound that might alert her to a loose piece of bark. Detecting the right spot, she pries under the edges and peels off the outer bark to reveal a pink inner layer, which she carefully teases off. Using her palm like a trowel, she gathers droplets of sap off the inner bark, pats the outer layer back in place to mend the injury, then hugs the tree and presses a long kiss on it. Indifferent to Rostam's complaining grunts, she traces her way back to the garden.

His heart heavy with concern for his daughter, Soleiman keeps his distance. Neda, no doubt, is different from other children her age, so much so, he sometimes wonders whether there is a seed of truth in Aunt Shamsi's belief that Neda is charmed because of her en caul birth. Whatever the reason for his daughter's exceptional behavior, it must be difficult for her to carry such a heavy emotional load.

He observes her drop the collected bark and sap in the mortar and begin to pound the mixture, the pestle gathering speed to the chorus of Rostam's mounting protests from behind the garden wall. Another half hour passes. She tests the consistency of the mixture and, presumably satisfied, removes her sweater and covers the mortar and pestle with it, then grabs a dandelion at her feet and runs to him.

He scoops her up in his arms and turns in circles, her grip around his neck a joy. "Thank you, Sweetheart, your Madar liked dandelions too. Make a wish. Blow. What are you making in the mortar?"

She throws her hands up as if he should already know. "I make Baba Magic for your pain."

He laughs. His daughter is like her resourceful mother, who had suggested he test the ointment on the gums of rabbits. "Is Madar helping you make Baba Magic?"

"No Baba! I make it all myself."

Her eyes are wide with fear or anxiety, so he does not probe deeper. "Ah! It must be hard to do this all by yourself. But you don't have to tire yourself, Sweetheart, because I don't have any pain."

"Why you lie, Baba? You have big smelly pain."

He lowers his voice, a more cautious tone. "Tell me, Sweetheart, what does my pain smell like?"

She throws her shoulders up. If she tells her Baba his pain smell bad like the beggar smell when he's hungry because he can't buy any foods, or like Aunt Shamsi when she's all sad because her beautiful Azar daughter died in black *abambar* waters, or like Baba Eleazar when he says people spit on him because his red hair is too much Jewishness, then she will make Baba even more sadder and then what will happen to Neda?

CHAPTER TWENTY

It is just before sunset on Thursday, and the Jewish Quarter is abuzz with covert coming and going of Muslim servants who scurry up and down basement steps to purchase forbidden wine and *aragh* from Jewish merchants, whose religion allows the brewing of alcohol.

Selling alcohol is a profitable business these days, when the populace craves temporary relief from the relentless assault of foreign warplanes in the skies, warships on the seas, tanks at the borders, and foreign boots in the streets. Then why, Eleazar the Redhead wonders, is no one knocking on his door? He arranges the blanket on the carpet-covered wooden cot he slept on the night before to periodically check the temperature of the stills in his basement, kisses his Tehillim prayer book, and tucks it under the pillow. It was foolish of him to exhaust his life savings on such expensive ingredients, all under the assumption that a few affluent clients would be willing to pay more for his superior *aragh*. Rich or poor, people don't care what kind of cheap poison they pour down their throats these days, as long as it provides the pleasure of an hour or two of drunkenness.

When Soleiman offered him financial aid on condition he retire his *shechitah* knife, he spent many sleepless nights kneading the proposal in his thoughts. In time, it dawned on him that becoming financially dependent on his son was more terrifying to him than opening his home to goyim and, in so doing, making himself more vulnerable to their wrath. He decided to dabble in the lucrative, but much maligned business of producing alcohol, which he had little experience in but hoped to make up for with ample creativity.

He borrowed money from Soleiman to purchase two oak barrels for the process of fermentation and two copper stills for distillation. He spent days studying the bazaar of wine sellers, visited one stall or another, asked questions, and eventually selected grapes harvested in late autumn from golden vines, which ripened in the moderate climate of Shiraz. Another week to choose herbs, spices, fruits, and the most aromatic of *sargol* saffron steeped in pure spring water to strip it off its reddish color and strong scent. Quince and pomegranate were added to one batch for customers who might gravitate toward more familiar tastes. The ingredients were crushed and left to ferment in barrels, mixed and stirred for three weeks to release the gasses, after which the brew was moved to copper stills where it went through numerous distillations to get the purest possible *aragh*.

The leftover pomegranate rind, quince, cherry pits, and grape skin he mixes with dirt and garbage and dumps in the pit to conceal the evidence of his activities from Muslim thugs.

At every step of the process, he devotes extra attention to a barrel with a brew of the finest of ingredients. This particular *aragh*, he is saving for Soleiman's future wedding. *Enshallah*. May it be *Hashem*'s will.

Eleazar the Redhead sits on his cot and holds his head between his hands. If his business continues like this, he will have to admit failure, sharpen his *shechitah* knife again, and begin the back-breaking jobs of slaughtering chickens, watering gardens, and shoveling snow off roofs.

At the sound of urgent banging at the door, he labors up the steep stairs. Remembering one of the many lessons he learned from his granddaughter, he hesitates behind the door to pay attention to the surrounding scents and sounds, which hold a wealth of information. Another three knocks. Nothing like the angry pounding associated with Jew-haters or the quick, impudent rat-a-tats of the frog-eyed pawnbroker, who torments him at odd hours. Nor are they Soleiman's kind-knuckled taps, but insistent and somewhat anxious. Eleazar opens the door.

"Here he is! The famous Eleazar the Redhead who makes the best whiskey in the whole entire universe!" Shamsi announces to the man behind her, as if she has the faintest idea about the difference between whiskey and *aragh* or remotely approves of the business of selling alcohol. Struggling unsuccessfully to imitate a sophisticated Muslim accent, she explains that she was in the bazaar to purchase loofa and pumice stone, when she heard this fine *Agha*, asking around for Eleazar the Redhead. "Price is not an issue at all for the honorable *Agha*," she adds with a discreet tilt of the head.

Eleazar the Redhead might not be a good businessman, but he is able to recognize a wealthy client when he sees one. The soft kid boots, the rich folds of his trousers, and the cashmere flow of his cape are enough proof. As is the confidence in his eyes that shimmer like polished ore above a wrapping of his silk turban, which covers his lower face.

Eleazar introduces himself with a slight bow of the head. "Most honorable *Agha*. I do not have whiskey here, but I brew the purest *aragh* you might find in all four corners of Tehran."

Shamsi rolls her eyes at her brother. "Poison is poison," she murmurs under her breath as she hurries away, leaving Eleazar alone with his customer.

"Eleazar the Redhead!" The stranger surprises Eleazar with two hearty kisses on his cheeks. "The merchants in the bazaar are jealous of you."

At the show of such unexpected familiarity, suspicion drills deep into Eleazar's marrow. What does this man want from him? In fact, if he set aside his own eagerness to make a sale, he will see how out of place the presence of such a dignified man is on a Thursday in the Jewish Quarter, when the task of purchasing alcohol is delegated to servants. Eleazar steps back into the house but before he has a chance to close the door in the stranger's face, he has stooped in with obvious difficulty and is looking down into Eleazar's eyes. "Am I too tall," he asks, "or is your door lower than most?"

"My door is lower than yours, *Agha*." Eleazar swallows the urge to spit out the explanation of a law that requires Jews to build lower doorposts to force them to bow to Muslims when they step out of their own houses.

Oblivious to Eleazar's bitter tone, the man removes the draping from his lower face, grabs a bunch of cardamom seeds from his pocket, and drops them into his mouth.

At the sight of the face he has seen more than once in the bazaar, Eleazar the Red Head tucks his astonishment and suspicion out of sight, pats his hair and *aba* into place, and prays with all the might of his faith that his hard work will pay off, at last, and this new client will change the trajectory of his life.

Although his eyes do not display the expected makeup, nor is he wearing his normally colorful clothes and jewelry, there is no mistaking the handsome eunuch of the governor general, whose love for the alcoholic drink is known to every Jew in the Quarter. In fact, anyone with a stash of savings somewhere under a stained mattress or a torn kilim under his feet has tried his hands at distilling *aragh*, in hope of seducing the most discerning Muslim palate in the Big City.

"Tell me the truth, *Agha* Eleazar, do you really have the best *aragh* in Iran? My boss is particular, and I cannot disappoint him."

"Follow me, *Agha*, please, and you can decide for yourself." Struggling to remember the eunuch's name, Eleazar leads him down the stairs and into the cellar.

Surrounded by the purr of fermenting fruits and spices, the eunuch walks around and strokes each barrel as if that will reveal the quality of the *aragh* inside. He sits on the carpet-covered cot and fills his lungs with the scent infused into the fabric of the cellar. "You must be a wizard, *Agha* Eleazar. You might have to chase me out because I can spend hours caressing my senses here."

Eleazar the Redhead allows himself a moment to savor the unexpected praise bestowed upon him. "You're infinitely kind, Tulip *Agha*," he says, remembering the eunuch's name. "But I don't think you'd want to spend hours down here. A nice Friday night dinner upstairs might be more pleasant."

Tulip bursts into laughter. "Why not? A dinner of lamb kebob and *aragh* sounds lovely."

"Not kebob, I'm afraid. That would require firing the chargrill, and I don't touch fire on Shabbat." Eleazar the Redhead falls silent—how utterly foolish of him to blurt out such a presumptuous invitation. How utterly foolish of him to entertain the prospect of sharing a meal with the governor general's eunuch, who cuts the banter by opening the flaps of his coat and producing an antique, gold-flecked crystal flask he has been carrying in a leather pocket fastened around his waist.

Eleazar smells the flask and then holds it up to the light to make sure it is clean and nothing will contaminate the purity of his *aragh*. He fills the bottle and hands it back. "Please, *Agha* Tulip, bring a clear glass container next time. It would be a pity not to appreciate the clarity and pureness of my *aragh*."

CHAPTER TWENTY-ONE

In the wild juniper grove, which the governor's staff affectionately call *Agha* Doctor's Clinic, now live in sporadic harmony two plump hens, a proud-necked rooster that keeps pecking feathers off the hens, and a bearded goat Soleiman received as compensation for suggesting a paste of vinegar, camphor, and salt to eradicate a guard's head lice. *Neda would have loved the goat to roam in her garden*, Soleiman muses, *if the animal didn't have the irritating habit of mounting any moving creature in his path, constantly licking himself between the legs, and marking his face with his own urine.*

It is past ten-thirty, and no line of patients has formed yet, promising a quieter day. He will feed the animals, take care of the governor, and be on his way. On one of the tree stumps where he usually spreads his medical instruments, he notices an open notebook and a silver filigree pen studded with tiny turquoise. A folded onion skin note with Velvet's bold handwriting in purple ink flutters out of the linen pages.

> *"Choose Love, Love! Without the sweet life of Love, living is a burden."*
> (Rumi)

He riffles through the notebook, the pages all blank. He is disappointed. Perhaps it is her response to his silence. How could she know that he read and reread the note she left in the flap of the poetry book, picked up his pen even more times to compose a reply, to tell her he is breaking in the seams. He lifts the pen, and, knowing full well he is adding more fuel to *barout* dynamite, he begins to write.

My Dearest love,

You stole into my heart like an uninvited guest. I see you everywhere, my love. Your silver eyes in the reflection of the moon. Your golden hair in the rays of the sun. I see you in the innocence of children. And in the strength of Ruth. You have made a home in my thoughts and in my dreams. You make me laugh with joy and cry in desperation but most of all—

A warning cough. A glimmer of bright colors approaches between the juniper branches. Soleiman tucks the pen between the pages of the notebook and puts it in the inner pocket of his medical case.

Tulip appears dressed in a red and gold kaftan, girded at the waist with a sapphire-studded sash. The wind has undone his turban, and, as Soleiman is the only one in the grove, he removes his turban and shakes his long, auburn tresses, which he keeps vibrant with a mixture of coffee, lemon juice, and sunshine. He touches his hand to his eyes. "*Salaam*, *Agha* doctor, forgive my intrusion."

"Not at all," Soleiman says, "I'm happy you came. I have good news for you." He takes Tulip's hand and closes it around a box of pills. "Here is the medicine I promised you." After months of research and hard work, he succeeded in creating a special compound of pills that might strengthen the eunuch's compromised bones and teeth, an inevitable side effect of the loss of his testes. "It is experimental, but I believe it will give you relief."

Tulip addresses his feet. "May your hands be painless, *Agha* doctor. I'm already a new person because of you. But as much as I want to, I can't accept any more favors from you."

Soleiman rests an affectionate hand on Tulip's shoulder, surprised how deeply he feels for him. "Why not, my friend? It took a long time. I made it especially for you."

"I owe you so much already, *Agha* doctor." The distraught Tulip wipes a tear from the corner of his eye. "I've begged and begged His Excellency again and again, but he won't change his position and—"

"About the visas?" Soleiman attempts to conceal his disappointment. "Don't worry, I'll find a way." His only hope now lies with the Queen, but that, too, is fading with each day he is not being summoned.

Tulip drops the box of pills in his gold-trimmed pocket then plants a respectful kiss on each of Soleiman's shoulders. "May I bother you for a different favor?"

"Yes, of course. Do you want me to check your teeth?"

"No, *Agha*, my teeth are still healthy, Allah be praised. It's not about me." A sudden weariness washes over him, bone-deep and so gray he wants to yank his hair out and walk down the mountain, never stop until he finds a more hospitable place to dig roots. "No, *Agha* doctor, it's not about me. It's Velvet *Khanom*—"

"What's wrong?" Soleiman's voice is louder than he intended. "Is she ill?"

"I'm not sure. She's been complaining of this and that pain, bless her heart. Perhaps you'd agree to see her."

"Absolutely. The sooner, the better. Pain shouldn't be ignored. Why don't you go fetch her? It's quiet here, and I've another half hour before I see His Excellency."

Tulip shuffles from one foot to another. "*Khanom* wants to see you in private. In your office, maybe...is that possible? Does your office have two doors for her to enter and leave without being seen? His Excellency is very strict in that way and won't allow her to see a male doctor. So, I'd understand if you find this too dangerous or decide to—" He holds his breath. He has done his part. Kept his promise to his mistress. Hopefully, the doctor will have the sense to do the right thing.

The air around Soleiman shimmers with possibilities. Why not? Why not see Velvet in private when this is what they both want? Somewhere far from this place, where the governor's ire is less of an immediate threat. A rented room in a tea house in the outskirts of Tehran is a possibility, or the remote inn—. His jaws clenched tight,

Soleiman gives the eunuch a friendly squeeze on his arm. "Velvet *Khanom* is lucky to have you. Please tell her I care too deeply for her to put her in such danger."

"Thank you, *Agha* doctor. Forever your servant. I will see you when you are ready for His Excellency." A sigh of relief, a grateful bow, and Tulip winds his colorful way out of the gathering of trees.

Soleiman looks around to make sure he collected all his medical paraphernalia. From one of the sacks at the foot of a tree, he grabs a fistful of sunflower seeds and scatters them around for the rooster and chickens. He taps the toe of his riding boot against a barrel of water a bald field worker who suffered from intestinal parasites gave him as compensation. The goat loses interest in licking himself and walks to the barrel.

He removes the stethoscope draped around his neck. No matter how often his patients are reminded that he is a dentist, they still expect him to cure whatever illness they are afflicted by. He drops the stethoscope in the medical case with his dental tools.

Velvet ducks under the trellis of dense branches, tosses her chador over a tree stump, and sits on it. "Why won't you see me in private, Doctor Yaran?" There is no blame in her soft voice.

"It's too dangerous, Velvet *Khanom*. But you are here now. How can I help you?"

She shifts to make space for him at her side. "I need emotional help, Doctor Yaran, and you're the only one I dare come to."

They spend moments sitting in silence next to one another, the only sounds the rustling of leaves, the hiss of the breeze, hens pecking on sunflower seeds, and the goat chewing on the underbrush.

Soleiman recalls the first time he saw her blaze a path through the red poppies, her yellow chador flapping about her like angel wings, her riot of hair a deeper silver than her eyes. If he had known then that in two years his every cell would yearn for this woman, he would have turned Rostam around and never looked back. Yet. Here he is, tuned to the rhythm of her breathing, the flavor of her unspoken words, sensing her sorrow, drinking her feminine scent of roses that multiplies his longing. "How could I possibly be the only one you can go to, Velvet *Khanom*? What about your friends, siblings, your parents?"

"I am an only child. My parents are in Bushehr, and I'm not allowed to travel there to visit them." Her voice cracks with pain. "I am in a loveless marriage, Doctor Yaran. My husband is in love with another woman." Her entire face blushes, but when she raises her eyes there is fire in them. "Does that make me a free woman?"

Soleiman clutches the watch in his pocket as if it is the governor's neck he is breaking. "I wish, Velvet *Khanom*. If only we were both free." He does not have the heart to tell her that they both are prisoners of her husband. She, up here in the mountains. And he and his people down there in the Jewish Quarter. He cups her warm face in his hands and plants a kiss on each of her salty eyes, breaking away the instant she gasps with pleasure.

CHAPTER TWENTY-TWO

Last year's dried pods crunch under Velvet's feet like nutshells as she walks across hectares of leveled land, where poppies yield tons of opium, which will find their way to smoking pipes around the nation, the purest and the most potent of the batch reserved for her husband. She grabs a fistful of poppies, crushes the scent against her palm, and tosses the bruised pods behind her.

Tulip quickens his steps to catch up with her. A playful smile, and he yanks a poppy from the roots and gives it a good kick. Much is communicated between them with a minimum of words, a survival tactic they have honed to perfection. "I went to the Jewish Quarter," he says, aware that his mistress is hungry to learn about Dr. Yaran's world, which is nothing like the image she has polished in her mind.

Velvet's grip tightens on Tulip's arm. "What kind of a place is it? Can anyone go there? Did you see Doctor Yaran?"

"It's an ugly place, *Khanom*, narrow alleys, small houses, low doors, nothing like your beautiful mansion. No, I didn't see Doctor Yaran. I went to the bazaar to find *aragh* for His Excellency, unaware that Jews brew the best *aragh* in their cellars. After much probing and bribing one or another merchant, I found out that someone called Eleazar the Redhead makes the best *aragh* in the Jewish Quarter, which made it more difficult, since no one seemed to know or want to show me where the man lived. So, in my desperation, I waved a wad of *toumans* in the air and, don't even remember what I shouted, when a woman with a strange accent stopped me and said she will take me to Eleazar the Redhead. I tell you, *Khanom*, the heavenly smells in his cellar made me drunker than a spinning dervish." Once again that push and pull of wanting to please as well as protect her, wanting her to experience love, which he has been deprived of, yet hoping and praying that what she is consumed by is no more than a fleeting obsession. He grabs a bunch of cardamom from his pocket and grinds them under his teeth as he watches her pensive gaze roam across the fields and land on a woman working there.

She is tall, a head above any other woman in the fields, a graceful fluidity to the silhouette of her thighs and hips under her colorful skirt, which swings about her bare, calloused feet. As if she just stepped out of bed, her brown curls spring every which way as she moves from one plant to another to make shallow incisions, careful not to penetrate the hollow inner chamber of the poppy pods.

"*Khanom*?" Tulip asks. "What is it?"

"Tulip, I found her!"

"Who, *Khanom*? Why are you so pale? What's disturbing you?"

"I found the Friday Night Woman! Look there, look at the tall one. My husband is in love with a simple opium picker!"

One hand over his hammering chest, Tulip's other hand dismisses the woman with a flippant gesture. "To *Jahannam* with whoever she is! Don't let her upset you, *Khanom*. She is not worth a hair on your head, not one single nail clipping."

"That's not what my husband thinks." Velvet turns her back to Tulip and marches toward the hip-swaying harlot in the poppy fields who managed to destroy her married life.

Alerted by the crackling pods underfoot, the woman turns around, quickly drops her lancet, and takes long strides toward Velvet. "*Salaam, Khanom*." She clasps her hands and respectfully bows her head.

Velvet's hand jumps to her heart. She tosses an imploring glance back at Tulip, who wants to run to the aid of both women, but his legs refuse to move. So, he crosses his arms across his aching chest and remains paralyzed at the edge of the field.

In front of Velvet is a child of no more than fourteen, half her nose and upper lip melted into a grimace by the *salak* flesh-eating infection. Her innocent eyes, having withstood the ravages of the disease, are heartbreaking. Velvet fumbles for a way to assure herself that this can't be true. No. Her husband will not bed a poor child, not someone so young and helpless. Never. He is not capable of such cruelty.

She fumbles in her pockets and finding a few crumpled bills drops them in the girl's hand. "For your schoolbooks."

"May Allah protect you, *Khanom*," the girl murmurs in a sweet Shirazi dialect, "I don't go to school."

"But why not? At your age, you should be in school."

Tears well in the girl's molasses eyes. "I work in the fields, *Khanom*. I work in the refineries and at home. How can I go to school?" She smooths the money on her skirt, folds each bill carefully, and tucks it in her pocket.

Velvet looks into the girl's face, all hope and hunger and wanting. "Wait for me right here on Monday, early in the morning." She whispers, "I'll take you to Doctor Yaran. He will know how to take care of your face."

"He's already seen me, *Khanom*." Her sun-browned forearm wipes tears off her devastated face. "It's too late for a cure." She offers a stoic smile before retracing her steps to retrieve her lancet and continue to visit and revisit each poppy to make incisions.

His legs hardly able to support his weight, Tulip urges Velvet toward the mansion. They do not speak until they walk through the gates and up the terrace steps. He lingers at the door and, his voice grim and cracked at the edges, says: "Listen to me, *Khanom*, please. It is a sin to accuse innocent people. His Excellency is too careful to invite someone into his bed who works around his estate. So, don't go about looking for her anywhere around here. Banish the Friday Night

Woman from your thoughts, *Khanom*, or your husband will make sure you don't have a head on your shoulders anymore to even think about her."

CHAPTER TWENTY-THREE

Baba's hair and suit are dusty from his ride back from the mountains, and his temples angry jump under her fingertips. Neda wants to make Baba happy, but Baba Magic isn't ready at all. "Baba? Why you more sad?"

He tightens his arms around his daughter. "You're right, Sweetheart. I *am* sad. I want to take you to Palestine with Uncle Jacob's children, but one of my patients, people call him the Land Eater, doesn't want us to go."

Neda digs her face in his neck. "Why you take us away, Baba?"

He coaxes her head up. "Don't be upset, Sweetheart. I'm not taking you away. I want to take you to a good doctor in Palestine to fix your eyes."

"No, Baba!" Neda screams. "I don't see more doctors and more doctors with more bad lights in my eyes to make my eyes hurt. I don't go away to Palestine with Uncle Jacob's children. I don't go with anyone. I stay here with Aunt Shamsi!"

Neda's screams propel Aunt Shamsi into the garden. "God forbid you listen to your old aunt, Soleiman. Didn't I tell you to stay away from the widow's bad luck door? But, no, Ruby's corpse wasn't even cold in the grave, when you had to go and paint the door white like a shroud. So, here we are, the door's curse struck your child's eyes."

"Stop this nonsense!" Soleiman exclaims. "Or Neda will think it's true. Listen, Sweetheart, don't pay attention to Aunt Shamsi's superstitious—"

But Neda wriggles out of Soleiman's arms and runs to the box of Ruby's herbs she has resurrected with leftover tealeaves, crushed eggshells, lots of water, and love. Her chest jumping with subsiding sobs, she squats down and selects the healthiest leaves, separates them from their stems, and adds them to the concoction in the mortar. She lifts from the herb box a glass of *gol gav zaban*, a purple brew of Omani lemons and borage Aunt Shamsi prepared and pours the liquid into the mortar.

"Say what you want, Soleiman," Aunt Shamsi says. "But I taught Neda well. *Gol gav zaban* cures every known pain in the universe."

The Quarter Fool skids to a sudden halt by the gate, kicks it open, and throws himself in front of Soleiman. "Help me, *Agha* doctor, I am dying!"

"Stand up like a man, you fool!" Aunt Shamsi hooks two hands under his armpits and drags him up to his feet. "What's the matter with you?"

The Quarter Fool forces Aunt Shamsi's head down to his belly. "Listen, Aunt Shamsi. Listen to all the *Ifrits* singing my funeral song!"

She slaps the Fool's hands away and delivers a smack to his head. "So, this is what devils sound like? If that's not the racket of stuck *gooz*, then my burps sound like Bibi Golden Voice." Her knuckles drum on his bloated stomach. "What did you expect, you farting truck, to have a silent motor?"

"Calm down, the two of you," Soleiman says. "Go, ask Neda for a few sprigs of peppermint, it will cure you."

Tears carve fresh trails down the Quarter Fool's face. "I don't need peppermint, *Agha* doctor. Give me a big injection."

Aunt Shamsi grab's the Fool's shirt and drags him to the mushroom patch. "You know these mushrooms, don't you, constantly running in and out of here as if it's your private caravanserai. You know they've special powers, don't you? Good. What you don't know is they'll scare away *Ifrits* all the way to *Jahannam*." She snatches a few mushrooms and drops them in his hand. "Shove them down your throat, and you'll be as good as new. What are you waiting for? Eat them before they rot."

The Quarter Fool glances at Neda, who is busy with her concoction, her sobs replaced by stubborn hiccups. "Ask Neda's permission."

"I've God's permission, and that's more than enough. Stuff them down your stinking throat, I said, before you croak."

"Neda!" The Fool shouts, as if Neda is not right there.

"Eat the mushrooms, *Agha* Fool." Neda says as she pounds her pestle with rhythmic tenacity. "Aunt Shamsi makes everything better."

The Quarter Fool shoves the mushrooms in his mouth and swallows them in one gulp, cocks his long neck, and waits, his ears sharpened to the ebb and flow of his bloated stomach. "Listen, Aunt Shamsi. What do you hear?"

"Nothing! You're healthier than the day you were born. I'll give you a few more in case and off you go." Aunt Shamsi bends to pick some mushrooms. She stops, staring at a strange-glowing group of newly appeared ones that lurk like thieves among the violet mushrooms. She brushes soil off one of the red-dotted black caps, startled by a bunch of evil eyes glaring back at her. "Don't just stand there like a dummy," she orders the Quarter Fool. "Pull the nasty things out. They popped up from nowhere like the black plague!"

"Leave Neda's mushrooms alone," Soleiman says. "Sweetheart, promise not to eat them. Right? Good girl."

He turns away from the mushrooms, which look like a group of conferring elves, from his daughter who wants to banish his sadness with an odd concoction, from the Quarter Fool who is happily cured of his devils, and from his aunt who believes in spirits, coffee dregs, and amulets.

How little he knows about this, his daughter's world.

CHAPTER TWENTY-FOUR

Tulip stands back to review the gold ribbons he wove into Velvet's strands of hair.

"My husband will not approve of these in my hair."

"Enjoy it for now, *Khanom*, and take them out when you're with him."

She takes another look at her image in the mirror and smiles. "I like them. I will leave them in."

The mansion heaves with the muezzins' faraway call to evening prayers. Tulip checks his image in the mirror, centers his ruby neck-lace, and applies rouge to his cheeks. "I must be on my way."

"Don't go, Tulip," Velvet begs. "I can't bear being alone with my thoughts."

The recurring nightmare had her shivering under the covers last night—the Friday Night Woman lounged next to her in the same bed, her body cold as a corpse, a triumphant grin painted on a face as blank and white as bleached bone. Even now, running wild in her mind, are images of her husband and the woman entwined in acts of passion. "That poor girl in the fields. She is not my husband's mistress, is she?"

"I don't think so, *Khanom*. His Excellency can't be attracted to such types."

"Then who is she? Don't shrug me off, Tulip. I don't believe you!" Velvet cries out. "What kind of a friend are you? You know about everyone and everything here, know who comes and goes. How could you not have seen her even once in three years?"

"I *have* seen her. But she covers her face with veils. How could I tell who she is? Listen to me, Velvet *Khanom*, please. I beg you. When a problem doesn't have a solution, better to accept and live with it, or it will destroy you. Enough that his Excellency cares for you, makes sure you are comfortable and well taken care of."

She holds her head between her hands. "No, it isn't enough, and you know it. I have no one, Tulip, no one."

"Not so, Velvet *Khanom*. You have me, and you have your parents."

"My parents? I'm here, they're there. When have I seen them last? More than a year, two years maybe, I've stopped counting or I'll go mad." She recalls the day the Trans-Iranian railway fell into allied hands and her father, who was the chief engineer, lost his job. Bankruptcy followed when the monthly stipend they received from the governor general was inexplicably reduced, and, unable to pay their expenses, her parents returned home to the Southern port of Bushehr by the Persian Gulf. The war had elevated the importance of that port, and they expected to find respectable jobs, but that did not happen. They were forced to resort to scrubbing the underfoot filth of foreign sailors in American and British warships transporting heavy artillery to the Soviet Union.

Tulip wraps himself in his cape. "This specific problem, Velvet *Khanom*, has a solution. You have more power than you think. The fields were productive today, and His Excellency is in a good mood. Don't wait for him to call you tonight. Go to him early. Show him you need him, he'd like that. Then ask him for what you want."

* * *

Velvet riffles through her chest of undergarments—tulle, lace, chiffon, gauze, and baldachin—takes her time to lengthen her lashes with a mixture of kohl and charred rose petals, a drop of belladonna in each eye, a puff of rouge on both cheeks, a few sprays of the essence of bergamot and rose under her arms, in the folds of her thighs, the indentation of her neck. She takes a last look in the mirror at her seductive body, naked beneath transparent undergarments. No, this will not do. Her husband desires the Friday Woman, not her. And nothing will change that. She quickly changes into a brown wool, long sleeved dress, and a gabardine overcoat, then drops a black chador over her head.

She hurries across the corridor to her husband's quarters, crosses the threshold, and approaches his working desk.

The governor general regards her with suspicion. It is not like her to take the initiative to come to him. "What are you looking for on my desk?"

She moves a stack of documents aside and lifts the diamond-capped pen from the groove in which it is cradled. "For this," she says, brandishing his pen in the air. She removes the cap, runs the tip of the pen over her bare skin the way he does when the ink on the back of her hand fades and he darkens his name anew as if his worth depends on the shade of his name on her skin. Slowly, methodically, she traces the shadow of his name, makes it darker and darker, her anger fueled by each stroke as the tip digs deeper into her tender flesh, punctures her skin as he has never done, tattooing his name with black ink mixed with her blood and pain.

Struggling to temper her fierce expression, she lowers her voice. "Your name will never fade now. No matter where I am, you will always be with me, my husband, and everyone will know I am yours."

"Why did you do this?" he asks.

She casts her eyes down. "I'd like to visit my parents in Bushehr, if you'll allow me."

"Alone? You want to travel alone?"

"No, not alone." She lifts the back of her hand and shows him his bleeding name. "I'm going with you. Only for a few days, please."

He regards her standing in front of him like a regal empress, not a sign of pain on her face, the pen clutched in her firm clasp. He takes it from her and screws the cap shut, drops it in his pocket, and lifts his dark eyes to her. "Two days of travel, two days in Bushehr, four days at most. I will think about it. Now go take care of your hand before it festers. Try the pipe. It will help."

CHAPTER TWENTY-FIVE

Tiny bells chirp at the hem of Tulip's coat as he inspects dresses Zahra holds up on hangers, runs a hand over one, and feels between two fingers the fabric of another. He settles on a long-sleeved, emerald-green taffeta with mother of pearl buttons. A pair of black velvet gloves to protect his mistress's bruised hand.

Zahra takes necklaces, rings, bracelets, and earrings out of the jewelry box on the dressing table and displays them on herself for Tulip to choose. Having helped him adorn Velvet often enough, she knows her mistress prefers the simpler pieces, rather than the large glittering jewels Zahra covets and Tulip insists Velvet wear on her outings with her husband.

As Velvet never bothers to lock the jewelry box, Zahra, at every opportunity, tries on multiple necklaces, pins brooches to her apron, a few into her knotted hair, wears rings on all ten fingers, and, with child-like glee, twirls in front of the mirror, until another chore demands her attention.

The sun is struggling to emerge from behind the mist-shrouded mountains as Tulip accompanies Velvet to the gates, where the half-bald chauffeur, who seems to possess an endless flow of saliva, is spit-polishing the Lincoln Continental to a high shine. He stuffs the cloth into his pocket, clicks his boots with a wobbly army salute, and opens the door to the car, where the governor general, dressed in a maroon-colored, double-breasted military uniform, weighted with gold braids and rows of impressive-looking medals, waits in the backseat.

Velvet raises a questioning eyebrow at Tulip. She despises her bi-weekly trips in the Lincoln with her husband when he parades her around the city like a war trophy. But this is different. It is not like him to flaunt her before the city is fully awake.

"I don't know where you're going, *Khanom*." Tulip whispers as he slides his turquoise ring off his finger and drops it in Velvet's pocket. "Allah protect you. I'll be waiting for you."

The Lincoln makes its way down the dirt road to Tajrish Square. Vendors are in the process of removing canvas coverings from their roadside stands. Young girls in uniforms are on their way to school. Carpet weavers hang dyed wool to dry in the sun. Behind an outdoor counter with mounds of cucumbers, a man is calculating on an abacus. An old man with a henna-dyed beard steps out of a crowded bakery, sheets of *sangak* bread balanced on his head.

The vendors, carpet weavers, students, and pedestrians gather at the side of the road. They clap at the sight of the governor general and his wife in their American car, shinier than onyx, its trim, grill, and door handles made of solid gold, the wipers swaying ceremoniously on the spotless windshield.

The chauffeur jumps out at the entrance of the bazaar, bows with a flourish, and opens the door for the governor general and his bejeweled wife to step out of the car.

Velvet observes the large crowd that gathers around to clap and call out salutations as if the royal couple, themselves, have found their way to the bazaar. It is hard enough to be displayed in the Lincoln around the city, but to be flaunted like this in the bazaar is unbearable.

She trails the governor past doorless stalls that open into dirt-floored corridors with arched arcades. Merchants advertise the merits of their commodities—jars for pickling, handmade ornaments of brass and silver, prayer mats, henna to tint hair, beards, and nails, kohl to strengthen and darken the lashes. Customers haggle—veiled women as well as women sporting European style hats and dresses, businessmen as well as foreign soldiers.

Bearded mullahs in rusty, brown cloaks stroll about, discussing the laws of the Koran. They bow their turbaned heads, step aside for the governor general and his wife to pass.

A ruddy, heavyset man halts in front of them; a moment of confusion. If he bows, the heavy copper bowl filled with hot soup of sheep's tongue and entrails he carries on his head, will fall. He shouts, "Peace and blessings be upon our honored governor general and his wife!"

The governor stops in front of a stall in the bazaar of fabric sellers, less crowded at this early hour, when women are busy tidying their messy world. He waves toward bolts of fabric, piled high on shelves and counters.

A thick, handlebar mustache dances above the merchant's lips as, knees creaking with every move, he retrieves bolt after bolt—linen and gabardine, silk and damask, cashmere and brocade.

"I have enough fabrics," Velvet tells the governor and, unable to look at the bolts of fabric the merchant keeps unspooling in front of her husband, she turns her back to the counter and looks around, biting into a slice of persimmon a vendor offers her. If she could only escape the frenzy of hectic clocks and the nauseating stink of opium in the mountains, stroll freely around the bazaar, hear the metallic taps of Shirazi silversmiths and Esfahani coppersmiths, inhale the spicy scent of Hamadani tanners.

Her eyes fall on a man in the distance. His hair grazes the back of the starched collar of his shirt. His hand dips into his pocket and, certain it is for his watch, all fear and awareness melt away, as do the growl of her husband's commands, the creaking bones of the scrambling merchant, the cries of surrounding hawkers, and she follows the man's back as he wends his way around the thickening throng, stops in front of a stall, and runs a hand over a row of silver trinkets hanging from the doorframe. Her heart flips in her chest. It is Dr. Yaran, yes, he is buying her a gift. A few more minutes in front of the stand, he turns the collar of his coat up and without looking this way or that vanishes among the crowd.

"Velvet!" Her husband's voice startles her back to her senses. "Where did you go?"

She retraces her steps and gestures toward the stall of silver jewelry. "I wanted to look at these."

"Cheap nothings! Not worthy of *my* wife. Come, see if you like this."

She takes a long time to inspect the exquisite silk paisley threaded with gold filaments until her heart begins to settle, and, unable to utter a word, she grants her husband an approving nod.

With the paper-wrapped silk in her lap, Velvet sits next to her husband in the Lincoln as it makes its way up north toward the mountains above which a stack of white clouds drifts aimlessly. A warm breeze with the faint scent of dust and chargrilled corn drifts in through the window the governor rolls down.

A newspaper boy waves a paper above his head. He cries out that Hitler has risen as the Shiite Messiah and is marching with his army into Iran to annihilate every single Jew in his path.

Velvet's gaze follows the newspaper boy beyond the window. She feels for Tulip's ring in her pocket. If this news is true, Dr. Yaran, a renowned Jewish doctor, will be one of the first to be arrested and murdered. "Husband, did you hear the newspaper boy? Is it true? What will happen to your dentist?"

"I heard the news. It is true," the governor replies, taking a moment to consider the consequences of a Jewish massacre. "Rommel's tanks are not far from our border. But don't worry about me. If I still need the Jew, I'll know how to save him when Rommel gets here."

Announcing their arrival with a series of festive honks, the Lincoln turns into a narrow street lined with young *chenar* trees. Residents spill out of their homes—men in suits or pajamas, women wearing kerchiefs spotted with soot and cooking oils, their chadors wrapped around their waists.

The car comes to a halt in front of a red-colored brick house, aflame with purple bougainvillea.

"Where is this? Why are we here?" Velvet asks.

"Honk louder," the governor orders the chauffeur.

The door to the house opens and out step Velvet's thirty-six-year-old mother, Star, and her father, Mousa.

Such powerful joy explodes in Velvet's chest, it feels like pain. She wants to rush into her parents' arms, but she sits back and listens to her husband explain how he sent a moving truck with a messenger to the port of Bushehr to relocate Star and Mousa into this furnished house of bougainvillea he purchased in Tehran and arranged for them to receive a larger monthly stipend. "Much better than visiting them in Bushehr, isn't it?"

Velvet kisses the back of the governor's hand and, unable to wait a second longer, jumps out of the car.

At the sight of her daughter descending from the Lincoln, Star throws her head back and bursts into her deep laughter, which never fails to shock the governor, who is unable to fathom how a small woman with such porcelain-like features and an air of fragility is capable of such an immodest show of joy. If it were not for her lashing tongue and the fierce expression in her brown eyes, he would have found a way to put her in her place.

Velvet's father bounces on his heels and claps with pleasure. A soft-spoken man of average height, with a receding hairline, a loose gait, and an unassuming manner, Mousa might have gone unnoticed if it were not for his penchant—despite his wife's constant warnings to keep his mouth shut or risk his head rolling down a remote ravine—to trumpet his unconventional beliefs. Why aren't women allowed to have four husbands too? Why should they cover their hair? What type of a ridiculous law is the *sigheh* temporary marriage mullahs invented to legalize prostitution and to feed their own lust? Why shouldn't women attend mosques when they're bleeding? On and on he complains to anyone who will listen, until he is summoned back to the police station to be chastised yet again, because no one dares throw the governor general's father-in-law into prison.

Velvet runs into her father's embrace, then she is sobbing and laughing in her mother's arms, until her husband barks that the street is no place for such a spectacle, and they enter the bright, whitewashed house.

If not for Star's touch—lacy curtains and purple bougainvillea in brass vases, pistachios, dates, and cut melons in colorful, glass bowls—the living and dining rooms would have resembled a crowded furniture shop. And everywhere, on the dining room cabinet, on the mantelpiece, and on the coffee tables are framed pictures of Velvet—the four-year-old helping her mother stir rice halvah, digging a finger in the marzipan cake baked on her fifth birthday, on an outing in Karaj with her father's camera slung across her shoulder, wearing the pink organza dress she refused to give away until it tore at the seams, a teenager flanked by proud parents and showing off her first hat after Reza Shah banned the chador.

The governor struts from room to room to assess whether his deputy has put his hard-earned money to good use. Having decided he has; he takes his pen out of his pocket and waves it expansively around the rooms. "Velvet? Are you pleased?"

"Of course, I am. Thank you." Velvet snatches the despised pen out of his hand and drops it back into his pocket.

Star and Mousa exchange baffled glances. Star raises a questioning eyebrow at her son-in-law and, the governor general, who can't help but tread lightly around her, grabs Mousa's arm and leads him into the living room. He would rather hear his father-in-law's baseless rants about how unfairly women are treated than suffer Star's drilling inquisitions, which he was subjected to often enough when Star and Mousa lived in Tehran and he'd send the Lincoln to fetch them. The visits were short and far between, but despite his fastidious efforts to make himself inaccessible, Star would find her way to him in the large mansion and hound him with questions until, unable to take it anymore, he reduced their stipend at a time of war when inflation was high and living in Tehran became increasingly expensive. Yet, here he is now, back to where he was.

Velvet takes the wooden spoon from the kitchen rack and tastes the bubbling *khoresh* on the stove. She longs for the days she baked poppyseed and pistachio cake with Star. She wants to lean on her mother and cry. Instead, she swallows her tears, hands her the package, and tells her it is a gift from her son-in-law.

"But he's done enough for us!" Star objects. "No, I can't accept it."

"Open it, Madar, he chose it for you."

Star feels the fine fabric between her thumb and forefinger; traces the paisley designs, the gold threads. "It's lovely. I'll thank him." She raises Velvet's chin. "What is it, daughter? You've lost weight. Are you healthy?"

"Yes, Madar, perfectly healthy."

"And your hands? Why are you wearing gloves?"

"It's the fashion, Madar, and it keeps me warm."

Star pins her daughter in her grilling gaze. "It's warm here. Why don't you take them off?"

Velvet begins to remove the glove that conceals the throbbing tattoo on the back of her hand, the punctured skin where the wound of her husband's name still stings, to show her mother how she tattooed herself with black ink and blood so he will allow her to visit her parents. Star should know how lonely her daughter is in the mountains, her only company a eunuch and her impossible longings for a Jewish doctor. Star is a fierce woman. She will find a way to save her daughter. She slides the glove back up. Her parents will not accept aid from a son-in-law who treats their daughter badly.

Velvet meets her mother's eyes with the same intensity she inherited from her. "I am a married woman, Madar. I don't like being told what to do."

Star turns toward the stove, lifts the top of the pan, and stirs the *khoresh* with the wooden spoon. The kitchen is suddenly hot, and a thick cloud of steam clings to everything.

"I miss you and Baba," Velvet complains to her mother's back.

Star drops the spoon in the sink and turns to face Velvet. "What was that business with the pen, daughter?"

"I hate the pen with its flashy diamond. So pretentious to wave it around like that. Now stop worrying about me Madar, please."

The call of the muezzin for noon prayer can be heard around the city as Star holds Velvet's gloved hands lightly on her palms. "Why don't you give us a grandchild?"

"Soon, Madar, I'm not nineteen yet, we've time."

"You, maybe, but your husband is nearly forty. Have you seen a doctor?" Star arranges four filigreed cup holders on a tray, checks four small tea glasses for any sign of water marks.

Velvet takes the tray from her mother and smiles without a hint of joy. "I don't need a doctor, Madar, nothing is wrong."

"Look at me, daughter! I am not easily fooled. Remember that as long as your parents are breathing, you are neither alone nor helpless."

CHAPTER TWENTY-SIX

Velvet slaps shut the book of poetry and tosses it on the pallet in her chamber. She clamps her hands to her ears to block her husband's howls of passion. It is late Friday, and she has not been summoned. She ought to be relieved, but she is not. How naïve of her to have nurtured expectations that given time her husband would tire of his whore and send her away with her fancy veils, high heels, and garish jewelry. The hateful woman is here to stay. Why else would the governor general abandon all show of keeping up appearances?

Velvet jumps to her feet, tosses a headscarf over her hair, and, satin slippers stifling the sound of her steps, walks out of her chambers. "Good evening, gentlemen." She acknowledges the guards at the door. "Full moon out there. Take a peek from the east windows. Best view from there. We all need some good luck before the start of another month."

The guards lower their heads and murmur under their breath that the moon is too bright and the night too silent for her to wander too far.

She nods, presses two fingers to her lips. "Only as far as necessary, gentlemen, I promise." Only as far, she muses, as discovering what type of a woman could bring the cold-blooded governor general to such orgasmic heights that his howls could be heard all the way in her quarters.

Past the courtyard and toward the other wing of the mansion, she makes her way through the seemingly endless Hall of Precious Clocks, the odor of black walnut oil growing more insistent as she approaches her husband's private quarters. A shiver scuttles down her spine at the sight of a new clock installed above the door, its gold bowels churning like a mill behind a rounded glass on which numbered soldiers point the gilded eyes of their guns at her.

At the sound of a lock turning, the soft creak of a door, she steals into the room adjacent to her husband's. The room is furnished with the heavy, red-upholstered furniture the governor favors. A tall, burl walnut grandfather clock pounds in a corner. An arrangement of cut roses overflow in a crystal vase. The gall of the woman! To raid precious roses Velvet pampers with such love in her courtyard. A glass of dark tea sits on an antique plate, the imprint of painted lips on the rim. The Friday Night Woman must be spending her nights here.

The gong of the grandfather clock sends Velvet's heart into a frenzy. She should crawl back to safety. Foolish of her to allow anger to rob her of all reason. Nothing will be achieved, other than exposing the extent of her own vulnerability.

Mouth dry and bitter, hand cold on the door handle, she waits for her heart to settle. Peeks out from behind the slightly open door to check whether it is safe to return to her quarters.

The Friday Night Woman steps out of the governor general's bedroom and makes her way down the hallway. Dressed as she was on Velvet's wedding night, in sequined veils covering her head and face, her veils trail her like the iridescent tail of a courting peacock. She hesitates, returns to check the door handle, makes sure it is firmly shut, then removes her high-heeled shoes and rests her forehead against the door.

Minutes pass. Velvet senses a tickling in her throat. She ducks behind the door again and, finding it impossible to choke a sneeze in her chest, tiptoes further into the room, the beat of the clock's pendulum loud against her ribcage.

Sounds in the hallway. Once again, she crosses the room and peeps through the slightly open door in time to see the woman crumple into a sequined heap and begin to pound her head on the carpet. The sickening thuds muffle the loud banging in Velvet's chest, and she fears she might vomit her supper. Hand to her chest, hardly able to breathe, she waits.

The thumps of the Clock Master's approaching boots in the distance. The jiggle of his keys. The shadow of his hulk precedes him on the wall at the end of the corridor.

The woman's head jolts up. As do her hands to yank up her veils that slip off her head, revealing her tear-streaked face.

A silent scream erupts in Velvet's throat.

CHAPTER TWENTY-SEVEN

It is early afternoon and a sour odor of sin wafts off the sweating poppy fields. The surrounding mountains are all hard stone, painting everything with a veneer of sorrow.

Purple cape flapping in the wind like the wings of a flamboyant bird, Tulip is by the dirt road beyond the fields.

Velvet cuts a path past a contingent of laborers, steals behind Tulip, and gives him a brisk tap on the shoulder.

He spins around with a start. "*Khanom*! Out in this heat?"

"As you are, dear Tulip."

"Yes, I came to greet Doctor Yaran."

"How very kind of you."

He pulls out his handkerchief from his pocket and wipes sweat off his forehead. "Doctor Yaran deserves any favor I can offer."

"Of course, Tulip, of course. How could I forget how generous you are with your favors?"

He flinches at her acerbic tone. Has he inadvertently offended his mistress? Never has he seen her this upset with him. "Please, Velvet *Khanom*, go inside. There are spies everywhere. His Excellency won't—"

Velvet tilts her head toward the mountains. "His Excellency can go throw himself off that cliff. I don't care."

"You should care, *Khanom*. He loves you very much. Well, as much as he's capable of loving."

She grabs him by both arms and shakes him with such ferocity his carefully folded turban comes undone. "Make excuses for him if you must. He is a monster, and you know it. But if *you* enjoy his pitiful love, go ahead, grovel at his feet until you grow old and useless." She removes the turquoise ring on her small finger and plants it in his hand.

He stares at the ring he gave her, glances at her enraged face. "*Khanom*! Why are you so upset?"

"I'll tell you why. You promised to find a way for me to see Doctor Yaran in private and you never did. I'm going to do it myself, and you better keep your mouth shut. I am done living under the same roof with the Friday Night Woman. You know her well, Tulip, don't you?" She looks around, searches for a stone, but all around are only dried poppy pods and bloody flowers that mask nothing but destruction. She grabs a bunch of pods, flings them at him with all the force of her pain. Her sobs rise painfully out of her chest. "I saw you leave my husband's bedroom last night."

Horror contorts his face, and his lips tremble with the effort to smother his cries, but the tears come as fast as he wipes them off. "Forgive me, *Khanom*, forgive your servant. I've caused you such pain, you who are dearer to me than anyone else on earth."

His desolate image last night, thumping his head on the carpet, is seared in her mind, and she both hates and pities him. "I don't understand, Tulip. Who are you? Who is my husband?"

"I don't know what we are, *Khanom*." Tulip hits himself over and over again between the legs with his fists. "His Excellency is not a man, and I am not a woman. But he likes to pretend that I am a woman. We are both terribly wrong." He grabs his turban, throws it down. Wrenches from the roots a handful of his curls and screaming in agony tosses it underfoot. Yanks another bunch. Beads of blood break out on his skull as fistfuls of hair gather at his feet.

"Stop it!" The horrified Velvet shouts. "Stop right now!"

He lifts his turban from the ground, shakes off poppies and dried pods, drops it on his head, and, to her surprise, stands at attention like a soldier relieved to be reminded of his place.

Under a brutal sun in the center of a white sky, the reek of rancid poppies in the wind, she turns her back to him and, aware that nothing will be the same again, takes the path back toward the mansion.

* * *

Tulip enters Velvet's chambers to the evening call of muezzin from minarets around the city and stands in front of her with bowed head and arms crossed against his chest.

Decisions had been made for him all his life—by his stepfather, by his master, even by Velvet *Khanom*. But this much dreaded visit to her, he knows, has to take place before the end of this terrible day, or he will lose all courage.

In preparation, he had changed one outfit after another, smeared his face with a thick layer of powder, lined his reddened eyes with dark kohl, dusted his cheeks with two shades of blush, and sprayed far too much perfume. As if to erase himself, he had wiped the mirror over and over again. Who was he? Nobody! No matter how thick the makeup on his face or how lavish his jewels and garments, he remains a helpless puppet his master bends and contorts to the music of his own twisted demands.

Velvet raises her eyes from her book of poetry, lifts a glass of tea from a tray at her side, and takes a sip. She sets the glass back, examines a bowl of rock sugar on the tray, picks one, and drops it in her mouth. She shuts the book. Regards Tulip with a mixture of rage and sorrow.

"It's all terribly confusing," he murmurs. "But His Excellency owns me. It's been like this ever since he paid my stepfather to cut me clean the way he likes—"

"Cut you clean?" Velvet's voice is loud and unbelieving, and for an instant everything around her turns into a dark haze of confusion. "You said you were born like this. You said my husband saved you from your stepfather. No, Tulip! Tell me my husband is not this cruel. He did *not* do this to you."

Tears rinse his made-up face and stain his embroidered baldachin cape. "I lied to you, *Khanom*. I was Hassan once. I was a healthy ten-year-old boy when His Excellency paid my stepfather to cut me, so I'd not grow to become a man. It's not his fault, *Khanom*, he is suffering, too, constantly fighting his demons. He can't tolerate the truth of who he is. So, he made me look like a woman to deceive himself into believing he really is with a woman. I feel for him."

"How can you feel anything but hate for him?" She digs her fingernails into her palms as she struggles to collect the shredded pieces of her mind, absorb the implications of what she just heard.

With his small, unexpected acts of kindness, which they sometimes mistook for love, her husband had succeeded in developing an attachment between himself, his wife, and poor Tulip. No! This is not love. This is the cruelty of a sick man who has no pity for his prisoners.

Tulip regards Velvet with sad, wet eyes. "Here I am now, with no one to go to but you, *Khanom*. Tell me what to do, and I will do it."

"I wish I knew, Tulip. All I know is I will not live under the same roof with a monster who is capable of such an act."

"This is your home, *Khanom*, you can't give everything up for me. I'll leave first thing tomorrow, make myself disappear, and no one will ever find me. No, *Khanom*, don't look so worried, I'm good at disappearing, I promise. Even His Excellency and his army of men won't find a trace of me."

Velvet raises Tulip's chin to force his gaze up. "Don't you dare disappear on me, Tulip. I need you by my side. We are the only two people who know something about the governor general he doesn't want others to know. And that's a powerful weapon."

"I don't think so, *Khanom*. If His Excellency finds out we know, he will make sure to silence both of us."

"Then we will not let him do that. We are going to be careful, a step ahead of him. Didn't you say I am resourceful? You are, too, much more than I am. Shhh, Tulip, shhh! It's an order, no more talk of disappearing," she says as she walks into his expansive embrace.

CHAPTER TWENTY-EIGHT

1943

Two years have gone by since the occupation, and the Allied Forces have become more deeply entrenched in the country. The Soviets stand guard over northern Iran. British forces command the southern part. And American armed forces police all supply routes. The shah, having declared war on Germany, has relinquished Iran's status of neutrality.

Leaders of the British Commonwealth, the Soviet Union, and the United States of America are holding the Tehran Conference here, and the city, ill equipped for the heavy security in place to accommodate the Big Three—Winston Churchill, Joseph Stalin, and Franklin Delano Roosevelt—vacillates between frenzy and paralysis. Facts and speculations bounce like ping pong balls from one news outlet to another, one mouth to another. Tehran throbs with curiosity. Is the Conference held in the Russian Embassy to appease Stalin for the countless casualties Russia continues to suffer? Or to alleviate Stalin's distrust of Roosevelt?

Allegedly, both Stalin and Churchill extended an invitation to Roosevelt to lodge with them in their respective embassies, but Roosevelt, in order to avoid any appearance of favoring one leader over the other, chose to stay in the American embassy. Consequently, Churchill and Stalin agreed to conduct the meetings at the American embassy to accommodate the ailing president for whom it is difficult to travel from one part of the city to another.

But before the president had had time to rest from a tiring trip from Cairo, Russian envoys reported a German assassination plot against the president, suggesting he relocate to the Russian Embassy, where security is tighter. Neither the president nor his consultants took the threat seriously. It is, they assumed, a ploy to move the president to the Russian Embassy, where cameras are tucked in every niche and corner. In the end, seeing an opportunity to be close to Stalin so as to better understand him, Roosevelt accepted the invitation and moved to the Russian Embassy.

Soleiman steers Rostam around Baharestan Square and past the ornate brick and stone building of the Majles Parliament with its carved arches and capitals depicting symbols of the Sassanid Era. Finding the road blocked, he detours around the Parliament Library and Sepahsalar Mosque. The British and Russian embassies are chained off as well; he has no choice but to wait. His riding boots drum against the stirrups. Rostam flicks his ears back and forth, and Soleiman attempts to calm him. The Queen will not forgive him if he is late again for his appointment.

A motorcade of black cars appears at the end of the thoroughfare and sails through the gates of the Russian Embassy, where the Big Three are in the process of discussing how best to form a second front to fight Nazi Germany, the Anglo-American landing in France, as well as the extent of their involvement in the Italian, Balkan, and Burmese fronts.

A group of gendarmes arrives to remove the blockade and to guide traffic in an orderly fashion. Finding it impossible to do so, they abandon the mayhem of cars, trucks, and droshkies and amble toward the closest teahouse.

* * *

Trumpeting their arrival with a series of arrogant snorts, Rostam struts into the royal grounds as if entering his private stable.

Four uniformed adjutants lead Soleiman to the Rose Garden where the Queen, her eyes shut, is resting in a rattan chair.

Soleiman waits with his escorts, their crested helmets tucked under their arms. A cool breeze whistles through the garden raising the scent of damp soil and roses. It occurs to him that Neda, having stripped the weeping willow of its inner bark and bled it of its essential oils, would have loved to forage around these gardens to discover different florae for her Baba Magic.

A parade of soft-footed attendants walk into the Rose Garden with antique trays of sweets, dry fruits, pistachios, and tea, which they arrange on a rattan table before bowing their way out.

The Queen opens her eyes, adjusts the delicate net framing her hair, lifts the spaniel from her lap, and rests him at her feet, where he continues to peacefully snore. Her eyes flicker in Soleiman's direction. "You are late, Doctor Yaran. Is this a habit?"

"My apologies, Your Majesty," Soleiman replies, noting her pink-veined eyes. Has the Queen been crying? "The Big Three are meeting, and the streets around the British and Russian Embassies were chained. I had to wait."

"The Tehran Conference." A backward flip of her royal hand as if to chase off the three pesky leaders. "Insolent dictators with no respect for their host! They will not achieve much without His Majesty."

Queen Fawzia is offended. Her twenty-four-year-old husband is furious. The decision to confer in Tehran was relayed to the shah a mere few days before the arrival of the Big Three. Stalin and Churchill paid His Majesty a brief courtesy call in the Russian Embassy, instead of in his own palace. It is the third and last day of the conference, and His Majesty has not been invited to any of the meetings.

"They want to dictate our destiny." The Queen frowns at the doctor as if he is to blame for the crime of those leaders. "No one, Doctor Yaran, no one could tell."

His back straightens into rigid attention. "I don't understand, Your Majesty."

"No one could tell you worked on my front tooth."

"Your Majesty is pleased?"

"I am. As is His Majesty. And our governor general, is he pleased with your work? I promised His Majesty to ask you."

"Hard to tell, Your Majesty, the governor general is a difficult man to please."

The Queen wipes a smile off with her handkerchief. "You are being kind, Doctor Yaran. The man is an insufferable brute. Still, His Majesty is fond of him as he seems to accomplish miracles no one else can." The Queen gestures to the rattan chair facing her, and Dr. Yaran settles at the edge. "I wanted to see you, Doctor Yaran, to discuss the state of the Polish orphans."

Soleiman's hands lock in his lap. He quickly unlocks them.

"I have visited them in the makeshift camp in our private gardens. It is a sad sight. If this is their state here, it must be quite terrible in other camps. Yes?"

"Yes, Your Majesty, it is. Most need medical care, especially the younger ones."

The Queen observes him with moist eyes. "How old are they?"

"They are so malnourished; it is hard to tell. A child, who lives with a friend of mine, looks like a one-year-old girl, although she is three years old."

"As young as my daughter." The Queen's knotted eyebrows soften. "This child, is she under proper medical care?"

"Unfortunately, not, Your Majesty. Our specialists are not trained to address the traumas these children have suffered."

"Our country has not caught up with the modern world, I am afraid. Have you considered sending the children to Egypt?"

His hand dips into his pocket in an involuntary act of alarm. He quickly takes it out. Egypt will not welcome Jewish orphans. "Egypt would be the ideal choice, Your Majesty. But it is a temporary solution."

The Queen's voice is cutting. "Temporary! Are you saying Egypt is not equipped to help the children?"

"On the contrary, Your Majesty. They will be fortunate to receive care from such qualified doctors. But the children need more than medical care. Their long-term emotional well-being depends on settling in a permanent place they can call home."

The Queen crosses her slim ankles. "Where is that place, Doctor Yaran?"

He bows his head. The Muslim Queen will not react well to his suggestion. "Palestine, Your Majesty. Palestine is well prepared for such immigrants."

The Queen crushes her handkerchief in her fist. "Are you sure? Is it safe to dispatch orphans right into a battle ground?"

"It is a risk, Your Majesty. But what is the choice? They will not survive if left homeless and broken as they are."

The Queen sinks into her own thoughts. A deep silence engulfs the garden, and, even the nightingales, as if sensing the weight of the moment, cease their endless chatter. They sit in uninterrupted silence for a while, until the Queen turns to him and says, "We all have our own problems, Doctor Yaran. In fact, the greater our position, the greater our problems. I hope you are right, and the orphans find happiness in Palestine." She lifts the spaniel into her arms and rises. "Farewell, then, and my prayers will follow them." The Queen studies him with narrowed eyes. "Is there a problem?"

A trickle of sweat makes its way down Soleiman's hairline. "There is, Your Majesty. A plane is going to Palestine next week, and Colonel Motamedi, who is in charge of issuing visas, will not grant visas unless he receives authorization from a higher office. I will be eternally grateful to Your Majesty if you might grant your endorsement."

"As you well know, Doctor Yaran, the political situation is dire, and travelling is quite dangerous." A commanding snap of her manicured fingers summon the adjutant to her side. "However, I do believe that the orphans should be granted the opportunity every other child deserves."

CHAPTER TWENTY-NINE

Neda looks at her poor doll. All sad and broken little pieces on the floor. She lifts the small wood arm and pushes the sharp tip hard into her own finger. Her blood smells like the mortar she pounds Baba Magic in and like all the nails in Rostam's shoes. Maybe Madar's blood when Neda was born smelled like Neda's blood.

The clang of the metal gate, the clip clop of riding boots. Neda's Baba is home, and she jumps into his arms. Baba's jacket smells of dust and smoke and medicines of That-Cursed-Land-Eater man in the mountains, and Neda wants to cry, but it hurts because her eyes don't ever want to make tears.

"What's this?" Soleiman points to the fresh blood stains on his white shirt. He untangles his daughter's arms from around his neck and stares with alarm at her bleeding finger and the shard of wood she clutches in her other hand. "What's this, Sweetheart? Neda! I asked a question. Wood dolls break, too, so be careful next time. Does it hurt?"

Neda doesn't know if it hurts or not because it's all mixed up in her head. Why Baba doesn't like the hurt, but Aunt Shamsi is all mixed up about hurt and sometimes slaps herself hard on her own chest when she thinks of her dead Azar and sometimes, she puts medicine on Neda's scratched hands to take away Neda's hurt.

A strange tenderness wells up in Soleiman at his daughter's tearless display of defiance. With each passing year, she becomes more like Ruby—brave, almost impudent in the face of danger, and challenging anyone foolish enough to consider her in any way lacking.

"Look what you did now!" Says Aunt Shamsi the instant she enters. "What's with you, Little Leech, breaking everything you touch?"

"Give me the broom," Soleiman says. "I'll handle this. And it's time you called Neda by her name!"

Aunt Shamsi loud thumps out and Baba swish, swishes with a broom all the mess Neda made with her broken doll." Aunt Shamsi is angry because she raises Neda all by herself all of poor Neda's motherless life. "Baba, why Aunt Shamsi raises me all by myself?"

"You mean all by herself, Sweetheart, and that's not true at all. I am always here, too, to make sure you have everything you need." But is he? How can he be present for his daughter, when his conflicted heart and mind are at constant war with one another?

Neda keeps her big mouth shut because Baba is not happy right now, and his voice is soft like feathers Neda pulls out of her pillow. "Baba? You're always here?"

"Yes, Sweetheart, always. You're so wise for your age. You have no idea what a miracle you are!"

Baba's words are tiny kisses in Neda's ears, so she closes her ears so his kisses don't run away, lifts one of her dolls and whispers, "You have no idea what a miracle you are."

Soleiman taps a forefinger over the doll's eyes and chuckles conspiratorially. "She's pop-eyed like Aunt Shamsi. But don't tell her, she won't like it. If you want to you can tell your mushrooms."

Neda doesn't know if to tell her Baba that she talks not so much to her mushrooms but all the time to her Mushrooms Friend in all the purple mushrooms that feel nice and warm when she rubs them to her cheeks and imagines her Madar's kisses if she ever wants to kiss Neda.

When Neda is with Mushrooms Friend, Aunt Shamsi shouts, "They're mushrooms, Little Leech, they're the color of hell and who in God's name is out there that you suddenly chatter like a parrot? Enough already, we've got mushrooms coming out of our ears. And stop digging your face in them, or you'll turn into a purple clown." When Neda sees herself all the time in the mirror to see if she turns into a purple clown, Aunt Shamsi tells her not to stand so much in front of the mirror because it'll make her all stupid and vain like a peacock. So she ask what's peacock, and Aunt Shamsi say, "Peacock is a no-good bird with a fancy fan-tail of feathers that has nothing better to do than show it off to trap innocent peahens. So Neda ask again what's innocent peahens and Aunt Shamsi laughs and say, "Peahens are ugly girl birds that beautiful boy peacocks trick to make them open their legs too wide for their own good." Neda ask and ask to know why boy peacocks trick girl peahens to make them open their legs too wide for their own good. But Aunt Shamsi only comb Neda's hair with her own hand and say to Neda that she's her *fozoul* nosy Little Leech that she loves to death.

Baba washes Neda's face because dinner is ready and then fills Neda's plate with turmeric rice and lentils and *tahdig* crispy rice so Neda makes big crunching sounds with *tahdig* between her strong teeth so Baba will tell her what a miracle she is to chew hard crispy rice at her age.

Aunt Shamsi brings her oily smells to the table and clangs a spoon with big huff and pours two and three spoons of rice and cuts chicken soft flesh and hard bone and plops drumstick and breast on rice and fat-eats all the time and then pops salty pumpkin seeds that are so good for her digestion.

"Send a messenger to That-Cursed-Land-Eater, Soleiman, say you can't go tomorrow. Say you're sick, say anything you want, just don't go. It's *Ashura* and any Jew with a tumbler of sense in his skull won't even think of stepping out of the house, let alone all the way to That-Cursed-Land-Eater. The streets will fill with Muslim shroud-wearers who're ready to attack an infidel with their chains and knives."

"Enough, Aunt Shamsi. You're scaring Neda. Let her enjoy her dinner in peace." His aunt is right, no sane Jew should be out tomorrow when processions march in the streets to commemorate the martyrdom of Imam Hussein at the Battle of Karbala. The tense atmosphere is like dry tinder, the sight of a Jew enough to spark an inferno. But the governor has summoned him, and he must go.

Neda's ears swallow Aunt Shamsi's scary voice all at once with crispy rice that pain scratch her throat. Baba angry clicks his watch like Aunt Shamsi chop chops with her knife all the herbs she hates because they make her hands red like monkey *koon*. Neda's stomach jumps like the saltshaker Aunt Shamsi shakes on her foods until Baba tell her to stop already because her blood pressure is jumping high up.

"Sweetheart? Are you okay?" Soleiman feels Neda's forehead, her cheeks, counts her pulse. "Come, I'll tuck you in. You must be tired."

Neda's mouth opens wide, and everything in her stomach bursts out stinking on her plate.

CHAPTER THIRTY

On his way to the governor general, one moment the sun is ablaze in a cloudless sky, the next he is being pummeled by a rush of hail that disorients his stallion and leaves Soleiman drenched to his core. Unseasonal torrents have overwhelmed Tehran, adding to the woes of an already chaotic city that has no clue how to deal with the allied troops who have hijacked any semblance of normal life.

Lightning scurries across the sky, followed by the growl of thunder. Another flare of lightning, this one so close, Rostam shies from the glowing earth under his hooves.

"*Bargard!* Go back!" Soleiman calls to a stray dog howling at the stallion's heels. The dog lifts its bearded snout, lets out a pitiful whine and, instead of turning around, continues to trail them.

"Come back, stupid dog!" The Quarter Fool has materialized at the end of the Alley of Seven Synagogues. "Don't go, I said, it's *Ashura* out there!"

"You keep safe." Soleiman waves the Quarter Fool away. "Don't worry about the dog."

The stallion and his rider leave the Jewish Quarter behind and make their way toward the grieving city, where stalls are shuttered, and black shrouds cover roadside stands. No sign of skinned sheep carcasses hanging from hooks, nor steaming pots of sheep innards, or hills of warm bread on flat wooden trays.

"Ya Hossein! Ya Hossein!" The advancing chant of hundreds, perhaps thousands, shouting the martyred imam's name can be heard above the racket of thunder. "Ya Hossein!" The resounding slaps of an army of feverish men beating their chests in mourning for the murdered imam. "Ya Hossein!"

The mud splattered stallion blinks and rears up on his haunches, lifts his head to the heavens, and neighs his protest, a dramatic kick of the hoof, and he comes to a sudden halt.

Soleiman waves his riding crop back and forth in an attempt to clear his field of vision and assess his surroundings. He steers the grunting animal to the side of the road and the only possible hiding place in sight: a one-story, makeshift stall, squeezed between a shuttered juice stand and an empty lot dotted with heaps of reeking garbage. He pushes aside a flap of burlap at the opening and is faced with a sheet of plywood leaning against the stall's entrance. Rostam, as if prompted by his master, turns around and gives the plywood a strong kick with his hind legs.

The chants of "Ya Hossein!" get closer. "Ya Hossein!"

"*Bia*, come." Soleiman attempts to steer the skeletal dog into the safety of the stall. The dog sits on its haunches and turns its melancholy eyes toward the black crowd of approaching men at the end of the avenue.

Soleiman and his stallion are accosted by a strong stench inside the stall, where water leaks from between bricks set haphazardly on top of wooden planks to create a sorry ceiling. Humid fumes of mud and wool and dye rise from wet sacks of wheat stacked around in neat rows.

"Ya Hossein!" The procession has reached them and is passing in the middle of the road. "Hossein went to Karbala!" "Ya Hossein!" "Hossein!"

Their faces trance like, their shrouds torn, they slap themselves raw on their bare chests, thrash their backs with heavy chains, and slash their shaven heads with daggers. Blood streams down their head and runs under their feet to spill into *joub* at the side of the road.

With horror Soleiman realizes it is possible to see through the wet burlap the beads of hail skipping on the fallen plywood outside, as well as the stray dog, a few meters away, barking at the passing mourners.

A man steps out of the procession. He brandishes a blood-dripping *shamshir* scimitar. From a deep gash on top of his shaved head, blood pours down his tear-drenched face, which he attempts to wipe off with a furious gesture of a vein-knotted arm. His savage eyes shoot toward the flap of burlap, behind which Soleiman and his steed are paralyzed with fear. He hoists the scimitar above his head, lets loose a curdling bellow of "Ya'Allah!" and marches toward the stall.

Soleiman strokes the restless stallion, whose labored breathing through flared nostrils sounds impossibly loud, as do his own heartbeats.

This is how he will end, cut to pieces and left to rot in a reeking stall, his daughter doubly orphaned, no one to rely on but a superstitious aunt and an old grandfather. He watches the man stomp forward with a howl of disgust. His sharp blade slashes through the air and, with a single powerful blow, decapitates the dog. A shot of spittle on the severed head, a kick, and he runs ahead to join the procession.

Soleiman's mouth fills with bile. His legs brace against Rostam's shuddering flank.

Rostam lets out a low grunt.

Another half-hour passes. The thump of departing steps, and the chorus of anguish die down. Soleiman collects himself and ventures out of the stall, averts his eyes from the mutilated dog, and makes his way up Pahlavi Avenue and around Tajrish Square. Hail has given way to rain, and the cacophony of vendors has been replaced by the sporadic rush of flotsam foaming over the riverbanks.

The landscape has changed since Soleiman first led Rostam up this dirt road two years back. Where the brown shades of soil and stone could be seen once, the mountain is now carpeted with the red of opium poppies. The feral gardens look different, as well. Rain has washed the wild junipers of dust and filth. Leaves glisten, the gravel path shimmers, and the scent of bark and wild berries has replaced the biting odor of opium.

"It was a rough trip." Soleiman hands the reins to the groom, who has braved the deluge. "Rostam is upset. Please attend to him."

The groom runs a hand over his healed face. "Of course, *Agha* doctor, with pleasure." This is as much as someone in the service of the governor would dare show appreciation for being cured of the flesh-eating disease, the spread of which the doctor has managed to stem.

Soleiman climbs the stairs to the terrace. He lingers below the mansion's upper window, his ears trained on the window in anticipation of the sound of the turning latch, her delight at seeing him, her sweet smile. He tips his hat, looks around to make sure he is not being followed, and lifts his riding crop in a bold salute, a silent agreement between Velvet and himself, the start of which was on a rainy day when she could not leave the mansion without stirring suspicion.

Minutes pass, more time than is wise for him to linger, as he is, below her window. Nothing today but the silence of the rain-streaked window and the echo of his disappointment.

* * *

Velvet follows Dr. Yaran's every move when he enters the gardens, hands his stallion to the groom, makes his way toward the mansion, and stops below her window, unaware a leather glove has tumbled out of his coat pocket. She turns to Tulip, who, mute and helpless under the canopy of juniper branches, is balancing a large, colorful umbrella over her head.

"Don't keep the car waiting at the gate," he begs. "Let's go, *Khanom*."

"Fetch me the glove, and I'll be on my way."

What else is he to do other than remember his place and follow orders, Tulip wonders, as he wends his way around the trees, plucks the wet glove from the gravel, and hurries back to hand it to his mistress.

The Lincoln bumps down the mountain toward the Hammam public baths. The *joub* water canals on both sides of the streets are overflowing, and black-clad pedestrians step over muddy waters. A man wearing a sheepskin vest and wide pants leans against a thatched stall, his fists pounding on his chest. Stray dogs fight over a heap of sheep innards on the sidewalk in front of a shuttered butchery. Three feral cats and a bald rooster roam in and out of an empty tea stall. A pockmarked beggar with a milky eye and a screaming infant in her lap sits cross-legged at the side of the road.

Velvet searches for her wallet in the small suitcase containing after-bathing change of clothing and toiletries Zahra packed this morning. The car slows down next to the beggar, and Velvet drops five *rials* into her tin can.

"May Allah bless our honorable governor general's wife with many healthy sons." The woman's string of good wishes follows the departing car.

Velvet strokes the soft leather glove in her skirt pocket, the meticulous stitching too fine for handling horses, the edge embossed with his name. Soleiman. She never addressed him by his first name. "Soleiman," she rolls his name in her mouth. "Soleiman." The taste, the melodic pulse on her tongue, and the intimate warmth of his name makes her blush to her marrow.

CHAPTER THIRTY-ONE

Hail falls plink plonk on Neda's head as she fusses with the garden gate so her fingers won't get caught in the hinges, kicks the gate open, jumps up three stairs to the street, walks past the empty property with the becoming-sick willow tree where Rostam sometimes sleeps, waves bye-bye to Pary's door, and runs with her nose open to save her Baba. Aunt Shamsi behind her smells like fenugreek, onion, and fear, so Neda walks faster toward her Baba's leather glove smell mixed with smells of Rostam and roses that Neda doesn't ever have in her garden.

"Wait until I tell your Baba. You stubborn mule! Where are you going with crazy Muslims all over the city? Look at me, drenched to my marrow. We're going to catch our death in this Noah's Flood."

Hail drums on roofs and pockmarks the earth under their feet. Neda's hair is pearled with hail, and Aunt Shamsi's wet kerchief is slicked against her head.

"Don't you dare go in there." Shamsi, who has chased Neda for two blocks to the public baths, bends over to catch her breath. "Stop! Or they'll cut your head off! What are you sniffing around for?"

"For my Baba," Neda calls behind her back.

"In this rich Muslim's hammam? Never! He's not there." Aunt Shamsi raises her pleading arms to the heavens, which has turned a violent shade of purple. Another downpour of cold hail rattles her bones. "Neda! Come back. Please. If you come back, I'll show you what's inside my trunk. I'll show you the silver purse you like...okay, okay, I'll give it to you."

But Neda has disappeared behind a mantle of gathering fog.

* * *

"Little girl, why are you out in this weather?"

Too loud voice and rolling words in big person's mouth sound like words of soldiers from other countries Baba says are all bad thieves who get medals for stealing our foods and oils and everything else.

Neda springs away from the stranger man and runs in the fog toward the mud-smelling wall of the hammam, crouches low, and hugs her trembling legs tight to her frightened stomach, squeezing her eyes shut to make herself smaller and smaller until she disappears.

Suddenly hail no longer falls on Neda's head, and her eyes spring open with renewed panic.

"Here, come under my umbrella, my daughter. Are you lost?"

Neda's hand is suddenly in this other man's smoke-smelling hand, and he's asking where Neda's house is. She snatches her hand away from the stranger man with black beard and round black eyes and begins to circle around and around herself to find the hammam. But big splashing wet drops of rain fall from the sky instead of hail and swallow all the smells Neda depends on. She lost her Baba. She lost Aunt Shamsi. And she can't ever find her way back home. She'll drown in the rain like Aunt Shamsi's little girl drown in *abambar* waters and become all puffed-up dead and black and blue.

Neda bangs her head against the mud-splattered wall to make her nose open.

"*Allahu Akbar*! Stop hitting your head!" the man exclaims, lifting Neda in his arms.

Neda's strong teeth dig into the man's hairy neck.

* * *

The flustered eunuch having, at last, sent Velvet on her way to the hammam, retraces his steps across the gravel path and up the terrace stairs. He appears from behind a mantle of rain and plants a respectful kiss on each of Dr. Yaran's shoulders.

Soleiman steps under Tulip's colorful umbrella. "Strange weather, my friend. One minute we've rain, the next hail. How are you feeling? Does the medicine help?"

"*Moteshakeram*, thank you, your medicine is a miracle, yes, it changed my life. But I've more pressing problems than my bones today. His Excellency is in great pain, and, I'm very sorry, but everything's all wet today and—"

"He hates rain too? Tell me, dear Tulip, is there anything His Excellency particularly likes?"

"It isn't really about rain, *Bebakhshid*, my apologies, but I don't know how to say it. I apologize, but it's all about you being wet like this in his presence."

Soleiman's gaze sweeps across Tulip's face which, despite the rain, glistens with sweat. An instant of confusion before realization solidifies in his mind. How could he forget about a time, not long ago, when Jews were ordered to stay home on rainy days in fear of their contaminating Muslims. How could he forget that a wet Jew would defile a Muslim by dripping his *najes* Jewishness all over the carpet, smear it over the brute's skin, sully his rotten mouth? He shoves Tulip's umbrella away.

"I am very sorry," Tulip says as he moves the umbrella back over Soleiman's head. "I don't know what to say. *Agha* doctor. To me you're a most honorable man, more honorable than many I won't name. If you come in, I'll dry you faster than lightning."

Soleiman's hand seeks his pocket watch as pride and anger creep up and tear at old wounds. Velvet on his reeling mind, he observes the slanting rain. Broken juniper branches and stray roses from the hothouse rush down a stream of rainwater. He steps into the mansion.

Isfahan carpets muffle the clap of their steps as they walk toward an unfamiliar wing of the mansion, two steps down into a rectangular courtyard and pass through an arched portal guarded by massive men handpicked for their size from among hundreds of army personnel. They enter a domed room, the tiles inscribed with Arabic letters reflected in cut mirror walls. A small, turquoise-tiled pool in the center is being cleaned. This is where the governor general performs the ritual of ablution and purification after engaging in the sexual act. This is where he falls to his knees and, week after week, his forehead pressed to a clay tablet of medicinal soil from the holy city of Karbala, recites the prayer of repentance advised in *sharee'a*. Pleads for his sinful days to come to an end, at last, at which time his conduct on earth will be forgiven in the court of the Almighty.

And week after week, his arms folded across his chest, Tulip witnesses the governor fight his own demons, while he, Tulip, struggles with his own regrets. It is written in the Book that the instant the soul rises to the throat and the rattle of death begins absolution is granted. However. Were there a pinch of justice left in that other world, his master's sins would have to be considered beyond forgiveness.

With a series of discreet gesture of a hand and a slight nod toward the door, the eunuch sends the servants scrambling for towels, an ironing table, and a coal iron, after which he locks the door behind them to save Soleiman from further embarrassment. "Tea, *Agha* doctor? A glass of sherbet, perhaps? No? I apologize again, please, don't be angry. It makes me very sad. May I have your jacket and shirt?" He irons the shirt as fast as his hands will allow, struggles with the starched cuffs, not sure whether to fold or iron them flat. Steam hisses from the iron he shakes now and then to encourage a draft and keep the coals inside burning. He pays extra attention to ironing the tailored jacket, which is quite wet at the seams. "Here, *Agha* doctor, your shirt and jacket, *bebakhshid* pardon me...your trousers now, please."

Soleiman shoves his hands in the shirt sleeves, ripping a side seam, yanks off his trousers and tosses them on the ironing table. He struggles to wear his jacket, which feels tight around the arms and shoulders.

"I'll dry your boots as well, *Agha* doctor. Don't take them out. I will kneel. Good. Here you go. The governor general will see you now."

The Land Eater's image—forbidden in Islam to discourage idol worship—is nevertheless stamped on the copper door of yet another suite of rooms in this massive mansion. Tulip lifts the knocker in the mouth of the image and knocks once, presses one ear to the door, then pounds louder. Faced with silence, he arches a quizzical eyebrow and opens the door.

A cloying smell levitates about the room like layers of sheer fabric, behind which the governor general is seated cross-legged on a carpet-covered pallet. Welts on his chest from having flagellated himself are visible through his black, unbuttoned shirt. His silver-threaded hair shines in the glow of a copper brazier over which he is in the process of preparing an ivory pipe studded with gems and decorated with Arabic inscriptions. With the tip of a thin rod, he smears a pea-sized ball of opium in the ceramic pipe-bowl.

The clocks in the halls chime, then others farther away in other rooms. One of the clocks is not synchronized, and the effect is unsettling, as if time itself is confused.

The governor general attempts to rise, drops back into his cushions, and mumbles under his breath that he will punish the Clock Master. A heavy-lidded glance at the doctor. "Someone up there is playing a cruel joke, Yaran, linking our fates like this. I need you. You need me. And your daughter needs us both. So, don't stand there with that arrogant look on your face. Come fix this damned tooth."

The crackle of wood in the fireplace is too loud and the room suddenly too hot, and all Soleiman can think of is that Neda must be frightened by the downpour knocking hard on the windowpanes back home, and he might never see her again because his sleeves are not quite dry, and as often as he blots the shirt cuffs against his coat, they keep dripping.

He spreads a towel next to the pallet and arranges his instruments on it, lifts the dental mirror and holds it under the wisdom tooth.

Takes a closer look and, unable to believe his eyes, steps back, then comes close again and pulls the upper lip up to better study the molar next to the problematic wisdom tooth.

"Beautiful work, Yaran, isn't it?" the governor exclaims in a pleased tone.

Soleiman catches in his palm a drop of water dripping from his cuff. He quickly dries his hand on one of the cushions behind the Governor. "It certainly is, Your Excellency. I've never seen a glass eye implanted into a molar."

"It's not just a glass eye, Yaran. It is a masterpiece! It has the power to ward off any curse you might inflict on me."

"A masterpiece? Yes. Quite impressive. The work of an accomplished dentist, I presume. Why not have the same dentist take care of your teeth, Your Excellency?"

The Land Eater grins effusively, taps a forefinger on the doctor's chest. "Because you, Yaran, have the magic painkiller."

* * *

Fat pellets of hail shower on Velvet as she runs the short distance from the Lincoln toward the hammam, a grand architectural wonder of the Safavid era with intricate turquoise tiles and delicately wrought domes. She greets the chatting women inside who, wrapped in black chadors, with bundles of clothing and toiletries at their feet, wait for a bath to become available on this busy afternoon of public mourning, when bathing is believed to keep one forever healthy.

They fall silent, rise, bow their heads in deference to the governor general's wife as she is ushered through a corridor and across a public bath crowded with more than fifty women and children. It is a somber day. Not the usual echo of laughter and song and the beat of tambourines. No cracking open of watermelons or the filling of melamine bowls with yogurt and spinach, yogurt and diced cucumbers, or sherbets of grated apples in rosewater.

Children, innocent of the seriousness of the day, play with soap bubbles. Bodies surrender to the scrub of loofah mittens and clay exfoliates, Persian mud and mineral masks on faces, pumice-softened-feet, the reek of paste of lye to banish unwanted body hair. Cone helmets of henna, coffee, and egg yolk sit on heads of women.

What has not changed is the exchange of gossip, the venting of jealousies, the matchmaking. This is the news center of the city, where some girls are introduced to the community, and the future of others is crushed under vicious tongues.

Velvet's reserved bath with its own shower and adjoining dressing room is quiet, away from the hubbub. Here, she seeks refuge from her home which, despite her husband's efforts, is too high up on the mountain to have been installed with plumbing. She hangs her wet chador and clothing and, cold and shivering, waits for the bath attendant, a plump round-cheeked girl, to disinfect the bath—a messy affair of mixing in a bucket of hot water the purple crystals of permanganate to get rid of other people's dirt and contagious diseases. The attendant crinkles her nose at the stench and smiles at Velvet to assure her she doesn't mind performing the task. With a large plaid cloth, she dries her hands, which are stained red from the liquid she splashed on the tiled walls, floor, and platform. "May you soon be blessed with a son," she murmurs as she tiptoes out on calloused feet.

Velvet lies on the towel and shuts her eyes. Not even here is she allowed to escape the reality of a life in which she will forever remain childless. She traces the familiar outline of her body. What would it feel like if her stomach became round and full with Dr. Yaran's child? Her entire body flushes with pleasure, and she shuts her eyes to savor the warmth of the moment.

An emaciated *dalak* ushers in a gust of cold as she pokes her head in to announce her arrival.

A red and black tartan fabric tied around her skeletal waist, the *dalak* begins to knead her client's body, her pendulous breasts flapping to the rhythm of her lips. "Did you hear about Samar, Velvet *Khanom*?

The girl plucks her eyebrows, saw it with my own eyes, paints her cheeks like a *jendeh* whore. With those flat breasts like fried eggs, not a decent hair on her. Mark my words, *Khanom*, the girl's as good as pickled cucumbers, no boy worth his mother's milk will touch her. This other girl, Shohreh, you won't believe how her luck curdled overnight! All because her straw-brained mother let her wash in the bath pool right after a bunch of virile men bathed in there. And ta, ta tagh! She gets pregnant."

"What a blessing!" Velvet exclaims, shocking Fatemeh into temporary paralysis, which lasts all of five seconds.

"You want to hear about a real blessing, *Khanom*? They say Hitler is at our gates, at last, and he's on his way to behead all those filthy Jews who're multiplying like rats."

"Where did you hear this *mozakhraf* nonsense?"

"In the newspapers, *Khanom*. I read it with my own eyes."

Velvet's heart flaps like a restless bird in her chest. Could this be true? Could Hitler and his devastating army have reached Iran's borders?

"Congratulations, *Khanom*. You are pregnant. I've seen it myself; every pregnant woman goes pale in this heat. Don't move, I'll go bring you some rosewater sherbet."

"I'm fine, Fatemeh. Thank you. You can go now." The moment Fatemeh adjusts the sarong around her waist and waddles out, Velvet jumps up to her feet and makes her slippery way to the adjacent vestibule, pulls a towel off one of the hooks, dries herself, and dresses.

Hail as large as the pearls her husband gave her on their wedding night—Persian Gulf Pearls strung into a fancy rope too heavy to wear—assault her as she runs toward the waiting Lincoln. She hands the small suitcase to the chauffeur and steps into the car when a small girl grabs her skirt and pulls her out with the urgency particular to children.

"Forgive us, *Khanom*," Aunt Shamsi cries out, gasping for breath. "I don't know what got into this child, dragged me all over the place to trouble you like this." She attempts to pry Neda away from Velvet's skirt. "What kind of *bazi* game is this?"

"Not *bazi*, I go right now with nice *Khanom*." Neda squeezes closer to the nice *Khanom*'s pocket with Baba's glove full of smells of rain and hay and this morning's apple Rostam nearly munched off with Neda's fingers.

"What's your name, beautiful girl?" Velvet asks, charmed by the child's innocence.

"I've two names, *Khanom*. I'm my Baba's Sweetheart and everyone else's Neda. Oh! I forget. I'm also Aunt Shamsi's Little Leech."

"How lovely, you must be a very special girl to have three names. Why do you want to come with me, Neda? I don't think we've ever met. Have we?"

Neda's arms tighten around Velvet. "I don't know if we ever meet, *Khanom*, but I come with you right now."

Velvet's heart constricts with the realization that a child will never be safe in her sprawling mansion, which is in constant danger of turning into ash from a single spark from the refinery, from one of the many opium pipes and braziers, or from her husband's scorching rage. She hugs the child's bird-bones shoulders. "I'm sorry, Neda, I don't think it's a good idea to come with me. So, be a good girl and go home with your Madar."

"Not my Madar, *Khanom*. My Baba's Aunt Shamsi only."

"Only!" Shamsi grumbles under her breath, wriggling her numb toes in her wet slippers. "Her mother, bless her soul, passed away three years ago."

"I will drop the two of you home, Shamsi *Khanom*. Where do you live?"

"Thank you, very kind of you, *Khanom*." Aunt Shamsi gestures toward the road, where pedestrians are desperately waving for transportation. The problem is how to give directions without mentioning the Jewish Quarter, as the *Khanom* would certainly not want her fancy car around that area. "We live south of here, *Khanom*, close to the Circle of Cannons."

"Not far at all, is it?" Velvet asks the chauffeur. "We'll drop them off first."

Neda grabs Velvet around the waist and digs her face in her skirt. "No, no, *Khanom*, don't drop us...I don't want to drop. Please, please, take me to my Baba."

"I will, of course, don't worry," Velvet says. "The child wants to see her father, Shamsi *Khanom*. I am not in a hurry. I'll take you to him."

"No, *Khanom*, you really don't want to drive up that scary mountain to the governor general's mansion," Shamsi says.

"The governor general's mansion?" Velvet asks. "What does her father do there?"

"Wasting his time, if you ask me, since the cursed man has nothing better to do than make Soleiman's life miserable."

"Soleiman?" Velvet's heart gives a violent skip, then another, and another until she fears it will jump out of her chest. "Soleiman who, Shamsi *Khanom*?"

"Soleiman Yaran, of course, my nephew. He is a famous dentist."

Everything around Velvet begins to spin so fast, she has to lean on the surprised chauffeur until her world straightens up and she is able to breathe again. She nudges Neda out of the folds of her skirt and gazes at her with astonishment, notes the shiny dark hair, the strong chin, the wet lashes stuck together like tiny butterfly wings.

She takes the child's cold hand out of her skirt pocket, clasps it tight, and walks her to the Lincoln.

CHAPTER THIRTY-TWO

Soleiman leans over to take a better look in the dental mirror at the reflection of the governor's tooth who, having been moved into a throne-like chair, seems to be more in a coma than in deep sleep.

An abundance of problems confronted Soleiman in the past three years and most he managed to solve. But to pull a wisdom tooth compromised by a glass eye studded into the adjacent molar is an entirely different matter.

Soleiman feels the governor's forehead, checks his pulse, the rise and fall of his chest. The chronic abscess he has been draining for the last months has turned into an acute infection, and the man is burning with a high fever. There is no choice but to extract the tooth or the infection will enter the bloodstream and kill him. In no mood to wait for the governor to wake up from his narcotic trance to grant his permission, Soleiman decides to remove this last wisdom tooth and deal with the consequences when they arise.

"Don't, *Agha* doctor!" Tulip grabs Soleiman's hand. "I completely forgot. It's forbidden to pull teeth today. Can't have blood break His Excellency's fast. He'll become very angry when he wakes up!"

A sudden burst of hail pours out of the chimney as if hundreds of healthy teeth have been tossed around the silk carpet. Tulip looks out the tall window. "Never seen such violent hail. Velvet *Khanom* should be back by now."

Soleiman wonders whether Neda is kept warm and dry back home. She must be. Aunt Shamsi hates the wet weather and will not think of stepping out of the house, nor allow Neda to do so. "Where is Velvet *Khanom*?"

"She went to the *hammam*, and the streets are slippery now and cars can't be trusted and who knows if *Khanom*—"

A concerned glance at the crash of thunder beyond the windows, the pounding hail on the panes. "The chauffeur must know how to navigate slippery streets," Soleiman says, not confident at all. "Listen Tulip, whether he is fasting or not, the tooth has to be removed, or he might not survive. And he's smoking opium, after all, and this isn't much different. So, do something about the fireplace. It's hard to work in this heat. And come help me here. I need a witness in case the glass eye dislodges and rolls down the His Excellency's windpipes."

His eyes fixed on the downpour of hail that pummels the window, Tulip says, "I won't be any use to you, *Agha* doctor, so do what you have to."

Soleiman turns to the task at hand and begins to apply a thick layer of Ruby Magic to the governor's gums, taking his time to massage the area. Despite having done everything in his power to save the man's teeth, he will need dentures soon, which poses an added problem. With his porous gums, brittle bones, and jaws hopelessly out of alignment, a proper fit will be a challenge, and a poor one would wreak havoc, leading to sore spots, infections, and digestive complications that will forever send the man barking at his heels.

Soleiman clasps the molar with forceps. Slightly lifts the tooth from its socket. Rocks the molar back and forth with a slow steady pressure to break the ligaments, widen the supporting bone, and loosen the tooth, careful not to cause any fractures. He is attentive to any unusual sound, which proves difficult since the sky is at war with itself. It is crucial the root does not break off at the gum line, as the process of removing a root from the gums is nothing short of a major surgery, which could further spread the infection.

Winds have gathered force and bare branches claw like phantom hands at the rattling windowpanes, behind which bursts of lightning turn the pellets of hail into a shower of purple fireworks.

A gilt-turbaned, porcelain mullah with an enameled staff pops out of a clock on the mantelpiece. A bizarre box-like contraption brought in for the month of Ramadan to announce the hours of prayer and the beginning and breaking of the fast.

Soleiman continues to manipulate the wisdom tooth, which is proving surprisingly strong and unwilling to let go of the supporting bone. Another ten minutes of teasing until bone and ligament give and the tooth sways in its socket. He steadies the forceps in his grip. Gives a firm tug. And extracts the tooth.

He holds the forceps up to the dim light from the window. The wisdom tooth is out. But there is no sign of the root, which remains buried in the Land Eater's jawbone.

* * *

Soleiman considers leaving the root in place, rather than embarking on a painful oral surgery that will require a cut to pull the gum flap down in order to reach the root. To further complicate matters, the gums have receded, and the supporting bone deteriorated, so they will not heal properly, exposing the underlying bone to air and food, and causing bad breath and dry socket, a painful postoperative complication prevalent among opium addicts. The root, however, if left untouched, will damage the nerves, spread to the surrounding bone, and kill the governor.

Here is his chance to let fate take its course. Dismiss the Hippocratic oath he is bound to and turn his back on this godforsaken place. He studies the half-comatose Land Eater, whose face ignites with every flash of lightning through the glass window on which Tulip presses his palms as if to conjure his mistress. More than the Hippocratic oath and ethics bind him to this place. He will have to remove the root.

Until now, he had been depending on Ruby Magic to numb the pain as he worked on the governor general's ravaged teeth. But this painful operation will require Novocaine, which poses innumerable dangers to an opium addict—vomiting, tremors, swelling of the face or mouth, and even cardiac arrest.

He pries the governor's mouth open and is startled at the sight of the amulet which, having been dislodged from its shallow grave, glares at him like a blue-eyed fiend in the center of the governor's tongue. He lifts it with college tweezers and drops it in his own pocket.

"Allah be praised!" Tulip exclaims. "Here she is, at last." He takes a startled step forward to wipe the window and clear his field of vision.

Appearing indecently naked in her wet chador that has slipped off her head and twists about her like second skin, his mistress clasps the hand of a child and, with a sense of unquestionable ownership, struts ahead on the gravel path, lifts her eyes to the stunned eunuch behind the window, and shakes her hair free of the pellets of hail lodged there like jewels.

"For heaven's sake, Tulip, let me do my work." Soleiman holds the syringe of Novocaine up. "I'm about to inject your master with Novocaine."

The governor general stirs out of his opium stupor. Struggles to bring the world into focus. His mouth tastes like *zahreh mar* snake venom, his head is as bloated as cow tits, and his body feels as if it doesn't belong to him. He flexes his muscles, leans on one elbow, and prepares to drag himself up.

The doctor shifts the syringe away from the Land Eater's stare. "I had to extract your wisdom tooth, Your Excellency."

Tulip tears himself away from the window. "Don't be upset, Your Excellency, it was an emergency, and you were asleep, and, with your permission, I told the doctor to go ahead and pull the tooth."

"You did?" The Land Eater attempts to clear his fogged mind. "Another wisdom tooth, Tulip? Was it absolutely necessary?"

"Yes, it was," Soleiman says. "But we have another problem now. The tooth had a deep crack, so it broke during extraction. And the root remained in your gums. I'll have to remove it, or it will fester in your gums and make you very sick. I'll have to give you an injection first; it's necessary so you don't feel pain."

The governor's jaundiced eyes narrow suspiciously. "Is this another one of your conspiracies, Yaran?"

"I don't think so," Tulip interjects, "But let us defer to our Sufi poet, Oman Khayyam. He will tell us if we should allow Doctor Yaran to take the root out or not." With a great flourish of his silk clad arms, he lifts the gilt-edged book bound in Moroccan leather from the stand made of antlers. His emerald-ringed finger slips between the two pages he has dog-eared for occasions when a positive response is required from the poet.

"Let the book fall open as it may on my lap, Tulip. Perfect, my boy. Read this page to me."

The eunuch clears his throat and recites the poem in his melodious voice:

"Some yearn for the pleasures here below
Others yearn for the prophet's paradise to come;
Ah, take the cash and let the credit go/nor heed the rumble
of a distant drum."

"What do you say, Tulip? The message is clear, isn't it?"

"Clear as your conscience, Your Excellency, take the cash and let the credit go. It won't be wise to wait."

"Go ahead, Yaran! Do what you have to do. But not a drop of blood. I am fasting."

Tulip casts his eyes down. "A few drops of blood won't break your fast, Your Excellency. And, as you know, our religion exempts us from fasting if we're ill."

The clocks announce the approach of evening as Soleiman's hands race with urgent precision to spoon-feed a cocktail of painkillers to his patient after which he steps away from the man's field of vision, waits, until his grip relaxes on the arms of the chair, his eyes shut, and his mouth falls open.

Soleiman checks the vial of Novocaine and, finding no cloudiness, discoloration or crystalline particles, stabs the needle into the top plastic pad, pulls the plunger, and fills the tube. Drawing the needle out, he squeezes the plunger to release a few drops of the clear liquid, lifts the governor's upper lip and gives it a few fast shakes. He thrusts the needle in and injects the governor with Novocaine.

The door flies open, and Velvet and Neda charge into the room with Aunt Shamsi lumbering behind like a beast of burden. With the skies hollering outside and the chimney rattling inside, and the Land Eater sprawled like a dead man in a giant chair, Aunt Shamsi is certain the wrath of God has descended upon them all. "Tof, tof, tof." She spits behind her shoulder, grabbing a fistful of salt from her pocket and tossing it around.

Soleiman drops the empty syringe of Novocaine, sprints forward, and lifts Neda in his arms. "My daughter," he explains to the bewildered Tulip, "and my aunt. What are you doing here?"

"I come to save you from That-Cursed-Land-Eater man," Neda says, clinging to him.

Velvet reaches out wet, slightly trembling hands toward the doctor.

Neda in one arm, he draws Velvet close and holds her tight against him as if this is the most natural thing to do.

Velvet snuggles against Soleiman, not caring if her husband opens his eyes and sees her tangled with the doctor and his child, sees her all bare-wrists and bare-ankles and bare-faced.

Lightning casts an eerie shade across the sky. The rattle of hail echoes in the smokestack and a sudden rush clatters down the chimney, skipping and rolling toward them like luminous pearls.

Neda is shaking in Soleiman's arms. Aunt Shamsi is in a state of panic and incapable of a single coherent word and, any moment now, the governor general will wake up.

Soleiman breaks his hold on Velvet and steps back. He peels Neda off and puts her down. "Don't worry about me, Sweetheart. You'll have to go home now."

Neda grabs her Baba's scared legs that want to run away from That-Cursed-Land-Eater man snoring so close, his stinky breath make Neda want to vomit again. She lets go of her Baba's leg and shoots faster than a rabid dog toward the bad man and digs her teeth into his thigh.

Aunt Shamsi takes one look at the governor general and flees out the door as fast as her tired legs allow.

Soleiman sprints to Neda's rescue and lifts her up in his arms.

The governor staggers out of his seat. Eyes delirious, he shakes himself like a wild animal startled out of hibernation and stumbles toward Velvet, who grabs Neda and escapes.

The instant Velvet hurries out, Soleiman rushes toward the governor, who is struggling for breath, his bloodshot eyes unhinged in their sockets. A dry rasp springs out of his throat, and he drops flat on his back.

Soleiman examines the man's pulse. His heartbeat is anemic and will not last long. He is experiencing a seizure. A reaction to Novocaine.

He wipes mucous off the governor's face, fills his own lungs with air, and begins to administer mouth-to-nostril resuscitation.

* * *

The governor's gaze is fixed on the doctor in an attempt to make sense of last hour's events which, as hard as he tries, refuse to solidify in his brain. "Show me the root, Yaran!"

"It's not out, Your Excellency. There was a small complication, and my work was interrupted. But you're ready now, as I am."

"All these obstacles, Yaran, must be a sign not to spill blood on *Ashura*. Leave the root alone where it belongs."

"If that's your wish. But I'm obliged to warn you that your body will fight a broken root that doesn't belong in your gums, causing serious complications, even septicemia."

"There you go again," the governor general barks. "With your senseless words."

"Septicemia happens when your blood becomes dirty with bacteria. It's dangerous, Your Excellency, and if left untreated it will lead to death." He pauses. Hail has given way to rain, and a wave of oppressive humidity makes its way through the window. A piercing neigh can be heard outside, and he wonders whether Rostam, too, is aware of Neda's presence in this fort-like hell. Soleiman collects his dental tools. "Farewell, Your Excellency."

Pale, the turban he hurriedly adjusted threatening to unwind again, Tulip blocks Soleiman's exit. "Please, *Agha* doctor, don't go before we thank you for blowing life back into His Excellency's lifeless body. You don't remember, Your Excellency, but you couldn't breathe anymore, and, Allah forbid, you were about to die, when Doctor Yaran blew breath into your nose and, thanks to all the imams, you are here now."

His every cell revolting, the governor rubs his nose to erase the filthy imprint of the Jew's mouth. He slides the brazier closer, fans the coals until they crackle and rage, then takes his time to pack the pipe with glowing embers. Allah had lent an ear to his pleas, at last, and was ready to summon him to His side. Yet. The smug Jew had to interfere and bring him back to this miserable life of counting every second, over and over again.

He raises his arm and sends the pipe flying toward the doctor.

Fire sparks and ash land on the carpet at Soleiman's feet. He backs toward the door. "It's impossible to work in this environment. I'll have to excuse myself."

Tulip rushes toward the governor, who has abandoned the divan and is charging toward the doctor. A sweep of the governor's arm across the eunuch's chest propels him backward with such force, he lands on the glowing embers. The acrid stench of burnt wool and opium fills the room.

The governor stomps on the hot spots. Grabs Tulip and drags him to safety. Falls on his knees and strokes Tulip's cheeks. "Didn't intend to, my boy! I'm not myself these days. All this mourning."

"We are all mourning, Your Excellency. Please lean on me." Tulip coaxes his master back to the divan, lifts the pipe to his lips. "A puff, deeper, do it for me, thank you, mourning won't bring our imam back. Lie down now, careful." He stacks pillows behind the governor, adds a healthy dose of opium to the pipe, and cajoles him to draw deeper.

"May the doctor take out the root? Please say, yes, I'll die if a hair falls off your head."

"Yaran!" The governor's hand creeps toward the desk in search of the pen he clutches like a dagger. "Hand me the root in one piece. Or you'll suffer such hell and fire, you'll curse the day you were born."

CHAPTER THIRTY-THREE

Disheveled, shadows under his eyes, Soleiman follows Tulip across the dark-as-catacomb hallways. The consequence of visiting the governor's wife in her private quarters is not lost on him, but Tulip has made it clear Neda will not leave unless he comes to fetch her.

The operation on the governor general was successful. Soleiman went to work before the anesthetic effect of the Novocaine injection had worn off, and the governor, under the influence of opium and painkillers, did not require another Novocaine injection.

But despite his best efforts a small fragment of the root broke. Thinking fast, he cleaned and smoothed the broken edges and handed it to Tulip, who placed it on a silk cushion inside an enamel box and carried it to the governor with absurd pomp and ceremony. Having put the governor's mind at ease, they left him in his quarters with a smoking opium pipe and a contingent of maids and servants, who transported freshly fired braziers, brass trays of saffron rice, lamb, eggplant stew, roasted sheep tongue, raisins, and dates for him to break his fast.

The clocks announce ten, two hours past Neda's bedtime. Soleiman stuffs his hands in his pocket and walks faster. His touch grazes the amulet forgotten at the bottom of his pocket and, having suffered his fair share of troubles for a day, hands it to Tulip to deal with as he sees fit.

They enter another wing of the mansion strewn with brighter-colored Isfahan and Kashan carpets, vases bursting with hothouse roses, a dog-eared poetry book on a chair, china teacups left here and there. A yellow, gossamer scarf scatters her addictive scent.

They descend two steps into a sunken courtyard sprawled with dormant rosebushes prepared for winter, their bare branches like so many praying hands. Massive guards with waxed mustaches are stationed at an arched portal. They salute the eunuch but remain at their posts, blocking the entrance.

"It is necessary!" Tulip commands. "Khanom is in need of medical attention."

The room is warm with the scent of rice and herbs and freshly baked bread. Colorful shawls are thrown over ottomans and pillows. Amber candle flames are reflected on the surface of side tables and on sheer drapes. Antique vases of alabaster, opal, and gilded glass overflow with motley of hothouse roses. Books of poetry are stacked on both sides of a large gilt-framed mirror.

Neda, flanked by Velvet and Aunt Shamsi, is seated at a *korsi* low table, under which a brazier full of hot coals keeps the room warm.

At the sight of his daughter, happy and content as never before, Ruby's parting words acquire a fresh urgency. Has he been an absent, even selfish father, paid no heed to Ruby's pleas that Neda needs a mother? Jacob might be right, after all, he has been too immersed in his own scientific world, rigid and rejecting of every suggestion. Neda's attachment to her dolls, her imaginary friend in the mushroom patch, her concern for his happiness, and, most important, the problem with her eyes might stem from the absence of a mother in her life.

"You're here, at last." Aunt Shamsi bundles a bunch of mint in a piece of bread and squeezes it into her mouth, rises from the *korsi*, and shakes breadcrumbs off her skirt. "I thought this black day would never end."

Velvet kisses Neda's tousled curls. "Neda has been waiting for you, Doctor Yaran. Will you break bread with us?"

"Please, Baba, break bread with us. Okay?"

"*Salaam*, Sweetheart. We'll have to leave, I'm afraid, it's way past your bedtime. Thank Velvet *Khanom* for taking such good care of you and off we go."

"No, Baba, I don't go off now because I don't tell Velvet *Khanom* all of the everything I want to tell her."

"All right then, I'll wait until you tell her everything you want to tell her," Soleiman says, welcoming the pleasant warmth of Velvet's quarters. Night has fallen on this day of mourning, and the pelting of rain and hail has stopped, leaving streaks of running tears outside the windowpanes. In the absence of chimes, gongs, whirrs, and clangs of clocks, he takes his first deep breath of the day. "Go ahead, Sweetheart, tell Velvet *Khanom* what you want to tell her."

"I want to tell I'm a big girl, *Khanom*, and I talk like big people. My horse's name is Rostam with iron shoes and swishing tail and big-carrot-munching teeth that don't bite my fingers when he opens his mouth big for me to feel his slippery teeth. I've Mademoiselle cat with sharp nails and always-hungry stomach, not really mine but maybe she think she's mine. My Baba know how to fix everything in the world but don't know to fix his not being happy."

Velvet lowers Neda's fists from her eyes. "Don't be sad, darling. Maybe we can find a way to make your Baba happy."

Neda slides her hand in Velvet *Khanom*'s pocket and strokes Baba's glove with Velvet *Khanom*'s liking already stuck to it. "Please, *Khanom*, please become my alive Madar and make Baba very happy."

"What in *Jahannam* hell are you blabbering about, you impossible leech!" Aunt Shamsi shouts. "Apologize to *Khanom* and let us go."

"It's fine, Shamsi *Khanom*, the child wants a mother," Velvet says softly.

Neda squeezes her eyes tight, puts her head in Velvet *Khanom's* lap, and pretends to sleep, so her Baba will sit close to Velvet *Khanom* and put tiny pieces of bread with cheese one by one in Velvet *Khanom's* mouth.

"Neda's hungry," Velvet says, "You must be, as well, Doctor Yaran."

A cautionary shake of Tulip's head. "Pardon me, Velvet *Khanom*. His Excellency is breaking his fast. He might need you."

"Come, Doctor Yaran, the stew is delicious," Velvet insists, ignoring Tulip's warning.

Heart thumping in his ears, Soleiman tugs at the chain looped across his vest, pulls out his pocket watch, checks the time as if it will determine his decision. Nothing will shed off the events of the day better and heal his tired bones faster than sharing a meal with Velvet and his daughter in this warm atmosphere. Hunger suddenly claws at him, and he realizes he has had nothing to eat the entire day. He glances at the inviting spread on the *korsi* table—*dolmeh* stuffed with raisins and dried fruit, *fesenjan* pomegranate and ground walnut stew, *shirin* polo fragrant with slivers of orange peel and pistachio.

There is stillness in the air. The scent of roses, candle, wax, and expectation of what might come and what might not.

It will be foolish of him to test his luck, when he has already been allocated a larger dose of luck than he has a right to in one day. "Thank you for your gracious invitation, Velvet *Khanom*. Hopefully at another time and place."

"Listen to your Baba, dear girl." Tulip pats Neda on the shoulder. "It's been a long day, and he's tired. Time to go home."

"Come, Sweetheart, give Velvet *Khanom* a big hug for me."

Neda reaches into the folds of Velvet's skirt. She raises her arm high above her head and waves her father's glove like a victory banner.

Aunt Shamsi slaps her mouth shut with her palm before a storm of obscenities blast out.

The rings around Velvet's silver irises deepen with defiance, belying the glistening tear at the corner of her eye, which she dashes away with the back of a hand.

Soleiman takes the glove from his daughter, riffles through his pockets in search of the mate, flattens and folds the pair into each other and hugs them like one of her poems between his palms.

He bows low and hands Velvet both gloves. "To keep you warm, my lady."

CHAPTER THIRTY-FOUR

"I couldn't sleep all night." Aunt Shamsi scours a pot in the sink as if she is skinning the head of the governor general. Not since her daughter's death and her husband's subsequent desertion has she been faced with a catastrophe of such unimaginable magnitude. "I rushed out this morning to pay Yaghoobi the Chicken Boy to sacrifice a rooster and smear its blood across the threshold to stop this shame in its tracks."

"You did what!" Soleiman stabs his fork into a piece of eggplant and pushes his dinner plate aside. "Where was Neda when you did this crazy thing?"

"Busy with that mysterious friend of hers. And that should be the least of your worries." Aunt Shamsi wipes her hands on her oil-stained apron, removes and shakes it with a couple of noisy flaps, folds it into a neat square, and tucks it under her arm. "Don't ask me how Neda knew, but you sure needed saving yesterday."

He wipes his mouth with his napkin. Pushes his chair away from the table and stands. "Please, Aunt Shamsi, stop meddling in my private affairs."

"I will meddle, I certainly will. What are you thinking, letting that woman charm her way into your heart? A Muslim married woman! That Cursed-Land-Eater's wife! Don't you get all red in the face and glare at me as if I'm spitting blasphemy. How can you betray your daughter, your family, and every single Jew who made you what you are? It's gone to your head, Soleiman. But to all those goyim, you're still a lice-infested Jew from the bottom of the garbage pit."

"Thank you for reminding me, Aunt Shamsi. Is that all?"

"No! And I won't be dismissed like this. I'm your second mother, Soleiman, nursed you when your mother's breasts went dry on you. So, I've a right to know what's going on between you two and why your glove ended up in that woman's pocket."

"My glove, Aunt Shamsi, ended in Velvet *Khanom*'s pocket because I dropped it and she must have found it. Now put this subject to rest."

"Soleiman!" Aunt Shamsi calls after his retreating steps. "Wait a minute…please. Just a minute."

He turns around. Stops at the threshold to the kitchen. "I'm ending this conversation, Aunt Shamsi. You will not run my life."

"I don't want to run your life, Soleiman, I promise. It's just that I'm worried about Neda. The child is lonely and becoming angrier with every passing day. I'm not sure what's happening to her, but I've never seen a child have so many accidents, hurt herself so many times. I'm getting old and tired and can't be looking after her. She needs a young mother to take care of her. Think about her."

"Of course, I think about her," he snaps. "The rest is not your business."

Aunt Shamsi drops a plate on a stack of dinner plates in the sink. The crash of china reverberates across the kitchen. "It is my business, Soleiman, mine and Neda's and every other Jew, whose head will roll unless you come to your senses! Listen to me, son, I've been looking around. I finally found you the right wife. And the perfect mother for your daughter."

"Don't bother, Aunt Shamsi. I am not interested!"

"You will be when you hear what Neda said last night that stabbed me like daggers in my heart. She said no one loves her. She said her only friend in the entire world is that I-don't-know-what-to-call-it-friend in the mushrooms. She said she wants to go to her mother."

Soleiman groans through clenched teeth. "Why would she say such a thing?"

"You tell me, Soleiman, you're the one with fancy diplomas! What I know is that growing up motherless can break a child's heart and make her imagine terrible things."

A bitter surge of guilt. What has become of the young man who returned from Paris with idealistic dreams of improving his people's lot? The man who promised Ruby to take good care of her daughter. He should have broken away from Velvet before she became so inescapably part of him, before it became so impossibly difficult to extricate himself from her gravitational pull. "All right, Aunt Shamsi. Who is this 'right' wife for me?"

Aunt Shamsi rummages in one of the kitchen cabinets and pulls out two kebab skewers, twists her hair into a tight coil, and stabs in the metal skewers. "Daughter of Moshe Ben Avram and Talieh Bat Azizolah. Most reputable family with a house at the end of Grocery Street. I tell you, Soleiman, a palace is a hovel in comparison."

"I know Moshe Ben Avram, Aunt Shamsi. How old is his daughter?"

"Eighteen but doesn't look a day older than sixteen, wonderful cook too. She has a ninth-grade certificate, but no school will teach the kind of maturity this girl has. Go get your coat. We are going *khastegari.*"

"Now? What's the great hurry? Give them prior notice."

"They've been notified and waiting!" The lines around Aunt Shamsi's mouth deepen with determination. "Don't you give me that look again. I had to take matters into my own hands or sit back and watch you destroy our lives."

Aunt Shamsi marches out of the kitchen and straight into the garden with its high walls topped with cut-glass, grabs Neda by the hand, brushes dirt, leaves, and mushrooms off her skirt, and smoothens her eyebrows with saliva. Against Soleiman's complaints that it is inappropriate for the child to accompany them on such a visit, she lumbers out of the gate, holding her bewildered charge firmly by the hand. They make a sharp turn to the left and march past the empty lot with the old willow and its weeping trunk, the branches stripped of sacrificial leaves for Neda's potion.

Neda stops in front of Pary's white door, and no matter how hard Aunt Shamsi pulls, she will not budge.

The slap and pat of sweating palms on the door have raised the sweet smell of mulberry wood mixed with the sticky smell of sheep fat Neda steals from the kitchen to rub on the door when Aunt Shamsi naps in the afternoons. Neda has not seen the door cry, but if the Quarter Fool says the tears helped him cry his pain out at the approach of sunset, then Neda will bide her time until the door will cry for her, too, and her own dry, itching eyes will learn to make beautiful, fat tears.

The door turns on its heavy hinges and Mademoiselle shoots out, mewing gleefully and, behind her, is Pary, holding up a chocolate cookie. "Mademoiselle always knows when you're here, darling. Here, I've baked your favorite cookie. Where are you going?"

"Somewhere very, very bad," Neda replies.

"With Baba? Then it must be somewhere nice, I'm sure."

"We're on our way to *Agha* Moshe Ben Avram." Soleiman has an urge to spill out his frustration. "Aunt Shamsi says she found the 'right wife' for me."

Pary tilts her head to the side and, half a smile at the corner of her mouth, regards him with a mixture of compassion and understanding, then steps forward and adjusts his cravat. "Good luck, Doctor Yaran. Whoever *you* choose will be a lucky woman." That self-effacing gesture of the back of her hand across her face before she retraces her steps and shuts the door behind her.

"Send the cat back to the same *Jahannam* it came from," Aunt Shamsi orders. "I'm not going to Moshe Ben Avram with a black cat in tow."

"Let her bring the cat," Soleiman says.

Feet planted apart; Aunt Shamsi folds her arms across her chest. "No! The cat is not coming! I won't have the entire Quarter snicker and spit behind our backs."

"Then, we will do this another day," he exclaims. "Neda will stay with Baba Eleazar, and we won't have to worry about the cat."

"Over my dead body!" Aunt Shamsi exclaims, "Come, Neda. Bring the cursed cat."

The mustard-colored brick house at the end of Grocery Street, although far from a palace, is larger than most houses in the Jewish Quarter. Pots of carnation line the windowpanes and two balconies. At the door, three shabby women are begging for food and shelter, a common sight after thousands of Polish refugees were cast upon the Caspian shores. Moshe Ben Avram, who cannot in good conscience turn any Jew away empty handed, has sent his housekeeper out with bundles of clothing and earthenware containers of food.

"May they bury Hitler alive," Aunt Shamsi sputters. "Poor people, they're dying like DDT-sprayed flies. The coffin maker on Electricity Street became a trillionaire, the louse."

Moshe Ben Avram steps outside to welcome his guests. He is round-faced and ruddy-cheeked, his nose thrice flattened by Muslim fists, which has not deterred him from wearing a brand-new hat, which he respectfully removes.

Soleiman is fond of Moshe Ben Avram, who can be seen strutting around the Jewish Quarter on Rosh Hashanah with a new hat perched on his head in defiance of a fatwa forbidding Jews to wear new hats. Throughout the years, he has donated carpets and candelabras to the seven synagogues, has overseen the construction of a two-room house for the Quarter Fool, and has helped establish the Alliance School. Known as Father of the Bride, he provides a dowry to any bride whose family is unable to do so.

Now, Moshe Ben Avram, who normally gives without any expectation of return, prays with all his might that his charitable contributions will be rewarded, and Soleiman, whom he is leading into his living room, will find his daughter pleasing.

"Good evening." Soleiman bows his head to Talieh *Khanom*, who appears decidedly lost in her own home, which Aunt Shamsi appropriates, dropping herself in an armchair at the head of the room and holding Neda and the cat hostage in her lap.

"*Salaam*, son," Eleazar the Redhead who, dressed in his best Shabbat suit, has been waiting impatiently, tips his felt hat at Soleiman, and taps on the sofa for Soleiman to join him.

This morning, his sister burst into his house to tell him about last night, about the glove, about Soleiman and the Land Eater's wife. No details were left behind until, in his rage and disbelief, Eleazar began to pound on the brewing stills and then, in case Moshe Ben Avram needed extra coaxing to open his house on such short notice, he quickly dressed in his best outfit and accompanied Shamsi to Moshe Ben Avram.

For once in his life, Eleazar the Redhead decided to ignore all show of civility and told Moshe Ben Avram that if he were to go back home, he might be detained by a client or two and might not be able to return in the afternoon when Soleiman came. And Moshe Ben Avram, the gentleman he was, begged Eleazar to feel at home, served him another cup of tea, this one with a few drops of rosewater, and informed his wife they had a guest for lunch.

"What are you doing here?" Soleiman whispers the moment he sits next to his father.

"Isn't it clear, son? What were you thinking? You better fix this disgrace. Or the blood of your people will be on your conscience." He retrieves his shechita knife from his coat pocket, selects cucumbers from a serving dish in the center of the coffee table, arranges them on a plate, and begins to peel them with the same quick and precise movements he performs the kosher beheading of chickens.

The clang and clatter of pots and glasses in the kitchen. High heels click in the corridor. Aunt Shamsi tightens her grip around Neda and Mademoiselle. The cat yowls. All eyes turn to the entrance.

A tall, long-lashed girl, with tight brown curls perfumed with Moroccan oil, and the serious expression of a mature child, enters the living room. Her eyes are pinned to the silver tray she carries, which is heavy with six teacups and silver containers heaped with sugar cubes and dates. It is customary to serve a prospective suitor tea, without spilling a drop, but her hands slightly shake, and the tray is wet with tea.

"Let me help." Soleiman jumps to his feet and relieves her of the tray. "Would you like a cup?"

She looks at the tray Soleiman wipes dry with his handkerchief, lets out a grateful breath, takes one of the teacups, and settles between her parents.

"I go to Baba," Neda whispers to Aunt Shamsi.

"If you want a nice Madar for yourself, you better stay where you are and smile."

Neda sucks her nostrils tight. This Madar person with her poofy blouse and poofy skirt, smells like sour lemons and dead flowers, not like Velvet *Khanom*'s tasty smells of warmed sugar and roses.

Soleiman, having served everyone, lowers himself on the sofa next to his father and waits, as he knows he will have to, for his aunt and father to perform the perfunctory niceties, before they present the main subject, which is unnecessary, since it is amply clear why they've all gathered here.

Aunt Shamsi clears her throat. "First and foremost, with the permission of *Parvardehgareh bakhshandeh* the gracious Lord. And second with the permission of my dear brother. We are here, *Agha* Moshe and Talieh *Khanom*, to ask for the hand of your daughter, Farideh, in marriage to Soleiman, son of Eleazar."

Eleazar the Redhead removes a small satin box from his pocket and puts it on the etched brass coffee table, next to a bowl filled with *noghle* wedding candies. He smiles at his son, clasps his knee a bit too tightly. "As the eldest representative of the Yaran family, I wish to extend my heartfelt respect to you, Farideh *Khanom*, and welcome you with open arms into our family."

Aunt Shamsi releases her captives, adjusts the skewers sticking out of her hair like metal horns, and walks around the room offering everyone wedding candies.

Neda creeps up to her father's lap, presses both hands on the sides of his face, and whispers in his ear that if he won't take her right now to Velvet *Khanom*, she will scream so loud, he'll have to give her a good old spanking on her no good *koon*.

He wraps an arm around her. "Shh, Sweetheart, not now."

Neda snatches the small satin box from the coffee table and, to the cat's purrs of approval, drops it in her pocket, jumps out of her father's lap, and, her ears trained on her grandfather's disapproving grunt, Aunt Shamsi's rebelling stomach, and Farideh's quick breathing, she grabs the cat and runs out of the room.

Farideh's eyes dart up toward Soleiman, who comes to stand in front of her. He lifts her hand from her lap and cups it between his two hands. "I am twenty-eight-years-old, Farideh *Khanom*, too old for a lovely young lady like you, who has a bright future ahead of her. You deserve a fresh start, not a man who was married once and has a daughter to raise. I've no doubt one day soon, you'll find the right man who will offer you everything you deserve."

CHAPTER THIRTY-FIVE

1944

The Tehran Conference is being hailed as a success. Britain and America, having honored Stalin's request to invade France, have appointed General Dwight Eisenhower and Field Marshal Montgomery as Allied commanders. America has been victorious in the Pacific. Paris is no longer under siege, and Italy has surrendered.

The hysterical führer, despite having suffered multiple devastating defeats, continues to push his demoralized people to fight the military machine of the Allies, which grinds ahead with no other concern, than the destruction of the Third Reich.

The prime minister, Mohammad Sa'ed, has vetoed Russia's petition for more oil concession, and Dr. Mohammad Mosaddeq, the elected deputy of the *Majles*, has introduced a law, prohibiting oil discounts, mining concessions, or any other negotiations with Russia and America, unless the Allies honor their earlier agreement to evacuate their troops from Iran. Nonetheless, supporters of the Red Army have successfully acquired nine seats in the *Majles* Parliament and, having changed Iran's political landscape, sees no reason to evacuate. And, despite large demonstrations around the country, Soviet tanks and troops are a constant presence in the streets.

On this, his fourth visit with the Queen, Soleiman is greeted in a different wing of the palace, a magnificent room with a French tapestry on the wall, antique urns, and gleaming commodes awash in sunlight pouring in from floor to ceiling windows, flanked by velvet drapes a shade greener than the gardens they frame. There is no sign of the crows in the gardens, nor of the pellet-gun wielding guard. Soleiman hopes that the despised birds have not been poisoned.

Queen Fawzia is seated on a sofa with her dog in her lap. Her hair is pulled away from her face with two pearl hairpins. A pearl brooch is attached to the collar of her black, short-sleeved dress. She gestures to the sofa opposite the coffee table, which is laden with a variety of sweetmeat—saffron rice pudding, rosewater almond pastries, and cardamom pistachio puffs—and, his back never turned to her, he takes his seat.

The Queen lifts the dog off her lap and places it on the sofa next to her. It attempts to scramble back, but she utters an order in Arabic and the dog rests its head on its paws and stares at the doctor as if he is to blame for the dog's banishment from the Queen's person.

The Queen adjusts the silk hem of her skirt above her knees and crosses her ankles. She favors sandals, Soleiman notes, these with golden straps revealing her red toenails. Velvet, too, wore nail polish on her toes the night he fetched Neda from her private quarters. Barefooted and trailing the perfume of roses, she escorted him and Neda to the door, her scent stalking him for many nights as he lay awake in bed.

The Queen leans forward, her earnest face reflected on the shiny surface of the coffee table. For long, awkward minutes, she holds him captive in her intense gaze. "We are both outsiders, Doctor Yaran," she says, at last. "Yes?"

He analyzes the Queen's unexpected question as he would an aching tooth. Is she expressing a fact or asking a question? "How so, Your Majesty?"

"I am a Sunni Egyptian in a Shiite country, and you, Doctor Yaran, are a Jew among Muslims. As such, we sometimes face the same problems."

He bows his head in agreement. *How*, he wonders, *could the problems of a dentist from the Jewish Quarter be similar to the problems the Queen of Iran has?*

"What I will tell you next, Doctor Yaran, will be kept confidential. I have your promise. Yes?"

"Always, Your Majesty." His hand rests on his heart to demonstrate his loyalty.

As if the doctor has passed her test, a veil lifts from the Queen's eyes, and her gaze warms with familiarity.

He attempts to keep his expression neutral, suppress the creeping joy. The Queen has decided to order the issue of visas. And, understandably, she does not want anyone to know she is willing to support a group of Jewish immigrants.

"Write a prescription, Doctor Yaran. A dental problem that must be addressed immediately or it will cause great damage. Assert the importance of my traveling abroad to seek medical care. Do you understand?"

His throat full of quarreling, he keeps silent, until the Queen raises an eyebrow and scrutinizes him with narrowed eyes, and he coughs into his clenched hand and finds his voice. "Of course, Your Majesty, you are in great pain."

"It is a serious problem," the Queen adds.

"Quite serious. One that will require specialized oral surgery, which cannot be done here. It has to be taken care of or the infection will spread and threaten Your Majesty's health."

He expresses this with such earnest conviction the Queen touches her cheek as if she is indeed in pain. Soleiman removes his prescription pad from his case and composes a detailed note:

> *Her Majesty is suffering from periodontal gum disease, which has developed into an infection. Such local infections, if not addressed immediately, will lead to subsequent infections in other parts of the body, due either to the spread of the infectious agent itself or to toxins*

produced from it. An extraction is necessary, which could be done here, but Her Majesty will require endosseous implantation, a relatively new procedure in which no Iranian dentist is trained. Absent proper treatment, Her Majesty will lose her oral facility.

The Queen reads the note with great care, folds, and tucks it under a plate of sweets on the coffee table. She rewards him with a conspiratorial smile—a different smile than the one she shows to the rest of the world. Queen Fawzia Pahlavi trusted him with a personal request, and he has emerged more favorably in her eyes. He, too, will not leave empty handed. He will remind the Queen of the favor she owes him. But she rises to her feet and offers her hand for a kiss. He gathers the courage to touch his lips to the back of her hand, then lifts his head and looks straight into the Queen's inquisitive eyes. "With your permission, Your Majesty. May I revisit the matter of the—"

The Queen lifts a forefinger. "No need, Doctor Yaran. I did not forget the orphans. A military plane is being readied to transport one-hundred-and-fifteen of your children to Palestine. I hope you are pleased."

There is an instant of such relief and joy, the only thing Soleiman hears is one-hundred-and-fifteen children, until the Queen reminds him that there must be much work of planning the journey, and he finds his voice again and says, "I am deeply grateful to you, Your Majesty. Your generosity will not be forgotten."

"Thank you, Doctor Yaran, and farewell. I will be going back home, as well."

"Farewell, Your Majesty, and *bon courage*." Soleiman follows the Queen's retreating back, certain he will not see her again.

CHAPTER THIRTY-SIX

Jacob studies Soleiman's transformed living room, the air heavy with the scent of herbs, oils, and books. A droning ceiling fan casts shadow on everything. Books about mushrooms and herbs and potions are stacked under an open window facing the small garden. Neatly labeled mason jars crowd a shelf on one wall, miniature wood dolls line another shelf. Two red sofas face one another across a coffee table cluttered with glass apothecary bottles, small bowls of mushrooms, tinctures, herbs, leaves, oils, pieces of bark, and flowers. Willow branches in a copper kettle next to a small mortar and pestle. Dental tools that outlasted their use are spread on a side table next to a threadbare armchair, a half-full box of sesame brittle at the foot of another armchair. Boxes filled with toys give the room a chaotic warmth.

He pulls a pack of cigarettes from his shirt pocket, shoves it back in his pocket. His head jerks toward the living room. "Neda's winter workshop?"

"Yes," Soleiman replies, "She's on a mission to finish her Baba Magic brew. But this is not why I wanted to see you. I have good news, Jacob, far better than we hoped for." He gives Jacob's back an affectionate slap. "The Queen has arranged for a military plane to take one-hundred-and-fifteen of your children to Palestine."

"One-hundred-and-fifteen!" Jacob holds Soleiman by the shoulders, draws him into his strong embrace, releases him, and studies him with a wide smile. "You did it, my friend! Thank you. One-hundred-and-fifteen, you said. Yes?"

"Well, one-hundred-and-thirteen to be exact. I will take Neda to Palestine with the children. There are better doctors there and the sooner she gets help the better."

Jacob's brows shoot up. He lights a cigarette, blows out the smoke through his nostrils. "Yes, my friend, Neda needs help. But it is not the help you're thinking of. How many medical doctors have you already seen?"

"Far too many," Soleiman replies with faint detachment.

"How many more should tell you nothing is wrong with her eyes?" His voice up a syllable, Jacob attempts to grab Soleiman's lukewarm interest. "Open your eyes, Soleiman. I am talking to you both as a friend and a psychoanalyst. I've worked with children long enough to recognize the signs of trauma. Remember Anna and Ludwig? You saw them playing in my home. Anna's fingers went numb when she was separated from her parents. And Ludwig stopped talking when he was deported. Such symptoms, although uncommon, can occur when children experience events that are too painful for their young minds to bear. I've been having great success in accessing a child's inner world with the use of play in therapy. It's miraculous, the way we can uncover a child's traumatic feelings during play, and how the healing process can begin soon after."

A bitter smile darkens Soleiman's unshaved face. "Neda is not traumatized. She never experienced the horrors your orphans experienced."

A muscle in Jacob's cheek flutters. "Neda lost her mother at birth. Enough of a shock to trigger a series of subconscious reactions that could shut down one organ or another."

Soleiman studies Jacob with a measure of surprise and interest. "Neda has never known her mother."

"This might seem unbelievable to you, Soleiman. But we now know that a newborn's memory exists in the body, in the cells. That memory can retain early impressions of events outside of consciousness. A difficult birth. A mother's death. A challenging upbringing. These can send messages to the mind to shut down an otherwise healthy organ. A self-inflicted punishment, if you will."

The hand Soleiman clutches around his pocket watch is about to break, and he thinks his heart will too. "Neda has a father. She has Aunt Shamsi. She is taken good care of, always."

"Not always, my friend. You've been too immersed in your own problems. And Neda notices."

Beyond the garden walls, the fruit and vegetable seller is cursing his stubborn mule. Mademoiselle meows to be let into the garden. Aunt Shamsi's heavy-footed thumping across the hallway, the creak of an opening door.

Deep in thought, Soleiman walks past the floor lamp. He bends to grab a piece of sesame brittle from the box at the foot of the armchair, then stations himself at the open window where he gazes at Neda who is inspecting a small cluster of newly sprouted mushrooms.

She digs one of the mushrooms from the root and holds it up to the sunlight, turns it around for her father to see. "Look Baba! Mushrooms Friend send this for your Baba Magic."

Soleiman studies the mushroom with great interest, which is replaced with concern. In his daughter's hand is a single black-capped mushroom, dotted with red, and slightly glowing, which he does not recognize. Might a poisonous spore have found its way into the mushrooms? "Sweetheart! Do not eat it. I'll have to test it first."

"Make sure you don't eat it either," Jacob says as he joins Soleiman at the window, adjusts his perfectly folded pocket square, takes out a cigarette, and fixes it at the corner of his mouth. He puts his hand on Soleiman's arm to silence him as he turns his attention to Neda, who is having an earnest discussion with her imaginary friend in the mushrooms. "Neda! Who are you talking to out there?"

"Mushrooms Friend!" Neda calls back. "She's nosey like you, liking to hear little secrets. Aunt Shamsi says I'm nosey, too, and should stop with too much questions or my ears will grow longer than a donkey's. Aunt Shamsi says I won't be nosey anymore if I pee pee on my hands."

Jacob's hearty laughter travels out the window and bounces around the garden. "Of all the strange things I've heard this one's the strangest. Your Aunt Shamsi is very funny. But don't you pay much attention to the silly things she says."

Aunt Shamsi materializes in front of them with a foul-smelling spray pump she aims at Jacob. "I am saying silly things? Another word out of your mouth and I'll spray you out of our lives!"

"Please, Aunt Shamsi, *s'il te plaît!*" Jacob leans out the window and shoves the pump away from his face, sending Aunt Shamsi and her weapon toward Mademoiselle, who, having squeezed herself into the garden through the gate, is accosted by furious spurts of vinegar and pepper.

"Is this what you want for your daughter?" Jacob asks Soleiman. "Three years is a long time for her to live with someone like Aunt Shamsi. It is not normal for a child's sense of smell to be so closely connected to the emotional temperatures of other people. It is not normal for healthy eyes to stop producing tears. Neda is crying for help. You better take care of this now, Soleiman, or the older she is, the harder it will become to access her psyche."

Neda drops the black-capped mushrooms in the mortar and begins to pound with earnest attention.

"Nothing else matters to her these days," Soleiman says, "Except this Baba Magic of hers."

"I am not surprised. She feels your conflict and sadness. The struggle between your emotions and your logic. Your love for Velvet and how it's breaking you. And in her young mind she blames herself. So, all her energy is focused on fixing that, on making you happy."

Soleiman's gaze travels around the garden and lingers on each of Neda's charges—the mushroom patch cleaned of weeds and dried leaves, mushroom caps glimmering with pearls of moisture, Pary's herb box wet with a new coat of red paint, the young, green shoots of herbs, the pestle and mortar covered with an old sheet—all well-nourished and healthy. Yet. Has he, a father, paid as much attention to his own daughter? Jacob's words speed through his mind in a jumble before they land, one by one, in their proper place: a newborn can retain memories in her cells. A trauma can message the mind to shut down a healthy organ. Neda is crying for help. He turns to Jacob. "Are you saying that Neda remembers her mother's death in a subconscious way? That this memory is so traumatic it signaled Neda's mind to shut her tear ducts? That this is a kind of self-punishment?"

Jacob's smoke-tinted lips part in a gentle smile. "Yes, my friend, this is what I'm saying. A difficult concept to grasp, I know. But the human mind is complicated. Trauma should be addressed, or it will cause permanent damage. As I said, I've had great success in using play in therapy. Not a new concept, by the way. Thousands of years ago, Plato famously said, 'You can discover more about a human being in an hour of play than a year of conversation.' Freud used this approach, and Anna, his daughter, continues to do so. We are all doctors like you, Soleiman, but in a different field. Trust us."

Soleiman squints at Neda's mason jars behind him on shelves around the room, the tiny wood dolls, the clutter of apothecary bottles and bowls with their assorted mushrooms, herbs, and different flowers and leaves that are such a significant part of his daughter's life. Jacob is right. The medical field he, himself, knows and trusts, is not equipped to deal with a child's subconscious world. "Jacob, will you work on this with Neda?"

"I would have, if I didn't have to prepare my children for Palestine. But why not you, Soleiman? I will teach you everything you need to know."

"No. I am not the right person. I will have to take care of my own problems first."

"Yes, I understand. At any rate, a woman is better suited, since it's her mother Neda lost. But who? I would have suggested Sahar, my helper, but she is overwhelmed with last minute preparations. Who else, then? Who does Neda love, trust?"

They do not speak for a moment as they observe Neda who, without stopping the rhythmic thud of her pestle, orders Mademoiselle to be nice and stop snarling at something in the mushroom patch. But, paying no attention, the cat's frightened yowls become shriller as she desperately paws the mushrooms. Neda brushes her hands clean with an old sheet, tucks it around the mortar and pestle, then lifts Mademoiselle in her arms and walks into the house to rinse off the pepper and vinegar Aunt Shamsi sprayed on the cat.

A mixture of relief and excitement in his voice, Soleiman turns to Jacob. "Let's get to work. I have just the right person to work with Neda."

CHAPTER THIRTY-SEVEN

It is already afternoon; shadows are long, and the air in the Jewish Quarter is laced with odors of dinners simmering in neighboring kitchens. Tulip shuffles from one foot to another to stop Mademoiselle from licking his dust-covered boots. A small kick and the cat lets out an indignant yowl and scrambles off to Neda who is hiding behind her father.

"Sorry to disturb you at home," Tulip tells Soleiman, who is surprised to find the flustered eunuch at his gate. "Come right away, *Agha* doctor, please. Velvet *Khanom* needs you, and there's not much time. I have to get back to prepare the governor's brazier."

"Is *Khanom* sick?" Soleiman exclaims.

"Sick, not sick, I don't really know, *Agha* doctor." Tulip tugs at the silver-trimmed mantle that slipped off his shoulders. "No matter how often I warn her, she will not listen, so here we are."

Neda digs her face in Mademoiselle's fur and giggles. Velvet *Khanom* with all her delicious smells of cookies and honey is somewhere close by, and Baba is becoming a little happy.

Soleiman kisses Neda on top of her head. "Go in, Sweetheart. I'll be back for dinner. Run in now."

The instant he opens the side door of a canvas-covered droshky waiting next to Pary's house and steps up to take his place in the back seat beside Velvet, she places her hand on his arm. "Are you unwell, Velvet *Khanom*?" he murmurs.

"I hope you don't mind, Doctor Yaran, I had to see you." She touches him again, this time on his thigh, the imprint of her touch electrifying.

"I would have happily come to you," he says. But she presses a finger to his mouth to silence him, and he leans back for her to take him wherever she wants.

The dilapidated droshky bumps along the Alley of Physicians, jolting Tulip on a metal coil, which pokes out of the plastic front seat. He drops a bunch of cardamom seeds in his mouth and begins to chew ferociously. The reek of the droshky and its driver with his rattling lungs and stinks of sheep fat, garlic and cigarettes is intolerable, but bringing the Lincoln was not an option. Only after the Lincoln roared down the mountain to take the governor general to his meeting this morning did Tulip dare embark on the downhill hike to get a covered droshky, his aching back commiserating with the loud complaints he directed at the heavens above and the pebbles underfoot. And in the end, what did he manage to find but this half-covered drosky with its limping horse.

The horse tosses its head to the right and left as if sniffing something foul around Graveyard Street, into which the droshky has made a sharp turn. The coachman yanks at the reins to avoid a pack of yelping dogs. The lame horse loses its footing. The droshky swerves, veers, and wobbles precariously on two wheels.

The side door flies open, and one moment Velvet is about to fall out of the droshky, the next she is in Soleiman's arms as the clueless driver goads the horse on, and Tulip, unaware of the dangling back door, keeps cursing his luck.

Soleiman reaches out across the narrow width of the droshky and pulls the door on Velvet's side shut. He lifts her chador and shakes off pieces of straw and dust, then arranges it over her hair and draws her close.

From time to time, the canvas above them shudders in the trapped wind and Soleiman is able to glimpse the passing view through a lifted flap. "Where are we going?" he asks Velvet.

"To the safest place I could think of," Tulip calls out from the front seat.

The droshky leaves Graveyard Street behind and makes a turn toward one of the four banks in the quarter, which happens to be the house of Mr. Dardashti, who lends money to residents of the Quarter, his only guarantee the records he scribbles in his well-thumbed notebook and a verbal promise sealed with a handshake.

The joints of the droshky shudder and complain as the horse limps past a boisterous crowd of children congregating around the plum-juice stand in front of Fouladi Butchery, where fly-covered carcasses of sheep hang from hooks in the open entrance. Soleiman reaches up and shoves the droshky's tarp cover aside. The moment he realizes what street the droshky has turned into, he shouts, "Stop!"

Tulip digs his fingers into the driver's arm, and the man lets out a phlegmatic humph, drags a leather whip from under his seat, and lands it with a resounding smack on the horse, and, despite Soleiman's insistence to turn the droshky around, the animal shudders to life and clops ahead with sudden vigor. The instant the droshky comes to a bumpy halt, Tulip pulls out the folding steps and helps Velvet down.

Eleazar the Redhead recognizes Tulip's familiar knocks, but he is not expected today. He closes the Tehillim he was reading and places it on the cot in the cellar, where he had spent the day, one ear tuned to prayer and the other to the sound of fermenting *aragh*.

"Excuse my rudeness," Tulip addresses Eleazar the Redhead at the door. "But *Khanom* needs to discuss a secret matter with Doctor Yaran and, with your permission, of course, I thought your cellar is a safe place for them to talk."

The dumbfounded Eleazar observes Soleiman lead a beautiful woman toward the house as if she is some kind of breakable crystal. If he knows anything about his son, it is that when he is doing something unkosher he will not look into his father's eyes. "Son? Who is this *Khanom*? And what secret matter do you possibly need to discuss with her in *my* cellar?"

"I apologize, Baba," Soleiman says. "It won't take long, I promise." Hardly a few days have passed since Aunt Shamsi dragged him to Moshe Ben Avram's home to ask for his daughter's hand. Yet. Here he is, caught between his love for Velvet and respect for his father. He should have jumped out of the droshky, faded into Graveyard Street, and never looked back.

With growing terror, Eleazar observes the formality with which Tulip keeps a step behind the woman, bows his head in deference, adjusts her chador when it slides off her hair. Blood drains off Eleazar's face, and, feeling faint, he grabs the railing to keep himself from falling down the stairs. It does not take a *Hakham* wise man to recognize that such decorum only occurs between mistress and servant. This must be the governor general's wife, the woman Shamsi warned him about, the reason Soleiman has been refusing every eligible girl in the Quarter. His son will have to step over his father's body before he finds himself in the cellar with the Land Eater's wife.

"Please step aside, Baba," Soleiman tells his father, who, arms crossed over his chest, blocks the way down the stairs.

Looming silence. Father and son exchange blistering stares. Velvet shifts close to Tulip, and he gestures for her to remain silent.

"Please, Baba," Soleiman says. "Don't make me do something I will regret."

A mocking sweep of Eleazar's arm gestures toward the cellar. "You know your way to the cellar, son. Knock your father down and step over his dead body. Go ahead, attend to your secret business. Commit your sin in your father's house."

Fire in his eyes, Soleiman towers over his father and, attempting to control his voice, declares: "Nothing, Baba, nothing about my business with the lady is sinful." Having made his point, he apologizes to his father and lifts him out of the way.

* * *

Velvet plucks a straw from Soleiman's coat and rests her cheek on that spot. "Don't tell me it's dangerous to be here. I know all about danger."

The surrounding oak barrels and copper stills hiss and gurgle and burp their discontent, as if empathizing with Muslims in the North of the city, Jews in the South, and Tulip and Eleazar the Redhead arguing upstairs.

His breath against her lips more intimate than a kiss, Soleiman's thumb traces her cheek, her mouth, her plump lower lip trembling at his touch, her skin thirsting for the tenderness she dreamed of in her sleep and imagined when awake.

He lifts her off the ground, his senses succumbing to the longing in her silver eyes, the taste of her breasts, one nipple, then the other.

He gently sets her back down, cups her face in his hands, lifts a curl from her cheek, and soothes it behind her ear.

"Doctor Yaran," she whispers, his scent of leather and brilliantine filling her with forceful waves of wanting, and everything disappears, save for the warmth of his tongue in her mouth.

"Soleiman," he whispers to the rhythm of his strokes. "Soleiman."

"Soleiman," she murmurs over and over again, and the intimacy of his name is enough to bring her to her climax.

He buries his face in her hair, thinking this is what his daughter fell in love with, the indescribable perfume of this woman.

"Take me away, Soleiman, somewhere far away. We'll take Neda and Tulip. Anywhere you choose. Say yes, Soleiman!"

"Neda would be very happy. She can't stop talking about you."

"And her father?"

"Can't bear life without you," he replies, and the confession stirs fresh hunger for this bold woman who is moist and receptive to his touch.

He carries her in his arms toward his father's cot, crumpled sheets and blankets on the cot, a leather covered Tehillim left hastily on the pillow. Velvet is fragrant with desire in his arms. His nerves are tense with an urgency long forgotten, but loving her here would be an added insult to his father.

The ceiling shakes with the thump of steps and rising voices. Tulip and Eleazar are still arguing. Eleazar threatens to drag them both out of the cellar and throw them out of his house. Soleiman presses Velvet to his chest, a hand against her ear, but noise is amplified down here, and they can hear everything.

He gestures up to the ceiling. "This, my love, is the reality of my life."

"I don't care, Soleiman. You'll have to rescue me from my husband. Or I'll die up there in the mountains."

Soleiman brushes his lips against her temple. "I've to think about Neda, too, about my people. I wish it were different, my love, but I am a common Jew with nothing to offer you but trouble."

Her hands plunge into his hair as if it were her lifeline. "And I am a prisoner surrounded by trouble, but let's not give up so easily. I've learned something about my husband he doesn't want anyone to know. A weapon I'll use against him if he won't let me go."

"Your husband is a ruthless man, my love. He will never let you go." His healer's touch glides over and around her fragile bones as if to put her back together. "And as long as he needs me, he will not let me go, either."

"But you will find a solution, Soleiman, won't you?"

"There's only one solution, my love. Do it for you and me and for Neda. Next time, when I'm summoned to your husband, stay in your private quarters until I leave." He tugs at the chain threaded through the buttonhole of his vest and pulls out of his pocket Ruby's watch, which has been ticking like a second heart against his ribcage. He places one of the last two material tethers to Ruby in Velvet's palm and closes her hand around the watch. "I have nothing else of value to give you to remember me by."

CHAPTER THIRTY-EIGHT

The mushroom patch is tidy and cleared of Neda's paraphernalia. No sign of the mortar and pestle, willow bark and leaves, or Aunt Shamsi's potions. Not one yellow sprig in the box of Ruby herbs, not a dried branch on the mulberry tree.

Aunt Shamsi steps into the garden with stacked plates and cutlery in hand, goes back and forth to bring dishes of food from the kitchen, and arranges them on the table with extra care. She spent two days washing, chopping, and frying. Since Soleiman does not touch any kind of meat, she drizzled vegetables with olive oil and simmered them in saffron and lemon juice, added minced dates and pomegranate seeds to steamed rice, and parsley, spring onions, and eggplant to meatless stews.

Soleiman promised Neda he would purchase a miraculous ingredient to complete Baba Magic, and for him to show such interest in any miracle is cause for celebration.

Neda helps set the special-occasion silver spoons and forks with etching around the handles next to the scalloped plates with raised daisies scattered in the center. "Baba's late, Aunt Shamsi. I think he forget."

Aunt Shamsi adjusts the red scarf's floppy bow around Neda's curls. "Calm down, Little Leech, your heart's beating like a hammer. Your Baba won't forget."

The instant Soleiman opens the gate and steps into the garden, Neda is at his side wanting to know all about her Miracle Shabbat.

He gently takes her hand out of his pocket and tells her she has to be patient until Uncle Jacob comes because he'd want to be included.

Three raps on the gate, and Jacob, uncharacteristically solemn, strides into the garden and sits at the table next to Neda, who bounces with excitement in her chair. Behind him, the Quarter Fool prances in like a long-necked rabbit with a newspaper-wrapped package balanced in his outstretched hands. Skipping around the table, he announces the birth of Angel Benyamin's son, comes to a sudden halt in front of Aunt Shamsi, slaps his feet together, and holds out the package as if presenting her with a medal of honor.

"Don't tell me your *Ifrits* are back," she huffs.

"Gone, Aunt Shamsi, gone! I brought you something," he says, smacking her face with kisses. "Open it."

"Get your stinking mouth off me!" She shoves him away, rips the wrapping, and checks with interest the grainy, black-and-white speckled heap in the center of the newspaper. "What in *Jahannam* is this?"

Neda leans across the table and riffles with a forefinger through the Quarter Fool's gift. "Salt to keep *Sheitans* out of our house. *Espand* seeds to explode all the many jealous eyes, and…and…this!" Under the mound of salt and seeds of rue is an oval shaped object that smells like Baba's inkwell and wet newspaper. She brushes off salt and seeds and lifts a blue egg.

"Our friend must have painted it blue," Soleiman tells Neda.

"It must be a special egg for Neda," Jacob says.

"Yes, a very, very special egg!" The Quarter Fool chuckles. "Wouldn't ever paint it in a trillion years." He was walking past the Mirza Yaghoub Synagogue early this morning, he swears, when a plump hen ran out of the entrance and clucked at his feet. Then right out of its little *koon* fell the shiny blue egg he grabbed to give Aunt Shamsi to thank her for scaring away his *Ifrits*.

Aunt Shamsi, who has no use for the pile of salt and seeds, which she stockpiles in the pantry, wets a finger in her mouth and rubs the egg, but no color comes off. A blue egg, she is aware, is a good omen sent once in a generation to the most righteous of all people. She wraps the egg in a napkin and displays it prominently in the center of the table.

Soleiman brushes off fallen mulberries from a chair under the tree, brings it to the table, and invites the Quarter Fool for dinner. "All right then, let's rise and thank God for his blessings."

Jacob tugs at the collar of his shirt, sips the sweet kosher wine, tastes the challah. Blue eggs and magical mushrooms mean more to him than the rituals of Shabbat, which he once considered beautiful, comforting, and necessary. But he no longer attends synagogue on Shabbat or on High Holydays. No longer fasts on Yom Kippur. Or feasts on Sukkot. What use is his faith to him when the ash of his family blankets the floors of Hitler's crematoriums?

"Dinner's done!" Neda announces. "Baba has miracle ingredient for Baba Magic"

"Neda! Uncle Jacob hasn't finished his dinner," Soleiman says.

"I am done, thank you. Everything is delicious." Jacob slides his plate back. He has no appetite. His children are on the flight to Palestine, and he will not rest until the plane lands safely in Tel-Aviv. He lifts his glass of wine and announces that there is no better time to start Neda's Miracle Shabbat than right now, around this table and in the company of friends.

Soleiman thrusts his hand into his pocket. Neda's gift cost him more than any sane person has a right to pay in these difficult times. But if this will help complete Baba Magic, as Aunt Shamsi promises, then it will be worth every *touman*.

He puts the present in his daughter's cupped hands. "Rub it between your palms, just like that, in a circular motion until your hands become nice and warm. This, Sweetheart, is Persian *Pirouzeh*, turquoise from the highest mountain peak of Ali-Mersai. It is the most healing of all precious stones."

Neda smells the Persian *Pirouzeh*'s chorus of exciting scents, mixed with the green breath of Ruby's herbs, the earthy slap of the new mushrooms, the grassy smell of cucumber peels, and the bitter cherry bite of the purple mushrooms. Everything sounds like music to her—the Quarter Fool's string of questions about the *Pirouzeh*, the cling and clang of the plum and pomegranate juice man behind the gate collecting the portable counter he brought to the Alley of Physicians, and even Aunt Shamsi's protests about how the shameless juice man should not be doing business on Shabbat. Neda shows the *Pirouzeh* to the Quarter Fool and asks if Aunt Shamsi is right and it's good for Baba Magic.

The Quarter Fool grabs his head between his hands. "Don't ask stupid questions, Neda! Why will your Baba pay so, so much for a giant *Pirouzeh* if Aunt Shamsi isn't always right?"

"I've something else for you, Sweetheart, far more precious than any *Pirouzeh*." Soleiman guides Neda's hand into his other pocket. "Take it out yourself."

Neda pulls out of her father's coat pocket twelve gold bangles, wears six around each upper arm, and, her laughter ringing in the garden, lifts her hands above her head and dances.

"You dance just like your mother did when I gave her these bangles. They are very valuable, Sweetheart. And now, they're all yours."

Belly jumping sobs replace Neda's laughter. One by one, she slides the bangles off her arms and drops them in Soleiman's lap. "Take them back, Baba. Madar don't ever wants to give them to me."

CHAPTER THIRTY-NINE

Aunt Shamsi rummages among mushrooms, willow leaves, herbs, spices, and bark on the kitchen table, straightens her back, at last, and claps soil off her hands. "Everything is here, Little Leech, you've learned well. But we're still missing two ingredients for your Baba Magic. Weren't you listening when I told you what else we need?"

"I listen. For Baba Magic, we also need one Moses Half Fish ingredient and one Madar for Neda ingredient."

"Well! If Madar is an ingredient, then we need three. You help me talk sense into your Baba, I'll find you a Madar in no time. I already have the second ingredient tucked safe in my bra. But we don't have the rare Moses Half Fish. So, let's get to work. But, let me change that muddy string first." Aunt Shamsi cuts the red string tied around Neda's wrist, removes the hanging safety pin, which she locks and buries under a heap of eggplant peel in the garbage bin. "Remember to change your red string when it gets dirty. A dirty string can't ward off the evil eye. And make sure you lock your tarnished safety pins before you throw them in trash or instead of blinding evil eyes, they'd turn around and poke our own eyes."

"Good afternoon, ladies." Soleiman enters the kitchen and bows dramatically to his aunt and daughter.

Aunt Shamsi hurries to collect the safety pins and stash of red threads and drops them into a drawer.

"Before you put these away," Soleiman tells his aunt. "Tie one of them around my wrist."

"Make as much fun as you want, Soleiman, you'll believe me one day. Why are you here? Is it dinner time already?"

"I'm not making fun, Aunt Shamsi, on the contrary. I am here to ask a favor. We're in the holy days of repentance and promise, a good time to complete tasks we undertook this year. Neda has been working for a long time on her Baba Magic. Will you help her put the finishing touches on it, so it won't be on her mind in the New Year?"

Aunt Shamsi looks hard at Soleiman, certain the end of the world is in sight and the *Mashiakh* is on his way. "*You* are asking me to help Neda? No! I won't go about breaking my back, so you make fun of me."

"I am serious, Aunt Shamsi, and eternally grateful, of course."

"Finally, Soleiman, finally! Stay right here, then." Aunt Shamsi takes Neda's hand and stuffs it into her bra.

Under her giant breast, Neda finds a small pouch she carefully retrieves, pokes her nose into the widened mouth, and smells mothballs, planting soil, and old things.

Aunt Shamsi pinches a grainy powder out of the pouch. "Have a good look at this Soleiman, rarer than rare. Look at the deep sapphire color. Found it in the Bazaar of Relics. Crushed Stone of Heaven to add to Baba Magic. It is necessary so it will not curdle."

She wiggles her breasts to adjust them in her bra. "We have all the ingredients now. Except Moses Half Fish. And that is not easy to find. Go ahead, sugar, tell your Baba what it is."

In the center of the kitchen, standing at attention, Neda explains that Aunt Shamsi is searching everywhere to find a very, very special fish called Moses Half Fish. Its name is Moses Half Fish because Moses chopped it in half with his cane when he parted the Red Sea and that when Aunt Shamsi finds it, she'll dry it in the sun and then pound it like powder. "Guess with what, Baba?"

"Tell me, Sweetheart." Soleiman regards his daughter with as much interest as he can muster. If superstitious fantasies will strengthen Neda's belief in the healing power of her potion, so be it.

"With my Persian Pirouzeh! Aunt Shamsi says when I pound everything together with my Persian Pirouzeh, a pinch of Baba Magic will cure every disease on earth."

"Yes, every known disease! But we have to find the Moses Half Fish by Tuesday, or we're in trouble! Tuesday is our lucky day, the day *Hashem* 'saw it was good.'" Aunt Shamsi points a forefinger at Soleiman. "If after all this *zahmat* hard work Baba Magic doesn't make you happy, then nothing in the world will. Not even Ruby dancing out of her grave to an army of jingling tambourines."

CHAPTER FORTY

It is early morning, and the garden is fearfully silent. No voices in the alley behind the walls. No footfalls of pedestrians or barking of stray dogs. No braying of donkeys, clatter of carts, chatter of haggling women, or the bleating of panicked sheep being walked to the slaughterhouse. Not even the chirping of crickets or the first hum of morning prayers at Pary's door.

Neda and her father sit among the mushrooms with their familiar smell of damp earth, watermelon rind, and cucumber peel Neda salvages from the kitchen for her friend. There is an additional odor of the newly appeared mushrooms—a hint of decay, the sting of bitter almonds, crustaceans, and swamp.

"Baba, we forgot my dolls."

"Why do you want your dolls?" Soleiman asks, wondering whether it was a mistake to follow Jacob's advice and leave the dolls behind, so she'd draw him into her games with her imaginary friend.

"I want it for my Madar."

"What do you mean, Sweetheart?"

"Madar won't come now."

"But why, Sweetheart, why won't your Madar come if your dolls aren't here?" His question ignored, Neda rests her elbows on her knees and cradles her chin in her cupped hands as her gaze glides around the mushroom patch. Long minutes pass. A sigh of resignation and she shifts closer to him.

Something hisses in the dim light.

A squirrel scrambles up the mulberry tree, releasing a shower of mulberries on the table. A crow swoops out of the branches and fades in the diminishing darkness. A rodent scurries away at their feet, and behind it a rabbit cuts a fleeing path in the mushrooms.

His every muscle on alert, Soleiman locks his arms around his daughter and, in one wide leap, carries her out of the mushroom patch.

"Baba? Why you afraid?"

"I heard a snake, Sweetheart. Snakes are dangerous. Didn't you hear it?"

"I hear, Baba, it's my Mushrooms Friend."

"Mushrooms Friend is a snake? All this time, you've been talking to a snake? That's not possible, Sweetheart. Snakes bite."

"Mushrooms Friend is nice, Baba, and *fozoul* too. Come, let's tell her all about my *Pirouzeh*. Maybe she tell us where to find Moses Half Fish."

He hesitates, then makes his way back, his footsteps slow and firm for the vibrations to warn the reptile of his approach. At the perimeter of the patch, he pauses. Two wide strides and he stands paralyzed amid the mushrooms, his ears cocked, his gaze slashing through the lifting mist. Hardly a meter from his feet, he notices a rock, which was not there the day before, and wonders who had helped Neda carry it here.

The morning turns golden, and the jagged shards of glass on top of the surrounding walls sparkle in the rising sun. The surroundings are so still, he can hear Aunt Shamsi shuffle in the kitchen.

The rock begins to glide toward them, crushing mushrooms under its weight, a dome of radiant colors, magnificent in the orange-streaked light of dawn. The advancing half-hill comes to a leisurely stop at Soleiman's feet. A prehistoric head emerges, hooded eyes aimed at him like two match-flames, a soft smacking sound of the widening jaws, and the flicks of a marbleized tongue.

He recovers his breath and crouches among the mushrooms with Neda in his lap. "Sweetheart, your friend is a tortoise with a beautiful carapace. See the tortoise's small home? It's stuck to its back like a ball cut in half. That's the carapace. Tortoises like to come out in the sun. I've never seen such vibrant colors. I'm thinking, Sweetheart, about how you said your Madar doesn't come to play if you don't have your dolls. Maybe she's afraid of your friend."

Neda cocks her head to one side and thinks for a while. "No, Madar's not afraid. She plays with my dolls when Mushrooms Friend is here."

He lowers his daughter's fists from her eyes. "Surely she plays with you too."

Neda crushes a bunch of mushrooms in one hand and scatters the pulp on top of the tortoise. A dry, raspy grunt of protest and the tortoise withdraws its head into safety.

Everything around them hisses and moans and complains.

A stray dog slouches past the gate. In the wake of the dog's despondent howls, the thump of Soleiman's breathing is loud in his chest.

The head of the tortoise reemerges out of its bright-colored carapace.

"Look, your friend's head is out again. Shall we tell it why Madar won't come to play?"

Neda's fingers skip on the egg-shaped head of the tortoise, cool and rough, slightly spongy between the eyes. She is familiar with her friend's scaly outline, familiar with the neck bones like broken pieces of her doll, so she is always careful not to squeeze and make Mushrooms Friend die too. Neda tucks her hand under her thigh and shuts her eyes.

He embraces his daughter's hunched shoulders. "Look, Sweetheart, Mushrooms Friend is nodding its head. It wants to know why Madar won't come to play with you."

"Mushrooms Friend knows everything."

"But I don't, Sweetheart. Tell your Baba why and make me happy."

Clouds drift past the fiery disk of the sun, and the flash of sorrow in Neda's eyes is like a trapped animal.

"Madar won't play with Neda because Neda is very bad girl to poison her Madar when she was little in Madar's stomach."

"No, Sweetheart!" Soleiman's voice echoes around the garden. "You are not a bad girl! You did not poison your Madar!"

"Yes, Baba, I poison my Madar and make her die."

His grip on his daughter tight, his voice cracks with pain and anger. "Listen, Sweetheart. A child can never poison her mother. You did *not* make your Madar die. She died from some complications of... birth...it happens sometimes...she lost blood...she became sick."

He falls silent. It is getting hot. They have spent some hours among the mushrooms, soaking in their growing aroma of earth and bitter almonds.

"Sweetheart, did Aunt Shamsi say this nonsense about poisoning your Madar?"

"It's not nonsense, Baba! Aunt Shamsi know everything in the world."

"No, Sweetheart, she does not know everything. She is wrong. Very, very wrong!"

"But why Aunt Shamsi tell me something very, very wrong?"

"Because Aunt Shamsi is not educated. She has some wrong ideas in her head that she thinks is the truth. But it is not the truth, Sweetheart, not at all."

CHAPTER FORTY-ONE

Midnight comes and goes. A milky curtain of fog rises and wraps itself around the world outside. Rain pitter-patters on the windowsill. The battle to flee the treacherous shores of his heart and navigate his way to more stable grounds, stretches to dawn. The rain stops. Daybreak lifts the fog and arouses the cacophony of waking birds.

Soleiman buttons up his shirt and shrugs on the jacket he had tossed behind the chair last night, then heads toward Neda's bedroom to find her bed empty.

He steps into the garden, where Aunt Shamsi is sitting on one of the metal chairs around the iron table under the tree with Neda in her lap.

The air is heavy with the odor of ripe mulberries underfoot and the sting of vinegar and pepper Aunt Shamsi sprayed on Mademoiselle, who whirls around him like a dervish. The table is set with fresh goat cheese and warm barbary bread, fried eggplants, and browned Shabbat eggs that simmered all night in the stew of lamb tongue and hooves.

Aunt Shamsi heaps a plate with food and places it in front of Soleiman. "Cooked a king's feast. Sit before it gets cold."

He slides the plate away.

"What's with you Soleiman? Woke on your left rib this morning?"

He takes a deep breath, attempts to release his clenched teeth. "I am upset at *you*, Aunt Shamsi, very upset. How could you fill Neda's head with such rubbish? Ruby died because her uterus ruptured, because she hemorrhaged. Neda did not poison her."

"You stick with fixing teeth, Soleiman, and let me do my job. I know what I'm talking about. I brought hundreds of children to this world and none of them—"

Everything around Soleiman turns black. He hovers over his aunt, grabs a plate, and hurls it across the garden. Lifts his chair above his head and brings it crashing on the table; plates break and food scatters.

Neda can smell Baba's sweat, but she does not recognize his anger. Her Baba does not break things like this. He does not scare Mademoiselle and bang on the table to make it shake like earthquakes. Her Baba never stomps up and down the garden.

"Baba?" Neda whimpers. "I'm scared."

"I'm angry, Sweetheart! Very angry! But not at you."

Aunt Shamsi pushes her chair back and rises with Neda in her arms. "Stop it, Soleiman! You're scaring your daughter to death."

"Stay where you are," he says, and Aunt Shamsi drops back into the chair.

Sunlight hits the façade of the house, and the kitchen windowpanes glare at him like accusations. He is furious with Aunt Shamsi, furious with the world but, above all, he is furious with himself. He should have known that no matter how often he warned Aunt Shamsi to mind what she told Neda, she would continue her volley of superstitious garbage.

He marches across the garden and out of the broken gate and into the Alley of Physicians, walks toward the door with the knocker in the shape of a cat, which he pounds with such ferocity Pary drops the book she is reading and runs to open the door.

She takes one look at Soleiman and quickly shuts the door behind him. She guides him across the hallway and into her living room with the arched windows, books scattered everywhere, and Monsieur André's carved figurines on ledges and shelves.

She fluffs cushions against the back of a sun-faded sofa, and they sit side by side for a long time, listening to the murmur of prayers behind the door, the buzz of flies against the window, and the shrill cry of the Mattress Beater, promising to beat any old cotton-stuffed mattress back to life.

Once Soleiman finds his voice, he tells Pary about his anger at Aunt Shamsi, who made Neda believe she poisoned her mother, about his grief at his own inability to notice his aunt's influence on his daughter, and his own failure in finding a proper mother for her.

Pary listens to him in silence, because this is what he needs, as she did three years ago, when he helped her paint André's door white.

They sit next to each other until a chill creeps into the room and the books, figurines, and the brocade-covered armchairs take a darker hue, and, Soleiman, ready to face himself, presses a grateful kiss on the back of her hand and leaves.

* * *

Soleiman plants a kiss on each of Neda's eyes. "I'm terribly sorry about this morning, Sweetheart. My behavior was inexcusable. It won't happen again. But I am very angry with Aunt Shamsi because of all the lies she's been telling you. It's impossible for you to poison your Madar, Sweetheart, do you understand that? You were too small and helpless when you were in your mother's stomach. You depended on her to give you food and take care of you until you were born. Sweetheart, your Madar died because she became sick. Do you understand?"

"I understand, Baba. You happy now?"

He forces a semblance of a smile, tucks the blanket under his daughter's chin. "Now get some sleep."

CHAPTER FORTY-TWO

Mesmerizing in her role as Aschenputtel, the brave and resourceful girl in the fairytale, Pary imitates the voice of a child, wide-eyed, uncertain, pleading, and hopeful. Impersonating Aschenputtel's father, she straightens her back and broadens her shoulders, assuming a deeper and kinder tone capable of righting everything.

Eyes glittering like wet obsidian, she tells Neda that Aschenputtel asks her father for a twig to plant on her mother's grave, which she waters for long hours with her tears until it grows into a magical tree that will fulfill Aschenputtel's wish.

Neda claps, lifts herself on her knees, and plants a kiss on each of Pary's cheeks.

Pary giggles with joyful innocence.

Laughter in Soleiman's chest, the first in months. He, too, has an urge to applaud as he observes Pary and Neda sit cross legged on the carpet, heads tilted toward one another as Pary reads a book of fairytales. He leans back in the red sofa in his living room and watches Pary riffle through the cotton-lined basket she brought from home and, one by one, retrieve colorful wood figurines—miniature birds, longhaired dolls, dappled cats, hookah pipes.

"Here, darling." Pary hands a doll to Neda. "It's the Aschenputtel doll you like."

Neda rises from the carpet and drops herself in Pary's lap. Neda's palm rests on an artery at the side of Pary's neck, calculating the exact distance between each of the beats, the highs, lows, and rhythm of each stroke. She has checked Aunt Shamsi's pulse, the beat of Baba Eleazar's temples, and her Baba's jumping heartbeats, but none are as calm and truthful as Pary's. "Okay, Pary, you don't lie. So, give me Aschenputtel's tears for Baba Magic to make my Baba happy."

For a long week, Pary pored over the literature Jacob provided to educate her about play therapy. She has memorized passages about certain psychological distress or mental conflicts beyond a child's capability that can send messages to the mind to shut down an otherwise healthy organ. But there was no mention on how to react to a special child who knows how to gauge one's sincerity. "To make Baba happy, darling, you need your own tears, not Aschenputtel's."

Neda tosses the doll back into the basket. Gives the basket an angry kick. "I don't have tears, Pary."

"You're wrong, darling. You have many tears, it's just that they're stuck in your little heart." Pary puts the child's hand back on her own heart. "The keys to your little heart are made of words. Each word fits a different feeling. When you find the right key for each of your feelings, then the door to your little heart will open and all your tears will run out."

Neda counts the strokes of Pary's heart—little playful skips like Neda's scared heart when she sneaks her hand into Aunt Shamsi's big-lock chest to find that silver purse that she shouldn't touch. Maybe Neda's heart is full of many tears like the deep *abambar* where Aunt Shamsi's daughter drowned. Maybe she shouldn't open the door for all her tears to rush out of her heart and spill into the house and garden and out into the alley and make everything drown like Aunt Shamsi's daughter.

Aunt Shamsi peeks through the door and, afraid to address Soleiman, tells Neda it is time for the *Tashlikh* ceremony and to ask her Baba if she is allowed to go to the Fountain of Running Waters to cast off her sins before sunset.

Neda, who loves the rituals of *Tashlikh*, jumps to her feet. "Come with me, Pary, okay?"

"Of course, darling, I never miss *Tashlikh*." Pary studies Soleiman, who is known to avoid the *Tashlikh* ceremony. She tilts her head as if she expects an answer to her yet unexpressed question, but Soleiman is already up on his feet.

* * *

Carrying their heavy load of sins in cotton bags dangling from their necks, arms, or in burlap sacks slung across their shoulders, the populace of the Jewish Quarter gathers around the Fountain of Mercy.

Prayers climb into the starless sky, high and insistent and wanting. "He will take us back in love." "He will cover up our iniquities." "He will cast all our sins into the depths of the ocean." And in full view of friend and foe, the populace empties cotton bags and burlap sacks of stale breadcrumbs to wide-eyed fish in the pond, after which, the sin-infested water will drain into *joubs* at the side of the street, then empty into reservoirs of poorer communities further south.

The Quarter Fool's eyes skip back and forth in an attempt to count the fish to make sure none had jumped out of the bowl of water in which he brought them here before sunrise. His joyful cackle announcing his arrival, he had pranced from house to house and knocked door to door. Every door was opened. Every family dropped two or three or more goldfish into his clay bowl. The bowl held tight, he gingerly followed the path of a crude pipe that carries water from the main cistern toward the Fountain of Mercy and dropped fish of all sizes into the shallow pond at the foot of the fountain.

Now, his eyes dizzy in their sockets, he shrugs his shoulders and gives up the impossible task of counting the fish while they swim around in the pond.

Neda crinkles her nose at the stink of fish that smells like cabbage Aunt Shamsi boils for *dolmeh* and the stench of the Quarter Fool's torrent of *gooz*. "Pary? Why we throw bread for fish?"

"Ah! Today is the first day of our New Year, and we're supposed to throw away last year's sins. The small pieces of bread are sins we throw away in running water. And there are fish in the water because fish don't have eyelids, so their eyes are always wide open, like God who is always watching over us."

Aunt Shamsi gathers Neda's skirt and drops a handful of bread-crumbs in it. "Shake your skirt and throw your sins into the water."

Pary flings the last morsels of bread into the water, which is fast becoming clogged. "Neda has no sins, Aunt Shamsi. She's just throwing away the bad feelings in her heart."

"Like my tears stuck in my little heart?"

"Yes, darling. Open your little heart and throw away your stuck tears into the water."

Soleiman watches Neda shake her skirt to make sure there are no leftover breadcrumbs. Hears her ask Pary if there are any bad feelings stuck in her hair, and Pary's reply that every single bad feeling is in the water. The thought occurs to him that despite his pure and innocent love, he, too, should repent for the sin of falling in love with another man's wife.

"Be patient, darling, this is only the first step," Pary tells Neda who keeps brushing a hand over her dry cheeks. "Remember how I said there's a key for each one of your feelings? It takes time to find the right keys."

The Quarter Fool scoops water in his palm from the fountain and splashes it on Neda's face. "Hurry Neda! Keys like to get lost all the time."

A sudden commotion around the fountain. Aunt Shamsi's screams pierce through the hum of prayers. Everyone is struck with terror at the possibility of yet another massacre on the first day of Rosh Hashana.

"Stop it!" Aunt Shamsi shouts. "Pary! Where are you? Stop your cursed cat!"

"Mademoiselle!" Pary cries out. "*Arrête ça immediatement*!"

The Quarter Fool jumps up and down like a coiled wire. "Please, Pary, please just speak normal language so Mademoiselle understands you."

Aunt Shamsi shoves her way through the crowd, attempts to grab the cat, who has jumped into the shallow pond and is hunting for fish. "Get her, Little Leech! The nasty cat's looking for our fish. I saw it just now! I saw our Moses Half Fish swimming in the pond."

Neda sees Mademoiselle dart out of the fountain with a fish dangling from her mouth. She really wants Moses Half Fish for her Baba Magic, but she does not want to leave the fountain and run after Mademoiselle. Neda wants to be patient until she finds all the keys to her feelings to make her tears become unstuck and fall in the water. She looks hard at the jumping fish in the water and wonders whether they're gulping down her unstuck tears.

The air is spiked with the smells of dough, sweat, and the mounting bite of curiosity. But stronger than all the smells, is the wet carpet stink of Mademoiselle's muddy pelt, which Neda trails as she first walks and then runs after the fleeing cat. Finding that useless, she squats and calls Mademoiselle with low clicks of her tongue.

Mademoiselle pauses. Hind leg in the air, she twitches her nose as if detecting a rotten stink in the air, flings an indignant stare at Neda, and, the trophy clamped between her teeth, turns back and hisses right into Aunt Shamsi's clutch.

Aunt Shamsi triumphantly holds up the mutilated fish. "Grabbed it right out of the thief's greedy mouth. Come, Little Leech, we have all the ingredients we need!"

CHAPTER FORTY-THREE

Soleiman wears his starched shirt, ties his cravat, and buttons his vest, the absence of his watch in his pocket stirring fresh longing. He combs his hair back with brilliantine. His hair has grown longer and grayer, since he held Velvet in his arms, and she clung to him as if she was sinking. He takes one last look around his bedroom and drops a vial of activated charcoal into his coat pocket.

He intends to be punctual for his appointment which, according to Aunt Shamsi, has to take place on Tuesday, the third day of creation, when God mentions, "It was good," twice.

His daughter is seated cross-legged among her mushrooms, Ruby's scarf splayed at her side. She pinches from a small clay bowl at her side a dash of ground Stone of Heaven and from another bowl some powdered Moses Half Fish and sprinkles everything into the mortar, in which Baba Magic has turned the golden shade of saffron.

She smells the result of her hard work, the well-orchestrated woody notes of willow bark, a tang of spices, the lively scents of herbs, a hint of ripe fruit and a whiff of earth and crustacean. She is pleased. She wipes her hands on her skirt. "Baba Magic is ready! You are ready too, Baba?"

"I am. *Mobarak* congratulations," he says, rewarded by the smiling face she turns toward him like a petal.

She taps him softy above one eye, then the other. "Close your eyes, Baba, and feel all the time warm sun behind your eyes until I say open your eyes. Okay?"

"Okay, Sweetheart."

He shuts his eyes, hears the metallic click of the gate, the clack of it being kicked shut, the chuckles of the Quarter Fool as he plops down next to Neda, who scolds him for being late and orders him to be quiet and stop his fidgeting. He feels Neda's small hand untie his cravat and slide beneath his shirt, lingering over his heart to count the beats. He takes a deep breath to calm his heartbeat as she massages the potion in circles on his chest.

His thoughts travel back as far as he can remember to summon memories that might project a semblance of joy. They are few: graduating dental school in France, his too short a time with Ruby, the day he learned she was pregnant, the success of his own ointment in numbing gums, and the cherished moments he held Velvet in Baba Eleazar's cellar.

Time passes. His patience is running low, and he is not sure whether he can keep his eyes shut much longer, when he hears Neda say, "What to do, *Agha* Fool? Baba Magic's not so good, it makes Baba more sadder."

"Use your head, Neda, think a bit," the Fool's high-pitched voice replies, "People don't get happy from outside. Have him eat the stupid thing, *belakhareh*!"

"But Baba say to me don't ever eat it."

"Because you're little, Neda, old people are different. Just give it to him before it goes bad."

"Okay, *Agha* Fool, you know everything. Open your mouth Baba. Taste Baba Magic in your two cheeks before you swallow. Don't ever open your eyes until I say open your eyes."

He hesitates. This might be his biggest mistake yet, but he will have to take the risk, or his daughter will lose faith in everything she worked so hard for. He opens his mouth and follows her instructions, holds in one cheek the mixture her fingers spoon into his mouth, then shifts it into his other cheek, as if the taste might differ from one side to another. It is bitter and has a sharp odor and his guts heave in rejection, but he forces it down.

Hours or minutes speed by, he can't tell how long. Neda feeds him more of the concoction. Sunlight warms his eyelids. The donkey-pulled cart of the shah's Water Man jangles across the Alley of Physicians. Mushrooms Friend squashes mushrooms as it crawls around. The rustle of willow branches next door. Rostam's contented snorts.

Neda's hand ripples toward him underwater with another helping of Baba Magic.

"Enough, Sweetheart, your mushrooms are making me drunk." He retrieves the vial of activated charcoal from his pocket and drops it in her hand. "Pour it in a glass of water if I vomit and make me drink it."

"Vomit out your bad things," the Quarter Fool says.

His daughter's voice from somewhere faraway orders the Fool to be quiet before telling him to open his eyes.

Everything around him is magnified and intensified: the newly grown black-capped mushrooms, the sea-green of Ruby's herbs in the box, the silvery glare of mulberries hanging from the tree, the sunlit golden leaves, and the glint of the metal table and chairs. For a terrifying instant, he realizes he is about to embark on a mysterious journey, and his daughter is left in the care of a fool, who rests a hand on his knee and assures him he is not going anywhere.

Soleiman is blinded by the sudden light of a universe conjured in feverish shades, alluring, intense, and awesome, his only tether the Quarter Fool's mesmerizing hand, the veins blooming into brooks that flow into five mercurial ponds soothing their way down his own leg and into the rich soil in which Ruby's buried caul and afterbirth beat like one heart, its budding arteries weaving their way underground to feed the mushrooms.

Time loses its meaning. The tortoise braids a colorful puff of brilliant air around Neda's head. Geranium petals caress the foot of the tree. Mulberry Juice drips from one of the trembling branches on which Ruby flutters like a dizzy butterfly.

He struggles to abandon the mushrooms, to open his arms to welcome her back, but his arms remain heavy at his sides, the earth heaves like a leviathan under his feet and images change and shift before coalescing in his brain with a delay.

"*Bas*!" Ruby's once sweet voice is tinged with anger. "Enough! What do you think you are doing?"

Everything around him sprouts a red mouth and chants to him in unison—the gathering of mushrooms, the swaying mulberry branches, and the fire-backed turtle with its reptilian head and wide-open jaws. "*Bas*! When will you come to your senses? *Enough*!"

Her rush of copper hair ablaze in the burnished light of hundreds of candles, Ruby's words stud the air like diamonds. "I want to join my own world with my angels. But you and Neda are keeping me tied to your world. Do the right thing, Soleiman. Release me on this Rosh Hashanah."

CHAPTER FORTY-FOUR

"Good morning, Sweetheart. Why are you here so early?" Soleiman walks into the empty lot, where Neda is talking to the weeping willow.

"I take leaves and barks and everything for Baba Magic, so our tree become sad and sick. So I come to fix it. You can help me. Okay?" From a jar at her feet, she scoops out a fistful of Baba Magic she drops in his hand, tells him to rub it on parts of the tree where she had peeled off the outer bark to collect sap.

They work side by side as Neda smears the ointment on one side of the tree, Soleiman on the other. Neda hums *Ey Iran* under her breath, and he joins in when he remembers the tune to the patriotic song being heard everywhere these days, the lyrics inspired by the insult of witnessing Allied flags hoisted over Iranian army barracks.

O Iran! O jewel-studded land!
Your soil, springhead of artistry sublime!
May those who harbor you ill, banished be!
May you remain everlastingly strong!

Neda peeks at her father from behind the tree trunk and says, "Okay, Baba. Check tree with your ear like when you put it on my sick heart. See if tree is happy?"

He bends to press his ear to the bark, moves with patience and meticulous attention from one spot to another, until Neda taps him on the shoulder, and he straightens his back and assures her that Baba Magic is working, and the tree will recover in no time.

He lowers himself to the earth at the foot of the tree, where gnarled roots and sun-bleached branches are strewn, leans against the trunk with Neda in his lap. He shuts his eyes and rests his head against the bark of the tree. He is exhausted. No matter where he is or what he might be doing, he can hear Velvet's voice above the thrum of blood in his veins.

"Baba? Are you a happy doctor now?"

"Yes, Sweetheart, I am a very happy doctor now. All because of your Baba Magic. Thank you."

Neda giggles in her stomach. "You want to eat more Baba Magic, so you become happier?"

He throws his head back and laughs. "I had more than enough, Sweetheart." He takes a deep breath and adds. "Listen, Sweetheart. You made yesterday very special for me. But you know which part was most special. When your Madar came to me."

"Really Baba? You see Madar? Because you eat my Baba Magic?"

"Yes, Sweetheart, I saw your Madar because I ate your Baba Magic. She hugged you, told you how much she loves you. She wants you to know she comes to play with you, not with your dolls." His daughter listens intently, her eyes like blue torches in sunlight seeping through the branches. "Do you know what will make your Madar very happy? For me to find a good Madar for you. A Madar who will love you as much as your Madar loves you." Neda studies him with a determined expression he has a hard time deciphering. He smooths back a tumbled curl from her eye and waits.

"Okay, Baba, I'll make Madar very happy. I found a good Madar for me, myself. I want Velvet *Khanom*."

He smiles. Yes. Velvet will be a good mother for Neda and an ideal wife for him, but ideal is a luxury he has no right to. "I like Velvet *Khanom*, too, Sweetheart. But she is not a good Madar for you."

Neda jumps to her feet. "No, Baba! Velvet *Khanom* is my very good Madar. She let me come in her nice car all the way to That-Cursed-Land-Eater man to save you! She keeps your glove in her pocket all the time. I want Velvet *Khanom* to be my only Madar."

"But Velvet *Khanom* is already married to that bad Land Eater. They'll have children of their own one day."

"So, you marry Velvet *Khanom* too, and I'll be children of your own."

"Velvet *Khanom* can only marry one husband. If she marries me, too, the Land Eater will become very angry, and he'll try to hurt me. You don't want that, do you? I'm sorry, Sweetheart, I wish it was not like this, but sometimes we have dreams and wishes we have to give up. I know how hard it is, believe me, Sweetheart, I do."

Neda takes a moment to think about what her father just said. Her expression is heartbreaking, but she, like him, will have to come to terms with the shattering of her dream. "Baba." Her voice is so small he has to lean forward to hear her. "Don't be hurt and die."

"I won't die, Sweetheart, I promise. But you'll have to listen to me. Will you come with me to ask Pary to become your Madar? She'll be very happy to know you like her too."

When the sun climbs to the center of the sky and the tree exhales the sweet aroma of warm spices, Neda rises on bare, sun-reddened feet, turns her back to him, and walks across the lot. She stops, crushes dried leaves under her feet, kicks a branch, then continues her slow march toward the alley. Just before disappearing from his sight, over one shoulder, she tosses him her grudging consent.

CHAPTER FORTY-FIVE

Neda's gaze trails every step Pary takes back and forth from the kitchen to the living room to set fruits, pistachios, soaked walnuts, sour cherries, and almond cookies on the coffee table in front of Baba. All the colors are sad today. The cucumbers in the tray, once bright green like Pary's happy fairytales, are pale like Aunt Shamsi's stories. The tiny tongues in the pistachio shells and the heap of red cherries are the color of their sofas where people's *koons* rubbed the red off a bit. Pary's skirt floats back and forth like gray torn clouds. Maybe Pary is not wanting to become Neda's Madar because her voice has become even softer than geranium petals at the foot of their mulberry tree.

"Please come sit for a moment, Pary. We'd like to talk to you. Right, Neda?"

"Right Baba," Neda replies. "We'll be very nice."

"Oh, darling, you're always nice. Here, I baked a special cookie for you. See the key I drew on it?" Pary goes to a round table in the corner and brings a plate of cookies.

Neda takes a cookie and says thank you three times because this morning Baba said three times Neda should be nice because Pary is waiting for them in her house. Mademoiselle meows her way into the room and leaps into Neda's lap. She strokes the cat with one hand and feeds her the cookie with the other. Neda wants Velvet *Khanom* to be her Madar because she's full of exciting scents and keeps Baba's glove all nice and warm in her pocket. So why did Velvet *Khanom* married

That-Cursed-Land-Eater man who'll make bad things to Baba if he marries Velvet *Khanom*?

Pary studies Neda's eyes that appear to evade her. "Darling, are you worried? Is it about all the keys to your tears? Be patient, you'll find them, I promise."

"I won't find keys ever because *Agha* Fool says I'm not like everyone else because even one tear doesn't fall down from my eyes."

"Oh, darling, that's not true." Pary hugs Neda's face in her hands. "You have many tears like everyone else. It's just that your tears are waiting for the right time to fall."

Neda wipes cookie crumbs off mademoiselle's face, lifts her from her lap, and places her on the sofa. "Now, Baba?"

"Yes, Sweetheart, now." He scoops a box out of his coat pocket. "Here, why don't you remove the wrapping."

Neda squeezes the box between both hands. She feels the seams of the wrapping, which is not as soft as Baba's leather gloves. Baba must like Pary less than he likes Velvet *Khanom* because he gave her his two soft gloves to keep always for herself. Neda carefully peels the wrapping off, snaps the top of the box open, and scrutinizes the gold wedding band on satin.

The samovar on the round table steams and lets out a series of burps. Murmur of prayers behind the door. The Quarter Fool's shrill voice trumpets the birth of a lucky girl in the house of Batool the Laundry Woman.

Soleiman observes Pary in a way he never had before. Sitting as she is, in complete silence, her legs delicately crossed at the ankles, she possesses an ethereal quality. Her bronze hair, the burnished shade of the decorative bands and medallions on her door, is piled on top of her head in a tumble of curls he especially likes. It would be lovely to remove the hairpins and shake her hair loose. He takes the box from Neda. "Pary, will you give me the honor of becoming my wife? It would make me very happy."

Pary runs a finger around the ring in the satin slit. The last few weeks have been a whirlwind of surprising events. She pored over books Jacob gave her, studied play therapy and managed to lead successful sessions with Neda. But most unexpected was doctor Yaran asking for her hand on his visit the other day, when never before had he given her reason to believe his feelings for her went beyond mere friendship. Now, here he is, the warmth of his presence flowering between her breasts. Her parents would approve of him as much as they disapproved of Monsieur André.

Neda slides to the edge of the sofa, flaps cookie crumbs off her skirt, and, remembering she has to be nice, says, "Pary, my Baba says he'll be very happy if you become my Madar, because you're very nice *Khanom* that went to school to teach me to read and write. Even nicer than Velvet *Khanom* because she's wife of That-Cursed-Land-Eater man—"

"Thank you, Sweetheart," Soleiman says. "We will have to be quiet now, so Pary can think about our proposal."

Pary's hand is on her heart, which is beating in every part of her body. Love and temptation can burrow roots and flourish in the most hostile of circumstances, this she knows too well. She rises to her feet and goes to the samovar to pour herself a glass of mint-laced tea. Steam rises from the teacup she warms her hands around. "I can tell that Neda likes the governor general's wife. What about you, Doctor Yaran?"

His complexion pale with concern at Pary's mournful expression, Soleiman scrambles for a reply worthy of her honesty. "Pary, it is you I respect, you I want for a wife. Isn't that far more important than mere liking?" He removes the gold band from the box. "You are wise and beyond beautiful and very special to me. Please give me, and Neda, the honor of making you happy."

She glances at the ring Soleiman is holding, a simple gold band as customary in the Jewish faith. "You feel affection, Doctor Yaran? For me, I mean. This much you do?"

There's an instant of silence so heavy, so complete, it appears all three in the room have stopped breathing.

"Oh, my dear, Pary, much, much more than mere affection." He raises her hand to his lips, lingers on the pulse at her wrist and breathes in her fragrance of talcum powder and home.

CHAPTER FORTY-SIX

The alleys and streets of the Jewish Quarter are cleared of all garbage, swept, watered, and mopped. Windows cleaned with rags and dried with newspapers, doorsteps and window ledges brushed free of dust, dead leaves, and cockroaches. The garbage pit is emptied and hosed down with precious water from private cisterns. A large pump aimed at anyone crossing his path, the Quarter Fool sprays the alleys with mosquito repellent.

Not since the wedding of Rabbi Elihu the Compassionate, twenty-six years back, has the Jewish Quarter been so completely freed of the stench of rat and refuse.

Threaded flowers are strung across houses. Carpets spread along the path the bride and groom will take to Eleazar the Redhead's house, where Rabbi Elihu the Compassionate will conduct the religious *Ketubah* signing ceremony.

It is the Sunday following Omer, an auspicious time to hold a wedding.

Businesses are closed for the occasion. The populace is up before daybreak. Musicians have gathered at the house of Morteza Ney Davoud, the famed sitar player. Violinists tune their instruments, *dombak* drum-players improvise a rhythmic pattern, and flute players play scores up and down. Bibi Golden Voice sips warm orange blossom and honey sherbet to soothe her vocal cords, while the hairstylist sets her hair in rag curlers.

The Quarter seamstress is getting ready to deliver the bride's dress, copied from a photo in an old Time Magazine, which the greengrocer, having no use for it other than to wrap merchandise in the pages, was more than happy to give to Pary.

Hope is on the rise, Pary read in the magazine. The end of the war, at least in Europe, might be in sight. The Allies have succeeded in chasing the Nazis out of Paris, if not out of France. Despite the cold winter, lack of coal, food, and most every other merchandise, the magazine had struck an optimistic note and had presented the fall fashion shows in the recently liberated Paris. Some of the well-known couturiers such as Alix, Bruyere, and Molyneux are back with wide shouldered styles, small waists, and full skirts.

After much deliberation, Pary settled on a square shouldered blue dress, gathered at the waist with a delicate belt, the hips decorated with white lace. Blue, she decided, was more appropriate than white for a second marriage. The decision as to whether to conceal her face behind a drop of lace, a half-hat, or a wedding veil has not been made yet, which is a source of worry since the rabbi will not conduct the religious ceremony if the bride's face is not covered.

She chose Soleiman's tuxedo from a photograph in the same magazine, the style Charles Boyer wore at the premier of one of his movies.

Certain the tuxedo will look better on Soleiman than on the French actor, Pary showed the photograph to the tailor, who fretted about the difficulty of sewing such a complicated piece with peaked lapels, shawl collar, and a vest which seemed to be made from cardboard. But he was not about to turn down such an honor, so he wiped sweat off his glistening forehead and assured Pary he'd do a far better job than any French tailor.

Neda had to be coaxed into trying on her dress—a copy of the pink organza, multi-tiered dress Princess Shahnaz Pahlavi wore on her last birthday—which made Pary vacillate between despair that the child would never accept her and hope that every problem can be solved with time and boundless kindness. In the end, when Pary tied Ruby's red scarf like a belt around the waist, Neda agreed to wear the dress.

Aunt Shamsi, after recovering from the shock of Soleiman's outburst in the garden, suffered yet another blow: her nephew, the most eligible bachelor in the Quarter, was marrying a twenty-seven-year-old widow who was, like any other widow, not only damaged goods and un-marriageable, but came with the added burden of being associated with the bad-luck door.

Aunt Shamsi went to her brother, pulled at her hair, beat her chest, and tried to convince him to drill some sense into his son's empty head. When Eleazar told his sister he rather liked Pary and reminded her of the dire alternative, Aunt Shamsi demanded an emergency meeting with the Quarter rabbis to present her case. The rabbis skewered Aunt Shamsi with their collective stares, after which they informed her that Pary had donated her house with everything in it to Hakim Synagogue for religious classes to be held there. Her only condition was for the door to remain intact, to which the rabbis had whole heartedly agreed.

Aunt Shamsi's confusion lasted one long, sleepless night and a good part of the next day, until she concluded that if the wise rabbis were accepting of Pary, then who was she to contradict them. Once the matter was settled, she hired Lucky Hands Khayat Banou—happily married and blessed with eight healthy children and thirty-one grandchildren, all marked by nothing but good fortune—to sew her a triple-pleated dress, the more fabric the richer she will appear, and for Eleazar a double-breasted suit with four rows of buttons.

The Jewish Quarter is humming with final preparations now. Women pluck chickens and marinate lambs, sift through tens of kilograms of rice, chop herbs, peel and fry eggplants, stuff pumpkins, and slice onions to be browned to golden crisps. Bakery ovens produce sheet after sheet of rice and chickpea cookies, baklava and halvah, pistachio nougat, and cardamom *koloocheh* cookies.

Men go from house to house to collect chairs and tables, tablecloths, plates, cutlery, trays, and other necessities to transport to the house of Eleazar the Redhead on the Alley of Seven Synagogues, where Soleiman's wedding festivities will be held this evening.

Despite Soleiman's insistence that his house is fully furnished, and a dowry is unnecessary, four wealthy families have assumed the responsibility of procuring items worthy of their beloved doctor's household.

Porters are preparing for the *tabagh baran* procession, decorating large, flat wooden palettes on which the bride's dowry will be transported to the groom's house, which Aunt Shamsi has scrubbed and polished with such enthusiasm her nephew is loath to touch anything in fear of leaving a single fingerprint.

Neda, on the other hand, feels differently. The moment a windowpane is cleaned, her hands leave marks; the moment the floor mopped, muddy footprints necessitate another round of mopping; and the moment a tablecloth is washed and ironed, a fresh stain appears on it.

Grumbling under her breath, Aunt Shamsi retraces her steps and wipes the windows again, mops the floor, and washes the tablecloth. But when the tireless child refuses to dismount the devil's stubborn donkey, come to her senses, and accept the situation, Aunt Shamsi curls a forefinger and signals Neda to follow her across the hallway and into the bedroom where, for the first time in three years, she retrieves a brass key from between her breasts and unlocks her trunk in front of Neda, hooks two finger under the chain of the silver purse she inherited from her own mother, and dangles it in the air. "The purse you've been wanting all your life. Help me clean the house, and it's all yours."

But as soon as Neda begins to dust every single doll on the shelves, every apothecary jar, and every dental tool and encyclopedia, Mademoiselle's paw-prints appear on chairs and shelves, carpets, and laundered clothing.

Aunt Shamsi marches out into the alley and orders Pary to lock her cat away until after the wedding. What if the cat happens to find her way to the wedding canopy, God forbid, and tarnish its sacredness? Pary smiles, tells Aunt Shamsi the cat belongs to Neda, too, and it would be unkind to lock her away. Aunt Shamsi fires a string of curses, which lasts all of half an hour, until she remembers she will be moving back home soon and will not have to suffer the cat much longer.

Having made her peace with the feline, she aims a hose at the bewildered cat to remove the stink of vinegar and pepper, brushes and sprays her with rosewater, then ties a pink ribbon around her neck.

Dr. Yaran is getting married, and every man, woman, and child in the Jewish Quarter is contributing to the festivities, save for the groom and his father, who have been forbidden to raise a finger to help or dip into their own pocket to provide a single *rial.*

* * *

Soleiman studies his face in the bedroom mirror. Should he shave now or in the afternoon? As he intends to spend the day with Neda and prepare her for tonight, the crowd, the noise, and festivities, which might overwhelm the child, he decides to shave later.

Aunt Shamsi's head emerges from behind the half-open door to congratulate him, and, seeing he is already dressed, she pushes the door open, enters, and stands in the center of the bedroom with her hands on her waist. "Listen, Soleiman, I'll go back home to Eleazar before you bring your bride here. No, no, don't try to change my mind, it's decided. You don't want a bad luck woman, who lost a dear daughter and a coward husband to be in your house when your bride—"

"I understand and thank you for all your help, Aunt Shamsi. I'm sure Baba Eleazar will be happy to have you back," Soleiman says, failing to suppress a grin.

Before Aunt Shamsi has time to spew out a chain of complaints about how her nephew does not even have the decency to express a bit of regret and sorrow at her departure after having sacrificed her youth at his feet, a racket of banging at the gate sends the relieved Soleiman outside.

Tulip pushes the gate open and enters the garden, where servants are already setting borrowed chairs and tables for after the wedding ceremony, when an entourage of community elders will escort the bride and groom to their home to recite nuptial songs and prayers behind their bedroom door.

"I apologize for disturbing you like this, *Agha* doctor," Tulip exclaims in a breathless rush. "But His Excellency needs you—"

"No, Tulip! Not today!"

"Please, I know it's your wedding day, but His Excellency is very sick and might even die—"

There is a chill in the air, and Soleiman buttons his jacket. "Sorry, my friend. I can't help you today. So, don't waste more time standing here."

Tulip pulls a loose thread and begins to unravel the fabric of his sleeve as if it will solve his master's predicament. Tears brim in his eyes and spill down his face and cloak. "Either you come with me, *Agha* Doctor, or I will not budge from here until I take my last breath on this earth."

CHAPTER FORTY-SEVEN

The acrid stench of opium is intolerable, and the governor general, splayed on a divan in his private quarters, is laboring for breath. But there is no sign of the opium brazier or pipe in the room, nor any smoke in the air.

Arms bare and the outline of her naked body visible under the linen dress she had no time to change when she rushed to her husband's bedside, Velvet leans against the yawning leather trunk with silver tooling and oversized brass tacks. She has never found herself so close to a dying person, and her muddled feelings vacillate between longing for something to change and fear that it will. Now that her husband has been reduced to a helpless state, she remembers glimpses of his generosity. The way he shelters her and supports her parents, the way his eyes overflow with affection and remorse whenever he does something hurtful.

"You will save my husband, Doctor Yaran, won't you?" Velvet tells Soleiman, whose mind clicks like an abacus to calculate the time left until his wedding.

"I will do my best," he replies, not certain whether she wants him to save her husband or asking him something else. He rips the governor general's shirt open and presses his ear to his chest, lifts the man's eyelids to find the pupils down to pinpoints. He is half comatose, and the little breath left in him reeks of opium and alcohol. "Your husband is in respiratory distress, I'm afraid. I'm not sure I can help him, Velvet *Khanom*. He must have overdosed on opium."

Tulip's voice seems to rise from the bottom of a dark well. "He did, *Agha* doctor. He had five pea-sized pieces, maybe eight yesterday and more today, stuffed in dates. The rest, two rolls larger than my middle finger, mixed in ground kebab with half a bottle of *aragh*."

Footsteps in the corridor, someone stops behind the closed door. There is a knock, and a servant enters with a tray of food. Velvet waves him away. He takes a look at the governor's ashen face and trips over the carpet. The tray wobbles in his hands, and for an instant it appears he might crash to the floor with the hot food. But he finds his footing and quickly backs out the door.

Soleiman lowers his voice. "Why didn't you stop him, Tulip?"

His eyes pinned to the carpet underfoot, Tulip shuffles in place.

Three knocks at the door punctuate the grave silence. Velvet half opens the door and sends away a servant with a hot brazier and an opium pipe.

"Tulip? Say something," Soleiman insists. "What is it?"

"I gave him the opium, *Agha* doctor," Tulip cries out, overwhelmed with waves of guilt and remorse. "For two endless days, I crammed his food with opium. I thought I was granting his wish to go to heaven and find forgiveness, at last. But I'm not sure now. Not at all. Please do something, *Agha* doctor."

Soleiman attempts to harness his shock and anger. "How could you do that, Tulip! It might be too late now."

He retrieves his prescription notepad and writes the name of a trusted doctor. A moment of hesitation. Questions will be asked the instant the governor general is admitted to the hospital. Both he and the eunuch will be held responsible and reported to the authorities. The Jewish Quarter will be razed down. He drops the notepad back into the case and is about to screw the cap of his pen shut when the Land Eater's hand jerks up and grabs his wrist.

This is the moment the governor general has been preparing for his entire life. Right now, when his soul is in his throat and the rattle of death has just begun and the gates of heaven are opening for him.

But now that he is here, he has changed his mind and wants to live. He forces air into his lungs, opens his mouth, and begs with all his might for the doctor to breathe life into him as he had once before, but the words gurgling out of his mouth sound like a curse, not a plea.

The clocks echo in unison. Long-drawn bongs levitate in the rancid air. One hour past noon and eight hours to Soleiman's wedding. One by one and with great gentleness he unlocks the governor's fingers from his wrist.

"I am not sure what you want from me now, Your Excellency. Perhaps you want this?" Soleiman presses his pen into the man's hand and closes the icy fingers around it. "Not fancy like your own pen. But good enough for any last-minute instructions you might have."

The governor's lips move and every muscle shakes with the effort to raise his arms and plead for mercy, plead for a few more years, months, even days on this earth.

But what the doctor sees is a man who, even on his deathbed, is struggling to gain some strength so he could push the dirty Jew away and rid himself of his defiling presence. Soleiman steps closer. Wraps his hand around the governor's fingers to further secure the pen, then puts his other hand on the man's clammy forehead and keeps it there.

The governor's eyes roll down and the two men stare at each other. A Muslim desperate for a second chance at life; a Jew with little mercy for this man left in his heart.

Tulip falls to his knees at Soleiman's feet. "Do something, *Agha* doctor, please. I beg you. Save His Excellency. Breathe into his nose. Can't you see he wants to live?"

The room with its clocks heaves and shudders and waits.

Soleiman releases his hold and steps away from the divan. "I am sorry, Tulip I would save him if I could. But it's too late."

A series of spasms shake the governor, and the sheets under him stain with urine.

Velvet removes her chador and drops it on the cot. Alarmed the chador landed on her husband, she snatches it back and tosses it to a corner. Her husband is in agony, and she feels a need to comfort him, but she does not know how.

Tremors seize the governor general's body; a convulsion, then another. A long-drawn rattle gurgles out of his throat and with it a faint odor of rot. The pen tumbles out of his limp fingers and rolls down to land on the carpet at Soleiman's feet.

The marble eyes of the clownish clock roll back and forth in unison, dismissing them all—Soleiman and his roiling thoughts, Velvet and her unattainable wishes, Tulip and his shame and remorse, but most of all the Land Eater who, freed from earthly shackles, embarks on his journey to an elusive world, where he will be greeted by plump-breasted virginal *houris* of paradise or by the *devil's* consuming flames.

The clocks, having clanged and banged and mocked for years, settle into an ensemble of monotonous ticking. It will not be long before they will be yanked off walls and shelves and commodes, hauled out of rooms and down from the attic, tossed in a large shuddering heap in the center of the poppy fields and burned down to charred coal with the opium refineries and every last poppy.

Tulip raises his fists and thumps them down on his head. He cries out for forgiveness from the man who provided him with food and shelter and spoiled him beyond limit with his own kind of love. So relentlessly present was he in life, Tulip never thought of how his master's absence will leave them all vulnerable. He crosses the governor's arms gently on his chest, then turns to Soleiman and says, "What is done is done. So, take Velvet *Khanom* and leave before the entire city comes for you. Go, *Agha* doctor! I'll prepare the body, delay things to give you time. Take the Lincoln and drive far from the city. The two of you deserve some happiness."

Velvet leans on Soleiman's arm. "Is it true, Soleiman? Are you getting married?"

Once again, the shock of her touch, the unbearable longing to pull her close. He raises her hand to his lips. "Yes, my love, I am."

Velvet walks into Soleiman's arms, and they remain like that for a long time. The mountains turn into ghostly shadows against a purple sky, and the howls of hunting jackals rise above the united kicks of their hearts.

"Are you sure, Soleiman?" Her voice is so low he leans his ear to her lips to hear her. "Is this what you really want?"

"Yes, my love. This is what I *have* to want."

Velvet's hand on Soleiman's arm no longer shakes. "And Neda? Is she fine with this wedding?"

"No, she is not," he replies, and the mercurial glim of her eyes shatters him once again. "She wants you. So does her father. But this is as it must be."

"I wish I didn't love you," she says, her breath warm on his neck.

"You will forget. You will make your own poetry. You will thrive." Pain in his chest, he brushes his lips against her temple and breaks away.

The half-dome of the sun is beginning to fade behind the mountains, and the household will be preparing supper. How long, Soleiman wonders, will it take him to reach the Quarter and change into his tuxedo? He might be late for his wedding.

The feral stench of the governor's lifeless body, which demands attention, is already stifling the room. According to Islamic law, the burial must take place immediately. The body washed in warm, then tepid water before being shrouded in the purest of white linens.

"A favor, Tulip. Pack the body in ice. Don't announce the governor general's death until tomorrow."

Tulip pulls his mantle around his shoulders. "Don't go yet, *Agha* doctor. Give me a moment, please. I've something that might change your mind."

He goes straight to the stand of antlers in the living room on which leans the gilded Rubayiat book of poetry bound in leather, which he lifts to reveal a concealed drawer at the back. He slides over his head the gold chain and key he has been carrying around his neck for years, turns it in the small lock, and the drawer slides forward like a well-oiled tray in which lies an envelope sealed with red wax embossed with two cannons. He makes his way back and presents the envelope to Velvet. "His Excellency's will, Velvet *Khanom*. He gave strict orders to open it after his death."

Velvet's hand jumps to her breasts as if to catch her falling heart. "Read it aloud, Tulip."

A trapped whiff of opium wafts out of the envelope Tulip tears open. "'*I bequeath my wealth evenly between my faithful servant, Tulip, and my dear wife and lifelong partner, Velvet, on condition that my dear wife does not remarry, and my faithful servant does not abandon her.*

"My wish is that when I am long gone, generations to come will hail me as an honest and god-fearing man who conducted his life with moral rectitude and fairness." With this, his final act—unusual for even the most loving husband to leave his wealth to his wife—his master's intention was to establish his love for a woman and, by doing so, take his secret to the grave.

Unbelieving, Velvet grabs the will and hands it to Soleiman, who reads aloud the slanted, cerulean letters on vellum paper. With a few strokes of his jewel-capped pen, the governor general managed to make his wife one of the wealthiest people in the country, as well as to exact a cruel revenge. He regards the red curtains and heavy furniture, the fine leather chest with its silver tooling, the hill of gold coins—all, and so much more, for Velvet to do with as she pleases, on condition she remain single.

He folds and refolds the will into a small, neat square and slips it back in the envelope as if he is tucking Velvet's past away. His fingers unsteady, he takes out from his medical case the last batch of pills he made for Tulip, leaves the bottle with the envelope on the governor's desk, and, an ache in his heart, bows his head to Velvet and walks out of the mansion.

CHAPTER FORTY-EIGHT

The air is laced with the heady scent of roasting lamb and saffron, mint and tarragon. Musicians play tambourines and flutes and dance in alleys adorned with jasmine and carpets. Sitar and drum players follow Bibi Golden Voice, whose melodies about charmed loves and good fortune are rumored to heal all types of ailments, from weeping hearts to unbridled passions.

Seamstresses and tailors, greengrocers and butchers, bankers and lenders are out with their families in tow. The Quarter prostitute is here, too, her bleached hair a white halo around her powdered face, her red lips puckered in airborne kisses, her rhinestone-studded skirt flirting with her giddy hips.

Clad in handouts of sparring colors and jiggling a tambourine above his head, the Quarter Fool spins on the heels of his new boots. "*Mobarak* congratulations! Lucky *Agha* doctor to catch Pary from the Alley of Physicians with her sweet little nipples. May our groom be happy, *Insha'Allah*."

A painful pinch from Aunt Shamsi on his backside silences the Fool.

Flamboyantly attired in a navy-colored suit, red bowtie, and yellow suspenders, the ever-present cigarette dangling at the corner of his mouth, Jacob, the only trained fighter around, catches Soleiman's eyes and raises a fist in a show of strength.

Soleiman nods, smiles, but is not comforted. If a single maid or servant, worker in the opium fields, a guard, a gardener, or whoever else might have seen him enter the governor general's mansion earlier today is looking for an excuse to spill Jewish blood, there is no better time to do so than now, when the populace is out celebrating a wedding.

He feels for the knife in his tuxedo pocket. Not much protection against thugs looking for an excuse to invade the Jewish Quarter.

"You look especially lovely tonight." Soleiman clasps his bride's hand, who is radiant in her blue wedding dress and small hat with the drop veil, behind which her eyes keep seeking him.

Her gaze overflowing with wonderment, Pary tells him that he is even more handsome than usual.

"It's the tuxedo you chose for me." A small lie, since once he returned from the mountains, he barely had time to wash dust and longing off his face, before he wore the tuxedo, which feels too tight around the shoulders.

Prayers echo around the streets and alleys as the bride and groom are escorted to the Alley of Seven Synagogues, where Rabbi Elihu the Compassionate will conduct the wedding ceremony.

"May the Lord spread His protective shadow over us all."

"Amen!"

Marching ahead with a spring in their gait, eighteen muscular porters carry on their heads the bride's dowry on round wooden pallets—a sofa on one pallet, two armchairs on another, a set of dining chairs on two others, and a brass table on yet another, plus plates and pots and pans, sheets and pillows and blankets, and a pair of antique candelabra. Transported on its own pallet is Eleazar the Redhead's wedding gift to his son, a silver urn passed down from generation to generation.

Rostam leads the procession, on his back Aunt Shamsi's storage trunk secured with ropes. Intent on dispatching Aunt Shamsi with respect and on her own terms, Soleiman granted her wish to publicly deliver back to her own house the trunk with her belongings. Sensing the significance of the occasion, the stallion sniffs the air and tosses his head this way and that as if transporting Queen Fawzia's royal jewels in the steel banded trunk with its brass lock clattering to the tune of flutes and tambourines and the rattle of curiosity.

It does not matter that the international greed for oil is tearing Iran apart. It does not matter that America, despite her previous policy of non-interference, has settled fifty-thousand American soldiers and officers here. It does not matter that the Soviet occupation in the north has encouraged the ascent of the Tudeh Communist Party. It does not matter that Hitler refuses to declare defeat. It does not even matter that Iran is mourning the death of the shah's father in exile in Johannesburg.

What matters is that the joyous populace has come together to celebrate their beloved doctor's wedding.

The ring of ululation intensifies as the retinue enters the Alley of Seven Synagogues, which is tented with prayer shawls lent by the few blessed families who have escaped death and misfortune, the few families whose possessions are believed to herald good luck.

A white fedora on top of his freshly dyed hair, Eleazar the Redhead waits at the entrance to the wedding tent, which is adorned with silk-fringed blue and white prayer shawls. Having decided that his hair caused him enough misery, he changed the color with a concoction of coffee, egg yolks, henna, and walnut husks, which altered his rich mop of red curls into a helmet of washed-out yellows.

One hand clutching a rooster by the legs, the other brandishing a kosher *shechitah* knife, he says, "This rooster is to your health, son. I didn't think you'd approve of my sacrificing a lamb. May I? Then, I'll retire, I promise."

Soleiman nods, kneels to face his daughter. "Neda, Sweetheart, remember how I told you not to believe in Aunt Shamsi's superstitious nonsense? Baba Eleazar is about to do one of those silly things, so I want you to close your eyes."

Neda's head is dizzy with all kinds of thoughts. Her Baba doesn't want her to see Baba Eleazar make the rooster all dead. Aunt Shamsi's voice inside Neda's head wants Neda to be a good girl because it's Baba and Pary's special marriage. And Pary keeps asking Neda if it's okay to marry Baba. But Neda doesn't even want Baba to marry Pary, but Baba can't marry Velvet *Khanom* because of That-Cursed-Land-Eater. Neda shuts her eyes and waits for the poor rooster to not cry anymore.

Eleazar the Redhead, having performed the ancient ritual, discreetly disposes of the lifeless rooster by handing it to the *shamash* in charge of Ezra Mikhael Synagogue at the end of the alley.

Soleiman wraps an arm around his daughter. "You can open your eyes, Sweetheart. Take my hand and we'll go in."

The guests squeeze themselves into the wedding tent, which is covered with borrowed carpets and lit with lanterns, oil lamps, and candles of all sizes in silver candelabras on loan from the seven synagogues in the Quarter.

At his post on a carpet-covered dais built for the occasion, Rabbi Elihu the Compassionate inspects the round table on which Aunt Shamsi has sprinkled a generous layer of salt to ward off an army of evil spirits. The Ketubah marriage contract, a silver wine goblet, a bottle of kosher wine, and a silver-covered Torah is here, as well as the blue egg which, according to Aunt Shamsi, is a harbinger of good fortune.

The bride and groom take Neda by the hand, and the three cross the tent and climb the four steps to the dais. They face the rabbi, the child between them and their backs to the surrounding guests.

Rabbi Elihu the Compassionate shifts his skullcap on his sparse hair, twists his bushy eyebrows, and glares at Eleazar the Redhead, who is passing around in miniature glasses the special *aragh* he brewed for his son's wedding.

"After the ceremony, *Agha* Eleazar, not now. Please!"

The rabbi lifts the Ketubah above his head for everyone to witness the delicately rendered birds and flowers surrounding the Aramaic script, on which the scribe spent every hour of the last week to make sure it is befitting of the groom. He raises his voice so guests who couldn't fit into the tent would hear him in the alley. "This is a marriage contract in which the husband promises to provide food and clothing to his wife." His thick-nailed finger taps on the Ketubah. "In accordance with the Jewish law, the husband has numerous responsibilities, the most sacred of which is to perform his conjugal duties. And to pay the sum of 100 zuz to his bride in the event of, God forbid, may it never, ever happen, a divorce." He places the Ketubah back on the table and tugs at his prayer shawl that keeps slipping off his shoulders. His pink-rimmed eyes focus on Pary. "It would have been 200 zuz if the bride were a virgin. *Mobarak*, Pary *Khanom*! Congratulations!"

This is the part of the wedding ceremony Rabbi Elihu the Compassionate enjoys best, when he has the undivided attention of his guests. He goes to the table and pours wine into the goblet. Gestures to Soleiman to move Neda aside so the bride and groom may stand next to one another, but as the two refuse to let go of the child's hand, he changes course.

"You have the ring, Doctor Yaran. Put it on the bride's right forefinger."

To the rabbi's dismay, the bride is wearing the ring on her finger as if she is already a married woman. He shakes his head at this blatant disregard for an ancient tradition and waits for the bride to remove the ring and give it to the groom, who recites the blessing over wine.

Soleiman takes a sip of wine, then raises the cup to Pary's lips. She brushes the back of a hand across her black-diamond eyes, and he tells her there's no need to dismiss her feelings anymore because she is no longer alone.

Neda smells the cherry scent of Pary's lips close to her face, sees her lashes shadow her cheeks like thin blades. Pary says, "I'm becoming Baba's wife and your Madar. Do you want this, darling? Tell me, because I'll never do something you don't want me to do."

Neda nods with all the vehemence of her uncertainty.

Pary's delicate fingers reach out to Soleiman like a prayer, the nail beds like gleaming shells. He slides the gold band on her index finger and covers her hand with his. "Behold, you are consecrated to me with this ring according to the laws of Moses and Israel."

Rabbi Elihu the Compassionate chants the *Sheva Brachot* Seven Wedding Blessings: "Blessed are You, Lord, our God, Sovereign of the universe, who created joy and gladness, groom and bride, mirth, song, delight and rejoicing, love and harmony and peace and companionship. Soon, Lord our God, may there ever be heard in the cities of Judah and in the streets of Jerusalem voices of joy and gladness, voices of groom and bride, the jubilant voices of those joined in marriage under the bridal canopy, the voices of young people feasting and singing. Blessed are You, Lord, who causes the groom to rejoice with his bride."

The tent shakes with the cheer of ululation, the thump of tambourines, and joyous dancing. *Noghle* sweets and rose petals shower down like blessings on the bride and groom and on Neda.

"*Yaran mobarak baada*," Bibi's crystal voice rises above the ecstasy of flutes, violins, and sitars to float into the Alley of Seven Synagogues, where others dance and clap and ululate.

The Quarter Fool croons at the top of his lungs, "*Siman tov* and *mazal tov* to my brain for telling *Agha* doctor to eat Baba Magic."

Jacob grabs his pocket square and waves it happily above his head. His children, despite the bombing of the immigration offices in Tel Aviv, Haifa, and Jerusalem, and despite British searches and roadblocks, managed to find homes and have settled with different families around Palestine.

Rabbi Elihu the Compassionate returns the silver goblet to the table. A moment of confusion and shock. The goblet has landed on the blue egg and its putrid insides are running out of its cracked shell. He dries the goblet with shaking hands and covers the mess with a corner of the tablecloth.

The rabbi holds up a glass Aunt Shamsi wrapped in a handkerchief embroidered for the occasion. "Crush it with your right foot,

Doctor Yaran. A reminder that as long as we mourn the destruction of our temple our joy is not complete."

Soleiman reaches out for the handkerchief-covered glass, but the rabbi's arm is paralyzed in mid-air.

A chorus of frightened voices from the alley makes its way into the tent. Women rush to gather their children and men with grim expressions come to stand by their families. One last terrified note erupts from Bibi Golden Voice's throat. Musical instruments are silenced.

"Dirt on our heads!" The Quarter Fool shouts, neck swaying like an inverted pendulum. "Muslims!"

Jacob's hand slips under his coat to the pistol snug in its holster.

Soleiman slips the knife out of his pocket.

Murmurs canter about the tent, exchange of alarmed glances. The groom is holding a knife! Dr. Yaran, on whom they've always relied for protection, is paler than *Meyet*. And his pistol cocked, Jacob Mordechai is inching his way toward the entrance.

A vision of opulence in a gold-threaded cape with ermine-trimmed sleeves, the eunuch of the governor general stands at the entrance to the wedding tent. He clasps the large emerald pinned at the neck of his cape, regards the bride and groom on the carpet-covered dais, the child standing between them, the table holding the ornate wedding contract in Aramaic script. He hoists a burlap sack he carries over one shoulder and rests it at his feet.

All the guests—the bankers and merchants, butchers and fruit vendors, the shah's Water Man and the gravedigger, the rabbis and the *shochet*, the Quarter Whore with her red lips and rhinestone-studded slippers, and the Fool with his gnawed sugar cane—wither under the eunuch's gaze, which measures them with the terrifying greed of a predator.

"Pary, stay here with Neda, please," Soleiman says. News of the governor general's death must have reached Tehran. The eunuc must be here to warn him of imminent danger. "I'm going down to see why Tulip's here."

Pary draws the child close. "How bad is it? Are we in danger?"

"Stay calm, I'll take care of this." He drops the knife back into his pocket and steps down the platform.

There is no breeze, but candles sputter, lanterns and oil lamps waver, and Soleiman is unable to find his way to the far end of the tent, which is tossed into darkness. Then, as inexplicably as they were snuffed, the lights come back to life with added intensity to illuminate Velvet as she steps into the tent. Draped in a magnificent suite of emeralds, her sheer-sleeved dress cinched at the waist with a chain studded with yellow sapphires the shade of her wild hair, she adjusts her slightly askew sleeve with an impatient shrug of the shoulder and enters a wedding tent crowded with Jews who see nothing but a Muslim woman with trouble in her eyes and evil in her heart.

She makes her way toward Soleiman, and the crowd, in awe of her poise and confidence, clears a path for her.

Rabbi Elihu the Compassionate makes a feeble attempt to call the groom back, but not a single word makes its way out of his dry throat.

Eleazar the Redhead spits obscenities under his breath as he observes his son on his way to greet the governor general's brazen wife, who has done nothing but usher havoc in her steps.

And Jacob, betting on the triumph of reason over love, holsters his revolver.

Soleiman faces Velvet in the center of the tent, and, for an instant, it is only the two of them under the wedding canopy, Soleiman and Velvet, the woman who taught him it is possible to love again. She comes close, too close, her voice hardly a whisper: "The death has not been announced, Soleiman. The Lincoln is waiting, bring Neda and come with me."

The tent jolts with the murmur of his people. Raised eyebrows and jabbing elbows. What in the world could be transpiring between the Muslim woman and the groom? Can there be something unkosher going on between them? No! Tof, tof, tof. Not their beloved doctor. Never!

The Quarter Fool brandishes the limp piece of sugar cane above his head. "Stop staring everyone! Leave them alone!"

"What brings His Excellency's wife here?" Soleiman says, flinching at the flash of pain in Velvet's silver eyes.

Velvet holds up a small jewelry box studded with diamonds and emeralds. "*Mobarak*, Doctor Yaran."

She flips the top of the box open for him to see Ruby's pocket watch on a bed of satin inside, and the tenderness of her act devastates him anew. He might not be a married man, he muses, since he did not yet break the glass. Then again, all the prayers must have been recited, so he probably is.

From up on the dais, Pary observes the unfolding scene below. Velvet is more mesmerizing than a snake, and Soleiman gazes at her with an ache painful to witness. She could live with Ruby's spirit, but she cannot compete with this woman. She kneels to address Neda. "I'd like to go to your Baba. Do you want to come down with me?"

Neda's eyes inch their way around Pary's face, whose lips are like tiny cherries, the flash of her teeth white like snowflakes. The twist of a curl falls over her eye like a shiny corkscrew. Pary is full of fairytales and *khoshmazeh* cookies and beautiful small dolls she gives Neda, and Neda doesn't want to make her sad. But Velvet *Khanom*, with all of her smell of roses and happy colors and fun and play, is making Neda want to jump down and crush her face in her skirt.

The stench of fear is hiding everything, and it's hard for Neda to tell if Velvet *Khanom* is happy, sad, angry, or scared. She squints harder and suddenly sees Velvet *Khanom* all sad and wanting to cry and Baba not happy again, and Neda becomes even sadder because Baba Magic is all finished, and she can't make more.

Neda is suddenly scared. Velvet *Khanom's* face looks like its swimming in front of Neda's wet eyes.

"What's wrong, darling?" Pary says. "You don't have to come with me if you don't want to. You can stay here with Baba Eleazar."

Neda unties her mother's red scarf from around her waist and digs her face in to take away the odd sting behind her eyelids. She lingers for a long time in her mother's delicious embrace, the sheer fabric becoming moist and then all wet against her face. She weeps for her Baba who is sad again. She weeps for Aunt Shamsi who has to go back to Baba Eleazar. She weeps for Baba Eleazar who colored his beautiful red hair the awful color of Rostam's pee pee. She weeps because Velvet is married to That-Cursed-Land-Eater man and cannot become Neda's Madar and she weeps because Pary's voice jumps in her throat like a scared cricket. But most of all Neda weeps because the nice thing she has to do now is to say goodbye to Madar's red scarf.

"Neda? Are you crying?" Pary gently lowers Ruby's scarf from her face. "Oh, darling, you are. Look at all the fat, juicy tears running down your cheeks. You found all the keys to your feelings. I knew you would. Congratulations!"

"Pary, are you my new Madar?"

"I hope so, darling. Why?"

"You will marry Baba and make him happy?"

"I'll try my best, darling, I will."

"So now you take my Madar's scarf for yourself."

"No, darling, never. The scarf is always yours. That's what your Madar will want. Here, let me teach you how to wear it like a big girl." She ties the wet scarf in a fancy double-knot around Neda's shoulders, grabs the silver goblet from the table, and holding Neda by the hand, descends the platform and stands next to Soleiman.

Pary's heart jolts at the spectacle of Velvet running her fingers over and around the curves of Soleiman's pocket watch, as if she is stroking Soleiman himself. How could Soleiman give his most precious possession to this sharp-taloned woman? Pary coaxes the watch out of the bejeweled box Velvet is holding and places it in Neda's hand. "Here, darling, take good care of it. It will remind you of this special night when you found all the keys to your tears."

Holding the wine goblet by the stem, Pary points a finger at Velvet as if to demand her retreat, but the look directed at her is devoid of malice. She drinks from the goblet. Wipes the rim with her thumb and forefinger. Offers the goblet to Velvet. Her voice is smoother than molasses. "Honor us, Velvet *Khanom*, please share a sip from our wedding wine."

Every single gaze in the tent is pinned on Velvet. The governor general's wife will not drink from the same cup Jews drank from, kosher wine no less. She will never do that, no, not the Land Eater's wife.

Velvet cuddles the goblet like a treasure in her hands, looks straight into Pary's eyes, raises the cup to her lips, and drinks the entire contents. The tip of one finger wipes a drop of wine from the corner of her lips, and, as if contemplating her future, she gazes at the reflection of her face in the bottom of the empty cup.

The dumfounded crowd exhales a sigh of relief. The Quarter Fool shakes his tambourine once above his head.

Tulip drags the burlap sack toward Soleiman and places it at his feet. He unlaces the twine at the neck, unfolds the flap, and widens the opening. A dramatic flourish of one arm and, for an instant, his ermine-trimmed sleeve hovers like a furry water creature in the candlelit air.

"My husband's wedding gift," Velvet exclaims. "Gratitude, Doctor Yaran, for all you have done for him."

A murmur ripples about the tent and, curiosity chasing away fear, people dare sneak closer to discover what is in the sack. The bankers, who loaned money to Soleiman and have always received it back with fair interest and in a timely manner. The poultry man, who sacrifices a rooster for Soleiman's health every Yom Kippur, although Eleazar the Redhead does so too. The Water Man, greengrocers, dried fruit vendors, plum and pomegranate juice men, and the butchers, who had no qualms bartering with the doctor in return for his services until his Ruby Magic performed miracles and he was able to pay for the goods. Even Eleazar the Redhead and Aunt Shamsi creep closer to take a peek at the contents of the sack, as does the Quarter Whore, whose flirtatious eyes never tire of trailing Soleiman.

"Full of Gold coins!" The Quarter Fool announces as he grabs a gold coin from the sack, drops it in Neda's hand, and tells her she's the richest girl in the entire world now. He gets closer and pats her cheek with his palm, opens his mouth to call everyone's attention to the huge tears rushing down her face, but the room is silent again, so he clamps his mouth shut.

Soleiman takes an imperceptible step toward Velvet. "Thank the governor general, Velvet *Khanom*. But I cannot accept his gift."

Tulip kneels, gathers the neck of the sack, and knots it with the twine. The crowd is pressing around him, the young and the old, the poor and the rich, and the astonished children who have never seen anyone so lavishly dressed. He pushes the sack forward with one boot, leans over and murmurs: "Listen to your heart, *Agha* doctor, leave the gold for your people and walk out with Velvet *Khanom*."

Pary slips her hand in Soleiman's. "You deserve the gold, Soleiman, for all your hard work and endless sacrifices."

Eleazar the Red Head mouths to his son to accept the gold. And Aunt Shamsi—certain her nephew's senseless pride will deprive the Jewish Quarter of this unimaginable wealth, which is more than enough to build a new school and a proper hospital—is about to faint.

Moshe Ben Avram, whose daughter Farideh is by now happily married and pregnant with her first child, decides to take matters into his own hands. He comes forward and hauls the sack away to be stored at the Dardashti house until the elders of the community decide on the best use for the gold.

Neda is scared she might vomit the tiny butterflies that flutter in her stomach. Baba is inching too close to Velvet *Khanom*, and Pary is breathing like the bird with broken wings that Baba saved one day. Then Baba won't have a wedding, and what will happen then? Neda grabs Pary's hand and pulls her down. "Let's take Baba and go home.

Right now. I want to show Baba all the beautiful tears falling out of my eyes."

"Yes, darling, we will celebrate your tears when we go home with your Baba soon. I promise."

"Velvet *Khanom* too will go home soon? I think she's wanting to cry like me," whispers Neda.

"Yes, darling, she will go home too. She's going to be fine, don't worry," Pary murmurs as she refills Velvet's goblet.

The bittersweet tang of wine explodes in Velvet's throat, and the harder she attempts to stop her tears, the more insistently they flood her cheeks. She cries in front of Jews her husband despised. She cries in front of Neda, who will never become hers. She cries for all the years she lost and for the love in Soleiman's eyes, which she will have to let go. And she cries because there's nothing left for her in the mountains but the howl of wandering ghosts.

When not a single tear is left, she wipes her face, smooths her hair, and straightens her back. It will take a week or two to put everything in order. The field workers can have the leveled land, the Lincoln, and the mansion with everything in it. Then she will go back to Bouchehr with Tulip and her parents.

She holds Tulip's arm, and they retrace their steps out of the tent and down the Alley of Seven Synagogues, the crowd parting to let them pass.

Behind them, once they reach Ezra Mikhael Synagogue at the bend, they hear the crack of the glass Soleiman shatters under his right foot.

ACKNOWLEDGMENTS

Not until 2020, the year I intended to finish *Love and War in the Jewish Quarter*, did I consider writing to be a lonely profession. Yet, in the heat of the Covid-19 Pandemic, quarantined at home, my brain a haze of worry, I came to especially appreciate the importance of proximity, hugs, kisses, face to face chats. So, I owe a special gratitude to Nader, my miracle man, who has been by my side to support and keep me going. To Carolyn, Negin, David, Leila, Adam, Hannah and Macabee, my source of love and inspiration. To Ora, Nora, Laura, David and Sol, who are always there to encourage and support. And to my mother, Parvin, the grand lady herself, without whose guidance none of this would have happened.

Special thanks to David Ascher, a mensch of a man, and a marvelous problem-solver.

My gratitude goes to Marcela Landres, editor par excellence, whose suggestions have been instrumental in every stage of my career. And to the peerless staff of Post Hill Press: Anthony Ziccardi, Megan Wheeler, Aleigha Kely, Alana Mills, Devon Brown, Kelsey Merritt, Debra Englander, Devan Murphy, Bryce Mayon, and Shelby Kirby.

My colleagues, long-time friends and faithful readers, Paula Shtrum, of blessed memory, Joan Goldsmith Gurfield, Alex Kivowitz, and Leslie Monsour, what two years we put behind us! We laughed, complained, and cried together. You read and reread and then read and reread again. Your astute suggestions and encouragements kept me afloat.

I owe a special debt of gratitude to Jonathan and Ann Kirsch, whose friendship and support have been invaluable in the success of this novel.

Thank you, M.J. Rose, for guiding me in the right direction and Alan Dingham for the magnificent cover.

A million thanks, Emi Battaglia for your trust, for leading me to the right publisher and for your tireless efforts.